SHADOW MAN

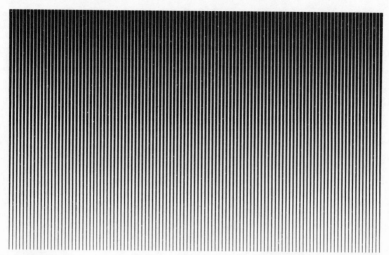

SHADOW MAN

JAMES W. KUNETKA

WARNER BOOKS

A Warner Communications Company

 A Warner Communications Company

Printed in the United States of America
First Printing: January 1988
10 9 8 7 6 5 4 3 2 1

Library of Congress Cataloging-in-Publication Data

Kunetka, James W., 1944-
    Shadow man.

    I. Title.
PS3561.U448S36 1988   813'.54   87-10403
ISBN 0-446-51358-X

Book design: H. Roberts

For the Old Ones

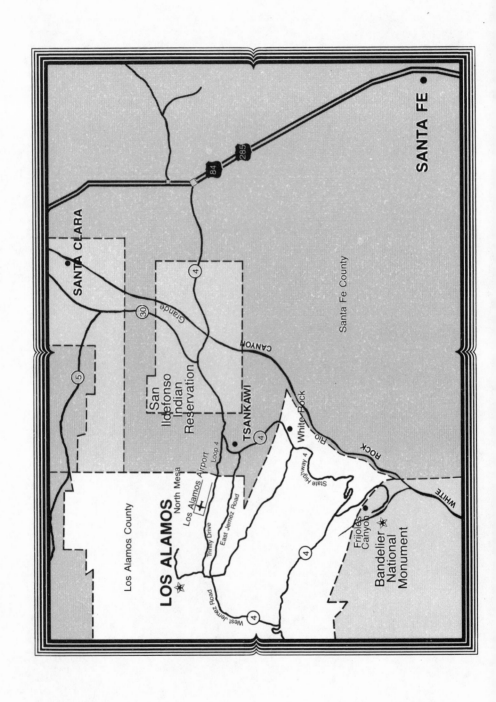

AUTHOR'S NOTE

Los Alamos and Tsankawi are real places, as are the Los Alamos National Laboratory and San Ildefonso Pueblo. The free-electron and X-ray lasers are more than scientific speculation: they are presently under development by the United States government.

The characters and events described in this novel, however, are entirely fictional.

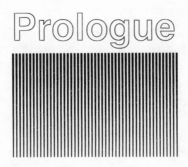

Prologue

SUNDAY MORNING

It was a soft sound and that surprised him. For a moment both men were frozen, the tall man in the dark windbreaker holding the rock, marveling at the sound it had just made, and the smaller man pausing wordlessly a moment to look at his attacker before slumping, unconscious, against the soft stone of the cliff.

The tall man watched his victim slide to the ground and pitch forward. He still gripped the rock, poised to hit again if there was any movement. He stood there for several minutes, very tense, breathing hard and feeling nauseous. He considered the sound of the rock hitting the back of the smaller man's head: it was a soft, dull *thump*, as if he had hit a watermelon, but more solid. There was no cracking sound, although he could see the rock had cut deeply into the other man's skull; blood was already gathering.

Suddenly it occurred to him that he could be seen standing there, next to the body. He quickly glanced around and was relieved to see no one; there were sounds in the distance, but he couldn't be sure if they were voices or just the wind.

He hurriedly took off his nylon backpack and laid it on the ground. Grabbing the body by one arm, he pulled it away from the cliff and then took hold of it by both armpits, fighting with the little man's dead weight. As quickly as he could, he dragged the body the short distance to the cave's entrance and bent low enough to back into it, pulling the body with him. Sweating heavily now, he struggled to arrange the little man against the wall in a sitting position, feeling the strain in his arms as when he lifted weights. For the first time, he became aware of the fetid smell of the darkened room. Then he remembered the tracks made by the feet; he had to be sure to smooth them out before he left.

Still cautious, he retrieved his backpack and stepped back inside. Watching the other man out of the corner of his eye, he took out his Swiss Army knife and selected a particularly sharp blade. He laid the knife on the ground, carefully put on a pair of kitchen gloves, and picked the knife back up. Squatting on his haunches, he lifted the man's balding head and, as hard as he could, ran the blade across the throat, immediately releasing a rush of blood.

He watched for a while, struck by the fact that he could feel the warmth of the blood even through the rubber glove. Finally he backed away and sat against the wall, forcing himself to remember everything he had been told to do. Her instructions had been very specific. He had to be quick, he knew, since he still had to make it back to his motorcycle without being seen and then to his office.

First he dabbed his right forefinger in some of the pooling blood and with it drew a wavy line on the man's forehead. He carefully cleaned his knife as best he could with a paper towel and then peeled off the bloodied gloves and dumped everything into a plastic bag. After placing it in his backpack, he picked out the other things he had been given and arranged them in front of the body as he had been told.

Before he left, he carefully swept the floor of the cave and then the outside pathway with a tree branch. Again glancing around, he took one last look at the dead man. He could still hear the *thump* the rock had made.

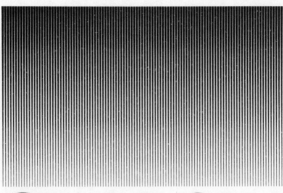

SHADOW MAN

chapter

1

SUNDAY AFTERNOON

The wind blew down from the north, touching the last of the snow on the Jemez Mountains, stirring the locoweed and wild snapdragons in White Rock Canyon.

David Parker could see the small petals and stalks move gently in the breeze. He lowered the window a little to let in more air and then leaned back in the leather seat. It was pleasantly cool outside but warm inside the Volvo with the sun pouring through the windshield.

It was an unusually clear spring afternoon in northern New Mexico. The sky was particularly blue, he thought, except for the heavy dark clouds threatening in the west. He stared out of his window down the highway and then out the other side.

Damnit! he thought. Elisha and Tevis should have been here fifteen minutes ago.

He was parked off the road in a graveled area that for a short distance paralleled a barbed-wire fence. On the other side of a dilapidated metal gate was a dirt trail that a led to the ruins of an Anasazi Indian community built and abandoned centuries before. All along the trail were dozens of caves and cliff dwellings. Next to the gate was a weathered piece of wood with peeling white and black paint: U.S. DEPARTMENT OF INTERIOR: TSANKAWI RUINS.

Behind him, to the north, lay the city of Los Alamos and the elaborate complex of buildings that belonged to his employer, the Los Alamos National Laboratory. To the southwest, maybe thirty miles away, was Santa Fe.

Parker pushed his head back again and tried to release some of the tension he felt in his neck. He closed his eyes against the glare of the bright sunlight. He had promised his son this family outing weeks ago, although it came at the worst possible time for him. At dawn tomorrow one of his scientific teams would test an experimental laser, and later in the day members of a Senate subcommittee would begin to arrive at the laboratory for what the Senate chairman was calling a "field meeting."

He rubbed his eyes, producing small, indistinct red images in the darkness of his inner eye. The work was intense these days, the politics ferocious as laboratories like Los Alamos and Livermore in California jockeyed for a share of the billions of dollars of government research funds for what newspaper reporters had dubbed Star Wars. Tomorrow's project was a crucial test of a laser with enough potential power to blast away incoming enemy missiles. Next week, another team of his would detonate a small nuclear bomb underground and attempt to produce enough X rays to do the same thing.

He opened his eyes and looked at his watch again. It was almost one-thirty. He had already spent a few hours this morning at his office. It had taken another hour to go home, change clothes, and then drive down to the ruins. Later this afternoon he would have to visit with members of his staff, who would be working through the night to prepare the giant laser for tomorrow's test.

Parker opened one of the manila-colored files that sat next to him on the seat; it contained interoffice memoranda asking for travel approval, staff reassignments, equipment requests, and all the bureaucratic demands that increasingly filled his time. At forty-three, he was the youngest associate director in the lab, but as he told his wife, in five years he had moved out of science into management.

From the rearview mirror he caught a reflection of himself. The eyes were still blue, but his brown hair had more gray in it. His face was still lean, like the rest of him, and his features were what his wife, Elisha, liked to call "handsome and clean-cut." It was an assessment he had heard all of his life, although the image in the mirror revealed a man who was perhaps working too hard. He edged closer and squinted into the glass and saw that his eyes were mildly bloodshot, with faint shadows appearing to hover underneath. All of the week's events came flooding back to him, and he fell back into the seat with a sigh.

Briefly he thumbed through the other folders containing unclassified project reports and lists of expenditures. Suddenly he smiled. One report was an estimate of new Defense Department funding for his laser project that would add almost thirty million dollars to his annual budget and increase his staff by another fifty scientists. *That* was very unlikely, he thought, given the hesitation Congress was expressing for the Strategic Defense Initiative.

Outside the car the sun seemed even brighter, although the dark clouds seemed to have moved closer. In that respect, Parker thought, Los Alamos could be like his hometown in California. There was little pollution in Stanford, and most days were sunny and bright. But that was the only similarity, he thought. Stanford was warm and flat and a tropical rain forest compared to the mountainous desert of Los Alamos. Growing up around the Stanford University campus, where both of his parents still taught, had never prepared him for the sort of life he and his family lived in New Mexico. To Parker, outdoor activity was tennis and jogging, both of which he disliked performing at an altitude of eight thousand feet. Hiking, the sort of thing he was going to do this afternoon, was not something he looked forward to.

Parker studied the landscape for a moment. It was, as everyone said, extraordinarily beautiful. The large volcano that had formed the area millions of years ago had created a series of mesas and corrugated canyons in earth colors of washed orange and yellow and brown. Scattered throughout, in weathered cliffs and on sun-bleached mesas, were the ruins of ancient peoples who had occupied the land in small communities well over a thousand years ago. This was the sort of thing he had learned from his archaeologist wife. Even Tevis, his eleven-year-old son, had taken a passionate interest in Indians and was now beginning to devour his mother's scholarly texts on the subject. Parker understood the beauty of the scene, but it was not beautiful for him. He looked forward to the day when he could leave Los Alamos and return to a university campus.

How much longer? he wondered. These days, his work was far removed from the laboratory and involved mostly management and institutional politics. And survival, he thought. Getting to the top in the small world of weapons development was more grueling than he could ever have imagined when he took the job ten years ago.

He had just settled back into the seat again when a horn sounded and the family Silverado pulled in next to him.

Parker pulled his lanky frame out of the station wagon and waited by his door until Elisha stepped down. Tevis sprang out of the backseat and rushed past him to the gate.

"Hey, Dad," he shouted. Elisha waved.

"Hello!" he said. "You're late."

"Hello, yourself. Are we?" Elisha smiled and looked at her watch. "Everything okay?" she asked.

It was almost two o'clock; he had been here nearly forty-five minutes.

"I hope so." He gave her a light kiss on the cheek. From the west, there was the faint sound of thunder. Parker turned to look; the possibility of sudden mountain lightning always scared him. In the mountains, he knew that lightning killed dozens of people a year. A few individuals—the lucky ones who weren't killed instantly, he thought—remembered their hair suddenly standing on end just before the lightning struck.

"Honey," he said, turning to his wife, "maybe we should call it off." He pointed in the direction of the dark clouds.

Elisha looked at the sky. "Oh, come on. Tevis is really looking foward to this."

Parker sighed and reached back into the Volvo to lock the door. He was tired, but he had promised.

"All right, let's go."

Elisha had already begun to climb to the mesa, which lay a mile away. Her otherwise slim shape was momentarily disguised by the large canvas bag she carried at her side. Parker pushed himself away from the car and started up the dirt trail behind his wife. It was hard to shake his lethargy; he had been to Tsankawi before, perhaps even several times. With Elisha he had been to a dozen other archaeological sites around Los Alamos over the years. They all looked the same to him.

Only intense lobbying from Elisha and Tevis had taken him from his office. All he could think of right now was the test tomorrow morning and the Senate subcommittee hearing a day later. Everyone from his boss on up to the director was waiting for the results. In his small universe of weapons research, no undertaking had greater priority these days than SDI.

Parker watched as his wife carefully examined something on the ground. Because of a earlier rain, the earth was a deep ocher color and the air was thick with the scent of piñon and juniper trees. Even from this distance, he could make out the elegant features of her face framed by short, blond hair.

He studied her with a mixture of affection and faint loss. They seemed to have no time for themselves these days. There was his work at the laboratory, and her career as a archaeologist specializing in the American Southwest—and there was Tevis, of course, who demanded more time than ever.

For a while they hiked, but even though the vistas of the ruins surrounded them, Parker kept talking about his heavy schedule at the lab.

Elisha stopped and turned to face him. "The Los Alamos National Laboratory leads the world, huh?" she asked, a slight edge to her voice. He knew her opinion about his weapons work and the demands it placed on his schedule. Most of all, he knew she took a dim view of his inability to put aside his professional concerns when they did have time together.

"I guess I am a little obsessive about the lab's progress right now," he said, reacting to her disapproving tone. "But the political pressure for success is intense, and the laser work looks particularly promising. Maybe more so after tomorrow. If it works, we really would lead the world—for the moment."

"I suppose Greenberg is watching all with more than a little bit of interest?"

"Like a hawk eyeing his last chance for a meal." Parker thought of his boss. Francis Greenberg was pushing sixty, and any breakthrough on Star Wars needed to come soon for his career to close on a high note.

"Is it going to work?" she asked.

"Maybe. Maybe not. Whatever happens, it won't be what everybody wants."

"What do you mean?"

"They want a superweapon. Something all-powerful that can't fail." He paused. "And my laser isn't that." He started walking again. "Even if it works."

They fell silent until they came to a point where the trail divided. Ahead of them, on the path that went to the right, they could see Tevis.

"Slow down!" she yelled to him.

Parker walked behind her, picking his way on a path that was a combination of Park Service construction and Anasazi footwork hundreds of years old.

Elisha stopped suddenly and pointed to a spot on a cliff to their left.

"What?" he asked, seeing nothing out of the ordinary.

"There! In that small patch of light stone. See? Petroglyphs."

Parker strained his eyes in the general direction of his wife's finger and finally made out a series of small stick figures that resembled deer or antelope. Nearby were a freshly carved swastika and the inscription "Joe + Marcia."

Tevis was still ahead of them, stationary for a moment as he poked with a stick under a rock. Such a bright kid, Parker thought. A gifted child, some of his teachers said, but an increasingly difficult one.

Tevis was always in trouble at school, mostly for disrupting his classes by showing off, or for telling wild stories, or for telling his classmates what they didn't know. This year he had twice been caught stealing books from a local bookstore. The psychologists—there had been two already—consistently painted a portrait of a bright, lonely child whose intelligence and imagination compensated for the inadequacy of parental love and attention.

Parker didn't know what to do. His laser work would take him through most of the rest of year. Elisha planned to spend part of the summer at an archaeological dig sponsored by the University of New Mexico. Just yesterday, he had heard Tevis ask his mother if he could go along. He would do anything, he pleaded, but he didn't want to be left with the maid all summer.

"You know," Elisha said softly, "there are hundreds of Anasazi sites in New Mexico alone, perhaps thousands. Most not as spectacular as this, but each one a place where people once lived and raised families." She looked beyond the trail into the valley. "And died," she added.

What opened in front of them in a broad sweep was a valley that seemed to run all the way down to the Rio Grande. The mesas, just coming out of winter, were still brown and yellow, not yet green with spring growth. The valley was greener, but not lush. Parker always thought Los Alamos to be a peculiar mix of desert and mountain, and because of its geography, a thoroughly questionable site for one of the government's most important scientific laboratories. Beautiful yes, but isolated and cumbersome compared to conventional laboratories in urban universities.

Ahead of his parents, Tevis walked along the path studying the cliff wall on his left. In some places it rose fifty feet or more almost straight up. In other spots, the cliff edge had eroded and dropped large boulders and other rubble down to the level of the path, forming a rocky slope to the top of the mesa. Tevis was looking for caves.

Although his parents didn't know it, he had been to Tsankawi before. Last fall he had ridden his bike down here and explored the ruins all by himself. He had learned in school that many of the caves around Los Alamos had been occupied by Indians, some of them a thousand years ago. Scattered throughout the mesas and canyons were old pieces of broken pottery shards and arrowheads.

Behind him, he heard his father's voice calling.

"I'm here!" he shouted back.

He waited a minute for his parents to catch up. Out of the corner of his eye, above him, he caught a movement. Looking up, he saw a figure in a dark coat dart between two large outcroppings of rock a hundred feet away. The image was fleeting, but for a moment the shadowy figure seemed to pause and look straight at him. Tevis concentrated his gaze. Nothing else moved. He couldn't be sure, but it looked like a man wearing something dark, with a hood. Perhaps it was an Indian from one of the nearby pueblos. Just then his parents turned the corner and walked next to him.

"Let's try to stick together, okay?" said Parker.

Tevis nodded, then looked back at where he had seen the shadow man. There was nothing there.

Tevis took off down the trail again. "Come on! Come on!" he cried.

On the mesa, Parker stopped to catch his breath; he was sweating and he could feel his shirt sticking to his skin underneath the nylon windbreaker. He reminded himself once again how much he disliked hiking in these damn mountains.

A dozen yards in front of him were the ruins of Tsankawi, now mostly earthen mounds heavily overgrown with weeds and grass.

"The Anasazi abandoned Tsankawi sometime around fifteen hundred," said Tevis. Parker noticed that he pronounced it "Sank-kah-wee." No doubt he was correct. Tevis looked up at his father. "The Anasazi, Dad, were the parents of the modern Pueblo Indians."

Parker smiled; his son sometimes seemed almost as well versed on the archaeology of the Southwest as Elisha. Parker had heard all this before, but he didn't want to spoil his son's pleasure. Tevis was jumping from one mound to another, spilling information as he did so. Actually, Parker thought, his son was lecturing. From whom, he mused, had his precocious son learned that?

"These are kivas, Dad," he said, pointing to two shallow pits in the ground. "Religious ceremonial rooms. They were originally below ground, and you got in through a hole in the roof. Only guys were allowed in."

There was a deep, low roll of thunder in the distance. Parker looked up and realized that the storm they had seen building earlier was now only minutes away. He thought again of lightning.

"I think it's going to rain," he said to Elisha. There was another low growl in the darkening sky.

Tevis was talking to him. "Dad, it's something. Once, you know, there were three hundred fifty rooms here. Maybe a thousand people. Maybe more." He ran off to another pile of overgrown stones.

Parker watched his wife search the ground with a practiced eye. Suddenly he remembered an image of her from college. It was early September of his last year, and they had been dating for almost a year. Elisha had been gone most of the summer, working on an archaeological excavation in Arizona, her first experience in the field.

She burst into his dorm room on her first day back, her arm in a plaster cast as a result of a hiking accident. She was tanned, her hair golden from the sun, and he thought that despite the cast no one could look more beautiful. For weeks, kissing was awkward, making love even more so. But for nearly eighteen years that image of her standing in the doorway had stayed with him.

There was another rumbling in the distance. Standing on an earthen mound and looking over a sea of grass, Parker made out the water towers of Los Alamos and even the outlines of some laboratory buildings. He smiled to himself. He had been startled on his first visit to Los Alamos to learn that nearly eighteen thousand people lived on the edge of a modern scientific laboratory. Just a mile or two away from where he stood was one of the world's most powerful linear accelerators, and not much farther the buildings housing his experimental electron laser.

"Perhaps we should start back, David."

He nodded and called to Tevis.

Elisha laughed. "Saved by the rain." She shook her head. "I know you don't like the outdoors." She lightly took his arm. "But you've already spent most of this morning at your office. It would have been nice to have had a little time together." Her voice was mocking, but not unkind.

Parker smiled. She should talk. She taught classes down in Albuquerque twice a week and spent weeks away during the dry months on archaeological digs. Thank God they had a dependable maid who stayed with Tevis when Elisha was away.

Tevis stood nearby, looking intently at one of the piles of rubble.

"He's extraordinary, David, so imaginative." She smiled. "The other day he made up this complicated story for me, something about a lost tribe of Indians living in an abandoned bomb shelter near Los Alamos."

"Another archaeologist in the family?"

Elisha lifted an eyebrow, not sure if he was being sarcastic. "Do you want another bomb maker?"

Parker forced a smile. Inside, he wondered how strongly she felt about his work. It had never been an issue before, especially since Elisha had her own career. He was often wistful, however. There was a time when all he wanted to be was a college professor, rising in the

academic ranks to head a physics department at a major university—
or better, directing a breakthrough research project, one whose
successes could be talked about openly.

"Let's go, Tev," said Elisha.

"Not yet, Mom, we just got here," protested Tevis.

"Look, it's going to rain," David said wearily.

Tevis looked as if he were suddenly going to pout.

"Let's *go*," Parker said, irritated as the weather grew more
threatening.

Five minutes later, it began to rain, just a few drops at first.
They covered another fifty yards before it began to pour in great,
heavy sheets. Parker stuffed his dark glasses inside his pocket. Nearby
there was a flash of light, followed swiftly by the crack and roll of
thunder.

Parker rushed up to his wife and grabbed her shoulder. "Let's
find a cave." Elisha nodded, a grim expression on her face. She ran
ahead and took Tevis's arm. He couldn't hear their conversation but
saw her point to the cliffs on their right. Fortunately, they were
pocked with dozens of small, dark recesses. Tevis immediately began
scrambling up the rocks.

There was another powerful flash of lightning, followed by an
even louder crash of thunder.

Jesus! Parker thought. *We'll be killed by the goddamn lightning*.

Above him, he saw Elisha disappear into one of the dark,
irregular holes and hover at the entrance looking for them. Tevis was
several dozen feet away, moving toward another cluster of black
openings. Rainwater, washing off the sides of the cliff, was beginning to run in torrents down the trail they had just left.

Bruising his hands and knees on the rocks and cursing heavily,
Parker finally made it to a small ledge and a cave; huddled inside was
Elisha.

Tevis was thirty feet away, making his way on a rough path
toward him.

"Stay there until the rain stops!" he shouted. Tevis clambered
into the nearest opening.

Parker stepped inside and sat down opposite his wife. His
windbreaker was waterproof, but rain had run down his back and
chest and he was soaked through. "Tevis is in another cave. I told

him to wait there." He leaned back against the wall and then put his head on the darkened surface; it looked black to him.

Watching him, Elisha said, "They built fires in these caves. You're leaning against a five-hundred-year-old fireplace."

He laughed, but he was wet and cold and miserable. Outside, the rain showed no signs of lessening.

Ten yards away, Tevis suddenly thought of snakes just as he began to move farther into the cave. He cautiously looked around. In the deeper darkness caused by the rain, the cave looked larger than it was, but it seemed empty. Then he realized that he could stand upright. With his hand he touched the moist, clammy roof of the cave. It was cold and smelled funny, like pee, he thought, and there was another smell he couldn't recognize. It wasn't until his eyes adjusted to the dark that he made out the figure of a man sitting in the corner.

Tevis let out a cry but didn't move. The man didn't respond. He sat slumped against the cave wall with his knees pulled toward his chest, his head resting stiffly against the wall, mouth open. He was wearing a tan jacket and brown shirt.

"Hello," Tevis said timidly, and then louder, "Hello?"

There was no response.

Tevis took a step or two closer. It was then that he realized that the dark brown shirt wasn't brown at all: it was dried blood from a wide slash across the throat. The man was dead.

Tevis stared but didn't move closer. The only dead person he had ever seen had been an uncle, but this man didn't look at all like him. The expression on his face—if it was an expression—was one of surprise. On his forehead was a dusky red jagged line. His hands, which were at his sides, seemed to melt into the dark earthen floor.

Tevis forced himself to stand very still, trying not to move even a finger. He was prepared to run out of the cave if there was even the slightest movement from across the room. Slowly, the shock turned to curiosity.

What finally brought Tevis closer were two small painted figures pushed partway into the soft dirt floor in front of the man's shoes. Scattered about them were pieces of cornmeal and twigs from a tree of some kind. Tevis studied them a moment and then pulled one of the objects from the floor. It lifted without a sound as he waited for any sign of movement from the man. There was none. He reached down and pulled up the second object, similar in shape, and examined both before he put them inside his jacket. He looked at the sprigs and tossed them into the corner of the cave.

He studied the body again. The man was older than his father, and balding. There appeared to be a large, dark bruise on the top of his head. Tevis realized that he had to tell his father about this. He carefully made his way in the rain across the slippery rocks to where he had last seen his father waving.

Inside, Parker sat in silence, miserably pressed against the damp wall. His mind was once again on his office and all he had to do this week. Elisha was leafing through the pages of her notebook.

From the corner of his eye, he caught a flicker of movement outside the entrance. Startled, he looked up to see his son.

"Tevis!" he shouted, "what the hell are you doing?" As he rose, he forgot the low ceiling and hit his head hard.

"For God's sake, come in! Didn't I tell you to stay put?"

"Dad?"

Elisha was up by now and took Tevis by the shoulder. "Are you all right?" she asked.

Tevis felt the objects in his coat.

"Dad. In the cave," he stumbled. He pointed outside.

"What?"

"In the cave. A dead man."

"What?" Parker was incredulous. What in the hell was Tevis talking about?

"A dead man. Covered with blood."

chapter

2

SUNDAY AFTERNOON

The man in the dark blue windbreaker paused for a moment, hidden by a large fissure in the face of the cliff. Now that the nausea had passed, he was surprised at how calm he felt. There had been only a moment after hearing the boy's voice to pull the hood of his jacket over his head and dart out of view. The kid couldn't have seen much.

He hid behind some large rocks and waited for the boy and his parents to pass by. When he thought it was safe, he stuck his head out carefully and looked. The path below was empty. As quickly as he could, the tall man scrambled up the face of the cliff along a break where the erosion made a natural pathway. When he reached the top of the mesa, he forced himself to walk slowly like any other tourist. He could tell from the dark clouds that it was going to rain soon.

It was still a half-mile to where his motorcycle was hidden behind some rocks. As a precaution, he took off his windbreaker and stuffed it into his backpack, just in case someone else came along. He made sure the flap fit snugly on the Velcro strip and felt the sides of the pack: the package of wadded gloves and towels were still there.

He wouldn't have picked this place to murder someone, of

course, certainly no place so public. But Berriman had forced his hand with yesterday's confrontation. He laughed. What a joke the little man had been! It never occurred to Berriman that any more was at stake than the possibility that his work was being pirated by another staff member. Certainly no suspicion that weapons data was being pulled off the laboratory's central computer from Berriman's own terminal. And no idea that the information was being sold to strange people in California.

As he walked, the man re-created the scene in the cave. With luck, when Berriman was eventually found, the manner of his death and the small objects at his feet would lead the police to suspect an Indian. If that didn't work, then the objects placed in Berriman's home by the man's girlfriend this morning would make them suspect Berriman was involved in a very expensive, and ultimately fatal, hobby.

The only thing left to do was to get back into the lab's computer and see if he could eliminate any record of his use of Berriman's terminal. He would have to think carefully about this, however, since a misstep might alert the security system built into the central computer. But he could work it out later.

All things considered, he thought, this business has gone rather well.

"You're sure?" Parker looked hard at his son's face.

"Dad! His throat is cut." Tevis made a broad sweeping motion with his hand across his throat.

"Oh God," cried Elisha.

Parker was silent for a moment. "Okay, we'll check it out."

He turned to Elisha. "Look, we don't know what's going on. You wait here. I'll send Tevis back as soon as possible."

"No way! I'm coming."

Tevis stood by the doorway, eyes wide. Parker wondered if his son was imagining all this.

As the three of them stepped outside, he noticed that the rain was easing up. *That* was something, at least.

When they got to the opening of the cave Parker stopped. "You two wait here."

"Dad! It's raining out here."

"All right, but wait right inside the entrance." There was no telling who or what was really inside the cave.

Parker edged into the chamber. At least the ceiling was a little higher than the last cave. Almost immediately he saw the body against the rear wall, its head jerked back and chin thrust awkwardly upward. The great slash across the throat was visible even from where he stood.

"Oh my God!" said Parker, feeling scared and sick at the same time.

"You see! It looks like he's wearing a brown shirt." Tevis started to move closer until his father waved him back. Elisha stepped in and gasped. Slowly she backed out into the rain.

Parker took another step and then stopped. There was no doubt that the man was dead and that someone had delivered a fatal whack to the poor man's throat. Parker looked around for a moment and then realized that something else was terribly wrong. He knew the man. He was a member of his staff.

Parker fought back his nausea. All he could do was stare at the lifeless form against the wall.

Tevis came up next to him. He looked at the man's feet to see if he had left anything. There were only two small depressions where the objects had been. He looked at his dad.

Elisha came up and took Parker's arm.

"I know him," he said, "he works for me." Then he caught himself. "I mean, he worked for me." They both stared for a moment. "Let's go." He took Tevis by the arm and pushed him out of the cave. "We need to call the police as soon as possible. Let's get out of here."

Tom Reyes was on Highway 4 halfway between his office at the San Ildefonso Reservation and Los Alamos when the police radio crackled and a voice came on. He had been monitoring the Los Alamos County police on his radio. Just a few minutes before, the dispatcher had reported speeding teenage motorcyclists near the Bandelier National Monument.

This call was a request for backup support. That mildly interested Reyes, since the request itself suggested something more than speeding cyclists. What really caught his ear was the mention of the

Tsankawi ruins. Reyes immediately turned the volume up. The ruins were bordered by his pueblo's reservation.

Reyes quickly learned that the requesting officer was already at Tsankawi. Of course, like most Anglos, he had mispronounced the Indian name, calling it something like "Sand Wee." Then Reyes heard the words "possible homicide."

He accelerated. Tsankawi was maybe ten minutes away.

Reyes had been at his job for less than a year. Before that, he had bummed his way around the country, living mostly on the West Coast. Before that he had put in nearly fifteen years in the Marines as a policeman. For five years during his Marine career he had been married to a white woman. Now he was forty, divorced, a recovered alcoholic, and living on the very same reservation that he had once tried desperately to put behind him. Life, he thought, had a strange way of turning out. Perhaps his old uncle was right: the white world was like a dazzling fire that was always cold the next morning.

Reyes mulled over his uncle's words for a minute. One thing was true. He had returned to San Ildefonso over a year ago, alone, with his life in pieces, and with no future to speak of. Perhaps "future" was more of an Anglo term, he thought. But his aunt and uncle, all that was left of his immediate family, took him back, as did the pueblo itself. They even gave him a job as policeman. As his ex-wife would no doubt say, once an Indian, always an Indian.

Reyes stayed on Highway 4 where it veered and split off to the right from another road that twisted its way to the east end of Los Alamos. The Tsankawi ruins were just a mile or so down the two-lane highway. The landscape at this point was some of the most dramatic in New Mexico, with the highway cutting through melon-colored rock that had eroded to form pylons. Dotting the cliffs were hundreds of small caves, like ink blots on a yellowed page. Most had been formed by the natural forces of rain and wind, while others had been carved hundreds of years before by hand.

Reyes pulled over to the left and parked beside the county police car. The only other vehicles were a new Silverado truck and a Volvo station wagon. All were empty. He speculated that the homicide, if that was what it was, had occurred somewhere in the ruins or perhaps along one of the trails that wound around the mesa. Now that he was here, he couldn't help thinking as a policeman.

He decided to take the cliff trail, which was longer but provided a number of naturally sheltered places where people could hide. As it turned out, it was the right choice. About three-quarters of a mile from the parking lot, he saw several figures standing outside of a cluster of small black holes in the cliff wall. They were maybe fifty yards off the dirt trail and up the sloping face of the cliff. As he walked closer, he realized that there was a child in the group.

Reyes left the trail and began to climb up a smaller, less-defined pathway. Although there were fresh footprints, they were probably those of the group in front of him. The heavy rain an hour earlier would have obliterated older impressions. Although he was in fairly good shape these days, he still felt the effects of the rapid climb. He was tall for an Indian, almost six feet, and while not slender, he had managed to lose nearly thirty-five pounds in the last six months. As he approached, he saw the Los Alamos police chief scowling down at him. Reyes was glad he was wearing his pueblo uniform. He waved but got no response. Son of a bitch doesn't like Indians, he thought.

"Afternoon, Chief," Reyes said matter-of-factly, making a point of standing back and not extending his hand. Bobby Smith was standing next to a couple and a young boy maybe ten or eleven years old. From their looks and clothing, Reyes guessed they were from Los Alamos. Everything they wore was expensive.

"Uh, Reyes," Smith said without expression. Reyes judged that on a scale of ten, this welcome was a one.

"I overheard your call on the radio for backup. I was in the area and thought I could help." Reyes formed one of his few smiles, no more than a slight upturn of his lips at the corners of his mouth. Reyes hesitated a moment and then added, "San Ildefonso land runs all along these ruins."

Smith raised one eyebrow. "Yeah, I called for backup. I need a coroner and a photographer." He shrugged and nodded behind him at a cave. "Take a look."

Reyes passed by the Anglo couple and said hello. They seemed more tired than shocked. Probably discovered the body, he thought. He stepped into the low overhang of the entrance and paused. The heavy rain had stopped almost an hour ago and the clear sky provided good light. He immediately saw the body slumped against the back wall. The man's throat had been slashed, and there was dried blood around his body.

This was more than just murder, Reyes thought. Someone had picked a damn messy way to kill.

He looked around the small, humid chamber and caught the sour smell of blood. There was nothing else in the room. The footprints he could see were mostly those of adults, although he could make out a child's tennis shoe in several spots. On either side of the body the loose dirt floor had been carefully swept, probably with a tree branch. The semicircular motion looked very fresh. Whoever had taken the time to cut the man's throat had also taken the time to erase his own tracks. The only exception were two small dimples in the dirt floor in front of the shoes.

Reyes studied the shallow depressions for a moment. Both looked as if something cylindrical had been pushed into the ground and then pulled out, something like the end of a stick or pole. Then he noticed the jagged line on the dead man's forehead; it had been drawn in blood. Reyes felt a slight shudder go through him. The line wasn't wavy; it had been deliberately drawn angularly, in a zigzag fashion.

Reyes backed out of the cave into the sunlight. Smith was talking to the couple.

"Reyes, this is Dr. Parker and his wife from Los Alamos." Smith had apparently softened.

"It's *Drs.* Parker," said the young boy. "They are both doctors." The woman smiled.

Smith cleared his throat. "Yes, the Parkers. They found the body about an hour ago."

"*I* found the body," said the young boy.

"Yes. He found the body first. This," he said, pointing to Tom, "is Officer Reyes from San Ildefonso." Smith seemed relieved to have the introductions over with.

He listened to Smith and Parker talk for a few minutes, then casually let his eyes search the setting. The cave was fifteen yards off the trail, up a fairly steep grade. In all likelihood, the man inside had been murdered here, or at least nearby. Dragging a body from the highway would have been impossible for one person, difficult for two. If he was killed in the cave, or immediately outside, there was no evidence of a struggle. Perhaps the victim and his murderer knew each other? Reyes turned back to the conversation.

"His name is Isaac Berriman," Parker said with a sigh. "He's been on my staff for several months now. I was only getting to know him. In fact, I saw him only yesterday at the lab. He was working on Saturday—we have a busy week coming up—but he did nothing or said nothing that would suggest he was part of something like *this*." He pointed to the cave.

"What kind of work did he do, Dr. Parker?" asked Reyes. He looked carefully at Smith to be sure he wasn't violating Anglo protocol by intervening.

"Well, he was a mathematician, a very good one. He was working on theoretical models of laser efficiency." Parker looked searchingly to see if his listeners understood. "The precise nature of his work is classified, of course, but he was very good."

Smith asked some other questions and made notes on a small pad. A few minutes later, the coroner and two deputies arrived. The inside of the cave was swept for objects and "pertinent evidence," as the chief called it. Photographs were taken, briefly turning the dark cave entrance brilliant white, and finally a portable light was set up to permit the coroner to begin a preliminary exam.

The coroner was a short, heavyset man named Ferry. Reyes decided that must have cost him considerable grief as a child. After a few minutes, he stuck his head out of the cave, sweating profusely.

Smith lit a cigarette. "What can you tell us?"

"Throat slashed, of course. But also a major blow to his head. I suspect he was knocked out first, then had his throat cut. Anyway, an autopsy will clear it up. No external signs of a struggle, however. Probably didn't know what hit him." Ferry paused, then added, "I'd say he's been dead two, maybe three hours."

"What about the blood on his forehead?" asked Reyes.

"I assume it's his blood," replied the coroner. "Too stylistic to be natural, though. Maybe a message of some kind?"

Smith frowned. "Jesus, that's all we need. Some crazy out here killing people and leaving a calling card in blood."

"Ritualistic murder?" Ferry looked at Reyes, who made no response.

"Let's just hope the newspapers don't pick up on this," said Smith.

Just then one of the deputies came out with a small rake and shook his head. "Nothing on the floor."

"Anything on the body itself?" Smith asked.

"Not a lot. His wallet is missing, but he has a camera and a watch. But we'll have to get him out of the cave to make a thorough check."

Reyes turned to Parker. "Did the man have a lot of money?"

"I don't think so. As far as I know, he's been at the laboratory for fifteen years or so. His salary was good, but I don't think he was rich." Parker found himself uneasy talking about Berriman in the past tense.

Smith seemed eager to go. He ordered the body taken out and put into a thick green plastic bag. Reyes watched the deputies shove Berriman into the bag, sweating and cursing as they did so. "Goddamn dead weight," mumbled one.

"Mind if I take one last look, Sheriff?" Reyes tried to make the request sound insignificant. Smith shook his head as if he didn't care and Reyes reentered the cave.

Reyes wondered if something had been missed. He carefully scanned the floor, then the walls for a sign of a scuffle. The deputy had raked the entire floor. With the blade of his knife he poked around randomly in the cave. Nothing. Then he moved closer to the spot where the body had sat. Again, nothing. He was just ready to leave when his eye caught a glint of yellow in the dirt near the entrance. With his blade he raked the floor; more yellow appeared.

Reyes bent down and went carefully through the dirt with his fingers. More yellow appeared. Turning toward the light, he realized he had bits of cornmeal in his hand. It was hard to tell its age, but it couldn't be too old. He stepped outside.

"Found this," he said, holding the cornmeal in his hand.

Smith looked at it and frowned. "What is it?"

"Cornmeal."

"What?"

"Bits of ground corn."

"Was someone eating it?" asked Smith.

"Maybe," answered Reyes. He was thinking something else. Cornmeal had a religious purpose among his people. But was that a possibility here? he thought.

Smith shrugged, disinterested. "Let's get out of here." He waved to his deputy. "Close it up."

Nails were driven into the soft stone on either side of the entrance and a yellow rope hung in between. A sign reading POLICE AREA—DO NOT ENTER was connected with thin wire. More photographs were taken.

Reyes held back a moment while Parker and the others began the walk back to the parking area. It was late in the afternoon and the sun would soon set. This murder, he thought, had to be more than robbery. Whatever the motive, Reyes had to admit that he was intrigued. He would come back.

On Barranca Mesa, one of the more expensive suburbs of Los Alamos, Tevis heard a car pull up, its engine stop, and a door slam. He glanced out the window and saw his father, looking tired, walking to the house.

"Dad's back from the police station!" he yelled.

In his bedroom, Tevis took one last look at the two objects from the Tsankawi cave. Both objects were similar and roughly the same size and consisted of a flat, wooden figure on a dowel that formed a handle. It had been an effort to keep them hidden in his windbreaker without making a sound or letting them show through the thin fabric.

He picked one up and studied it again. The figure was crudely shaped like a man with his hands extended upwards. Tevis could tell that it had been painted a long time ago, since now there were only traces of paint: red, green, black, and an even fainter hint of yellow. Cut into the center of the figure was a small bird. He couldn't be sure, but both objects looked very old, very worn by the touch of countless human hands. He guessed that they had been left as part of a ceremony of some kind, maybe a religious one.

He covered each one with a T-shirt and placed them in the back of the bottom drawer of a chest. He would have to find out what they were and what they were used for. Down the hall from his room he heard the front door open and close and his father shout hello.

chapter 3

MONDAY MORNING

A switch was flipped and a Klaxon wailed, its loud, piercing sound flooding every room in the complex.

Parker clenched the metal railing in front of him and shut his eyes tight, trying to ignore the sound. It was six-ten in the morning and he had been here since four-thirty. Through a glass partition to his left, he could see into a waiting room, and through another window on the far wall, he could see outside. It was still dark.

He had barely slept, tossing and turning throughout the night, replaying the scene at Tsankawi a dozen times in his mind. The image of Berriman in the cave in a pool of blood wouldn't go away.

Ten feet away from him, on the other side of the rail, was the elaborate control panel that coordinated the test. Every light on the panel was being scanned by technicians casually dressed in tennis shoes and jeans. Blue Los Alamos security badges dangled from shirt collars and belt loops. Soft drink cans were everywhere. Above them, visible to everyone in the room, were a dozen television monitors studying from a dozen angles the machinery in the warehouse-sized room next door. Both the metal rail and the floor beneath him vibrated with a pulsating rhythm.

Another bank of switches was thrown, and in another room more equipment sprang to life. The throbbing movement in the floor increased, and Parker noticed that the mechanical hum that pervaded the building went up by several decibels. On several monitors Parker was able to see pieces of the giant laser begin to vibrate slightly. The movement would have been undetectable except that the shaking equipment was the size of a small car. Slowly the stale smell of the air-conditioning began to mix with the newer scent of heating metal as electricity was consumed at a rate that would power a small city. Thousands of feet of black electrical cable crisscrossing the floor surged with power.

Parker tried to loosen up, releasing his grip on the railing for a moment. He looked around the room. He was one of the oldest men there. Most of the team were young men in their twenties and early thirties; even Gabriella, the only female on the project, was twenty-eight.

"System ready!" shouted one of the technicians.

"Hit it!" said the crew chief. Parker again gripped the railing hard.

Next door, in a room half the size of a football field, a sophisticated array of electronic and mechanical devices began to generate a beam of electrons. As the beam bounced off specially designed magnets, the electrons began to wiggle violently and give off light. Several of the monitors above the control panel suddenly went white as a brilliant glow filled the laser room.

On another monitor, Parker caught the image of a shaft of light exploding against a sheet of metal, dissolving it in a shower of melting alloy and smoke. Tiny bits of brightly burning metal flew off into the room in a flood of small stars. Not coincidentally, he thought, the metal was the thickness of a Soviet missile's skin.

Just as quickly, the noise level dropped and the vibration in the floor settled down. Parker looked over at the crew chief, who had monitored a bank of digital readouts during the experiment. The man looked up and slowly shook his head. "Minimal," he said, his voice barely audible over the general noise of the room.

Parker forced a smile. "Well, it worked," he said to the man next to him.

He walked outside the control room and down the metal stairs to the room containing the laser. The temperature was at least fifteen degrees warmer, and the smell of ozone mixed with the acrid stench of fused metal. At least the equipment was still in one piece, he thought.

He congratulated his staff, encouraging them not to be disappointed, and emphasized that the results were promising. That was the key word, he thought: *promising*. The problem was not one of making the laser more powerful, more destructive, but of making everyone understand that a lot of difficult, perhaps impossible, work remained to be done. He glanced around him. It would be a while before the huge device that filled this room was a true weapon that could be counted on to destroy Soviet warheads in space. Suddenly he thought of the Senate subcommittee. Would *they* understand?

"Berriman murdered?" Francis Greenberg shook his large head and looked out the window at the snow-tipped Jemez Mountains to the west. Some of them, he knew, were over ten thousand feet high; in his younger days he had climbed them often enough.

Parker sat uncomfortably in a standard-issue government chair: gray metal with tweed cushions long since worn flat by everyday wear. Today, after nearly thirty minutes in Greenberg's office, he fell into a slump with his feet on the floor and his hands folded against his chest. Every few minutes he shifted slightly to alleviate the sore spot in his back where the metal frame of the chair pressed into his shoulder blades.

Greenberg had taken the news of this morning's test calmly, refusing to be put off by the lackluster results. "It's just a matter of time before it's improved," he said. "What's important now is to be optimistic and push ahead."

Parker watched his boss stare out the window in silence. He wondered how Greenberg was reacting to the fact that the overworked division was now short one man.

He shifted in the chair again, looking for a comfortable spot. Greenberg's office was typical of the lab: metal furniture—a round conference table and four chairs—and various bric-a-brac that Greenberg and his wife had picked up on their many travels. On the desk was a small lucite cube containing sand melted into glass by the first nuclear explosion in New Mexico in 1945.

For the most part, Parker found Greenberg easy to work for. The Old Man, as Parker liked to call him, was intelligent, utterly committed to his work, and generous. Greenberg would never receive the credit he was due: his entire lifetime of scientific work was hidden under the red ink of a TOP SECRET stamp. Greenberg never complained, of course, and perhaps it never occurred to him that he should be known outside of Department of Defense circles. Parker often wondered how the man's background came into play: he was the only child of an Irish Catholic mother and a Jewish father.

Parker watched the older man finger his tie, something he did when he was concentrating on a problem or considering an airline schedule. Greenberg was large and bulky, shorter than Parker by an inch. His pudgy face was offset by a heavy beard that he often shaved several times a day. The round face was topped by a thick mane of wiry gray hair. Despite the fact that he had lived in New Mexico for over twenty-five years, Greenberg had never adopted the casual style of dress so popular in the mountain community. Born and bred in Boston, he still wore a coat and tie most days, occasionally a suit, and his only concession to Southwestern dress was a bolo tie. Today, he wore a silver slide set with a large piece of turquoise.

At sixty-two, Greenberg faced retirement in the next few years. He was associate director for national security programs at Los Alamos, and after a career of nearly thirty-five years, he was known as one of the best bomb makers in the business.

The last few years had seen him move into what was rapidly becoming the focus of the defense establishment: a comprehensive, foolproof system for detecting and destroying enemy warheads before they could hit the U.S. Greenberg had earned a leadership position and now hoped for a major breakthrough to crown his career. He considered Parker a key to that success.

"Security called first thing this morning." Greenberg turned around and looked at Parker. "A preliminary autopsy confirmed what you saw. Berriman was hit on the head with a hard object, probably a rock, and then had his throat slashed." An unpleasant expression crossed his face as he said it.

Parker nodded.

"The sheriff's office can't be sure of the motive," Greenberg continued, "but they believe it wasn't robbery."

"Oh?"

"Yeah. Berriman was still wearing his watch, an expensive Rolex his late wife apparently gave him."

"He was married?"

"Some time back. She was killed in a car accident seven, maybe eight years ago."

Parker suddenly realized how little he knew about the dead man.

"Lab Security is coordinating with the sheriff on this. We should have a preliminary report later today." Greenberg picked up his coffee cup, looked inside, and changed his mind about drinking whatever was left.

"David, I have to warn you that all of us can expect to be interviewed by Security. A death like that, of a man with the highest clearance, well . . ."

"Is it possible, Francis," David asked, "that Berriman could have been involved in something. Something illegal? Blackmail?" Parker wondered if the classified nature of his work could have exposed him to exploitation.

"I don't know. I only hope Security, or someone, gets to the bottom of it." Greenberg frowned. "David, do you think Berriman's work has been jeopardized in some way?"

Parker thought about it for a moment. "Do you mean *compromised*?"

"No. Jeopardized. Berriman was loaned to us from the theoretical division to head up the correlations on the latest laser developments. Was anybody working with him? He was your boy." Greenberg tapped his finger on the desk several times.

"He was assigned to me a few months ago. Maybe just a month, I don't really remember. I do remember that he asked for very little staff support and apparently that is a well-established practice of his. He had a reputation for it, in fact."

Greenberg tapped his finger some more. "Jesus," he said suddenly. "Who can pick up his work?"

"I'd have to think about it, but we could consider Schneider. Or maybe Rollins."

"That hippie? Forget it." Greenberg worked well with most people but always had one or two individuals that he made little secret of disliking. Bob Rollins was one of them.

Parker smiled. "Let me work on it. We have someone, I'm sure." The real question, he thought, was who could step in the quickest.

"What about the Senate subcommittee visit. Everything okay?"
"It's okay."

Greenberg's attention had now shifted to tomorrow's congressional briefing in Los Alamos. This meeting was part of a Senate subcommittee hearing on the state of the Strategic Defense Initiative. The president's chief science adviser would be there, as would the Air Force general in charge of SDI. Senator Tom Kearney, the subcommittee chairman, had specifically asked for reports from Los Alamos, Lawrence Livermore in California, and several universities and defense contractors. Kearney wanted the meeting to be "in the field," where he and his committee could visit laboratories and meet staff. Participants from out of town would start arriving at Los Alamos later in the day. The closed hearing, which meant classified matters could be discussed, would start the next day.

Greenberg began tapping his finger on the desk again. "I want you to be positive. None of this 'so-so' crap. I know some of these senators are opposed to SDI. They'll be looking for any weak link in the chain."

"I'll do my best." Parker knew what was coming next.

"Remember," Greenberg began, smiling for the first time that day, "that the 'best light' is the best policy." By which, Parker thought, he meant don't discuss the possibilities of failure.

It was this side of his work that Parker was least comfortable with. Somehow, science had become subordinate to the need for a final product, not just knowledge itself. He was the youngest associate director at Los Alamos, with a multimillion-dollar project under him. But the message was clear: there was no future without a product that sold. In this case, the buyer was the Department of Defense.

His name was also under consideration for appointment to a top-level presidential commission on long-term science goals for the nation. If he were selected, he would probably be the youngest member on the commission as well. But the prestige of the appointment could be his ticket out of Los Alamos to a major university.

Parker forced a smile. "Our work *is* positive, Francis. But I do think we should avoid being overly optimistic about the end results. There's a long road ahead, and—"

"And we don't have to dwell on those difficulties," Greenberg interrupted. "You can be sure that Livermore won't be here crying about their failures. Of which they have many." He got up from his chair and looked out the window again. "I know that ultimately this system may not matter. The president may only want a diplomatic bargaining chip, and Defense would be willing to settle for something that protects their ground-based missiles. But there are good things in this for us—for all of us—if we succeed."

Parker excused himself and hurried down the corridor to his own office. He was struck again by the blandness of the building, especially its hallways. And there was the smell; the laboratories always reeked of chemicals or heated metal, but the administration building smelled like an old book.

He nodded to Theresa, his secretary. "Any calls?"

"Hundreds," she said, smiling. "Want something? Coffee?" She arranged the loose ends of her hair and put on her glasses. She was an attractive and congenial middle-aged woman, whose easygoing temperament made her an expert in working with the group's many personalities. "And I need a yes or no on your trip to Las Vegas next week for the test."

"Yes to Las Vegas, no to coffee. Anything else?"

"No."

"See if you can get Rollins in here, will you?"

She nodded and picked up her phone.

Parker sat in his chair and tried to relax for a moment. His office was smaller than Greenberg's, although more expensively done. He had Elisha to thank for that. In front of his desk, underneath two metal chairs, was a colorful Germantown Navajo rug. It had been one of their first purchases when they moved to Los Alamos—made possible through Elisha's monthly trust check. There were two large, excellent Hopi pots on top of his crammed bookshelf. In the corner was a small conference table. Expensively framed watercolors by Santa Fe artists added color to the dirty white walls.

National Security Programs, of which his own Strategic Defense Research Group was a part, was centered in the main administration building. The division, however, had staff and projects located all over the sprawling acreage of the laboratory. The administration building was one of the oldest and least attractive buildings the laboratory owned. It did, however, carry a certain prestige, since the director had his offices there.

He mused for a moment over Greenberg's remark about careers. Having a career had always been important to Parker. Ironically, he had grown up thinking of himself as a university professor, like his father and mother. He had vivid memories of them discussing their specializations over dinner—his mother arguing gently the merits of "pure" studies such as linguistics; his father, applied studies like political science. For the first five years he was at Los Alamos, Parker expected to leave anytime for another job; for the last five he wasn't sure what he was going to do.

He thought of Elisha. She would be at home, probably working on the paper she intended to deliver later in the week in Tucson at a conference of Southwest archaeologists. *She* was a contrast, a poor little rich girl who embraced the academic world with a fierce energy that earned her a doctorate three months earlier than his own. Now she was reading papers at professional conferences and he was making presentations before senators and bureaucrats.

He dialed his home number and after six rings was ready to hang up when he heard her voice.

"Hello?" She sounded out of breath.

"It's me. You busy?"

She laughed. "I was in the garage, looking for some damn notes in a box."

"I'm tied up the rest of the day with the site visit. I won't be home until late."

"Have fun."

He laughed. "When are you leaving for Tucson?"

"Thursday morning or afternoon, I haven't decided. My paper is Friday morning. I'll be back Saturday."

"Maria is staying at the house?" Maria was the elderly maid who worked for them and babysat when Elisha left town overnight. She lived down at the Santa Clara Pueblo and drove to Los Alamos every day in a green Volkswagen beetle.

"She promised."

"Good." There was a brief silence on the phone when both of them began to speak at once.

"You go first," Elisha said, laughing gently.

"Going to make the club in Tucson?" This was their private joke. The "club" was actually Club 21, a restaurant in Tucson that both were convinced had the best Mexican food in Arizona and probably the world's best margaritas.

"Of course. I have reservations for six people on Friday night."

Parker smiled. In the early days of their marriage, before Tevis was born, they used to take vacations and do nothing but drive through the Southwest stopping at all the national parks, dozens of archaeological sites, and sampling as many Mexican restaurants as they could stand. Tucson always reminded Parker of those days. Even now, as Elisha laughed, he knew she was thinking the same thing. Suddenly, he felt her absence very keenly.

"We have to get back to Tucson together," he said, thinking of a small motel there.

She laughed again. "Sure."

The telephone intercom buzzed. "I've got to go," he said.

"You're forgiven," she said, and hung up.

David hit his intercom button. "Rollins is here," said Theresa.

Before Parker had a chance to say anything, the door opened and a tall, muscular man walked aggressively in and sat down in a chair opposite Parker. "Morning." Rollins appeared cheerful despite the news of Berriman's death. Parker wondered if he had heard.

"You hear about Berriman?" He studied Rollins's face.

"Yeah. What the hell happened?" Rollins looked directly at Parker with intense blue eyes. He was handsome in a rough way, with a characteristic that Parker always found a contradiction: Rollins had small, almost delicate hands.

"Well, apparently he was murdered. Someone hit him on the head and then slashed his throat. It happened in a cave at Tsankawi."

"Jesus."

"My son and I discovered the body."

Rollins shook his head. "Any idea who did it?"

"No. The police found only the body, nothing else."

"Nothing else?" Rollins had a curious look on his face.

"Nothing as far as I know. They raked the floor of the cave."

Rollins smirked. "Christ!"

"Lab Security is working on it now. Which reminds me, the

Security people are coming here sometime today to interview the staff. Help them out if they need anything, will you?"

"Sure." Rollins stared at the floor. "Anything else?"

"Yes. More important now is picking up Berriman's work where he left off. Could you take over, if necessary?"

"Of course. I should have done it to begin with. God knows, that cross-correlational stuff is more my field than his. And his preliminary analyses were off."

"You've seen his report?" Berriman was reputedly tight with his work until it was nearly finished.

"Oh, part of it. I tried to help. You know, suggest some new computer techniques, but he wanted to stick with his old programs. Don't worry, his death won't slow us down."

Parker couldn't be sure, but it sounded like Berriman and Rollins had had a squabble of some kind. It was typical of Rollins, whose arrogance often put his colleagues off. He was a brilliant mathematician, but psychologically immature.

Parker didn't know that much about Rollins except that he'd been a mathematically gifted child. He had grown up in one of the poorest white ghettos of Los Angeles only to win scholarships to Stanford and MIT. As far as Parker knew, Rollins had breezed through school with exceptional grades and no friends. For all of his academic success, Rollins maintained a raw edge that even his live-in girlfriend had never been able to soften. The two of them lived on several acres of land outside of White Rock, a small town below Los Alamos. They grew much of their own food and lived, as Rollins liked to say, in "planned naturalism." Their life-style reminded everyone of hippies in the sixties.

"For God's sake, Rollins," Parker said softly, "the man is dead. He was doing important work."

"Forget it. The man was a quiet little creep. I tried to help him out and he told me to buzz off." Rollins looked irritated.

Parker could imagine Rollins's offer of help, no doubt something like a bull in a china shop.

"All right. Just be prepared to take over if Greenberg approves."

Rollins nodded and walked out, failing to shut the door as he left the office. Parker heard him whistling as he disappeared into the hallway.

Theresa knocked on the door. "Lab Security called. They want to talk to you about Berriman."

"I've only known him for a few months."

"I know. I told them that and that you were entertaining the senators tonight."

"And?"

"And you would talk to them on Thursday or Friday. Okay?"

Parker nodded, then quickly added, "Try for Friday. I'm on my way to Weapons for meetings and then to meet our guests."

"Sounds like fun," Theresa said.

chapter

4

MONDAY AFTERNOON

Tevis Parker thanked the librarian and stuffed the books into his nylon backpack.

He was out of school early today with permission to attend his scheduled appointment with the psychologist. But from the drugstore across from school he had called the doctor's office and politely told the secretary that he wouldn't be in because of illness. He had agreed to come later in the week.

Tevis smiled to himself. His homeroom teacher was only too glad to see him go to a psychologist. She was a nice woman, actually, and more understanding than most teachers, but he resented her insistence that he learn to fit in with the other kids. She had expressed that concern to his parents, and as far as he could tell, they had agreed, because shortly thereafter there was talk of signing up for soccer. Eventually they dropped the idea and he was left alone again.

As he unlocked the chain on his bike, he mentally calculated that the ride down to Tsankawi would take thirty, maybe thirty-five minutes. Most of the trip would be downhill. It was now two o'clock.

What he had learned in the last hour of reading was that the wooden figures from Tsankawi were called prayer sticks, or *pahos* by the Indians, and used in kiva ceremonies. Maybe the books in his backpack would give him some clue to the meaning or purpose of the figures, and why they had been left in the cave with the dead man. What power they had, if any, wasn't clear from what he had read so far.

He did remember what his mother had taught him: The Pueblo Indians saw unity in all things. The earth, sky, human beings, and plants were connected in some fundamental way that Pueblo life and ritual struggled to keep harmonious. And everything was suffused by a dual principle that made objects, forces, even the stars, either male or female. The wooden objects therefore had to be connected in some way to the struggle for harmony. But how?

Tevis smiled. The evening star, he remembered his mother telling him, was female; the morning star, male. He would have an hour or so at Tsankawi before he made the trip back to Los Alamos. That, he knew from experience, would take an hour. He wanted to be home well before the evening star made her appearance.

Ed Poole handed the county coroner's preliminary report back to his assistant.

"Well, hell, we knew all that." The report was only a couple pages long and repeated the details of Isaac Berriman's death: a blow to the head, sufficient to render him unconscious, or at least daze him, and then a severe laceration to the throat. Massive bleeding. No sign of a struggle. Death due to loss of blood. Et cetera.

Poole found the report of little help. It was true, as director of Security at Los Alamos for nearly ten years, he had never found himself reading a coroner's report. Most of his daily concerns involved processing security clearances, checking for violations, and lately, with preparing for the possibilities of terrorist attacks. Only in his FBI days had he dealt with murder.

Berriman's death had been reported to Poole's office last night as a formality, of course, since the laboratory was the dead man's employer. But it wasn't until this morning that a routine background check on Berriman revealed his present job assignment and security clearance. It was then that Poole saw the case as possibly something very important: Berriman was involved in one of the lab's top-priority programs.

"Nothing else?" Poole looked up from the report and across the desk at Raul Castro, his assistant. He encouraged Castro and other members of his staff to call him Ed.

Castro looked half awake. "Nope. You got it all."

"Well, what are we doing?"

"We've pulled his file, of course, and we've begun to interview his friends and co-workers. His office has been closed off." Castro, who always sat stiffly in a chair, spoke slowly and deliberately, as if he were measuring the length of each word before he spoke it.

"What do we know so far?"

"We don't think it was robbery. His wallet was gone, but there was cash in his pocket and a Rolex watch still on his wrist."

Poole shook his head. "Have we found his car?"

"It's at his house. We don't know how he got down to Tsankawi."

"What about the man's private life?"

"Quiet. Lived alone."

Poole interrupted. "Queer?" If the motive wasn't robbery, maybe it was blackmail.

"Not that we know of. He was married once and had a child. They were killed some years ago in a car accident. On the road to Santa Fe, in fact. Since then, he's lived by himself. No police record of any kind, not even a speeding ticket. And from what we can tell so far, he was a highly respected math man, hardworking and dedicated."

Aren't they all, Poole thought, at least until you really knew them. He leaned back in his chair and revealed a middle-age paunch, which he unconsciously covered with one hand. For years he had been trying to trim it through diets and walking—to no avail. At fifty-six, he liked to say that it wasn't vanity that made him concerned about his weight, but a holdover from the strict codes of his FBI days.

"Hmm. Sounds like the model citizen. Has his family been notified?"

"The lab's personnel office is taking care of that. I don't think he had any relatives in Los Alamos, however."

"What about his home. Anything?" Castro had just come from a search of Berriman's house.

"Nothing obvious. No sign of a struggle there, either. I made a preliminary check for classified material, of course, but I didn't find anything. We confiscated his home computer diskettes. And Sam and one of his guys will make a complete search of all of his papers as soon as the county police are through photographing and dusting the place for fingerprints."

Poole frowned. If there was anything to Berriman's murder beyond robbery, he didn't want the local police involved. As far as he was concerned, they were amateurs.

"And what about his office?" Perhaps there was a connection there, Poole thought.

"We've sealed his office for the moment until we can make a thorough search. We have to check his classified safe, of course, and determine what sort of classified materials he kept. His division leader and his immediate boss have been notified that we're coming. Interviews will start this afternoon."

"Good." Poole had to admit that Castro was thorough. He had been a security officer for a major defense contractor before Los Alamos. Both he and his wife were from Española, about twenty miles away. Poole's only gripe about Castro was that he spoke so damn slow and smoked.

"What about his life-style? Anything?"

"We'll check on that during interviews. But right now, not much. He was a loner, especially after his family was killed, and apparently his only interest was in collecting Indian things and in making clay models of archaeological ruins."

"Models?"

"Yeah. Clay or plaster models several feet wide and about a foot high." Castro gesticulated with his hands. "Lots of details like caves and kivas. He even put trees and little people on them. Apparently he was known for making these models. Some of them are really nice."

"And the Indian things?"

"You know, pots, kachinas, a few Navajo rugs. That sort of stuff. The sheriff's office is making a complete inventory." Castro stopped to light a cigarette even though Poole was known to dislike it.

"I'm not an expert, Ed, but I think a few of Berriman's pieces were pretty expensive. Those were found in a closet."

"How expensive?"

"I mean a couple of hundred to maybe a couple of thousand dollars."

Poole whistled. Maybe this was the connection. "Was he rich? He worked for the lab, for God's sake. How much could he make working here?" Poole reached for a copy of Berriman's personnel folder and began skimming through the collection of personnel action forms, letters of recommendation and promotion, sick leave requests, and the like.

"Looks like he made forty-seven thousand a year. Not bad." Poole was always amazed at what scientists earned. For what they did, which Poole likened to playing with toys, he thought they were overpaid.

"What about his bank account? Savings? Things like that?"

"We'll get a court order as soon as we can. But nothing in his house would suggest that he had a lot of money. His car, in fact, is an eight-year-old Mazda." Castro thought for a moment. "Maybe he's got family money. Or insurance money?"

"Possibly." Poole realized he needed to slow down. It was easy to move too fast in a case like this. It was always possible to miss the obvious and end up with a dead end.

"Who does he work for?"

"According to Personnel, he was assigned six weeks ago to the Strategic Defense Group under National Security Programs. Dr. Greenberg, who heads the division, knew Berriman only professionally, and we haven't interviewed Dr. Parker, his immediate boss, yet."

"Who did Berriman work for before Parker?"

"A man named Gerald Sandys, one of the British old-timers who first came here during the war. He retired a few months ago and lives here in Los Alamos. We've arranged to interview him right after lunch."

"Good. Maybe he can shed some light on the late Dr. Berriman."

Castro suddenly smiled, something he didn't often do. "I might be wrong, but I think Sandys is an authority or something on Indian art. I think he gives talks every now and then on the subject."

"Well, maybe he can tell us something about Berriman's collection." He paused. "And how he paid for it."

The phone rang on Poole's desk. He pushed the intercom button.

"Yeah?"

"It's Farrell Doty in Albuquerque," said his secretary.

"Damn." He turned to Castro. "It's Doty with FBI."

Castro rolled his eyes and remembered the strained relationship between his boss and the regional FBI director.

"Doty. What can we do for you?" Poole forced himself to sound friendly but realized that he had failed to even say hello.

"Ed, long time no see." Doty sounded casual but Poole knew that it was anything but that. Was it possible that he already had word of Berriman?

"Yeah. Things going okay for you?"

"Keeping busy, Ed, you know the life."

Poole took that as a jab on his past. Eleven years ago he had been cashiered out of the FBI on medical grounds. A small stroke, in fact. Although he was given a pension, he still missed his days with the Bureau.

"Life's good up here, Farrell. Lots of clean air and quiet living."

"That's not what I hear, Ed."

Poole paused for a moment. "Oh?" he said noncommittally.

"I heard you had a nasty little murder up there yesterday and that it was one of the lab staff."

"It's true, but how did you hear?"

"Los Alamos police. What's the deal?"

Poole realized he would have to play this easy or he would have the FBI in Los Alamos in an hour.

"We don't know a lot just yet. One of the lab's employees was murdered yesterday morning. It's possible that robbery was involved. We're working with the local police, but of course we've initiated our own internal investigation."

"Want some help?" The voice on the other end of the line was baiting.

Poole forced a friendly laugh. "Not yet, Doty. Why don't you let us brief you in the next day or so. I'll have a lot more to tell you then." Poole knew damned good and well that Doty and the FBI could step in anytime they wanted. What Poole wanted, however, was a chance to investigate this business himself. Bringing in the FBI would only make it the FBI's case. Los Alamos would be relegated to a subservient role.

"Ed, this sounds like something we might be interested in. I really would appreciate being kept abreast of what you find out." The pleasant voice on the other end paused for a moment. "You'll call me this afternoon or tomorrow?"

"Tomorrow, Farrell, by noon or early afternoon. You have my word."

"Good. Talk to you then." The line went dead.

Poole leaned back in his chair and put his hands behind his head. He could feel a headache coming on.

There was no guarantee that Doty wouldn't get involved anyway, tomorrow's deadline or not. There was something about Doty's voice that Poole didn't like, something artificially pleasant, like the automatic voice that told you your car door was open.

"Damn it, Castro, let's get on it. I know these guys, they'll be up here in no time if they smell something interesting."

He sat back in his chair again, revealing his stomach. Another thought hit him. Doty had to have a reason for being interested.

"Check the Spook Shop, will you? See if anything is going on there." Poole referred to the small contingent of Los Alamos staff who worked at the laboratory but were paid by the Central Intelligence and National Security agencies to interpret foreign intelligence data for scientific value.

"What are we looking for?"

Poole thought a moment. "See if they're aware of anything that the FBI would be interested in." He thought again. "See if there've been any leaks or breaches of security."

Castro nodded and left, a cigarette still smoldering in the ashtray. Poole found a pencil with a broken point and began to jab at what remained of the butt. He knew it would take hours for the smell to go away.

Reyes pulled off the highway into the small parking area outside the entrance to the Tsankawi ruins. He noticed that the metal gate was now locked and bore a new sign: CLOSED—U.S. PARK SERVICE. Good, he thought, there shouldn't be anybody else around.

Reyes got out of the pueblo's police car and locked his shotgun in the trunk. Then he locked the car and looked for a spot in the barbed-wire fence he could climb through. About fifteen yards away he saw a part of the fence where the rain had created a small gully under the lowest line of wire; there was almost three feet of clearance. It wasn't until he was almost there that he saw the thin, fresh tracks of a bicycle.

He crawled under the wire and stood for a moment and looked around. Fifteen feet ahead, behind a small clump of juniper trees he saw it. The bicycle was chained to one of the trees and appeared to be expensive. He couldn't be sure of its value since the last bike he owned as a youth was a large tubular affair with thick, wide tires. It had been given to his parents, instead of being thrown away, by a wealthy Anglo family in Santa Fe for whom his father did some work. This one was very lightweight and had multiple gears. The small metal tag under the seat identified it as registered in Los Alamos.

He started on the trail that led to the cave where the dead man had been found. On the way, he tried to remember what he knew.

The manner of death was obvious; the motive was not. The ruins were hardly the best place to murder and hide a body given the possibility of tourists. On the other hand, maybe the body was meant to be found. Robbery was possible, but more likely another motive existed. Reyes suddenly wondered if there had been more than one murderer. Lots of questions, he thought, and no answers.

As he climbed the path and made his way through a natural passage in the rock, he remembered the last time he was here with his grandfather many years before. The old man spoke to him mostly in Tewa, their Indian tongue, and sometimes in English or Spanish. Some of the stories were about the first Tewas, the Ancient Ones, and how for hundreds of years they had lived on the mesa, eking out an existence geared to the seasons and the generosity of the great forces that ruled the earth and its occupants. Other times, the stories were really lessons on the purpose and meaning of ceremonies and customs. Images of the dances he had danced as a child came to mind: for rain, for a good harvest, for making visits by the kachinas, or spirits, possible.

This was after the war, when his grandfather was still alive, and when Los Alamos was only a small community fenced off from the rest of the world. The ruins of Tsankawi, Bandelier, and the many others in this part of New Mexico were reachable over clumsy dirt roads that discouraged sightseers. Most of the land around Tsankawi wasn't fenced in back then, and a young San Ildefonso boy could roam for miles, hiking the ancient trails or playing in the elephant mud along the river and creeks.

Reyes stopped for a moment and sat on a rock. A flood of memories came back to him: his parents, his family, his youth, even the first time he brought his former wife to New Mexico. The smell of Tsankawi made him remember things he hadn't thought of for years. It was only now, after many years away, that he was trying to understand what it meant for him to be an Indian. No matter how far he traveled, it seemed, he could never quite leave the pueblo without its force of myths and rituals drawing him back.

He wiped the sweat on his brow and saw the shadow of his hand move on a nearby rock. Suddenly he thought of something else and smiled. In Santa Fe, like much of the Southwest, he was rarely taken for an Indian. Perhaps it was his height, maybe even his coloring. But very often people approached him and spoke to him in Spanish. Once at the border in El Paso, he had been detained as an alien until he produced identification. Well, he thought, his grandfather always told him that he would live in two worlds, that the day when an Indian could live only in his own had passed long before.

His reverie was disrupted by a flash of red movement in the distance, and Reyes remembered the bicycle. The red shape moved again and fell behind a clump of rocks near the cave where the Anglo had been murdered. Reyes quickly moved off the trail, out of view, and thought a moment. Whoever it was was not concerned about being seen. Perhaps, like Reyes, they thought that no one else would be here.

Reyes edged closer and saw the figure in the red coat again. This time he knew that it was a child. He decided to approach the cave openly.

Fifty yards away, Tevis was unaware that anyone else was watching him. Finding the ruins closed had been helpful; it meant that he could visit the cave and explore on his own. At least this time it wasn't raining.

Tevis had run almost the entire way to the cave from his bike,

his heart beating furiously as he scrambled up the cliff to the cave
itself. He was very excited, feeling a mixture of dread and awe as he
made his way along the worn pathway. It wasn't just the specter of
the dead man, but also the realization that Indians had once lived
here and performed their ceremonies in the caves and on the mesas.
In his mind, he could make each pile of stones and every empty kiva
tell its own story through the ghosts who still lived in the ruins.

Tevis was sure that his psychologist would think he was crazy,
but sometimes when he visited these old ruins, he heard voices and
people moving about. There was never anyone there when he
looked, but somehow he knew he heard parents calling children or
old men in dark kivas telling young boys the secrets of their people.

Right now he settled back against the exterior wall of the cliff,
just off the entrance to the dead man's cave and out of view from the
trail below. The sign put up by the police was down and crumpled
on the ground, the cave itself now empty. He pulled the library
books out of his backpack and began to thumb through them.
Somewhere there had to be information that would help explain
yesterday. Tevis was convinced that there was a connection between
the man's death, this ancient cliff dwelling, and the objects he had in
his possession. Perhaps, he thought, the man was guilty of violating
a Pueblo taboo.

He was so immersed in his book that he failed to hear Reyes
approaching. The older man made it to the rocks that hid Tevis, and
looked over. He recognized him as the young boy from the day
before.

Tevis suddenly looked up and gasped.

"It's okay," said Reyes, who adopted a soothing tone. Both of
them were quiet for a moment.

"You're the policeman from San Ildefonso?"

"Right." Reyes looked around and nodded toward the cave.
"Find anything?"

Tevis started to say no and stopped. "I haven't looked," he said,
and then added sheepishly, "Well, I only peeked in." Tevis stood up
and dusted off his pants.

"I'm gonna look around," said Reyes. "Your parents know
you're here?" He knew the answer.

Stooping over, Reyes entered the cave but stopped just inside.

The rake marks from yesterday's search of the floor were still intact. The young boy had told the truth; no one had been inside. He stepped back out.

The boy was still there, although whatever he was reading had been stuffed into his blue backpack.

"What were you reading?"

"Oh, books." Tevis shuffled one foot slightly.

Reyes nodded. "What kind of books?"

Tevis pulled one of them out and handed it to Reyes. It was a book called *The Tewa World*.

"Heavy reading for a ten-year-old, isn't it?"

"I'm eleven, and I'm a good reader."

Reyes glanced through the book; he was impressed. This wasn't a typical eleven-year-old boy.

He handed the book back. "Interested in my people?"

"Yeah."

Reyes sat down across from Tevis and pulled out a cigarette. For a moment he thought of offering him one, just to see if he'd take it. Then he laughed to himself; his grandfather thought nothing of offering him a cigarette when he was this kid's age. That was many years ago, when grandparents lived next door.

"Any particular reason for reading a book on the Tewa here at Tsankawi?" He watched Tevis formulate the answer.

"Well, this is where the guy was killed, wasn't it?"

Reyes nodded. "Apparently." He waited patiently for the young boy to continue.

"I just thought there might be something to the way the guy was killed, I mean, with his throat cut and everything."

"Do you think that has something to do with this place?"

Tevis thought for a moment. "Maybe nothing to do with *this* cave, but with the people who live here."

"What people?"

"You know, the Indians. You're one, aren't you?"

Reyes wondered what the boy meant. "Do you think an Indian killed the man from Los Alamos?"

Tevis only shrugged. "What if his throat was cut and he was left in this cave for a purpose. Maybe to tell others that he had done something bad?"

Reyes shook his head. "I don't know." It was odd, but he had wondered the same thing.

"Do Indians cut people's throats for a reason?" asked Tevis.

Reyes had to smile. "Not that I know of. I think that's an Anglo custom."

"Oh." Tevis seemed disappointed. "Well, do you leave anything with the dead?"

"What do you mean?" He was struck by the realization that this was a very strange conversation to have with an eleven-year-old boy, even if he was an Anglo.

"I mean, do certain things have any meaning if they're left with the dead?" Tevis seemed genuinely curious, Reyes thought, but not in the way whites often were about life-styles they considered primitive.

"Well, as a rule, the dead individual is buried with only his clothing or maybe a personal item or two." Reyes searched his memory. "Sometimes, if the family is very old-fashioned, the individual's moccasins are reversed and a bit of his favorite food is placed under one of his armpits." He couldn't remember if it was supposed to be the right or left armpit. "And there are other practices."

Reyes knew that all of them were a part of his people's long heritage and beliefs. They would seem strange to an Anglo, even to this unusual child. But it would be inappropriate to discuss them outside of the pueblo. In fact, they were hardly mentioned at all, for when someone died, things simply were done by members of the family, who just *knew* what to do. And always, the rituals associated with life and death were a mixture of Indian and Catholic beliefs.

Tevis was quiet for a moment. "Are there any sacred things that are used? You know, like a crucifix or something."

Reyes shook his head. "Not formally." Suddenly he wondered if this boy was holding something back.

"I don't remember hearing your name yesterday."

"It's Tevis. Tevis Parker."

Reyes thought of the small dimples in front of the dead man's feet and the pieces of cornmeal scattered on the floor of the cave. "There was cornmeal on the ground, and sometimes that's used in our religious ceremonies."

Tevis nodded again. He remembered the cornmeal and the small tree sprigs. "I think I saw the cornmeal." He hesitated. "And some small branches from a tree. Like twigs."

The policeman took a long drag on his cigarette. He hadn't seen the twigs, but both items were commonly used by Pueblo people as part of religious practice. Was that a coincidence? Maybe an Indian *was* involved. These signs were small—invisible, in fact, to Sheriff Smith—but there nonetheless.

"Maybe he was a bad man," said Tevis. "Maybe he wasn't supposed to be here."

Reyes sensed that this wasn't the moment to press the child for more information. Instead, he asked about Tevis's father.

"Doesn't your dad work for the laboratory?"

"Yeah. He works on Star Wars. Do you know what that is?"

"Well, a little."

"My father's very important. He works on lasers." Tevis smiled broadly. "Do you believe in Star Wars?"

"I'm not sure, Tevis. I don't know much about it."

"Is that because you're an Indian?"

Reyes laughed. "Maybe. You see, to the Tewa, you would place nothing where it wasn't needed or where it might cause harm. Unless you wanted to, that is. That wouldn't be in the natural order of things. The sky, for example, is considered a deity, a god, called Sky Old Man, who is married to Earth Old Woman. Can you imagine what they'd think about Star Wars?"

Both of them smiled, and Reyes searched his memory for more of what he had been taught as a youth.

"The earth and the heavens are linked in very important ways. Rain comes from the clouds where the kachina spirits are said to live."

"Really?"

"Yes, it's said that if you look up, you can sometimes see them. And in the Tewa universe, the sun and moon move in paths across the heavens from east to west, finally setting in a lake and reemerging the next day from another lake. Why would you want to risk disrupting that cycle by putting something like a weapon in their path?" He pointed up.

Tevis seemed deep in thought for a moment. "Are kachinas the same thing as angels?" he finally asked.

"I don't know, Tevis, maybe." Reyes had no idea how Tewa kachinas compared with Christian angels. Suddenly he was amused at the thought of choirs of kachinas singing songs of praise to a man in a white beard.

He studied the boy for a moment and then looked at his watch. It was nearly five o'clock.

"I think we should go, don't you? Your parents will wonder where you are."

Tevis nodded.

"How about a ride home? At least you won't have to pedal up hill."

"Yeah. I'd like that."

They began the walk down to the parking lot. Tevis told Reyes about his interest in Indians and that his mother was an archaeologist. They were less than fifty yards from the car when Tevis saw something shining in the distance.

"What's that?" He pointed to a rim of gleaming metal shielded by branches. They walked over and found a bike flat on its side, deliberately covered over with pine branches. Suddenly, Reyes knew how Isaac Berriman had come to Tsankawi.

"Don't touch it," he ordered. Very carefully, using a stick, Reyes lifted up one of the branches and read the Los Alamos bicycle registration tag. Without disturbing the position of the bike, he lifted another branch or two and looked for signs of blood or an accident. There was nothing. Then he jotted down the registration number and told Tevis they had to go.

"Do you think it belonged to the dead man?" the boy asked.

"I think that is a very good possibility."

chapter 5

TUESDAY AFTERNOON

The high-speed jet printer sputtered for only an instant before it silently began to spew a series of numbers across the moving sheet of computer paper. Several seconds later it finished a page of computations and, with a loud "whap," jerked another sheet of paper into the machine.

The curious "whap-whap" sound of lightning-quick printers was the dominant noise in the large room; even through the walls of his adjacent office, the director of the laboratory's computer complex could hear their screeching. It was a sound he was used to, and other than the voices of his staff, the only distinct sound he could easily pick out from his desk. The huge CRAY computers were in another room, sealed off by a thick door, and were protectively maintained year-round at a temperature that never rose above sixty-five degrees. The entire complex lay deep underground, built of concrete and swathed in lead to protect it from both saboteurs and small nuclear weapons. "The Mole," as he was known, wasn't sure just how safe he and his computers would really be if the Russians lobbed a bomb or two at Los Alamos.

Through the glass window that formed part of the wall, Lee Willows could see members of his staff sitting at computer keyboards or huddled over a printout as it noisily emerged from a printer. Everyone and everything was bathed in the constant glow of fluorescent lighting that never varied throughout the day. Only the bright blue walls broke the monotonous effect of working in an underground concrete bunker.

For an instant the pudgy man caught his reflection in a framed poster on the wall, where he was reminded of the fact that he was rapidly growing bald. Squinting into the glare, he carefully patted what was left of his red hair and turned back to the computer printout on his desk and his can of diet soda. He was interrupted by a junior member of his staff standing at the doorway.

"Got a minute?" The young man in a sleeveless ski jacket hesitated for a moment and then clumsily sat down in one of the office's two extra chairs. The laces of one running shoe were untied.

"We have a problem."

"Like what?" Willows finished off his soda.

"Well, I don't know what everything means, but we have some unauthorized entries."

The director lifted his eyebrows and brought his body forward in his chair. "What?"

"Well, you know the man who died, uh..."

"Berriman?"

"Yeah. Well, in retiring his access code I ran the usual scan of his computer use for the last month, for security purposes."

"And what?" Willows was suddenly concerned. The news about Berriman was all over the lab.

"Well, I ran a scan of both his computer time and the computer time used by the terminal assigned to him." The young man nervously paused again. "I don't know what this means, but there's a record of that terminal accessing several different files using three different computer passwords."

The director relaxed for a moment. "So what? Someone else used his terminal. It happens all the time."

The young man looked at the ground. "They weren't authorized."

"Not authorized?"

The younger man shook his head. "I checked. Each password owner denied using Berriman's terminal; one guy was out of town on the occasion during which his code was used." He paused. "And all the files accessed were 'top secret.'"

The director tensed in his chair. "What made you check all this out?"

"It just seemed strange, that's all. The passwords were assigned to guys in other divisions. And it gets worse. Berriman seems to have found a way to subvert the automatic protect system for certain data files." The young man continued to stare at the floor as he spoke. "As far as I can tell, this guy found a way to trick the system into letting him have access to areas that are for specifically designated terminals only. There aren't a dozen of them in the lab."

"Shit!" The director straightened his body in the chair, forcing the air in the cushion out with a tired wheeze.

"Which data fields?"

"The Sigma Level stuff."

"Jesus," he muttered. All computer fields were assigned classification levels beginning with Alpha, the most accessible. Sigma had the highest, most restricted access. That meant maybe two dozen people in the lab, thought Willows.

"How did you find this out?"

"I found two cases where his terminal tapped the 'no access' areas, all within the three days before the guy was, uh, killed. I don't know what he tapped, only that the terminal made an entry. He may have pulled data, but I can't be sure; obviously, he found a way of entering."

"We know when anyone enters these data areas, right?" asked the director.

"Yeah, usually. And we know what they look at. But this guy shows computer activity with no *specific* files listed. This could mean he was in the process of covering up his tracks." He looked up from the floor. "Maybe he ran out of time."

"Could Berriman have done this? Programming wasn't his thing, was it?"

The young man shrugged.

The director talked for a few more minutes and then sent his staff member out to run a complete search of Berriman's activities for the last year. The young man was at the door when he was called back.

"Listen, let's keep this in-house, okay? I'll need to get Security here right away and call the boss. But let's not discuss this out of this office."

He pulled his laboratory telephone directory off the shelf and looked up several numbers. The shit was going to hit the fan, Willows thought. If his assistant was right, Berriman had used his terminal to pull data from several top-secret projects. He did that using passwords assigned to other individuals. How in the hell did Berriman get the passwords? But worse, he tapped into files that were theoretically impossible to access with his terminal. There was no telling what else he had done.

And now, the pudgy man thought, Berriman was dead and the object of an intense security investigation. The shit was going to hit the fan, all right.

Parker tried to smile although he had a terrific headache. The all-day meeting of the Senate Subcommittee on Strategic Defense was just over, and both senators and scientists stood milling around in the modern conference room of the Robert Oppenheimer Center. He stood next to Greenberg, who was talking with two Air Force generals.

Parker had been the last witness of the day, sitting for over an hour in a metal chair at a long table with a starched white tablecloth. The water pitcher in front of him had been empty since that morning.

He had begun his presentation innocently enough, with a review of yesterday's laser test in Los Alamos. But just minutes into his talk, however, he had been preempted by a verbal battle between the pro–Star Wars subcommittee chairman and another senator known for his criticism of defense expenditures. One moment Parker was being ignored at the witness table and the next he was being asked scientific and technical questions that ranged far beyond his responsibility at the laboratory.

Several times he had been pressed by the opposing senator into admitting that in his opinion the technical problems in Star Wars were immense and perhaps unsolvable, at least in the next twenty or thirty years. *That* admission had fueled an intense debate between members of the subcommittee for almost half an hour. Frustrated and mostly ignored, Parker listened to the bickering, never sure how much of any individual's argument was really political posturing for some unknown audience beyond the conference room. What *was* clear was that no other presenter that day—and there had been ten of them, representing defense contractors, universities, and research laboratories—had been anything less than totally optimistic about the eventual success of Star Wars.

Now, standing with Greenberg and making small talk, Parker wondered how much the senators really understood or cared. The bulky and disheveled subcommittee chairman was off in a corner with his opposition, and although he couldn't be sure, it looked as if both men were laughing. Just ten minutes ago, the two men and their colleagues behind their inquisitor's table had engaged in a heated exchange over American scientific know-how and dedication. Parker had the distinct feeling that these men had reduced the enormous technical challenge of SDI down to a simple matter of "If America wants it, America can do it!"

One wall of the conference room looked out into the Jemez Mountains, where the late afternoon sun was pulling away. The patches of green and black were turning darker by the minute.

"A little rough, Dave?"

Parker turned to see one of the scientists from California's Lawrence Livermore Laboratory talking to him. He nodded and forced a smile.

"Thank God it was you and not me." The man laughed and walked off.

Parker suddenly felt anxious and very tired. He still had his headache. Obviously, Greenberg was grooming him to take over the division and a good showing today would make that step on the ladder easier. Had he screwed up? Greenberg would probably rate this a "so-so" performance. Parker felt his stomach tighten. Greenberg's rule for situations like this afternoon was inviolate: Always be positive, always sound certain. Parker surmised that he had probably failed on both accounts.

In another part of the room several Air Force majors were disassembling a huge magnetic display board perhaps eight feet wide and six high. On it were horizontal lines representing the levels of space above the earth and dozens of brightly colored plastic cutouts in the shape of satellites, strange futuristic-looking weapons, large reflecting mirrors, and enemy warheads. Across the bottom was an exploded map of the United States and the U.S.S.R. with hundreds of colored dots representing missile silos and submarines. The display had been used throughout the day by the Air Force general in charge of the nation's Strategic Defense Initiative program as an aid in his explanation of how Star Wars would work.

During the day's presentations, Alan Merritt, the laboratory's director, expressed enthusiasm only once: when the Air Force unveiled their giant magnetic board. "Look at that," he whispered to Greenberg.

Parker briefly studied the faces of the military men in the room. They all looked like university professors instead of professional soldiers. He knew some of them well; a few had doctorates in engineering or science from major universities. Suddenly, he realized that every person in the room was male. He wondered what Elisha would say about that?

Another display—this one consisting of a huge, very accurate drawing of an electromagnetic rail gun shattering a Russian satellite with its projectile—was being taken down by staff members from the nation's largest defense contractor, a company with hundreds of millions of dollars at stake in Star Wars research. Los Alamos had its own photographs as well, as did almost everyone here. As Greenberg saw it, a congressional hearing was as much public relations as information. His view was that money flowed to institutions in direct proportion to the quality of the dog and pony show.

Parker felt a hand on his shoulder and turned around to see Dick Lawton, a member of the subcommitttee staff and administrative aide to the California senator who headed the subcommittee.

Lawton was also a good friend from Stanford University days.

"Still on for tonight?"

Parker nodded. "Sure. Where?"

"Seven-thirty at the Los Alamos Inn. Downstairs bar."

"There's only one bar."

"That's the one. See you there."

Lawton said hello to the generals, whom he obviously knew, and shook Greenberg's hand. "Good session, gentlemen."

The generals nodded. Greenberg forced a smile. "We'll have to keep Parker here out of trouble next time, won't we?" said Lawton. Greenberg's dour look remained unchanged.

Lawton laughed. "Now, Francis, this is the Senate, you never know what's going to happen." He patted Parker on the back and moved away to another group of scientists from Livermore.

Parker noticed that Greenberg didn't look his way but instead motioned to another small group several yards away. He started to walk over when Parker grabbed his arm. "Remember, I'm having dinner with Dick."

Greenberg nodded, and acknowledged a hand wave from a member of a nearby group with a smile. "Good. Talk us up."

Farrell Doty loved the view from his third-floor office. From one corner he could look east toward the Sandia Mountains and watch the light change the texture of their surface and the color throughout the day. North, behind him, he saw the city of Albuquerque spread out for miles until it disappeared into the haze.

There was talk of moving the FBI's regional office to another building, one considered less susceptible to terrorism. Doty had opposed the move, and for the moment he had one of the best views in Albuquerque.

Mounted on the wall to his right was a large plaster cast of the FBI seal, and in the corner an American flag. Underneath the seal, resting on a wood and glass parson's table, was a series of photographs of his family. There was one of his wife and him taken three years ago on their twenty-fifth wedding anniversary, as well as a single photograph of himself when he ran the Albuquerque Ten

Thousand Meters Race last year. It was one of his favorite shots. Looking at his trim jogger's frame, it would be hard to guess that he was fifty-one years old. The rest of the photographs were of his four children, taken at various ages, all looking remarkably clean-cut and Mormon. The two, Doty often thought, were synonymous. After all, his was a third-generation Mormon family that, as he liked to say, he had raised with a zeal and commitment to both Mormon and American ideals.

For a moment he studied his desk, straightened the pencil holder at one end, and then quickly read through several memos organized for him by his secretary. He wanted to be through with administrative matters in order to be able to focus his attention on the events in Los Alamos.

His suspicions had been triggered as soon as the news had come in yesterday from the county police. The murder of a high-level scientist with a top security clearance was an automatic alert.

He had been right. After communicating with Washington, he had been given shocking information: there were indications, from recent CIA and National Security Agency intelligence, that the Soviets were learning details on the American weapons program from deeply placed sources within the defense industry—despite the successful crackdowns in recent years by the FBI. There was reason to believe that one of the sources was an individual or maybe a small group in one of the government's national weapons laboratories. That included Los Alamos.

Doty looked at a large map of New Mexico mounted on one wall. Red pins indicated government defense research installations. There was a pin for Los Alamos, of course, but also pins in Albuquerque where the Sandia National Laboratory was located, as well as pins in Las Cruces and White Sands. Blue pins, indicating military installations, were stuck in Albuquerque, Clovis, Gallup, Alamogordo, and even El Paso on the Texas border. The Soviets could have someone in any of these places, he thought.

From his desk Doty picked up a list of names associated with the murdered scientist. That was one place to start. Another was to plug into the agency's vast computer files of known terrorists, left-wing activists, and foreign agents. Even the employees of Los Alamos would need to be checked, in a search for anything out of the ordinary that had made it into the electronic data banks: financial or personal difficulties, trouble with the law, security violations, even an unusual number of traffic tickets. It was unlikely, Doty thought, that someone spying for the Soviets would have so obvious a flag in their background. But still, you never knew. It was worth checking.

Doty scanned the police and coroner's reports that had been wired to him. There appeared to be nothing particularly informative in either report beyond the bizzare nature of the man's murder. *That*, however, might bear further investigation. What little they knew about Isaac Berriman didn't suggest a great deal. He was in his late forties, widowed and childless, and a longtime employee of Los Alamos. No police record of any kind; no mention of any extraordinary political or financial activity. On the surface at least, not the type to spy. But of course it was always possible that he was working with someone else. Someone more clever and with the means to connect with the other side.

For the moment, Doty would have to content himself with pulling the files on Berriman and everyone he worked with, and then waiting for his agents to report on their preliminary field investigation. It was difficult to tell if the security office at Los Alamos would be useful or not. The director was an ex-FBI man, but he had been out of service for a number of years and was undoubtedly out of touch with the Bureau's techniques and procedures.

He buzzed his secretary and asked her to organize a meeting later in the afternoon with his two senior agents. At the same time, he gave her the list of names at Los Alamos and asked her to initiate a deep background search. That, he thought, would take a day or two. In the meantime, he would put pressure on Poole in Los Alamos; a man in a soft job like that wasn't likely to move too fast.

Parker would not have picked a bar in one of the local motels for conversation. Especially since it was small and loud. Lawton was off buying a pack of cigarettes, leaving Parker to defend their small table.

He spotted Lawton making his way through the bar, stopping a few times to shake hands and make brief conversation. His friend looked tired; he had the look of a man who worked too hard and drank too much. One of the cocktail waitresses waved, and Lawton smiled and waved back. Parker wondered if this was part of his friend's recent divorce.

"I'm back." Lawton sat down and opened the pack of Merit menthols and lit one.

"Friend of yours?" Parker nodded in the direction of the waitress.

Lawton smiled. "Just met her last night." He took a drag. "Understand you had a messy incident in Los Alamos." He smiled again.

"Like what?"

"Like murder?"

Jesus! Parker thought. Did everybody know? "You heard about that?"

"Today. From the people at Livermore."

"How in the hell did they hear about it? It just happened a few days ago."

Lawton shook his head. "Don't know. Is it a problem?"

"I don't think so. The man was doing important work, but we've already picked it up." At least he hoped they had.

Lawton, however, changed the subject. "Enjoy yourself today?"

"Sure. Lots. Senate site visits are a blast."

"You did pretty well."

"Pretty well?"

"A little uncertain, perhaps. And unenthusiastic."

"Dick, for God's sake! I was being quizzed about developments I know very little about. *Cross-examined* is a better description!" Parker finished the last of his vodka tonic and signaled the waitress to bring another round.

"Look, David, most of the subcommittee doesn't know shit about Star Wars. They think all scientists are alike and that all of you do the same thing." He leaned forward and smiled. "The chairman knows his stuff, but the rest, well, they're interested in what SDI can do for their state. We're spending over two billion in California alone on these projects."

Parker was quiet for a moment. "This whole Star Wars business is complex, risky, and may never even get off the goddamn ground. You know that."

"I know what you people tell me. Livermore thinks it will work. A lot of people do. Even a small, less complex version of Star Wars would be useful against the Soviets."

Parker looked around to see if anyone was listening. "Tomorrow the guys from MIT are going to report on computer research."

Lawton nodded. "So?"

"So that may be where this whole business falls on its ass, Dick. We have no computers at the moment, and none in the immediate future, that can coordinate all of the elements of a space defense system."

Parker leaned closer. "You're talking about a master computer *and* a computer program maybe twenty, thirty million lines long. It not only has to coordinate every action, but it has to decide which incoming warheads are real and which are decoys. Who in the hell is going to write that program? And who or what is going to test it to be sure it works if and when a real attack comes?" Parker eased back in his chair; he could tell that Lawton didn't want a lecture.

Lawton looked up from his glass. "I thought this was what big-time science was all about?"

Parker shook his head. "We aren't doing science; we're doing weapons." He didn't have the energy to try to explain what he meant.

Lawton looked straight at Parker with a wry smile. "Well, David, it's a buck."

Parker took a sip of his drink and tried to wave away some of the smoke with his hand. "That it is."

"Don't forget that Kearney wants to nominate you for the presidential commission. If you get it, you'll be hot shit around here."

"A big fish in a small pond?"

"You sound less than enthusiastic, David. Maybe you should go back to a university. Teach freshman physics or something."

Parker looked at his friend. It was hard to tell if Lawton was joking or not.

"Look," Lawton said, "here it is. A fact of life." He ground his cigarette out in the ashtray. "Your lasers are clever, but they're big and expensive. Rail guns and killer satellites are cheaper and ready now. You're gonna have to move your ass to keep the money coming in." He waved to the waitress and asked for the check. "This is on me. You buy dinner, which unfortunately for me can't cost you very much in this hick town."

As he threw down some bills, Lawton said, "I have one bit of advice." He looked at Parker.

"Yeah?"

"If you testify again, be positive. Enthusiasm! *That's* what they want to hear." Lawton stood up and waved again to the cocktail waitress.

"Come on. Let's find a fabulous restaurant here on the Hill." He grabbed Parker's arm and guided him out of the bar. "Nouvelle cuisine. Very expensive. Why don't we use some of Elisha's trust fund to pay for it?"

chapter

6

WEDNESDAY AFTERNOON

What was left of the coffee was strong and bitter. Reyes winced as he swallowed, and remembered that it had been made in the morning.

So far it had been a quiet day at the pueblo. He had intervened, with little success, in a domestic quarrel between old man Dominguez and his wife. The man had been gone all night and returned home drunk, which wasn't new. Someone else had reported their car stolen, but it turned up at a nearby cousin's. And there had been the Anglo tourists who ignored all the signs and tried to climb into the pueblo's ceremonial kiva to take photographs. Looking out of his window, he could see half a dozen cars, most with Texas license plates, and several couples stumbling about the plaza looking for Indian crafts. The huge cottonwood tree that dominated the plaza in front of his office was just now beginning to bloom.

In the back of his mind, going this way and that all day like an erratic wind, was the murder at the ruins of Tsankawi. Something about it had caught his interest and wouldn't go away. Part of it was the setting, which seemed an unlikely and risky choice. Another element was the *deliberateness*—that was the word for it, he thought—of the murder, the care that had been taken to kill the man and leave the impression that some dark ritual had been followed. The red line on the man's forehead was still vivid in his mind. Even the young Parker boy seemed to sense this.

It wasn't that murder, even violent murder, was new to him. After all, his years in the Marines had given him a very thorough, if not depressing, view of the human capacity for violence. He rarely talked with others about his work, but last night, at dinner with his aunt and uncle, he mentioned the murder and the gruesome particulars. His aunt, at least, looked shocked and mumbled something in Tewa to herself. His uncle had simply shrugged and said that he didn't think it was one of their people, that it was probably a white. Something about the situation convinced Reyes that the executioner wanted to convey a particular impression or a message. If his uncle was right, the author wasn't an Indian.

Reyes had just decided that the coffee was undrinkable when the telephone rang.

"This is Richard White at Dewey Galleries. I don't know if you remember me?"

"Yes. What can I do for you?" White ran Santa Fe's best-known gallery for Indian arts and museum-quality artifacts.

"Something happened today that I thought you might want to know about." There was a pause on the other end. "A young Indian came in to see me this afternoon. I think he was from San Ildefonso."

Reyes waited for White to explain what that meant.

"Well, I can't be sure, but I believe I've seen him with his grandmother here at the gallery. He didn't give his name, but offered to sell me several objects that almost never come on the market."

"What kinds of objects?"

"I would say that they were religious objects, old ones, perhaps used in kiva ceremonies."

Reyes was stunned. Indians regarded the objects used in religious ceremonies as sacred. They were never sold to outsiders, not even duplicated for commercial purposes. In fact, most ceremonial objects that he knew of were handed down from one generation to another, or from one clan to another, as part of a continuing tradition.

Reyes sat up in his chair. He knew that a substantial underground market existed for antiquities, most of them stolen, some even dug up from the graves of the Anasazi. On his desk was a bulletin from the Department of Interior reporting on the destruction of ancient burial sites throughout the Southwest; in some cases, tractors were used to plow the earth for a few pieces of pottery.

"I want to make it perfectly clear that this gallery does not trade in stolen goods. And we respect the pueblo's interest in preserving the privacy of religious practice."

"I appreciate that. Did you have an opportunity to see the objects themselves?"

"No, not directly. The young man showed me photographs. You know, the kind taken with an instant camera."

"What were they? Could you tell?"

"Yes, I believe so. There was a paho, or kiva prayer stick, that I would say dated from the last century. And some large stone fetishes. I'm not sure about the fetishes, but the prayer stick looked like something typical of the Rio Grande pueblos." White paused and then added, "As you probably know, there is an illegal market for these sorts of things. For the young man to approach me suggests that he, ah, isn't very experienced."

"What did you arrange?"

"I told him I'd have to see the objects. The young man said he would get back to me in several days. I gather he didn't have the objects immediately available."

Reyes wrote down White's description of the young man and arranged to visit the gallery in Santa Fe. For a moment after he hung up, Reyes stared at the telephone.

For many years, he had been indifferent to his religion. Or rather, to his religions, since he had been raised believing elements of both traditional Indian and Christian faiths. But for some time now he had felt himself drawn increasingly to his Indian half. Even if he didn't quite *believe*, he was angered that for money, outsiders would violate something others held so sacred.

With the description from White, it might be possible to track down the youth. It would make it easier if he were from San Ildefonso, but harder too, since he would have to contend with someone from his own people. Either way, it was going to take some luck, and Reyes had been around long enough not to count on anything like that.

*   *   *

It only took a few minutes for Gerald Sandys to find Isaac Berriman's house again. It had been six months, maybe seven, since he had last been there, but then most streets and houses in Los Alamos were easy to find.

Los Alamos had changed a great deal since Sandys first arrived on a cold March day in 1944. He was one of the first members of the British team to arrive at this remote mountain laboratory. Those years, when he had been in his twenties, had been the most exciting of his life. After the war, he had been given an opportunity by Robert Oppenheimer to stay or return to England. He had chosen to stay.

Sandys pulled up to the house and parked behind the official laboratory car. He was nervous; the visit from the lab's security office Monday afternoon had upset him. He wasn't sure of all the details, but apparently Berriman had been murdered. The news had been a shock: Berriman had worked for Sandys for over ten years, and as far as he could remember, the poor man had no enemies. True, he was a man of few friends, especially after his wife's death, but that wasn't uncommon here in this community of known eccentrics.

He had expressed considerable trepidation, of course, at Security's request that he make a preliminary appraisal of Berriman's Indian art. To his knowledge, the man had very little of importance. As Sandys remembered, he was fond of those gaudy kachina dolls that were popular among uneducated tourists, and of "affordable" Navajo rugs. Sandys scoffed. If anything was "affordable," it was likely of dubious quality and worth. He didn't expect to find anything.

Overall, Sandys thought this whole business was rather sad. Berriman was an inoffensive man and a very good mathematician. So to be murdered?

Sandys stopped at the open front door. He knocked once, then several times, as loudly as he could.

"Officer Castro?" There was no answer. "Officer Castro?" Sandys walked in and stood mutely in the living room.

Castro appeared from behind a door and startled Sandys.

"My God, man!"

"Sorry, Dr. Sandys. Please come in."

I *am* in, you bloody ass, thought Sandys.

"Thank you for coming. We appreciate this. The family will

probably want their own professional appraisal, but we need to know the value of Dr. Berriman's collection as soon as possible."

"Of course." Sandys was tempted to tell Castro what he normally charged for estate appraisals.

They made a tour room by room, with Sandys calling out rough dollar values for individual items and Castro making notes in a small black book. As he suspected, most of what he had seen so far was of little value.

In several rooms were small clay and plaster models of local archaeological sites. Each model had been meticulously sculpted and carved to duplicate actual scenes around Los Alamos. In one room was a model of the famous Bandelier cliff dwellings; in another was a model of some ruins called Puyé. Each one had been painted and detailed with small trees, rocks, and even creeks and roadbeds. Several had miniature human figures dressed like tourists. In Berriman's den was an unfinished model of Tsankawi; scattered around were photographs of the cliffs, the tourist paths, and the ruins and caves. To Sandys, the models looked like the miniature dioramas you saw in anthropological museums.

"Is this it, Officer? If so, I really must be going."

"There are several items in the hall closet, Doctor." Castro spoke slowly and appeared in no hurry. From a wall switch Castro flooded the small walk-in closet with light.

Sandys was stunned at what he saw. Sitting on the top shelf, above a collection of ski gear, was one large polychrome pot from the Ácoma Pueblo outside of Albuquerque. It was in beautiful condition and dated from the late nineteenth century. It alone was worth eight, maybe nine thousand dollars! And there were several Hopi kachinas, at least seventy-five years old, and among the most beautiful Sandys had ever seen. They would bring three to four thousand dollars each.

But what shocked Sandys was a much smaller object, at first hidden behind the large pot, ten inches long and cylindrical. It was a Pueblo deity stick, something used in religious ceremonies and almost never available to collectors. This particular object, however, had once belonged, just briefly, to Sandys. He had sold it and several others to a collector for just under five thousand dollars.

He picked it up to be sure it was the same one. The chubby

stick had been carved to resemble a phallus, and no doubt some Anglos would consider it mildly obscene. The Indians themselves would never see it that way, of course, since to them it was only a representation of human fertility.

Sandys felt weak. How in the hell had Berriman come by it? An object like this was not only beyond the man's financial means, but was far too subtle an object to be regarded as collectible by such a tourist as Berriman. Though the original colors were still faintly visible, it was on the whole extremely crude compared to the other items in this small room.

A wave of claustrophobia came on him. He backed awkwardly out of the room.

"Are you all right, Doctor?" Castro saw the small man's body suddenly tighten.

"Yes." For a moment he couldn't say anything more. "These objects, they..." He fumbled for words. "They're very rare."

Castro smiled to himself. He had been right; he readied his black book.

Sandys went through his estimations. "Why, there must be twenty, maybe twenty-five thousand dollars' worth of objects in here. I can't believe it." He repeated it. "I just can't believe it."

Castro took extensive notes on each object. Sandys urged him to immediately photograph each item and then remove it for safekeeping.

"Several questions, Doctor. Where do you find or buy items like these? And how do you sell them?"

Sandys thought for a moment. He had to be very careful. "You could buy most of these at a good, reputable gallery. And the same gallery would probably buy them." He paused. "The exception is this smaller piece." He started to pick it up again and then changed his mind, although he realized that his fingerprints were already on it. "This is a very rare piece, even though it may not look like it. It's called a 'deity stick,' and they are used even today in Pueblo religious ceremonies. They almost never come on the market because, understandably, the Indians themselves regard the objects as sacred and don't wish to have them outside the hands of their own people." He hoped the security man grasped what he was saying.

Sandys left with Castro's promise to lock everything away. For a brief moment, he thought of indicating that he would be interested in buying the collection should the estate wish to put it on the market. Then he changed his mind. Discretion was important here. He shook hands and walked to his car.

His mind raced as he drove home. He summoned all the will he had to control the trembling in his hands. He certainly couldn't let his wife see him like this. Of course, like everyone in Los Alamos, she was eager to hear what he had learned about Berriman, since the rumors were fantastic.

What frightened him now was the prospect of exposure. For years, ever since his arrival here in Los Alamos in the forties, he had been an ardent collector of rare Indian objects. He was known to have one of the finest private collections of ceremonial objects and a small but exquisite collection of pottery.

All of these items had been carefully acquired, each chosen for its rarity and beauty. He had bought and sold thousands of items over the years, carefully keeping only the best. Twice, no three times, he remembered, he had been involved with items that undoubtedly had been stolen or acquired in some questionable way. While he never kept any of them for long, nor inquired about their origin, he had assisted in their sale to, well, discreet hands. That had been years ago.

Thank God he had never been caught, and his fear of this had lessened over the years—until today! He had to think carefully. He had to collect his thoughts and determine what, if anything, he could do.

It was a quarter to five and the hallway was already beginning to fill with people going home for the day. The tall man was unaware of the time; he had been at his computer terminal for almost half an hour and was beginning to feel the muscles tighten in his back and neck. Without losing sight of the monitor, he moved his shoulders up and down to relieve the tension. It helped only a little bit.

The problem was that he was getting an "entry denied" line on his screen. None of the elaborate tricks he had developed during the last few weeks worked now, and his sense of alarm was growing. Almost certainly, the people in central computer had discovered his illegal entries into data storage. If that was true, the mainframe's security system would have tagged his terminal at this very moment.

He paused, his fingers just hovering over the keys; it looked like he was going to have to abandon his search. But there was one thing he needed to know before he employed his last wild card.

He quickly typed in a series of commands and waited for the computer to give him a "go ahead" prompt. After a moment, the word "proceed" appeared on the green television screen. He typed in another series of commands and waited. He had his answer without a trace of message on the screen other than the flickering prompt character. It was taking too goddamn long for the computer to respond! The mainframe had been alerted.

"Shit!" he said out loud, and for a brief moment he was tempted to smash the damn keyboard. He formed tight fists with both hands and hit his thighs hard, once, twice. "Shit!" he said again.

He had to act fast. The series of procedures he had so carefully worked out to access the central computer were now foiled by some recent change in the system. That had to be it! Perhaps it was related to Berriman, but the man with the powerful arms couldn't be sure. It didn't matter now, anyway. If the computer had identified his terminal, it would lead Security to him. What mattered was to make the computer think something else!

From behind him he heard voices, and instinctively he pushed himself close to the monitor. The voices continued for a moment in the hallway outside of his office; it was a man and a woman talking. In front of him, the screen suddenly came alive. The words "no access—repeat authorization code" came flooding across the green field letter by letter. He had to act quickly, just in case someone on the other end was visually watching a screen or printout.

"Working late?" The voice behind him made him jerk and sit up in an instant.

"Jesus!" he shouted.

Parker laughed. "Just a little preoccupied, maybe?" He cleared his throat. "Just on my way out. Everything okay?"

The tall man eased down in his chair. He turned around and forced a small laugh.

"Yeah. Just heavy into some calculations. You scared the shit out of me." He sighed and tried to relax and, as casually as possible, cover the screen with his body.

"Don't overdo it." Parker started out the door. "Good night."

The other man sat stiffly, staring at the doorway, until he could hear Parker's footsteps disappear down the marble hallway. Jesus Christ! he mumbled.

But then the idea hit him. He reached quickly over the desk for the telephone and dialed an outside line and then his home number. Jesus! I hope she's there, he thought. The chances were slim; she probably was still in California. The screen continued its urgent, unrelenting request for identification.

He let the phone ring ten times before he slammed the receiver back into the cradle. Through the crack in his door he could see Parker's secretary turning out the lights in their suite of offices. He looked back at the screen. He may have already waited too long. He was going to have to make this decision by himself. Christ! he hoped she understood.

He quickly typed a series of word and number combinations and waited briefly for the screen to clear. When it did, he typed in a series of commands, waiting each time for the appropriate response before proceeding to the next step. Each time it worked, he smiled. Few people at the laboratory remembered that part of his background was in computer security systems. What had started as a game months ago to break into the central data banks had evolved into much more these last few weeks.

The card he was now playing was one of the most sophisticated computer tricks he had ever created. By using a hidden "back door" to the computer—something he had discovered a few weeks ago—he was now directing the computer to read both a different identification code *and* a different terminal. Unwittingly, Parker now volunteered his.

The last series of numbers appeared on the screen and the man smiled again. He typed one last command and saw the words "exit," "account," and "time utilized" spill across the screen along with several lines of data. Then with a flick of a switch, he turned his terminal off. If everything had gone as it should, the computer had dissolved a record of most of the last hour's activity but left, deeply buried, a telltale record of use on Parker's terminal.

He sat back in his chair and exhaled deeply, trying to force his body to relax. He would have to work out hard tonight to ease the tension in his body.

There was still one other thing to do. An image of his girlfriend lecturing him came into his mind. He shook his head to break the thought and reached across the table to a stack of computer print-outs, some of them three and four inches thick. From the middle of one he pulled out four small reports typed on regular paper. Each one had a heavy cardboard cover sheet on it with the edges outlined in heavy red stripes. Across the top and center of the cover sheet were the words TOP SECRET, printed in large red letters. Below that were a series of lines with a few names indicating who had checked out the report and the dates. On all three documents the last name, with the return date still empty, read Isaac Berriman.

The hall was empty in both directions. It would be at least half an hour before the night cleanup crew arrived. He walked quickly across the floor into Parker's suite of offices with a small briefcase in his hand. If he was caught at this point, he could always say he was looking for a nonclassified report on the secretary's desk. It was ironic, he thought, that the laboratory's security system favored his plan.

The entire administration building was a secure area, which meant that no one could enter the building without the appropriate ID badge. A system like this meant that classified material could be handled during the day without fear of compromise. At night, all materials not returned to the central library were locked up in special filing cabinets that were actually safes with combination locks.

He moved the door within a few inches of being closed; there was just enough of an opening to hear someone walking down the tile hallway. The man smiled to himself. It had been easy to break into Berriman's office safe using a list of combination numbers that Parker's secretary kept. He had entered the man's office on Sunday, after the murder at Tsankawi, and opened the safe in less than a minute.

As quickly as he could, the tall man found a spot behind some books on Parker's shelf where he carefully arranged three of the reports stolen from Berriman's safe, holding them with his handkerchief. Somewhere he had read that experts could take fingerprints off of paper.

His last step was to fold the remaining document lengthwise and stuff it flatly inside his pants. It fit comfortably and unobtrusively along his lower abdomen.

He had one last task. Mentally recalling Theresa's safe combination, he opened the top drawer of her safe and pulled out the list of all safe combinations in the group and slipped that into his pants as well. Later he would burn it; hopefully that would focus attention on Parker and his secretary.

With the hallway still empty, he walked out of the office and took the stairwell down to the main floor. Stopping at the security gate for an ID check, he offered his attaché case for a search and the guard waved him on. After saying good night, he walked casually out to his motorcycle.

He wasn't sure what to do next, but that was something he could discuss with her. He was mildly sorry at involving Parker, but right now he was just glad he had been able to cover his ass.

Parker pulled into his driveway and parked next to Elisha's Volvo. He had just seen Lawton, Kearney, and the other senators off at the small airport at the edge of Los Alamos. In spite of everything, the two-day subcommittee meeting had gone well; Kearney left pleased with what he had heard and with promises for a new push in Congress for more funds.

Elisha was in the kitchen making dinner and Tevis sat watching television. He changed clothes and made a drink. He always thought of bourbon as a summer drink, but tonight it was just what he wanted.

"You need to talk to Tevis again."

"Now what?"

"He cut school Monday afternoon and rode his bike down to Tsankawi." She expertly diced a tomato. "He even cut his session with the psychologist."

"Jesus."

"I'm worried that he's taking the business on Sunday too hard. He's been awfully quiet. We talked on Sunday, before you got home, but it must have upset him."

Parker suddenly wondered how Sunday had affected Elisha. She couldn't even say the word *murder*, it seemed.

"I'll talk to him," he said, and walked over to Tevis in the living room.

"I know what you're going to say, Dad."

"You do?"

"Yes. And I promise I won't do it again."

"What is that?"

"I won't cut school."

"And?"

"And I won't go down to Tsankawi again."

"Good. After what happened last Sunday, that was a pretty dumb thing to do. And you'll keep your appointments with the psychologist?"

He nodded. His psychologist was a woman named Eileen, but at least she was better than the last one.

"Why did you go?"

"Well, Dad, uh, I wanted to see what was there."

"What do you mean, 'what was there'?"

"Dad, see, there was cornmeal in the cave, and little twigs from a tree."

Parker frowned. "So what?"

"So, Dad, the Indians use that sort of stuff in their secret ceremonies. It's sort of, well, magical."

Parker shook his head. "How do you know that?"

"Mom told me about some of it, and Reyes, uh, Officer Reyes, the Indian policeman, also told me. It could have something to do with the murder, Dad."

Parker didn't like the sound of that; there was something spooky about a mix of murder and magic.

"Yeah, Dad, he's neat. We talked about a lot of things that the Pueblo people do."

"That's nice, but no more of this crap. You stay in Los Alamos. Understand?" He hoped he sounded firm. Then it struck him that even the Indians had more time for his son than he did.

"Okay." Tevis adopted his most angelic look. "Dad?"

Parker looked skeptically at him; he had seen that look before.

"Could we set up the telescope tonight, Dad. Just for a little while? Huh?"

Parker started to say no. After all, he was tired and Tevis probably deserved some kind of punishment. On the other hand, he had spent so little time with his son recently.

"Okay. But just for a while."

Later they hauled out the heavy metal tripod and set it up on their outside deck. The porch was just high enough so that the telescope cleared the tops of the trees; on a clear night, there was excellent visibility in most directions.

Parker attached the short, thick telescope to a special mount. First he centered the scope on the North Star and then made a smaller adjustment that brought it toward true north. With the built-in motor drive, the special eight-inch mirror and lens assembly could accurately follow any star or celestial object as it moved across the night sky.

Parker found two small smudges of light in the finder scope and then focused the objects in the larger telescope. He turned it over to Tevis.

"What do you see?"

Tevis took a look. "M81 and M82!" he shouted, "both in Ursa Major." He used the astronomical "Messier" designations for two nebular clusters millions of light-years away.

"Good." Parker found another object.

"M44 in Cancer. The Beehive Cluster."

"Excellent."

This was Parker's favorite father-and-son activity. While he disliked hiking and most outdoor sports, this was one activity that he enjoyed from his own childhood. He always remembered the warm evenings in California spent with his father staring up into space and the tiny pinpricks of light. Fortunately, Tevis seemed to enjoy this as well. Parker sensed that Tevis would soon know more about astronomy than he did.

"Dad?"

"Yeah." He was trying to focus on another, dimmer cluster.

"Will we be able to see the Star Wars thing with our telescope?"

Parker smiled to himself. "Star Wars is actually lots of things, Tev. And although the individual components in some cases will be as large as houses, it's unlikely that we will be able to see them from earth."

"Why not?"

"Well, although a space station or giant laser might be large to us, it will still be far away. At best, it will look like a small spot of light."

"Will there be a lot of lasers and things in space?"

"If the government has its way, there will be."

"Will it get in the way of anything?"

"Not that I know of." Parker wondered what his son meant.

Tevis was silent for a moment. "Will we still be able to see the stars, Dad?"

Parker smiled again. "Yes. Besides, there may not be a Star Wars system."

"Why not?"

"Because if it doesn't work on earth, it won't work in space. And maybe we won't need it."

Tevis was quiet for a moment. "That might be good, huh, Dad?"

"Why?"

"Because then everything will be the same as it is now. Undisturbed."

Later that night, in bed, Parker couldn't go to sleep. Elisha was turned on her side, away from him. They had barely talked that evening, and there seemed to be so much to tell her. Maybe she could help him put his uncertainties into perspective. His performance before the subcommittee, Lawton's talk with him, Berriman's violent death—all of them raised doubts about what he was doing. He gently put his hand on Elisha's shoulder.

"Elisha?" he said softly.

There was no response. It was Elisha's turn to fall asleep first.

chapter 7

THURSDAY MORNING

The director sat silently at the head of the large conference table in his office, his round, gold-rim glasses resting on the lower half of his nose. He was waiting patiently for the last of his associate directors to arrive. It was 8:28, and Alan Merritt was known as a director who started meetings on time.

Parker couldn't be sure, but Merritt seemed edgy, just a little less composed than usual. Maybe it was no more than the way the man nervously pushed his glasses back on his nose, but Parker sensed something was disturbing the normally taciturn director.

For a moment, Parker's attention was drawn to Merritt's wall, where six elaborately mounted color photographs hung. Several photos were of lasers firing; another was of a giant solar panel angled dramatically against the blue New Mexico sky; the others were closeups of electronic equipment that produced intricate geometrical patterns. All were taken in laboratories in Los Alamos. It always amused Parker to see the photos, which Merritt had changed regularly. None of them were of weapons; all of them looked like pages from *National Geographic*.

Parker sat next to Greenberg, who seemed uncomfortable. He could tell this wasn't Merritt's ordinary management meeting. Except for Ed Poole, who sat at the end of the table opposite Merritt, he was the low man on the pole. Parker knew it had something to do with Berriman.

On top of everything, Theresa told him this morning that something had been taken from her safe. It was the list of combinations to each one of the file safes in the group. Crying, she told him she was *sure* she hadn't lost it; she had seen it only as recently as yesterday afternoon. By the time he arrived, she had already reported it to Security.

This would mean a reprimand from Security, and worse, each safe would be sealed, reopened, and inventoried, with new combinations issued by Poole's office. No one, including Greenberg, was going to like that.

Merritt nodded regally and his secretary left the room, noiselessly closing the door behind her.

Parker studied the director for a moment. He decided that in an earlier era, Merritt would look exactly the same except that he would be wearing pince-nez glasses; with a moustache, he might look like a thin Teddy Roosevelt.

Without any formality, Merritt turned to Parker and spoke. "David, I've asked you to attend because Isaac Berriman worked for you." With that, he turned to the table at large.

"Gentlemen, you all know of Isaac Berriman's death last Sunday?" Everyone around the table nodded.

"Well, I'm sorry to say that we have reason to believe that he may have been involved in, ah, something of considerable harm to the laboratory and national security."

Jesus, Parker said to himself. His worst fears were coming true: Berriman's death was more than murder. By the look on Poole's face, it was something big.

"What we've learned, gentlemen, is that Berriman accessed data from our central computers. Apparently, he tapped data from several different divisions, the results of which would give him a rather thorough understanding of our most sensitive work. This includes data on the X-ray weapon configuration scheduled for test next week in Nevada. Isn't that right, Willows?" He turned to the director of the computer center, who was nervously pulling at the ends of his string tie.

The pale man nodded. Right now, he was very conscious of the fact that his colleagues called him "The Mole" behind his back. He assumed that the nickname was a reference to his underground office. "We have confirmed that Berriman, or his terminal at least, accessed data from several divisions, and that he attempted access to several other sensitive areas." On orders from Merritt, he held back from revealing the full extent of the investigation—and his findings.

Merritt continued. "What this suggests is that Berriman may have pulled data on other occasions, and on any number of projects. What we don't know is how he learned the appropriate passwords or a way of subverting the computer's internal security system." He shot a glance at the uncomfortable computer director.

The elaborate computer system at Los Alamos was among the largest in the nation and was used entirely for weapons work. Certain divisions and groups within the laboratory had access to the computer over secure telephone lines that ran through metal pipes welded at each joint to prevent unauthorized tapping. Access to the computer, and the considerable information it stored, was through a special terminal that required a set of keys to open and then a series of passwords to engage the computer itself. As a rule, individuals were unable to access more than their own research data. Berriman had been able to open the entire system.

"Ed, why don't you tell us what you know so far."

"Yes, sir." Poole leaned forward and rested one arm on the table and fiddled with his collar with the other. He had been up since five this morning preparing his presentation.

"We know that Berriman was authorized access by Dr. Parker to Level Five data just five days after being assigned to the Strategic Defense Research Group. A secure terminal was then installed in his office. His password, which we have now retired, enabled him to pull information on a broad range of activities. Somehow he was able to obtain other operable passwords that gave him access to data beyond Epsilon Level. We do not know if he learned these passwords on his own or found some method of tricking the computer into giving him access. We do know that his last access time was Saturday morning, before his death."

Poole stopped for a moment and took a sip of his coffee, oblivious to the anxious effect his delay caused around the table. He shuffled several pages of notes in front of him. What he was not telling was that the laboratory's Sigma files had been penetrated.

At the head of the table, Merritt sat quietly in his chair, letting his coffee grow cold. Methodically, over and over, he traced small circles and then boxes on the pad in front of him; each time he paused, he pushed his wire-rim glasses up the bridge of his nose.

"We also have verification," Poole continued, "that Dr. Berriman instructed the computer to run at least one hard copy on the special printer connected to his secure terminal. As you know, the ribbons for these printers must be checked in and out each day and accounted for by our security personnel. This, of course, prevents theft of classified materials through carbon ribbons."

The director grimaced. "The report appears to be a compendium of recent scaling data on our laser work. Not only did it cite previous test results, but all of the innovations incorporated into the weapon to be tested next week in Nevada." He cleared his throat. "We have been unable to account for the document."

"You mean a copy of our latest data is floating around somewhere?" Greenberg was visibly upset. Berriman, after all, was a member of his division. "What about his house? His car?"

Poole shook his head. "So far, we've found nothing. We've thoroughly searched his house, his car, and his office. There's nothing."

Poole looked around the room; for once, Merritt's staff seemed to understand the importance of security. "We have inventoried the contents of Dr. Berriman's safe. There are four classified documents unaccounted for and which have not been returned to the central library." Poole let this sink in. "A list containing the combinations to each safe within Dr. Parker's group has been lost, and it is possible that the security of each safe has been compromised."

Parker heard Greenberg gasp and felt his face flush. He leaned over and whispered, "It just happened. I learned about it only thirty minutes ago." He could feel all eyes on him.

"We did find this in his desk here in the lab." He held up and then circulated the torn half of a standard-size sheet of white paper. It had been folded several times to make a small square. Now it was flattened and encased between two sheets of plastic. "We believe the first column of numbers to be dates, the second, times. In part, it matches the list of entries compiled by the master computer." Poole looked around the room. "We think it was prepared by Berriman since the writing on the bottom of this page is in his handwriting."

When the sheet came around to Parker, he studied it for a moment. In someone's handwriting, it read:

4-23	11:40
4-23	17:10
4-23	18:05
4-24	11:33
4-25	16:33
4-25	18:09
4-26	15:45

At the bottom were the words "authorship," and "to settle." Parker found it strange that Berriman would keep something like this in his desk. If he was doing something wrong, it was incriminating.

Poole continued his briefing, mentioning Berriman's background and surprising collection of artifacts. Merritt straightened his glasses. "Is there anything else?"

"I don't think so, except that the FBI is now involved in the investigation. It's quite likely that they will interview a number of individuals." He looked at Greenberg and Parker and then gathered up his papers.

Parker sensed mixed emotions from around the table. Mostly it was shock, but another one, barely recognizable, was a sense of disapproval directed at him. Perhaps he was overreacting, but the message seemed to be: You're responsible because this man worked for you.

"This," said Merritt, "is a bad situation and comes at a particularly unfortunate time." He was referring to several recent and well-publicized cases where American citizens had sold highly classified defense information to the Soviets. The press had covered all of these events in great detail.

"I must ask all of you to keep this information strictly confidential. Obviously, the fact that he was murdered is public, given the public's propensity for ghoulish news. But it isn't necessary, I think, to spread the fact that Berriman has, or apparently has, illegally obtained advanced weapons data."

Several people nodded agreement.

"One other thing, gentlemen. We have to consider the possibility that Berriman was working with someone else. I don't want to
suggest a witch-hunt, but we need to look closely at security in all of
our programs."

As the meeting was breaking up, Merritt signaled Parker and
Greenberg to stay. Parker felt exhausted and overwhelmed. It was
already nine-thirty and in his office were a thousand things to do,
including pacifying his staff as their safes were inventoried.

"How do you think the Senate briefing went?" Merritt asked.

Parker wondered what he was fishing for.

"I think it was great, Alan," said Greenberg.

"David?"

"Good. The Senate, of course, would like to have a flat yes or
no on whether SDI will work or not."

Merritt didn't respond for a moment and then began slowly
gesticulating with one hand. "I was impressed by the Air Force's
visual display. You know, the large magnetic board. And Livermore
had better graphics than we did." He looked at Greenberg. "We need
to upgrade our stuff and have more colorful art. And large scale."

Greenberg nodded.

"And also," Merritt began, looking at Parker, "we need to be as
positive as possible about our work."

There it was, Parker thought. The message. Next to him,
Greenberg maintained a stony silence.

He studied Merritt's smooth, boyish face as they stood around
the large conference table. He fit anyone's description of an Eastern
prep-school graduate, which, as Parker realized, the man was by
breeding and education. The contradiction, perhaps, was that this
youthful man with the clean-cut good looks directed an institution
that spent nearly half a billion dollars a year, the majority of it going
to research on sophisticated nuclear weapons.

Merritt let Greenberg and Parker get as far as the door. "And,
David, you'd better get your house in order. There's no telling where
this Berriman business is going to lead, but we don't want any
skeletons in the closet."

Greenberg was unusually quiet as they walked back to their

offices on the second floor. Parker was prepared to leave Greenberg at his office, but the older man motioned to him to step in.

"This is a helluva business, David." Greenberg slumped down in his chair, making it creak as he settled his frame in it.

"I wonder what's next?"

"I don't know, but we need to be sure that nothing else happens. How in the hell could you lose a list of safe combinations?" Greenberg waved his hands dramatically. "Are you supposed to even keep a list?" He leaned forward in his chair and looked directly at Parker. "I want you to check and double-check everything Berriman was working on and who, if anybody, worked with him. In fact, let's find out who he talked to regularly, and even who he ate lunch with. That kind of thing." Was this, Parker thought, the beginning of the witch-hunt Merritt denied he wanted?

Parker didn't know what else to say but agreed to get on it right away. As he stood up to leave, Greenberg halted him.

"And, David, I didn't like the way you handled yourself during your presentation."

"But, Francis—"

"I don't want to talk about it now. But you weren't up to snuff. You equivocated and you were just too damn negative." He shook his big head. "Just too goddamn filled with doubts. It wasn't our job to raise policy questions. Our job was to make Los Alamos look like it knows what it's doing. We don't want to lose anything to Livermore or to a goddamn defense contractor."

Parker just stood there, silent, unable to say anything.

"Next time better, okay?"

"Sure."

Back at his own desk, he stared out the window at the mountains; he could see all the way to the very top of the towering Jemez and make out the dark line of trees that ran across the ridge.

It was silly, he knew, but he hoped that somehow someone would find an explanation for Berriman and the computer taps and that the whole business would be settled and go away. Maybe then life would get back to normal.

Returning to his office, Poole closed the door and sat down slowly in his big chair. The tension was back in his neck. He checked his messages. There was a call from the county coroner. That probably meant something on Berriman's death. There was a call from Doty in Albuquerque saying he would be in Los Alamos later in the day. That probably meant trouble. There was a note that Castro wanted to see him at his convenience. Castro would have to wait.

The FBI had moved with surprising speed; in one day they obtained a court order to examine Berriman's finances and sent agents to interview co-workers and even individuals in Poole's own Security division. One agent was already hanging around the administration building, and it wouldn't be long before they established an office in Los Alamos, thought Poole. They had moved in like a pack of hungry relatives.

He called his secretary on the telephone and asked her to come into his office. When she stepped in the room, he noticed she was chewing gum, something that ten years ago he and the Bureau would never have permitted staff to do on the job.

The Berriman business was very puzzling. The news on the illegal computer taps was scary, very scary and very unlike Berriman. But that's what puzzled Poole most about the whole business: it didn't seem to fit what he knew about Isaac Berriman. Poole didn't especially want to believe it, but there was the possibility that Berriman was working with someone else, someone more sophisticated. He had suggested that possibility to Merritt. Maybe the man was innocent, Poole thought. Maybe he was being made the patsy.

There was only one thing to do right now, and it was the same thing the FBI would be doing. "Ask Castro to pull the files on everyone in Parker's group. And see if we can get their personnel files as well."

There was silence on the other end for a moment. "But that's probably fifty or sixty people, Mr. Poole."

"That's right," he said. He massaged his neck. He would do this the old-fashioned way—start at the top and work his way down. He would start with David Parker.

The weapons lab was actually a complex of buildings hidden behind a series of high security fences and electronic sensing devices. There were rarely nuclear weapons there. The few that existed from time to time were experimental models designed as prototypes, or Air Force warheads modified for use in the laboratory's underground testing program. They were always called "devices" by their designers.

Parker went through several security screenings before he finally entered the building he needed. He found Jerry Hoffman, his assistant group leader and test director, and then convened an informal meeting with members of the project staff.

"Everything okay?" Parker looked at Hoffman.

"So far. It'll be shipped out tomorrow and flown to Nevada on Wednesday and reassembled over the weekend for preliminary evaluation."

Behind Hoffman and the others was a heavy tubular steel platform six feet wide and half as tall as a man. On it, laced with dozens of cables, was the test weapon. Because the bomb would rest on its special scaffolding until the moment of detonation, it had only a simple metal cover, like a canister. Several key elements of the device were missing, locked away, to prevent any possibility of a detonation. Now it looked like something from an oil refinery instead of a nuclear warhead from a Titan missile.

Not far from the platform were a dozen pieces of equipment varying in size from a suitcase to a small car. Some rested on their own skids and others sat impassively on the floor, connected to a master console that would coordinate the complicated experiment a thousand feet underground. Also nearby were dozens of special metal pipes bound together on dollies; they were designed to receive energy from the detonation and in turn direct it toward a phalanx of special monitors. Each piece of equipment was designed to work only once—that was the only life it had—and to interact with the thermonuclear explosion itself and thereby test the feasibility of X rays as a weapon. Special monitors had to gather in a fraction of a second as much information as possible before they, too, were destroyed in the explosion.

Parker knew this weapon had only one purpose. It needed to generate, in concert with the metal rods, a very intense X-ray laser. An earlier prototype had worked, but this one incorporated substantial improvements. One Star Wars scheme his team had imagined called for thousands of these X-ray weapons to be placed in orbit in space, each one able to be controlled from the ground to aim at a specific Soviet warhead.

Parker studied the array of equipment and listened to Hoffman's briefing. His assistant was barely five-and-a-half feet tall, and stocky. Parker wasn't sure how old he was, perhaps fifty, but his full beard had been white for as long as Parker could remember. He was, however, one of the best bomb designers in the nation.

"We're expecting something like ten to twelve thousand tons of yield," he said. That, thought Parker, made the explosion almost as powerful as the weapon dropped on Hiroshima.

Parker looked at the thermonuclear device, the source of the experiment, and studied it. Swathed with cables and smaller pieces of electronic equipment, without its conical shield, it could be something designed by a group of mechanical engineering students as a graduate experiment. From any angle, it didn't look like a weapon that could destroy a small city.

Parker touched it with one hand; in another week it would be detonated underground. Thank God, he thought, that's all it would do.

chapter 8

THURSDAY AFTERNOON

Reyes looked at his watch: it was a quarter to nine. He had fifteen minutes until his appointment with Richard White at the gallery. It would take him only a few minutes to walk the three short blocks in Santa Fe from Tia Sophia's Restaurant, where he sat by himself.

Sipping coffee from a beige cup, he tried to sort out the rich smells of the restaurant: the smell of his coffee was overlaid with green chili and eggs, and very faintly he thought he could pick out the posole. As he paid his check and started down the street, he brought his thoughts back to the young man at San Ildefonso.

The discreet inquiries made around the pueblo during the last few days had produced nothing, no knowledge of sacred objects missing or stolen. No word of a youth, or youths, involved in stolen goods. A talk with one of the pueblo caciques, or leaders, however, revealed that other pueblos had had trouble.

"I heard the Hopis had problems," the man told him in his old, rasping voice.

Reyes sat quietly at the man's dining room table, sipping raw, black coffee made from boiling the grounds in water.

"Problems," the man repeated.

"What sort of problems?" asked Reyes.

"The Two Horn Society at Mishongnovi had two *alosakas*

stolen. Maybe it was Indians, but they think whites." The older man didn't look up from the table.

Reyes searched his memory for the meaning of "*alosaka*"; as best as he could remember, it was a figure carved from cottonwood root and used in a ceremony. The old man seemed to sense his uncertainty.

"They're used in the New Fire Ceremony to bring rain and make the corn grow." He referred to a Hopi ritual, one of the most important since it began the annual cycle.

"Could it be one of their own people?" asked Reyes.

"Maybe. The people are poor and if there is money..." Those words had stayed with Reyes.

White was a tall, congenial man who was well known for his knowledge of Indian artifacts, both old and contemporary. His gallery, which occupied several floors, contained everything from gleaming silver jewelry to old Indian baskets several feet wide. White sat behind his desk in a cramped upstairs office filled with books and art magazines. On the walls were rare Hopi kachinas. As he talked, Reyes studied a series of small photographs.

"As you can see, the objects are quite old and of course very valuable." White settled back in his chair; he seemed more comfortable face to face than talking over the telephone.

The objects in the photographs were similar to some Reyes had seen in his own pueblo, but there was nothing to specifically tie them to San Ildefonso. At least, not without looking at the objects themselves. *That* was a relief, of sorts, since perhaps the objects had come from somewhere else.

"Do these sort of things come on the market often?"

White shifted in his chair. "Rarely. And when they do, they usually come from established collections." White paused again. "In other words, we know where they've come from and that they aren't stolen."

"What made you suspicious in this particular case?" Reyes looked hard at White.

"Mostly, that they were offered to me by an Indian. And a young one at that." White looked around his office. "You have to understand that we are approached every day by Indians, by traders, by private individuals, either to buy their goods or to take them on consignment. When we buy from Indians, it's usually pottery or jewelry or rugs that we buy. Most, if not all, of the older stuff comes from traders or from private collections."

Reyes considered White's explanation for a moment. "Why do you think this man approached you?"

White shrugged. "It's hard to say, of course, except that the gallery is well known for handling classic pieces. But most of all I would say the young man was very inexperienced in these matters." White leaned forward and dropped his voice. "I can't be sure, but my feeling is that these items are part of a private collection." White softly cleared his throat. "I may have scared him off, however."

Reyes looked at him. "Why do you think that?"

"He hasn't been back." He shook his head. "He may have changed his mind or gone somewhere else."

"You think these items were stolen?"

"Yes, but I can't be sure. There have been several robberies in the last eight or nine months in the Santa Fe area. One or two of them were thefts of major collections."

Reyes made several notes on a small pad. Once again, he asked White to describe the man.

"In his twenties, I'd say. Heavy, but not fat. Maybe five-six, five-seven." White paused for a moment. "I don't remember anything extraordinary about him, if that's what you want. But I do remember that he had tattoos on three knuckles of his left hand. No. Maybe it was his right hand." He shook his head. "I can't remember."

"Do you remember the tattoos?"

"They were letters. It made a word, I think. It was a simple word—like 'mad,' or maybe 'sad.' Again, I'm sorry, I just can't remember."

Reyes wrote it down. "What makes you think he was from the San Ildefonso Pueblo?"

"Do you know a potter named Isabel Martinez?"

Reyes nodded.

"This man may be a grandson, maybe a nephew. But I'm almost certain I've seen them together here in the store. We bought pottery from her."

Reyes wrote the information down and thanked White, who promised to contact him as soon as the young man came back. *If* he did.

As he walked out of the store, he noticed an older couple with matching baseball caps complain about the cost of an elaborate silver bracelet set with beautiful hunter green turquoise stones. The attractive sales woman only smiled and deftly drew their attention to a less expensive piece in another case. As the young woman moved around the corner of the wooden showcase, Reyes noticed she was wearing a long denim skirt that half hid a pair of mauve-colored boots. This was Santa Fe, he thought.

On the way back to the pueblo, Reyes considered the possibilities. One was that the young man was simply unloading stolen merchandise. Another was that he was part of a gang that targeted well-known collections. But if that was true, why was he jeopardizing his anonymity by going directly to a well-known dealer in Santa Fe? Another possibility—and this one upset Reyes the most—was that this young man was offering to sell items stolen from the pueblo, or from his clan, just to raise a few easy dollars.

He turned off on Highway 4 to his office at San Ildefonso; the cottonwoods along the road were as full and beautiful this spring as he had ever seen them. It was hard to imagine anything bad happening on a day like this, he thought. And for the first time all day, he smiled.

Heat drifted out of the vents with a muffled, rasping sound that choked the air and made the small room noticeably stuffy. For a moment Parker considered opening the window to let in some air but changed his mind when he considered his visitors. Across his small conference table sat Poole and Castro.

Parker noticed that the director of Security wore a faded green coat that had an iridescent sheen to it. At first he thought it might be the light in his office until he shifted in his chair and caught a glimpse of Poole's pants; they were green but of a different material.

"Let me see if we have this right," said Poole, flipping the pages of his notepad. "You were in your office Sunday morning for a brief period—let's see—you arrived about nine A.M., you think." He flipped to the next page. "And then you left at approximately eleven-thirty."

"Yes, that's it."

"You left directly for the ruins called, uh, Tsankawi?"

"Yes. I mean, not directly. I went home first. And then to the ruins."

For the first time in nearly an hour, Castro spoke up. "Isn't that somewhat out of your way, Doctor?"

Parker stared at them for a moment. "What the hell difference does that make?"

Castro only stared back. "Only that it was out of your way."

"Well, yes, it's out of the way. But I had to go home first. It's maybe fifteen minutes from this office to my house." What were they digging at? Parker thought.

"We're only interested in accounting for everyone's time, Dr. Parker," said Poole. "It's standard procedure." He forced a smile.

"Well, I went home, organized some papers to read, and then drove down to Tsankawi. That took maybe twenty minutes."

Both Poole and Castro made notes. "Did you see Dr. Berriman that morning?"

Parker shook his head. "No. That was Saturday morning. Or maybe afternoon. As I told you, he was working on his terminal. I don't think he even saw me." He thought for a moment. "Since it was Saturday, I signed in at the guard station. They'll have a record of my times. Sunday too, for that matter."

Poole made another note. "If we could go back over the computer practices of your group, Doctor?"

Parker rolled his eyes. "They're the same procedures as any other group in the lab. Berriman's work cleared him for access to all classified data generated by the project. As part of his job, like a half-dozen others here, he had a terminal assigned to him in his office and a password by which he could link up with the central computer system." Parker pointed to a terminal in the corner of his office. "I have one too."

"About his use of passwords? ... "

Parker cut him off. "I don't know how he learned anyone else's. Unlike safe combinations, we keep no list of passwords. The project is billed for all time used, and I see a printout each month that tells me what we're using. In the short time he was here, Berriman used what I can only describe as a 'normal' amount of computer time."

Poole started to ask a question, but Parker continued. "There was no way of telling what Berriman was doing by looking at the monthly billings. Short of watching him every moment, there was no way of knowing his activities. As I understand it, most of these unauthorized taps occurred only in the last month or so."

"That we know of," corrected Castro.

"Yes. As you know, any individual with a password can access the central computer from any terminal. The exception is a certain level of data not generally available to staff. Only specific terminals and special code words access *that* stuff."

"Can your terminal access the Sigma files?"

"Yes. But even so, I can only access a portion of the data stored at that level." He looked over his shoulder at the white monitor and keyboard with the special lock. "I haven't been in the Sigma files for over a month."

Poole made another note. Other than the director and a handful of others, including himself, no one knew of Berriman's breech of the lab's supersecret files. But something didn't jibe in all of that, he thought. Something had happened under Parker's nose.

"Is it possible that someone else used your terminal during the last week?"

"I don't think so. It would be damn difficult."

"Why?"

"Poole—Ed—there are people in and out of here all the time. But my staff does not make a practice, even a rare one, of using my office for their work."

Poole nodded. "And the list of safe combinations?" he inquired.

"Yes, I told you. I know now that this was inappropriate, but several of my staff barely use their safes and some of them forget the combinations. We kept a list to help them out, but it was never circulated and no one knew anyone else's number."

"Well, you did, Dr. Parker," said Castro benignly, "and your secretary."

Poole intervened. "If they had problems, they should have contacted my office," he said.

"I know, but our job is to design weapons and not spend all day with bureaucratic details." Parker tried to calm himself. They had been over this earlier in the conversation. Clearly he had made a mistake permitting such a list—but Christ! He felt the same subtle disapproval he experienced this morning in Merritt's office. "As far as we know, the list has been missing for only a day or so. Theresa remembers checking the list the day before. It's part of a daily ritual, I think. But the important thing is that the list was missing less than twenty-four hours."

Poole started to mention that such a list missing even for a few minutes was potentially dangerous but he held back. Instead, he handed Parker a copy of the handwritten list of dates and times found in Berriman's desk. "Do you have any idea why Berriman would single out these particular times?"

Parker shook his head.

"The computer center has confirmed that Berriman's terminal was in use on each of these occasions. We don't know why he made such a list, however."

"I don't either," said Parker. "Berriman used the computer a lot. This list could mean anything. Or nothing."

"Did Berriman have any special expertise with the computer?" asked Castro.

"He was competent with them, I think. In fact, he used the computer extensively in his work. As I told you, he mainly conducted large-scale analyses." Parker sighed. "That is, he crunched numbers. But I wouldn't consider him particularly knowledgeable about computer hardware or programming for that matter. There are others who are more expert."

"In your group?"

"Yes, I'd say so." He thought for a moment. "Schneider, Walker, maybe Kronkosky. And probably others."

Poole made notes. "And yourself?"

Parker laughed. "Not an expert by any means," he said.

Poole thought for a moment. "I think that's about it." He flipped the pages of his notepad back to the beginning. "I don't want to burden you, Dr. Parker, but I'm sure we'll be back with more questions. And no doubt with some for members of your staff."

Parker waved his hand. "Whatever we can do."

Poole stood up and looked briefly around the room. "Do you collect Indian art, Dr. Parker?"

"Not really. Most of these things were selected by my wife."

"She collects?"

Parker nodded. "Yes and no. It's her business, really. She's an anthropologist and her specialty is the Southwest."

Poole smiled and made a mental note to check out Mrs. Parker. "She has good taste," he said.

Both men stood by the table and stared at the printout.

"Are you sure?" asked the balding man. He could barely hear his staff member over the sound of the printers.

"I'm afraid so." The younger man tentatively pointed to a series of entries on the unfolded printout. "Right there," he said. "As far as we can tell, it happened yesterday afternoon just after five o'clock."

"What did he get?" asked the computer director.

"We don't know. All we know is that someone attempted to access the Sigma stuff. There's no record of what he got."

"How in the goddamn hell did he do it?"

The thin man shook his head. "I don't know. The only explanation is that he found a window somewhere."

"That's impossible. We altered the system after the Berriman trouble. It's tight, absolutely tight."

"There has to be something, a window somewhere that he could manipulate."

The older man shook his head. "You're sure we don't know what he got?"

"No. Only that the system was compromised. He may have gotten nothing, but the only record we have is of the terminal making contact with the mainframe."

"How could he get past the security interlocks?"

The young man couldn't answer. At this moment, he was thinking only about his job.

"Holy shit." The director walked over to a chair and fell into it, his hands falling between his legs. "I just don't know how someone could get into the system now. Not after the changes we installed."

"It has to be a window somewhere."

"Why in the hell didn't we find it yesterday?"

"Somehow the computer was instructed not to alert us." The thin man waved his hands. "It made a record of the attempt but didn't trigger the security alert. It all came out today in the normal record of computer usage."

"Who else was using Sigma?"

"No one in two days."

"And we don't know whose goddamn terminal it is?"

"Not yet, but I think the answer is in there." He pointed to the CRAY computers.

The director shrugged. "Why?"

"I think there's a record of the terminal in there somewhere. We just have to find a way of digging it out." The young man searched for words. "See, the computer keeps a record of all requests and information going in and the same going out, including the terminal involved. I don't know for sure, but I think only one-half—the incoming half—was wiped clean, but the scrambling procedure the guy used sent the remaining half to some other file."

"So somewhere there's still a record of the terminal?"

The man nodded.

There was hope yet, Willows thought. He grabbed his assistant by the arm and spoke very closely to his ear. "Work on this. As much as necessary. But don't tell anyone. Understand?"

The young man nodded.

For a moment, all the director could do was stand there, fingering the ends of his bolo tie. This needed to be reported immediately. He didn't know what was going on in the laboratory, but whatever it was, he *did* know that it hadn't stopped with Berriman's murder.

Outside, it was getting dark. From his chair in the living room, Tevis could see the failing light pull away from the sky. In the kitchen, Maria was making dinner.

Tevis always liked it when Maria stayed over at their house. She was easygoing and always straightened his room whether it needed it or not. When she made lunch or dinner, she made everything from scratch: the tortillas, the spicy salsa, even the seasonings she ground up from the contents of the little plastic bags she brought with her. Most of all, Tevis liked talking with her, especially about her life at nearby Santa Clara Pueblo, where she had been born and lived all of her life.

She loved to talk about her family, which, given her age, now included several great-grandchildren. She had wonderful stories about her life as a young girl, growing up in the pueblo and being courted by the young men.

What was not easy to do, thought Tevis, was to get Maria to talk about what she *believed*. She regularly crossed herself or uttered some Catholic phrase, but rarely did she talk about her Tewa beliefs. Once when he asked her about what went on in the pueblo's kiva, she simply said she didn't know since women weren't allowed in. It was for the men, she answered, and said no more.

She was more talkative when Tevis asked her questions about the origins of her people, which Maria explained in terms of stories told to her by her family. She also told him about the spirits that inhabited her world. Occasionally, she would break into Tewa, mixed with a little Spanish. Tevis couldn't always follow the complicated history she spoke of, especially when she talked about the emergence of First Man and First Woman. He learned the Tewa names for the four major directions, though, as well as the colors and animals that went with each cardinal point. North was his favorite, since its color was blue and the animal a mountain lion.

From his chair, he could hear Maria humming to herself. Whatever she was cooking smelled very good. Outside, it was black except for the thinnest line of milky orange at the horizon. The only light inside the living room came from the TV, which was showing an old *Star Trek* rerun.

From the corner of his eye, Tevis thought he caught a movement outside the large picture windows. He quickly sat up in his chair. The only sound was the dull blaring of the television. At first startled, and then curious, Tevis got up and walked to the window. The wind was blowing, and he couldn't be sure, but at the edge of the backyard, just at the line of trees that hedged the rim of the canyon, he thought he saw a shadowy figure. He put his head next to the glass, breathing on the clear pane and feeling the warm breath returning back to him as it made a foggy circle. There was nothing.

He walked into the kitchen, where Maria stood cleaning carrots over the sink. A window above the sink faced the backyard.

"Did you see anything, Maria?" He pointed to the backyard.

She looked out the window and back to Tevis. "Nothing. What did you see?"

"I'm not sure. Maybe a man, maybe something else."

She laughed. "Another ghost, *niño*?"

"Maybe," he said, and wondered if he should tell Maria about the fleeting image he had seen at Tsankawi. Maybe, he thought, the Shadow Man was looking for the two objects in his bedroom?

Instead, he grabbed a piece of carrot. "When do we eat?" he asked.

chapter

9

THURSDAY NIGHT

The sun had fallen well below the horizon, leaving only a band of
light; above it, the sky turned from violet to black. Reyes cursed to
himself: he was driving on the outer edge of the pueblo on the dirt
road that he couldn't see well and which hadn't been graded since
winter. Even at fifteen miles an hour, the car bounced up and down
in the ruts.

He had spent the last couple of hours talking with residents of
the pueblo, looking for some clue to the identity of the young man.
Most of the afternoon's work was unproductive. People were either
telling the truth when they said they knew nothing, or they weren't
telling what they knew. The man he was looking for might be a
nephew or maybe a grandson and therefore nothing would be said.
Of course, the fact that he was a policeman didn't help, even among
his own people.

Only the last stop had been helpful. A middle-aged woman
whose husband worked in Los Alamos thought she had seen a
young man matching the description driving a pickup to Mary
Naranjo's a mile or so away. She couldn't be sure, but she thought he
was a nephew, or maybe a cousin. She had no idea what his name
was.

In the distance he saw a faint light which, he realized as he drove closer, came from the window of a mobile home. He honked his horn several times to alert the occupants, although Reyes couldn't imagine that he was unexpected with the noise the car made on the road.

As he pulled up, he saw the door open and a child's face look out from behind a screen door. As soon as he stopped, the face disappeared and was shortly replaced by a woman maybe in her thirties. Reyes wondered if she could be the young man's mother? She stood protectively behind the black metal screen.

"Good evening," he said, standing casually by his car. He wanted this woman to know that he wasn't planning to arrest her or barge into her trailer. The woman nodded.

"I'm trying to find someone." He paused. "And I was told that Mary Naranjo could help me." He noticed that the small child peeked out from behind the woman's turquoise blue pants. From the look of the apron, she was in the middle of cooking dinner. Reyes knew he would have to be brief.

"That's me."

He nodded and took a few easy steps toward the door. "I'd like to ask you a few questions about someone who might be a relative." Even from a distance he could feel the warmth of the home escaping into the chilly early evening air.

"Who you looking for?" The woman opened the screen door and stepped down to the rickety wooden steps. Reyes could tell that she had once been attractive but years of childbearing and hard work had taken a toll. She smiled to reveal a broken front tooth.

"I don't know his name, only a description of what he looks like."

"What's he done?"

"Nothing. I only want to talk to him about some of his friends." He thought it wise to say no more. Probably the woman wouldn't believe him anyway. Briefly he passed along the description given to him by the gallery owner in Santa Fe. After only a few sentences, he saw the woman's smile disappear. She shook her head.

"I think you want my sister's boy. That one is trouble," she said, and started to go back inside the mobile home. "You can talk to my mother."

The woman bent down and said something to the child that

Reyes couldn't understand. From inside the trailer he could hear a television.

"Do you know him?" he asked.

She stepped back inside without answering, and Reyes could hear low voices. After a few moments an old woman with a cane appeared. She made no effort to go beyond the doorway.

Reyes spoke to her in Tewa. She listened impassively, especially to the part about the tattoos on the knuckles. Reyes sensed that she knew whom he was speaking of; he also sensed that she didn't buy the story that he wanted only to "talk" with the boy. But then she changed her mind and began to speak.

"It could be," she began, "that you describe my other daughter's son." She paused for a moment, as if to weigh what she would say next. "He lives at Santa Clara, where his father is from." She gave his name and then spoke of her other children and the fact that two daughters had married outside of the pueblo, one of them to an Anglo in Albuquerque. She lived here with her youngest daughter, she said, because she was too old to live by herself and she had little money. These days she did no pottery. Finally she asked, "Is Johnny in trouble again?"

"I don't know," he said, "but he may be involved with bad friends." He wondered what sort of trouble she referred to.

The old woman described as best she could where her daughter lived at Santa Clara. The pueblo was adjacent to San Ildefonso, and he could go there tomorrow. She shook her head slowly. "He was a difficult boy, even as a child, but always he came to see me. I told him what he should know, but you understand how it is today."

"Times have changed," Reyes said, sharing for a moment the grandmother's pain.

"My daughter did the best she could," the old woman said. "She lost one husband to the Army, and her man now drinks too much." She said it with a finality that had no trace of bitterness.

He thanked her and got back into his car. In one of the windows he saw the curtain move and the young woman's face appear and then disappear when she caught him looking at her. It was dark now. It suddenly hit him that he hadn't eaten since this morning. He would eat something and then go back to the office to do some paperwork. Tomorrow, he would visit Santa Clara and try to find the young Indian who had sacred objects to sell.

Bob Rollins fluffed up his pillow and then fell back naked into the bed and closed his eyes. From the bathroom he could hear the shower running and Angela moving in and out of the spray. Her scent still lingered next to him on the bed, a clean smell that he always associated with freshly cut vegetables. She wore no perfume and no makeup but concocted her own creams from herbs and plants.

Dressed in her long terrycloth robe that revealed the pale color of her skin, she had been waiting for him this evening when he drove down from the laboratory. She had been back from California for only a few hours, and he could tell from her eyes that she had driven straight through from Los Angeles. They had talked and eaten vegetables from their garden and then made love.

For a moment he thought of asking her to do it again but then realized she wouldn't be likely to agree. It was just as well, he thought, since now he would have time to work out with his weights. The water stopped, and when he opened his eyes, Rollins could see steam, highlighted from the bathroom light, escaping into the bedroom. The same light reflected on the chrome frame of his weight bench in the corner.

"You sure about what you did with the computer?" she asked. The door opened and she stepped into the room wearing her robe and a towel on her head.

"Yeah," he replied. He wasn't absolutely sure, but he didn't want to upset her by saying anything else. His first mistake was in assuming that Berriman would never discover that his password and terminal were being used. His second was in not clearing the record of computer use once Berriman was murdered. He should have done something last Sunday, or Monday at the latest. But he hadn't and now it was too late.

"You *sure* it'll pick up Parker's terminal?" She sat down next to him; this time he could pick out the faint scent of the glycerine soap she used.

"Yes. They'll have to work for it, but I left the terminal ID in the data; they just have to break the loop." Unconsciously, one hand went to his crotch and touched the slight pressure he felt there.

She looked at him for a moment, and he realized she didn't understand what he was talking about. "If they check," he said slowly, "they'll see that someone tried to break in, but they'll have to get around my block to see *who* tried to get in."

She sat back in the bed and closed her eyes for a moment, apparently thinking about the possibilities. Rollins wanted to reach over and touch her, but he didn't dare. It was their understanding that when they finished making love, it was over until the next time. She decided when.

"I guess it was necessary," she said slowly, never opening her eyes.

"It was," he said firmly. "When I tried to close out, I saw that they had detected the earlier attempts to pull data. I had no choice and I needed to identify someone." He wasn't sure she bought the explanation; it was his poking around that made it clear to the lab that the computer break-ins had not ended with Berriman.

She said nothing, and Rollins could sense that she was practicing her breathing exercises. The bed trembled ever so slightly each time she inhaled and exhaled.

Berriman had forced his hand, Rollins recalled, with the discovery that someone was using his terminal. He had confronted Rollins Saturday afternoon with a telephone call and, in a nervous, high-pitched voice, accused Rollins of stealing his latest work. That was partly true, although even now Rollins found it amusing. He wasn't stealing the data to claim authorship, but to sell to people in California. Even funnier, Rollins had never touched Berriman's terminal; he had only made it look that way by giving the proper instructions from his own terminal.

Berriman had discovered that a hard copy existed of his latest work; that discovery apparently led him to check all the entries for his terminal. It had never occurred to the little man that someone was using his terminal's ID to pull top-secret data off the central computer. Instead, Berriman deduced it was Rollins and accused him of stealing his latest theoretical work on the Nemesis weapon.

Rollins looked over at Angela. She sat composed and still next to him, with her hand flat on her stomach following the rhythm of her breathing. Thank God she had been in town that day. It was she who came up with the plan to get rid of Berriman and implicate him with the stolen objects. If the plan had gone right, the man would have been suspected of dealing in stolen goods and murdered by an Indian.

Images from the weekend came flooding back to him: the tense telephone call on Saturday and their agreement to talk it over Sunday afternoon; tracking Berriman to some ruins where he said he planned to take photographs Sunday morning; the confrontation outside the cave and the knife and blood; the race back to the lab to estalish an alibi; Angela stuffing the pot and kachinas in Berriman's closet. He even remembered the sound of the rock on the little man's head. Suddenly, it didn't seem all that okay anymore.

"Angela?" he said quietly. He reached over without thinking and touched her hand. Her deep breathing stopped and she snapped her head to stare at him through intense green eyes; a wisp of red hair spilled out from beneath the towel.

"I'm practicing," she said coldly.

"I mean," he stumbled, "what do we do now with Parker?" He searched for words. "And everything else?"

Very slowly her look eased. "We keep calm and wait," she said. Surprisingly, she reached over and took his hand and held it. "We wait and see what happens." She looked out into the darkened room and closed her eyes again.

"If you're right, the lab will discover Parker and go after him. What we need to do now is be *sure* that he's connected with Berriman in some way." She still held his hand.

Rollins sat up in bed and unconsciously flexed the muscles in his chest and arms. That was something Angela always liked for him to do in bed.

"I've already done something," he said quietly.

"What?"

"I've done something. I've tied Parker to Berriman." He thought of the documents taken from Berriman's safe. There had been no time to put them back in Berriman's safe after copying them; that's why he had been forced to hide them in Parker's office. He had been so nervous about the computer access record that he had forgotten to tell Angela about that.

When he explained, she smiled. "Good," she said. "And we have one report left over for good measure." She placed her hand on his chest and slowly massaged it.

He started to undo her robe, but she got out of bed and walked to the desk and began looking through the mail. He was about to say something when she spoke up.

"You *were* going to tell me about this, weren't you?" She continued to look through the mail as she talked.

"You've only been back a few hours. Of course, I was going to tell you."

"Good," she said again, and walked into the next room.

Rollins sat in bed for a moment, relieved that she hadn't been angry. He got up and put on a pair of shorts and went to his weights.

She was damn moody, he thought, but then, so was he. Despite all their differences, they had been together almost three years. Her work, if you could call it that, he thought, took her all over the country. But each time she came back and they made wild love and took hikes and worked the garden and he felt good. Until she left again, and then he would start worrying all over.

He lay down on the bench and did a set of presses using 150 pounds of weight. *Inhale, exhale.* He did the exercises with a vengeance. Shit! he thought with the last repetition, how in the hell had all his happened?

First it was her work he had had to accept. She traded and dealt in black market antiquities, mostly Indian things, sometimes trekking to California or the East Coast in her van with a hundred thousand dollars' worth of pots and jewelry and things. And then it was her idea to sell information on his work at Los Alamos to someone in California. Just to raise money. That was just a few months ago. At first he resisted, but then, under pressure from her, he relented. God, what a bad time that had been. The things she had accused him of, her hot and cold moods. Jesus, he was glad that was over.

In the beginning it was only low-level stuff, which got them enough money to pay for the greenhouse out back. But then they—whoever "they" were—wanted more, better data, which they offered a lot more cash for.

He rested the barbell on the frame and sat up, sweat dripping down his forehead. He should never have told her about Tommy. He had never told anyone about what he and Tommy had done together, and now she knew about them, and he knew that she would bring it up again someday.

Rollins could hear Angela moving around in the living room, putting on one of her strange, "new age" records. God! he hoped that she was right and everything was okay.

Poole put his hand on the glass windowpane; he calculated the temperature had already dropped at least ten degrees in the thirty minutes since it turned dark. Outside of his office, down the tile hallway, he could hear the night cleaning crew banging their metal carts against each other.

He was alone in his office. Everyone else had gone home, except for the night shift who manned the twenty-four-hour security office down the hall. Poole sat back down in his chair. He had just let his head rest against the back of the chair and closed his eyes when his telephone rang.

Startled, Poole sat straight up and for a brief moment tried to understand where the sound was coming from. When the phone rang a second time, he quickly saw that it was his special outside line that avoided the laboratory's central telephone system. It must be his wife, he thought.

"Hello?"

"Ed? Farrell Doty."

Poole grimaced. "Yeah, Farrell. What's up?" Doty was the last person he wanted to speak to now.

"I'm coming up tomorrow and wondered if I could stop by and talk with you." The voice on the other end sounded to Poole as calm and mechanical as ever.

"Of course. What time do you plan to be here?"

"I could be at your office at eight in the morning."

Poole paused. If Doty were to be here by eight, that meant he would be leaving Albuquerque at five-thirty in the morning.

"Sure. Stop by. I'll have coffee ready."

There was a chuckle on the other end. "Don't bother. See you then."

Poole hung up and wondered what in the hell Doty meant by that last comment. Then he remembered that Doty was a Mormon.

He looked back down at the stack of papers on his desk. There were a half-dozen reports from members of his staff on the Berriman matter as well as the personnel files of the individuals who worked with Berriman. The top file belonged to David Parker.

Doty was coming to talk about Berriman, of course; the news from the computer center strengthened everyone's suspicions that Berriman was working with someone else. The question was: With whom?

The news on Wednesday's computer break-in had been transmitted to Doty within the hour by Poole. Doty's only comment was "That's what we thought." With those words, Poole knew that the FBI had more information than he did.

He looked at the stack of file folders: Parker, Thompson, Kronkosky, Schneider, Rollins, and a dozen others. All of them individuals who worked with Berriman or who were in a strategic position to know what the man was doing. Was Berriman working with one of these individuals? Was Berriman killed by one of them? Poole had a dozen names, but the laboratory employed several thousand people.

Poole considered that fact for a moment. It made sense to assume that anyone associated with Berriman, either as a collaborator or a murderer, was someone close by. And after today's news from the computer division, it was someone familiar with the laboratory's central computer system. Right now, there was no news on who made the attempts on Wednesday to enter the computer; *that* information would be a big help, if they could get it.

He picked up Parker's file and leafed through it. On the surface, a least, nothing seemed extraordinary. Parker had an excellent track record, starting with good grades at Stanford, a stint on the defense project in California and then Los Alamos, where he had quickly risen to head his own group. Not bad, thought Poole, but something bothered him about Parker. Mainly, that he was careless. Keeping a list of safe combinations, for example, and God knows what other rules he ignored. He was also uncooperative and treated this investigation as if it were no more than a search for missing library books.

Poole threw the file back down on the desk and massaged his temples. Then he remembered the stuff in Parker's office.

He made a mental note to tell Castro to make some discreet inquiries about Parker and the other names he had on his desk. Any expensive purchases. Maybe talk of unusual political or religious views. Or maybe disenchantment with weapons work.

Outside, Poole heard the metallic creaking of the cleaning carts. The janitorial crew was outside his office. He looked at his watch: it was seven-thirty. He was late for dinner and his wife would be mad at him.

chapter 10

FRIDAY MORNING

Santa Clara Pueblo lay to the north of San Ildefonso, off Highway 30. The paved road into the pueblo turned to dirt just thirty feet off the main highway.

Reyes bounced up and down inside the cab of his ten-year-old pickup truck. He made the decision this morning to drive his own truck to Santa Clara; to use his pueblo's police car would make him too conspicuous.

The directions he had were vague, and it took him nearly thirty minutes and one stop to find the house. He asked a pair of young girls carrying red lunchboxes where the house was. He didn't ask for Johnny but for Johnny's mother. The young girls giggled and argued among themselves for a moment until they finally agreed on the location. Reyes asked how he would know it.

"You'll know it," one giggled.

"It's half and half," said the other in Tewa.

He smiled and winked at the pair and drove off down the road. He was surprised to see that the house was just like the young girls described. It was a duplex where the right half was new, maybe two years old, and built of cinder block and plastered to resemble adobe. The other half was fifty or sixty years old and built of thick adobe bricks. Although it was old, it was well cared for. Broken plaster had been replaced in several places, and the contrast between the old and new plaster resembled lines of jagged lightning frozen permanently into the mud-colored wall. From behind the house, a column of dark smoke rose into the early morning sky.

Reyes pulled up to the strange house and stopped the truck. He took off his holster and .38 pistol and locked it in the glove compartment. A mangy brown dog stood guard on the porch of the new half. As soon as Reyes opened the door of his truck, the dog began to bark and wag its tail at the same time.

He stepped down and waited by the truck for a few minutes. The dog cautiously made its way to him and sniffed his pant leg. As soon as Reyes bent down, the dog jumped away and took a cautious position by the corner of the house.

He knocked on the door several times and waited. There was no answer. From the corner of his eye he saw the dog move to the back of the house. He knocked again and tried to peer through the small square window in the upper door; unfortunately a piece of white fabric covered the window and obscured the other side. He was about to knock again when he heard a woman's voice behind him.

"What do you want?"

Reyes quickly turned around and saw an attractive young woman in a straw hat staring at him; she was pulling off a pair of dirty work gloves. Her smooth brown face was glistening with sweat.

"What do you want?" she repeated.

"I'm looking for Johnny," he said slowly.

"What for?" She wasn't exactly friendly, Reyes noticed.

"I just want to talk with him."

She stared right at him, although her eyes were hidden under the shadow of the rim of her hat. "You police?"

He nodded. "I just want to talk with Johnny. That's all."

"Yeah? Well, he's not here. Hasn't been here in a while."

Reyes tried to get a better look at her face under the hat. She was young, too young to be Johnny's mother.

"Are you his sister?"

"No. I'm his grandmother. What do you think?" She gave a throaty laugh.

Reyes just stood there for a moment, silent. Johnny's grand-mother had said the night before that her grandson had been by to visit in the last few days. Was this girl lying?

"I spoke with your grandmother. She said Johnny had visited her in the last two or three days."

"Johnny comes and goes. He's not here now and I don't know when he'll be back." She started to turn but then stopped, perhaps to see what Reyes would do.

"You don't sound like you come from around here," said Reyes. It was true. The woman didn't have the same singsong cadence in her voice that he noticed in women raised and living in the pueblo.

"I've been away at school a lot." She continued to stare.

"College?"

She nodded. "UCLA."

Reyes whistled. "California, huh?"

"Yeah, but that was a few years ago." She adjusted her hat, revealing a pair of large, dark eyes. "Look, if you want to talk, then talk in the back. I'm firing some pottery and I need to watch the burning." She headed for the back of the house.

Reyes followed, struck by her independence and poise. Califor-nia. That would explain her accent, or rather, the lack of it.

The source of the smoke was a small pile about four feet wide and two high. In the tradition of some potters, the young woman was smothering the fire with dung; that would make the pottery a rich black in color. The air was pungent with its scent. She quickly inspected the pile and used a long metal pole to arrange or compress parts of the smoldering structure.

"No one else home?" he asked after a few minutes of watching her.

"No. Just me. My mother is at work in Española, and I don't know where Johnny is." She poked one corner of the pile. "My stepfather hasn't been here for a year, and Johnny does a lot of traveling."

Reyes wondered what he did for a living, if anything. He also wondered why this young woman had come back to the pueblo. "Do you know when he'll be back?"

She shook her head. "Nope."

"One other thing. Does he have some letters tattooed on the knuckles of one hand?"

"How did you know that?"

Reyes smiled. "What do they say?"

"Oh hell, I can't remember exactly. I think it reads 'bad' on one hand and 'man' on the other. Johnny had it done when he was thirteen." She eyed him carefully. "You know a lot about him?"

"Look, I don't want to arrest him. Just talk with him."

"What about?"

"It's possible that he's involved with people who are dealing in stolen Indian artifacts."

She looked up at Reyes but didn't say anything at first. "What sort of artifacts?" she finally asked.

"Religious ones. Objects used in the kiva, for example."

The woman was quiet a long time, never looking up from her fire.

"My brother has been in trouble a lot. But I don't know anything about this." She backed away from the fire and wiped the perspiration from her face. "Last time I saw him was last week. He spent the night here and a woman picked him up the next day."

"A woman?"

"Yes. An Anglo. With red hair."

Reyes thought about this for a moment. "Do you know who she is?"

The young woman shook her head. "No idea. I got the impression maybe Johnny did some work for her. But I don't know what." She wiped her forehead again. "Want some coffee?"

He smiled. "I'd like some."

"Okay." She put her pole down and went inside through a badly worn screen door. From inside he heard her shout if he wanted anything in it.

"Just black!"

A few minutes later she kicked open the door with her foot and came out with two steaming mugs in her hands.

"Thanks." He watched her sit down on an old wooden crate against the house in a position where she could watch the smoldering pile of horse manure. Nearby was a table with potting equipment, and stored underneath were bags of finely meshed clay and one of finely ground dung. On a piece of tin four feet square were a half-dozen pieces of cooling pottery, their dark black color even darker than the wall of shade behind it.

Reyes took a sip of the hot coffee before saying anything. "What were you studying at UCLA?"

"Art."

"When did you finish?"

"I didn't. I had to leave and come back here in my junior year."

"Too bad."

"Yeah. Family stuff and all that." She took a swallow of coffee. "I've kind of liked being back, though. I'm doing traditional pottery again and I love it."

Reyes looked at the pieces cooling on the tin sheet. "Yours?"

She nodded. "Yeah. It's black on black." She pointed at the smoking pile in front of them. "This batch is traditional too."

After a while, Reyes spoke up again. "Do you think you can give your brother a message?"

The young woman shrugged. "I'll try."

"Tell him I'd like to talk to him. No hassle, okay? Just to talk."

She nodded.

Reyes looked back at the house. He couldn't be absolutely sure that the kid wasn't in the house at this very moment. But he couldn't just bust in. Besides, he lacked jurisdiction here at Santa Clara.

"Look. Your brother might be on the edge of doing something very stupid. And if it involves the pueblo's religious stuff, then..." He let his meaning sink in. "Maybe we can help him." He gently stressed the "we."

The girl nodded and looked at Reyes. "He could use the help," she said.

Reyes wrote his name and phone number on a piece of paper and gave it to her.

"My name is Reyes. Tomás Reyes. I'm a policeman at San Ildefonso."

She looked at the paper. "I'm Jenny Vargas."

He nodded in the direction of the smoke. "Good luck."

"Thanks."

He walked around the side of the house and startled the dog, who began barking furiously at him. As he drove out of Santa Clara, he wondered how much older he was than Jenny Vargas.

Looking at his notes, and then the board, Castro neatly copied a series of numbers into the empty squares of the matrix. Poole watched from his conference table, amazed that anyone who always dropped ashes when he smoked could be otherwise so neat. When the man finished, he carefully put down the chalk, wiped his hands on a handkerchief, and sat down.

"That's about it," he said.

Poole studied the numbers and then the list of eleven names down the left side of the board. In a highly synthesized form, the information on the blackboard represented everything they knew at the moment about eleven individuals and their whereabouts during the week preceding Berriman's murder. As far as Poole could tell, these individuals appeared to be in the best position to know what Berriman was doing.

"There's lots of holes," said Poole. Half the small squares were empty.

Castro nodded and lit another cigarette. "Three of those people were gone the entire week before the murder. Business or family trips. Another six were absent during some of the computer dates listed by Berriman. Verified absences."

Poole nodded. That seemed to let them out; there was no way they could have used the computer unless they were in a laboratory building.

Castro studied the board for a moment. "Parker was here during all dates and left his office last Sunday at least three hours before we can confirm his presence at Tsankawi. Two, maybe one-and-a-half hours if you believe that his family was with him for part of the time."

Poole shook his head. "I believe his family was there." He looked down the list of other names. "What about Schneider?"

"Sick earlier this week and unavailable for interview until this afternoon; claims he had bad diarrhea all week." He looked at his notes. "Spotty verification on his activities last week."

"What about computers?"

Castro searched his notes again. "Only four have their own

terminals; only Parker has a terminal with access to Sigma." He read off the list of names: "Parker, Schneider, Silverstein, and Rollins. And Berriman, of course."

"What about Greenberg?"

"All of his time is accounted for, and there's no terminal in his office. In fact, he says he doesn't use a computer." Castro put out his cigarette and looked across the table at his boss. As carefully as he could, he raised a point that had begun to trouble him. "Isn't the Bureau doing this same thing, Ed?" He was perplexed over Poole's interest in the case; as far as he could tell, the FBI had it all under control, and they were duplicating the Bureau's work.

"Probably." Poole fingered his notes. "But it's still our problem."

What *was* the FBI doing? he wondered. They already had a task force assembled in Albuquerque, and Poole knew the pressure was on Doty from his superiors in Washington. Los Alamos had been relegated to support—at least in the eyes of the Bureau. That much was certain.

He looked at the board. Maybe it was a waste of time, maybe not. But somehow Poole didn't feel comfortable with the direction the FBI's investigation had taken; it couldn't hurt for him to continue with a little digging on his own.

"Okay," he said, "let's try filling in these holes." Poole stood up and motioned toward the blackboard. "And, Castro, wipe this clean. I don't want anyone to find even chalk dust."

Reyes hadn't planned to visit Los Alamos this morning but decided on the spur of the moment after talking with Jenny. Now, on the outskirts of the town, just past an abandoned security tower, he realized that he might get absolutely nowhere with the Los Alamos County police.

Police headquarters was right off Trinity Street, the town's major thoroughfare. It was a massive brick building near a small pond that dated from the years before the war when Los Alamos was an exclusive boys school. San Ildefonso's police building was only a fraction of the size of this complex. He pulled up to a visitor's area and parked his truck. From his glove compartment, he retrieved his .38 and a small printed sign that read POLICE VEHICLE. He put the sign on his dashboard, although he had no idea if anyone would look beyond the dented bumpers and faded paint job. Then he replaced his leather coat with his official San Ildefonso police jacket.

He found his way to the chief's office and politely asked to see him. The female clerk was pleasant but discouraging.

"The chief's out. Wanna see someone else?"

Reyes shook his head and started to leave when he saw Smith's deputy walk into the room. He waved.

"Hey, Reyes." The big man took off his sunglasses and stuffed them into a pocket filled with several pens.

"You got a minute?"

"What do you need?"

"Just a little information. About the man murdered last Sunday."

"You ain't heard?" The tall officer motioned him over to an empty desk in the corner. There were only the two of them and the female clerk in the room. From another room, behind a wall, Reyes could hear a police radio crackling.

The officer walked over to a small table and poured two cups of coffee into styrene cups. "You heard about the FBI?"

Reyes flinched and the officer smiled.

"Hell, they've just about taken over. Along with Los Alamos Security."

Reyes tried to look calm, but inside he felt a rush of excitement. "What the hell's going on?"

"Looks like this Berriman dude was stealing secrets or something." The man leaned forward as if to share a great confidence. "We haven't been told directly, but the word is that this guy was pulling information off a computer when, you know, only a few guys were supposed to have that shit."

"Shit?"

"I don't know. Bomb shit, I guess. Anyway, lab Security dropped in and asked for a lid to be put on the case. Then the FBI showed up and they're watching over everything with an eagle eye."

Reyes lifted his eyebrows.

"No shit, man. It's heavy these days."

"What do they know about the dead man? Berriman."

The deputy waffled one hand. "A lot. A little." The man looked around to check the room. "We found some real expensive things in the guy's house."

"What kind of things?"

"Indian stuff. Pottery. Some antiques, I think."

Reyes's pulse quickened. "You're kidding?" He immediately thought of the photographs in the Santa Fe gallery.

"No. I hear some of the stuff is worth thousands. No one knows how Berriman paid for the stuff. At least, on his salary."

Reyes now thought about Johnny Vargas.

"Word has it that Berriman was the quiet type. You know, no bad habits like drugs or women." He laughed loudly. Reyes wondered briefly what else he was thinking of.

"Any chance of seeing the file on this?" Reyes tried to look as innocent as he could. The deputy hesitated.

"Look, the murder involved Indian land." Well, he thought, it was Indian land once.

The officer looked around again and walked over to a file cabinet and pulled a manila folder. He handed it to Reyes. "You got five minutes."

"Thanks," he said, taking the file.

He thumbed quickly through the paperwork. The coroner's report confirmed most of what he had deduced last Sunday and the police reports weren't any more informative. There was no mention of the cornmeal on the floor of the cave.

Another report covered the search of Berriman's home. Reyes looked through this more slowly and then thumbed through a series of eight-by-ten glossy photographs, mostly shots of the dead man's home. Reyes could make out what looked like small clay models in several shots. That intrigued him. In other shots there was a shelf with several objects on it, including a large Ácoma pot.

Reyes carefully put the photos back into the file folder and whistled softly. Berriman had some expensive stuff at his home, all right, but something was odd; the best items were jumbled together on a small shelf in what looked like a closet.

Another series of photographs showed Berriman in the cave as he had been found. Closeups revealed the deep gash in his throat in vivid detail as well as the shirt and light jacket stained with darkened blood.

The rest of the report consisted of interviews of the Parkers and of neighbors. No one had seen or heard anything on the day of the

murder. The only thing everyone agreed on was that Berriman
wasn't the kind to be involved in something bad. "Seen enough?"
asked the deputy.

"Yeah, thanks." As he handed the file back, Reyes noted Berriman's
Los Alamos address.

Reyes briefly studied the map of Los Alamos he kept in his
glove compartment, and drove straight to Berriman's house. It
wasn't hard to find once he located the street: a city police car and an
unmarked government vehicle were parked in front. Just as he got
out of his car, he saw Smith and two other men gather on the front
porch. Reyes recognized at least one of them: it was Ed Poole of
laboratory Security. He waited until Smith went back inside and
walked over and introduced himself to Poole.

"It's a strange business, isn't it?" he said.

The pudgy man nodded. "Yeah," he said. "You were there on
Sunday? You see anything?"

"There was something," he began, "but I don't know what to
make of it."

Poole looked at him. "What?"

"Two things, really. The first is that I found cornmeal on the
floor of the cave where Berriman's body was discovered." He paused
to study Poole's reaction. There was none. "Cornmeal is sometimes
used in Pueblo religious ceremonies. The point is, the cornmeal was
fresh. That could mean that an Indian was involved."

"We've thought about that," said Poole.

"I also talked with the young Parker boy the other day, and he
told me that he found small sprigs of greenery around the body.
That, too, could have religious significance."

"What are you saying? Was there some sort of ritual involved?"
Poole remembered the photograph of Berriman's forehead and the
smear of blood there.

"That's possible. There's another thing, though, something I've
got no proof for." Reyes hesitated for a moment. "I wonder if some
of Berriman's collection of Indian art isn't stolen, or if he was
involved in the black market for this stuff."

Poole looked at Reyes. "That occurred to us too."

Poole and Reyes talked for a few minutes until Poole said he had
to go. "I'll get in touch with you," he said from the door of his car.

Reyes wondered if any of what he had said had made sense. It was difficult to discuss the potential importance of the cornmeal and sprigs in the cave; by themselves, they would mean nothing to an Anglo.

Reyes walked to the front door and knocked. Smith was standing in the living room with his deputy.

"Chief?" he called out.

"Reyes?" Smith looked surprised. "What the hell you want?"

"I wonder if I could take a quick look at Berriman's art collection?" He briefly related the story of the telephone call from the Santa Fe gallery. "Maybe there's a connection."

The chief shrugged. "Help yourself. We're boxing up the expensive stuff. It's in the kitchen."

"By the way, who was the man with Poole?"

"Farrell Doty. FBI regional in Albuquerque. A real hard-ass."

Reyes walked through the dining room, where a table was heaped with neat piles of magazines and art supplies. It had been a long time since Berriman had used the table for dinner. On one edge was a small model in clay of a Pueblo kiva. It was perhaps six inches high and eight wide.

In the kitchen a deputy was preparing cardboard boxes. Sitting on the small table in the center of the room was a large, beautifully decorated pot, several kachina figures, and a cylindrical stone object ten inches long. Reyes let out a soft whistle. The pot and kachinas had to be worth thousands if he remembered correctly some of the prices for similar items at the Dewey Galleries in Santa Fe. He could see the faint, black remnants of police dusting on all the items.

He looked carefully at the stone phallus that he recognized as a deity stick. It was a religious object, of course, and obviously quite old. Although he couldn't be sure, the object looked Hopi; at least it wasn't from San Ildefonso. Behind him, he heard Smith walk into the kitchen.

"What do you think?"

Reyes thought for a moment. "Looks like Dr. Berriman spent a good piece of change on this stuff."

Smith gave a high-pitched laugh, like a tittering sound. "We figure twenty, maybe twenty-five thousand."

Reyes looked around the room and then at the door leading

back to dining and living room. "What about the rest of his collection?"

Smith shook his head. "Small stuff. Nothing valuable." He walked to the kitchen table and picked up the stone deity stick. "Wonder how they used this, huh?" He made his high-pitched laugh again.

"We had a local man come and evaluate the collection," Smith added. "These are far and away the most valuable items; the rest is apparently junk."

"Who?"

"Someone named Sandys. English guy. Used to work at the lab but retired not too long ago." Smith put the stick back down on the table. "Apparently collects the good stuff."

"Any chance of seeing the rest of the house?" asked Reyes.

"Help yourself."

"Where did you find these?" he said, pointing to the objects on the table.

"Hall closet, back of the house."

Reyes walked back through the living room, pausing to study several of the clay models.

He was fascinated. The models were finely detailed, down to small twigs made to resemble trees. On some of the completed models, painted and arranged with artificial vegetation, there were small plastic figures glued to the surface to resemble tourists. One unfinished model was instantly recognizable: Tsankawi. Suddenly, Reyes realized that Berriman had been at Tsankawi for a reason. He hadn't wandered there by accident. He had gone to study the ruins and caves.

A few feet away was the hall closet; he flipped the light on and peered into the small room. On one side was a collection of old coats and outdoor clothing; on the other was ski equipment. The room's single shelf was empty; presumably, the valuable objects in the kitchen had been found here. On the floor, heaped in a pile, were old boxes and clothing. Reyes checked another closet and found it neatly organized. He walked back into the living room and found Smith standing in the doorway.

"Seen enough?"

Reyes nodded. He thought of the clay models and messy closet. "Appreciate it," he said.

Reyes sat in his truck for a moment before starting it. Although Berriman's house was cluttered, it wasn't messy; the closet was the exception. And the value of any one item there far exceeded the value of the rest of the collection put together.

Was Berriman killed for something in his collection? Or was he killed for buying something he couldn't pay for? Then he thought of the cave at Tsankawi. Had Berriman been murdered for something done there?

Reyes looked at his watch and saw that it was nearly noon. Then another thought hit him: Maybe Berriman's murder had nothing to do with any of the objects in his house or with Tsankawi. But that, he thought, opened a very large can of worms.

chapter

11

FRIDAY AFTERNOON

The road beyond the guardhouse turned sharply to the left and then straightened out to run for almost a mile through trees and cliffside. The laboratory's huge linear accelerator complex lay at the end, hidden from the road by a slight rise in the mesa.

Parker pulled his Blazer into the parking spot labeled LABORA-TORY VEHICLES ONLY and got out. He ran the risk of getting a five-dollar fine, but he was in a hurry.

He was here to meet with Greenberg before the Old Man left for a weekend trip to California. At the security desk he showed his ID badge and walked into the concrete building. A few hundred feet away lay the laboratory's massive block-long meson accelerator. An underground tunnel fed a beam of radiation from the central acceler-ator path to a special target room beneath the building Parker was in.

In this minicomplex, neutrons were hurled against nuclear warheads, missile guidance systems, and other electronics; the effect was to bombard them with radiation similar to that generated in nuclear explosions.

Parker found Greenberg in the control center talking with an assistant. On a television monitor, he could see a team of men in white sterile clothing making final adjustments on a piece of equipment. The room they were in was shielded by lead and concrete.

Just then a Klaxon sounded, and Parker heard mechanical equipment shuddering into action underground.

"Parker. Good. You're just in time for the Air Force test."

On another monitor, he could see the missile warhead on its special target platform. This test would duplicate a burst of neutrons from a theoretical Soviet space weapon. Red warning lights flashed and the noise level rose slightly. Then, just as suddenly, the noise subsided and the test was over. Now technicians would wait until the radiation levels were safe before examining the warhead.

Greenberg relaxed. He gave the "okay" sign to the staff. "Let's talk," he said to Parker.

They walked down the hall to a small office and stepped inside. The glass window next to the door allowed a view of the corridor. Greenberg peered down each direction and then shut the door. Parker wondered what was up.

"Something else has happened," he said, his voice tense.

Parker had a sickening feeling in his stomach.

"Merritt just told me this morning. There was another attempt to enter the central computer. Apparently they were digging around the Sigma stuff."

Parker just stared at him.

"They don't know who or why, just that it happened. That means..." he began, but didn't finish his sentence.

"Berriman wasn't the only one."

"Right. And they're going to be looking real hard at our division and particularly your group. You have a Sigma terminal."

"Jesus." Parker sat down on the edge of a desk. "What next?"

"I don't know, but it can't be anything else in our division." Greenberg fingered his tie. "I've heard you've been critical, too critical, of our laser effort," he said flatly.

"What the hell!" shouted Parker, then caught himself and lowered his voice. "Are we back in the McCarthy era?"

"It's just talk, David, but it's not helpful to anyone right now." He cleared his throat. "Especially with everything that's going on."

"Jesus, Francis, of course I've been critical. It's our job to be critical until the goddamn thing works like we want."

"I don't mean that kind of professional skecticism, David. I mean the sort that says the lab's wrong for even doing the work."

Parker shook his head, momentarily stupefied. "Not me," he said, "I haven't said anything like that." Right now, he wanted to know who was spreading this crap about him, although Greenberg was not likely to tell him.

Greenberg eyed him carefully for a moment in silence and then forced a smile. "Do you have an offer from somewhere?"

Parker was incredulous. "Are you kidding?"

"I mean it. Do you have a university offer you haven't told me about?" Then another possibility hit him. "An offer from Livermore?"

"No. Nothing. You'll be the first to know."

Greenberg relaxed. "All right, let's just be careful." He started out the door. "No more missing lists, okay?"

Doty adjusted the bottom of the flag one more time until the red and white stripes were more equally exposed. He eyed it carefully for effect and then sat back down.

"What about the people he worked with?" he asked his agents.

"Nothing unusual. Everyone looks clean." The young man in his thirties skimmed the file he had in his lap and read the names of over twenty individuals interviewed at Los Alamos; all had worked with Berriman before his death.

Doty listened to the names and matched the brief summary of each interview with what he personally had gleaned from reviewing FBI background files. His agent was right; all of them appeared to live very ordinary lives. One, maybe two of them, had elements in their files that might warrant further investigation. Doty leaned back in the soft chair.

He knew something that his agents didn't: the latest Class I intelligence from Washington. In a secure telephone conversation yesterday with the Intelligence division, Doty had learned that there was further evidence that pointed to Soviet penetration in the government's weapons laboratories. There was no information on who was involved or how deeply they had been able to work, but the evidence pointed to either Los Alamos or Livermore.

Intelligence only knew that the Soviets were considerably more informed about Star Wars than they should be. Doty had no idea what sort of information the Soviets had been able to acquire, nor did he care. Despite his own top-level security clearance, he had no interest in scientific or weapons data. The only fact that mattered was that the other side had somehow found a way in. Doty could only tell his agents that the events in Los Alamos were in all likelihood tied to more extensive enemy activities.

"Anything unusual reported before or since Berriman's death?" · Doty looked up from his desk at his two associates.

The second agent, a man in his forties with a graying crew cut, sifted through his notes.

"The classified reports missing from Berriman's safe have not been recovered yet," said the younger man.

Doty shook his head. "God knows where they are now."

"As it turns out, the classified safes in Berriman's group were not secure in any case."

"What do you mean?"

"The group director kept a list of combination numbers in his secretary's safe, which remained opened during much of the workday." The agent cleared his throat. "The list is missing and still unaccounted for. As I understand it, Los Alamos Security has been forced to seal each safe until it can have the combinations changed and recertified."

"The group leader permitted this? What's his name?"

One of the agents looked through his notes. "David Parker. Berriman's immediate boss. He's the one who's been critical of the weapons program."

Doty looked through the stack of papers on his desk and pulled the computer printout on Parker and set it aside.

"What about Berriman?"

"Well," said the younger man, "his collection of Indian art was appraised by an authority to be worth over twenty-five thousand dollars."

"What's unusual about that?" asked Doty.

"Most of that value comes from less than five objects, none of which Berriman owned for more than six months."

Doty leaned forward. "What's our source on this?"

One agent leafed through his notes again. "An individual named Dr. Gerald Sandys." He read quickly through his notes. "Sandys is a retired Los Alamos scientist and a well-known collector of Indian artifacts. He was called in to appraise Berriman's collection." He leafed some more. "He did this several days after Berriman's death. Interestingly, he was familiar with the deceased's general collection but was surprised at the value of five objects found in the man's house. He reports that in his estimation, Berriman was unlikely to invest such an amount in those items. Apparently, the subject collected mostly popular and inexpensive items."

Doty relaxed back in his chair. "Who is this Sandys?"

"The man is sixty-six years old and retired less than a year ago from Los Alamos. He does consulting for the laboratory and still retains his 'Q' security clearance. He came to the laboratory during the Second World War. He has been collecting Southwest Indian art for several decades and has a reputation for being an expert." The young man took one last glance. "He was also Berriman's boss for some years before his transfer to Parker's office."

"That's interesting," said Doty. He made a note on a pad on his desk. "Let's look a little more into this Sandys fellow. What about the objects? What are they?"

"A large pot about a hundred years old and some wood figures called kachina dolls. And a stone object used as part of a religious ceremony."

"*That* is worth twenty-five thousand?" said Doty, taken aback.

The agent nodded. "Apparently to other collectors."

Doty was surprised at the dollar figures. He had been in the Albuquerque office for six years now and had never understood what tourists—or natives, for that matter—liked about pots and rugs and little dolls. His taste ran more to antique clocks.

"And we have no information on how he paid for them?"

Both men shook their heads.

"Are they stolen?"

"It's a possibility, although it will take some time to try to match each item with reports on file of stolen goods."

"I think these pots and dolls are a dead end. I'll bet you anything Berriman was working with someone else. What about the computer break-ins?"

"Still no information on which terminal tried to access the computer. Apparently the lab has people working on it trying to recover some of the data."

Doty looked at his agenda. "Okay. Let's stay with it." Then he caught the last item. "And let's finish those psychological profiles as soon as possible."

There was no safe time, he reckoned; it might as well be now. He hoped that Angela was right, that the best approach was the most direct one.

Rollins pulled his motorcycle into the driveway and cut the engine. Naturally they had two expensive cars, he thought, and for sure the Volvo belonged to Parker's wife; it fit his image of her as a rich bitch.

Under his coat, stuffed between his undershirt and an old woolen shirt, was the final document from Berriman's safe. At home, tucked away in one of Angela's art books, was the red-striped cover with the TOP SECRET label on it. Angela had plans for it later, she said.

The plan tonight was simple. If he had a chance, he was to plant the document somewhere in the house. But, as Angela cautioned him, it had to be put somewhere that made sense. Parker might find it if it were in his desk, for example. Angela was more optimistic about this venture than he was, but then, he was the one at Parker's house at eight o'clock at night.

He walked to the small porch in front of a set of ornately carved doors and pushed the small button to the right. From inside he heard a soft, melodic sound.

It seemed like a long time before he heard the sound of shoes and then the deadbolt. The door opened briskly, and Parker stood there blinking into the bright yellow glare of the porch light.

"Rollins!" Parker looked startled.

"Yeah, David. Got a minute?"

"Sure. You all right?"

"Yeah. No problem. Just want to talk about running some analyses on Berriman's data while you're in Nevada."

Parker nodded, and led Rollins into the living room where Parker's son and an old Indian woman sat watching television. "Want something to drink?"

"Beer?"

"Fine," said Parker as he disappeared into the kitchen.

The young blond boy looked up from the TV and said, "Hi."

"Hi," he replied. This was the kid he had seen at Tsankawi, but there was no sign that the boy recognized him. The old woman didn't bother to look up from the TV.

Parker came back in with a Mexican beer and handed it to Rollins along with a glass. "Sorry. It's all I've got."

"It's fine."

"Why don't we use my study?" said Parker, pointing to a hallway that led to another part of the house.

The study was impressive. At one end of the large room was a fireplace, and another wall was lined with books and a collection of Indian pots. Several large Navajo rugs covered most of the carpeting. Two large desks sat back to back, both sharing light from matching lamps with sheepskin shades. Parker led them to a small couch and chair.

"My wife and I both use this room." He made a sweeping motion with his hand. "Actually, she uses it more than I do, since she works at home."

Rollins sat down and stared for a moment at the rich contents of the room. He tried to make a quick assessment of the possibilities. Unless he could get Parker out of the room, he would have no chance to hide the document. There was no chance of hiding it somewhere else.

"Well, what do you need?"

Rollins delivered his prepared request, honed by recitation to Angela; he tried to remember to make it sound like it had been on his mind a lot.

"Well, sure. Move ahead on it if that's what you think we need."

Rollins nodded.

Parker looked at him oddly. "Why didn't you just ask me this on Monday, before I left?"

"Uh, well, I didn't know when you were leaving, and I wanted to be sure I checked it out with you." He smiled sheepishly. "Besides, I was still up here in Los Alamos. It wasn't any bother to stop by."

Parker smiled and sat there for a moment waiting to see if anything else was on Rollins's mind. Suddenly the man got up and said that it was time for him to go. When he stood up, Parker realized for the first time how muscular he was.

Just then, Rollins noticed something on Parker's desk that was round and shiny like an old watch. On the surface was a series of initials.

"What's that?" he asked.

"This?" said Parker, picking up the brass object. "This is my father's Boy Scout compass. He had it when he was a kid." He handed it to Rollins. "Hit the small button."

Rollins did and the top flipped opened to reveal a working magnetic compass. His face lit up like a child's.

"I always wanted one of these when I was a kid." He closed the lid with a snap. The letters read BSA. He handed it back to Parker. "Yeah, well, I'll keep you posted," he said roughly as he started out the door.

"Good," said Parker.

Rollins was halfway to his motorcycle when he heard the heavy front door shut behind him. He wasn't sure what Parker thought of his visit, but it didn't really matter now. There had been no chance to plant the document, and Angela would just have to understand. They would have to find a better moment.

Five minutes later he was at the edge of Los Alamos, just before he left the mesa and dropped down to the valley that led to White Rock and his house. On his left was the huge complex operated by the laboratory to fabricate plutonium for weapons. The buildings lay behind several widely spaced chain-link fences and guardtowers that were flooded with the yellow-orange light of sodium vapor lamps. Together with the lights from Los Alamos, the mesa threw up a fountain of incandescence into the cloudy night sky.

The Parkers seemed to live very well, he thought, very well indeed. He remembered the pots and rugs in David's study. But then, didn't those all-American types always do well? They always had looks and money and storybook childhoods.

God, how he hated rich people, he thought.

Parker slumped back into the most comfortable chair in the living room and sat without moving for several minutes. It had been a hell of a day.

Tevis was asleep, and Maria had finally stopped puttering around in the kitchen and was downstairs in the guest bedroom. The fire had spent itself into glowing embers. It wasn't all that cold, but Tevis had wanted toasted marshmallows; even from his chair Parker could see little ribbons of black stuck to the brick hearth that Maria had failed to clean up.

For a while, memories of his own childhood moved through his head: scenes of picnics and outdoor marshmallow roasts, star-watching with his father, and naked midnight swims as a teenager in the cold backyard swimming pool. The reverie stopped with the image of Berriman dead in the cave.

What was happening to him? His work, which had been his life for so long, now seemed to have taken a wrong turn, leading to a dead end. The business with Berriman and the subsequent revelations about the computer appeared ominous and threatening. He was even losing touch with his staff, who were looking for reassurance that everything was okay. Like himself, maybe they wanted to know that their work meant something.

Parker got up and threw another log on the fire and positioned it with an antique poker that had been a gift from Elisha's parents. It was heavy and ornate and had been made in England in the last century.

He fixed himself a drink and settled back into the oversized chair. The recently added log tumbled to the front of the grate, but he couldn't manage the effort to get up and fix the fire.

Elisha and he seemed to be drifting apart as well. It wasn't just that their individual careers gave them so little time together—although that certainly was part of it. Over the years they had reached an understanding that the time apart was a necessary evil for the ultimate satisfaction only a career can bring. No, it was more than that. Deep inside, he was of two minds about her career: proud on the one hand, and envious, even threatened, on the other. Her success was so public, so open for all to see. With an edge of bitterness that surprised him, he wondered what would become of his laser research at the lab. Would it end up as a weapon in space somewhere or disappear in a flood of papers stamped SECRET and lost on a shelf?

Was that why he found himself unable to put his work out of his mind in the few moments they *did* have together? Maybe he was reacting in a very basic and childish way, making clear the message that *his* work was most important.

Now he tried to put it all out of his mind. Elisha would be back tomorrow or the next day, and he would make an effort to be with her in mind as well as in body. Maybe they could go down to Santa Fe for dinner, just the two of them. And he would spend more time with Tevis. Even his son seemed to have something on his mind.

Outside, the wind picked up and Parker could make out the dark shapes of the trees swaying back and forth. For some reason, a prayer his mother taught him as a child came into his mind:

> There are four corners on my bed,
> And four angels at my head,
> Matthew, Mark, Luke, and John,
> Bless the bed that I lie on.

If only that would work, he thought.

chapter

12

SATURDAY MORNING

The photograph was taken maybe fifty years ago. The young Indian boys were dressed for a ceremonial dance, their faces, chests, and legs painted with black and white designs. It was fall or winter, because the trees had no leaves, and off to the side, in the shadow of the kiva, stood a line of old men with masks.

Reyes stared at it for a long time. It was taken at San Ildefonso before he was born, and appeared in a book he was reading on Pueblo dances. Except for his age—he was too young—he could be any one of those young boys. He remembered the ritual dances he performed as a child, especially the ones in winter, at dawn, when the air was so cold it hurt when you breathed.

He looked at his watch. He had been in the Los Alamos public library for nearly two hours skimming through books on archaeology and anthropology.

He wasn't sure what he was looking for. In part, he hoped to educate himself a little better on the ruins at Tsankawi; perhaps there would be something that would connect with the murder there. Another part of him wanted to know more about his own heritage, beyond the stories his grandparents and parents told him when he was young. But now he was tired of sitting.

Had Reyes not stood up from the reading table to stretch and look for a water fountain, he would have missed the boy. Standing at the checkout desk, putting books into a backpack, was Tevis Parker. Reyes grabbed his coat and his dark glasses from the table and walked toward the front of the room.

"Hello."

The young boy looked up, only a little surprised. "Hi."

Reyes watched silently as the librarian opened each book and ran an electronic pencil across the bar code. When she finished, she smiled and pushed the stack toward Tevis, who turned to look at Reyes. "Do you use the library here in Los Alamos?" he asked.

"This is the first time."

Reyes held the door and they walked outside to where his bike was chained. "I've been wondering, Tevis, if maybe you had a chance to think about what you saw last Sunday on Tsankawi. If maybe, you remembered anything else since we talked?"

Tevis was quiet for a while. "I don't think so."

Reyes tried to formulate his next question carefully before he asked it.

"You see, I'm interested in what happened because it took place on Tsankawi. The way the man was killed—his name was Berriman— might mean that you were right: that he was punished for something. And I have to consider the possibility that an Indian was involved. That's why anything you can remember could be very helpful."

Tevis stopped for a minute, lost in thought. "What if the man did something bad?" he said pushing the hair out of his eyes. "You know, something that broke the rules and death was the punishment?"

Reyes thought for a moment. "I don't know of anything like that, Tevis. Not at San Ildefonso. Not at any pueblo."

"Oh." Tevis seemed disappointed.

"Why do you ask that?"

"I mean, the way he was killed and everything. Maybe he took something he wasn't supposed to." In his mind, Tevis was thinking about the two prayer objects, like the voodoo dolls on Caribbean islands he had read about, and the jagged line of blood.

Tevis suddenly imagined a parade of ghostly figures, some dressed like kachinas, others like the dancers he had seen on special holidays at nearby pueblos. They wore different costumes, some with paint on their bodies, others only partially clothed and wearing the branches of trees. None had any faces, either hidden behind masks or painted dark like the shadowy figure Tevis had seen at Tsankawi.

"What if he wasn't killed by a man?"

Reyes looked down. "What do you mean?"

"I saw someone that day."

The older man dropped down to squat at Tevis's level. "Who did you see?"

Tevis seemed to fumble for words. "I don't know. It was a man maybe, high above me and looking down." He waved his hands excitedly. "His face was dark, you know, black like a shadow." Suddenly he developed a sheepish look. "I just remembered."

"What else do you remember, Tevis? Think hard."

Tevis closed his eyes tightly, oblivious to the passersby who stared at the native policeman and the small, blond white boy stopped dead in the middle of the sidewalk.

"That's all. I only saw him for a moment."

"How do you know it was a man?"

Tevis opened his eyes. "Well, it just looked like a man. A man with a bump on its back."

"What was the man wearing?"

Tevis searched his memory again, trying to resurrect the fleeting image in the cleft of the rock. The image kept changing, however, because in his head sometimes it wore only a dark piece of cloth, like a shawl, and sometimes it had a mask with deer horns like the dancers at the pueblo.

"I'm not sure. Maybe a hood of some kind, dark, maybe a mask." He looked at Reyes. "Horns?"

"Is he all right?" It was the voice of an elderly woman standing next to them holding a bag of groceries. Reyes could feel her eyes fixed on him.

"Yes," he said, "he's fine."

The woman stood there for a moment before she walked slowly away, turning once to check on the two of them.

"Was the man wearing a mask, Tevis? Could you see that well?" He watched the boy's face for a reaction. "Could you tell if it was a white man or an Indian?"

"Yes. Well, no, not that clearly. The guy was on a ledge in the cliff." He paused, confused. "But his face was dark, hidden by something. I couldn't tell what kind of man it was, an Indian or anyone else." Tevis looked up from the ground at Reyes. "I only saw him for a second."

"But you think it was a man?"

"I think it was a man, but maybe it wasn't human."

Reyes paused for a moment. "What do you mean?"

"Maybe it was a kachina."

"A ghost?"

"You know, a spirit of some kind. From the ruins above the cave." His eyes widened. "Maybe from inside the cave."

Reyes tried to control his exasperation; the boy was confusing what he had seen with some fantasy in his head. If the basic story was true, Tevis had seen a man—probably a man—wearing a hood or something, maybe to cover his face. And the man had a bump on his back, or was wearing something which looked, from where Tevis stood, like a bulge. Reyes *knew* it couldn't have been anything but a human. And yet he couldn't entirely dismiss the child's dual interpretation. Something about what Tevis was saying struck a chord deep inside of him, something that sprung perhaps from his childhood.

"I've, uh, been reading these books see, and I know that caves are important to the Tewa. They lead to the Underworld, the Below Place, were spirits live."

"That's true," said Reyes.

"Well, you see, maybe it was something from below. A spirit sent to punish Berriman."

A name suddenly came to Reyes. It was one of the spirits he had been told about as a child called Tsave Yoh. Once a year, men of the pueblo dressed in old clothes or rags and impersonated this spirit who was believed to live in a cave, emerging to find and whip wrongdoers with a tree branch.

"What about the blood, the snake on the man's forehead?" Tevis pulled his sleeve. "You know, the kind of snake you see on Indian pottery."

Then it clicked. Reyes had sensed the same thing without knowing precisely what seemed familiar about the line of blood: it could be the Avanyu, or feather serpent, design that many potters used as decoration. It was an old design, but a powerful one in Indian legend. If it *was* the serpent on Berriman's forehead, then the murderer was someone who knew at least that much about Indian mythology.

Reyes didn't feel comfortable with the realization. It increased the possibility that an Indian was involved.

"Tevis, think hard. Where did you see this man, this figure with the mask?"

"It wasn't far from the cave where the dead man was. You know, just after the trail turns the corner but before you climb up to the ruins."

Reyes tried to place the spot in his mind. Tevis could be accurate or he could be off by half a mile.

"Why didn't you tell the police this after you found the body?"

"I don't know. I just remembered." Tevis stared down at the ground.

The two sat on the bench for a moment in silence. "Mr. Reyes? If it was a kachina, and if it killed the man, would it have left something behind as a warning to others?"

"Perhaps. But I think you saw a man, very possibly the same man who killed Dr. Berriman."

"Maybe the kachinas left something behind?"

"What would they have left, Tevis?"

The boy shrugged.

Reyes walked Tevis back to his bike. "Look, Tevis, I want you to know that you can come to me anytime you want, with anything you want to talk about."

Reyes reached inside one of his pockets and pulled out a card. "I'm going to give you my telephone number. You call me if you remember anything else."

Tevis nodded.

"Be careful," shouted Reyes as Tevis sped away on his bike.

Reyes walked to his car, parked a half-block away, trying to make sense of the conversation. The boy had seen someone, or something, and for some reason kachinas or spirits seemed to be a part of what Tevis had experienced.

All of a sudden Reyes thought of his grandfather. It was ironic, he thought, but that old man shared something with the Anglo boy: the two of them could believe in a world in which both spirit and human lived side by side, struggling over good and evil.

*   *   *

The herbal tea gave off a pungent smell, faintly like flowers that had lost their perfume and would soon begin to rot. Rollins tried to put the smell out of his mind as he sipped it. Across the table, loosely wrapped in her terrycloth robe, sat Angela. She seemed indifferent to the early morning chill, although she grasped her teacup with both hands as though to take its warmth.

Rollins studied her without trying to be obvious. She disliked being stared at, she said, often shouting at him when she caught him at it. This morning, however, she seemed oblivious, still groggy with sleep. She had been gone most of yesterday and last night taking a delivery to El Paso. He had heard her drive up sometime around three in the morning and stumble in to take a shower before falling into bed. He had missed her and wanted to talk, but she only shed her robe and fell into bed saying, "Not now."

She was, he thought, as beautiful as ever, even with her half-closed eyes. She was a tall woman, almost five-nine, with a thin body that seemed incongruous with her ample breasts. Her face, which Rollins always liked to look at, was angular and boyish. When he first met Angela, she had short, close-cropped red hair, heightening her tomboy quality. Now her hair was shoulder length, usually gathered and tied simply in the back of her head. Right above her right eye was a small mole.

He knew very little about her past, considering they had lived together over three years. She almost never talked about her family, her parents, or anything about her earlier life. She sometimes said she had been born in college. About all Rollins knew was that she was an only child and that her mother was dead and her father was a wealthy California car dealer. Every now and then, one of her strange friends from California or New York would show up and, during the course of the evening, make some casual reference to her wealthy father, or to some great and irreparable break with her family. When they came, sometimes in twos or threes and always looking like refugees, they talked politics late into the night.

It didn't seem necessary to Rollins to know more. Knowing more might threaten their relationship. Besides, there was much about his own family and past he never talked about. Growing up poor and fighting for everything he wanted had its share of bad memories. Angela more than returned the favor: she never asked at all about his childhood or his family. His only mistake was in telling her about his relationship with Tommy; she had thrown that back at him during their bad fight two months ago. No matter how much he loved her, he vowed he would never tell her anything so personal again.

He briefly thought about Tommy; he would be in his fifties now, fifteen years older than himself. It was Tommy who introduced him to weights and working out, who taught him to believe in himself when no one else would. There were other things too, the sexual things, but he didn't want to think about that. That was one thing Angela did for him that no one else had ever done: she made him forget that part of his past. Tommy would never intervene again.

"So?" Angela asked between breaths on the hot tea.

Rollins looked at her; she was awake now, the thin veil of sleepiness gone from her eyes. "So what?"

"So tell me everything that happened."

Rollins told her everything he could remember about Parker's house. He particularly described the Indian pots and things he had seen.

"Good stuff, huh?"

He nodded.

She laughed. "Too bad. I might have sold them something." She pushed her hair back behind her ears and poured more tea into her cup from the brown clay pot. Even from across the table, Rollins could smell it.

"Can you get anything else from the lab?" she asked.

"I don't think so. Not from the computer anyway. Too hot right now." He pushed his cup away and wished he was at his office where he could pour himself some coffee. He wasn't quite telling the truth, he thought, since he still had a copy of Berriman's unfinished report on Nemesis. *That* he was holding just in case Angela hassled him. Given the situation at the lab, it was probably the last thing he could deliver. But he knew he had to maximize his advantage with Angela; something told him that more difficult times were ahead.

"Why Parker?" she suddenly asked.

"What do you mean?"

"I mean, why him? Why not someone else?"

He thought for a moment. "Simple. He has a secure terminal, a special one that no one else in the group has. It's the sort of machine that can enter the really deep data on the lab computer. Besides, he had access to the list of safe combinations in each office, including Berriman's. And right now, three of those reports are sitting on his bookshelf. It was simple." The real truth, he thought, was that Parker's name was the first one to come into his head.

"Nothing's ever simple," she said after a while. She spoke flatly, without emotion, but Rollins knew it was a criticism.

"What else could I do? You weren't home and I had to act."

"You should have waited and checked with me. There might have been someone else. Someone more suitable."

"I couldn't wait. I was on-line with the computer."

Angela shook her head. "It doesn't matter now, but you might be compromised." She looked wearily at what was left of her tea. "You may have to leave." She got up from the table and walked to the counter to leave her teacup. He noticed that she put it in the sink without washing it.

Looking out the window, she said, "I warned you this could happen. Be very careful at work and don't do anything out of the ordinary." She turned around and looked directly at him. "Leave the rest to me." With that she left the kitchen.

Rollins was left sitting at the table. She wasn't pleased, he thought. But hell, what else could he have done? He'd been compromised from the first moment he took classified information out of his office and let her copy it. That was only three months ago, and it seemed like a joke then. And now she was talking about leaving; *that* had never crossed his mind.

In the next room he heard Angela talking on the telephone. From the context, he knew it was one of her contacts for Indian goods. It sounded like a meeting had been arranged. A second telephone conversation was much shorter and more subdued.

Rollins started to clean up the table, carefully gathering the dishes and taking them to the sink to be washed. It was a task he had done all of his life, one of the few family chores he could remember his stepmother praising him for. When he turned around, he saw Angela standing in the doorway.

"I've made some calls," she said, "and there are some things that I have to do today that are very important."

Rollins frowned; she had only been back a few hours and she

was leaving again. Her "errands" often took a full day. He turned back to the dishes.

"I want to get rid of the rest of the collection I took to El Paso. We could use the extra money." She gathered her robe around her neck. "But first, there's something you and I have to do." She put her hand on the back of his head, in the same spot where the headaches always started. She slowly turned him around to face her, her green eyes taking on a grayish tinge from the morning light coming through the window. Her hand moved down his chest, and then slowly, very lightly, to between his legs.

All of his concern and anxiety washed away in a flood of desire.

"We need to go back to bed now," she said.

He couldn't decide whether to telephone or just drive up. Ojo Caliente was a small village only thirty miles from Los Alamos.

Sandys paced the worn brick of the sun porch, back and forth, occasionally stopping to listen for his wife. She knew something was wrong. She had quizzed him several times already, but each time he sloughed off her concern saying he was working on a new idea. Probably she didn't believe him, but it didn't matter as long as she didn't press him.

For days now he had been brooding about the stolen deity stick he had seen at Berriman's house. The same object he had come by several years ago and sold to another collector in Ojo Caliente. Damn! he thought, how had it ended up in Berriman's closet? And now, to learn from a close friend at the laboratory that Berriman was suspected of stealing classified information.

A massive investigation would no doubt take place; in fact, he assumed it must be under way. But would it lead to an investigation of the objects found in Berriman's house? *That* was what concerned him.

Through the window he could see his wife spading their small vegetable garden. Now was the time, he decided. He walked to the telephone directory and thumbed through several pages before he found the name and number he wanted.

The phone rang six times before someone finally answered.

"Arthur? It's Gerald."

"Yes, hello."

"Something's come up and I need to see you straightway. Can I come up?"

"Just a minute." Sandys heard the other man cover the telephone mouthpiece with his hand and talk to someone else.

"I have someone here at the moment, but I'll be through in twenty or thirty minutes." The voice was polished and sounded to Sandys like East Coast American.

"That'll be fine, Arthur. I'll see you in an hour if that's all right with you?"

"See you in an hour."

Sandys hung up the phone and went outside to tell his wife he needed to run to Santa Fe to visit a gallery and look at some new acquisitions. Fortunately she had lunch plans and wouldn't want to go with him.

He walked through the den and stopped for a moment. The bulk of his collection, amassed since the forties, was here. Even in the darkened room the pottery gleamed and shone. His collection of tablitas, or headdresses, took up nearly one entire wall. God! he thought, so many beautiful objects had passed through his hands over the years.

The best approach to Arthur, he thought, was to be direct but careful. There was no need, he reasoned, to mention the theft of classified information. His point would be the likely investigation by the police of the expensive artifacts found in Berriman's house. They could be linked to old reports of stolen art conceivably still on file in some police computer.

As far as Sandys knew, the deity stick came from a large collection held by a California collector and looted in a particularly daring robbery. He was worried about Arthur, who, Sandys knew, bought from a variety of sources, not all of which were discreet. In their business, *that* sort of indiscretion was dangerous, he thought.

An hour later, on the edge of Ojo Caliente, Sandys spotted the huge adobe walls surrounding Arthur's expensive home. The man was well known for his collection, and the security system was elaborate. Actually, "collections" would be more accurate, he thought, since Arthur maintained a large and impressive public collection and a variety of smaller ones composed of items whose origins were questionable.

He pushed the small white button on the speaker box and watched two remote television cameras whirl in the direction of his car.

"Yes?" squeaked the small box. The voice had a heavy Spanish accent.

"It's Gerald Sandys. I'm expected."

A few seconds later, the huge wooden gates slowly parted in the middle and revealed a two-lane gravel driveway. Coming toward him, in the opposite lane, was a four-door truck driven by a young woman. It wasn't until she paused, letting him drive by, that he got a brief look at her face. She looked familiar, Sandys thought, but he couldn't immediately place her. As he drove past, he noticed in the rearview mirror that she had a California license plate. Ahead of him, on the steps of the entrance to the elaborate adobe-style house, was the generous physical form of Arthur.

"Welcome, my friend," he said as Sandys slowly removed himself from his Buick Electra.

"Who was that? She looks familiar."

"Just a friend," he replied.

They walked into the house, through the foyer and into a large living room with a huge fireplace at one end. One entire wall was covered with shelves with some of the most exquisite Indian pottery Sandys had ever seen. Any one piece would be worth five or six thousand dollars. Scattered around the room were old Apache baskets, in beautiful shape, and dozens of smaller objects like kachina dolls and small figures. Another wall contained a pair of elaborate Hopi deer masks. Sandys knew that what he saw was only a part of Arthur's collection.

"Would you like some coffee?" Arthur said, pointing to a silver coffee set on the table.

"Yes, thank you. Black."

Arthur handed him a cup and sat back in the chair. "Well, what *is* this urgent thing you must tell me?" Arthur lit a cigarette and held it daintily with his fingers. Sandys immediately saw that he wore two large rings on each hand.

"Something has happened that I believe you should know about." He cleared his throat. "A man was killed last week in Los

Alamos, a colleague of mine from the laboratory. He was murdered actually."

"How dreadful." He took another deep drag on his cigarette and crossed his legs.

"A search of his house by the police revealed a small collection of very expensive Indian pieces, items far too expensive for this man to collect. One of them, I'm shocked to say, was the deity stick I sold you three years ago."

Arthur's eyebrows lifted.

"I didn't know you had disposed of that item, Arthur."

"I didn't actually dispose of it, you see. It was stolen about six months ago. Awful experience."

"What?"

"Yes, it was an unfortunate incident. I was using several, ah, secondary items from my collection as part of a trade for a large turn-of-the-century San Ildefonso pot by Maria Martinez." Arthur paused to take another puff of his cigarette before snuffing it out in a silver ashtray on the table.

"Unfortunately, I sent them down to Santa Fe with one of the young men who works for me. When he stopped for gas, the items were stolen from the car. I fired him, naturally, but needless to say, I never recovered my goods. And your little penis stick was one of the items stolen."

"Did you report it to the police?"

"No. Under the circumstances I didn't think it would be wise. If that's what concerns you, I don't think you need to worry. That special item can't be traced back to me."

Sandys settled back against the cushions, relieved, at least for the moment.

"Come see what I just bought," said Arthur, walking toward a low set of double doors.

Sandys got up and compliantly followed the other man into a long, windowless room that served as a study. Above him, set near the ceiling in the corner of the room, was a television camera and a series of small boxes along the lower walls; Sandys guessed they must be some form of motion detector. Beyond an ornately carved desk was a large table on which sat a cardboard box. The wooden floor was almost entirely covered in some of the most exquisite Navajo rugs Sandys had ever seen. The room, he thought, was a vault.

Arthur very carefully began pulling out objects from the box, each one crudely wrapped in crumpled newspaper. What he finally revealed was a collection of five religious statues, each a foot or more high, called santeros. Each was hand carved, representing the figure of Jesus or a saint, and delicately painted; some had silver or gold crowns on their heads and other pieces of jewelry.

"They're beautiful," said Sandys, feeling a rush of pleasure at seeing such beautiful handiwork. "Are they nineteenth century?"

Arthur smiled. "Only these two. The other three are seventeenth." His voice managed to convey both arrogance and condescension at the same time, thought Sandys.

"Expensive, Arthur?"

"Of course. But I managed to get a good price for the lot. It seems the seller wanted to make a quick deal, and I just happened to have a few extra dollars this month." He laughed wickedly.

"I must say, that young woman looked familiar."

The other man suppressed a giggle. "You might as well know. She has things like this for sale from time to time. I gather she needed the money; she took an unbelievably low offer."

"I really think I've seen her before."

"I'm not surprised. Apparently she lives with one of your type."

"My type?"

"You know, a cerebral Los Alamos scientist."

Sandys tried to place her but could not. Where, he wondered, had he seen her? In Los Alamos?

Both men walked out to the living room and then back to the foyer. Arthur seemed anxious to get back to his acquisitions, and Sandys felt a sense of uneasiness spreading within him. This man was careless, he told himself. There was no telling how much of the collection had been pieced together from black market sources. There were a number of ceremonial objects that the Hopi or local Pueblos would no doubt be furious to learn were in Anglo hands.

"Well," said Arthur, "we must talk again." Someone pushed a button, and the large gates began to open before Sandys had even reached his car.

Driving home, he tried to reassure himself that everything was okay. There seemed little chance that the object in Berriman's home could be traced back to Arthur and therefore to himself. There *was* the question of the young woman.

Sandys slowed down and let a pickup truck pass him. Rapidly he tried to consider the possibilities. Would the woman have recognized him? Would she connect him with Arthur and his collection in some way?

It was that last thought that provided some comfort. After all, if she was dealing in stolen art, she would be unlikely to contact the police about anything. *That* made him feel better. Perhaps, he thought, he was overreacting. Part of an American expression came to him, one of the first he learned when he came to New Mexico in 1943: something about making a mountain out of a molehill.

Just to be safe, however, he would try to find out more about her. And just what she was selling. He would make a few inquiries with friends at galleries saying he was interested in a few more "good" pieces for his collection. Then he would mention that word had it that a young woman had things to sell. Perhaps then he could assess how much of threat she might be.

The four of them had been sitting for two hours, although Poole felt like it had been all day. On the table were several small piles of manila folders.

Even though it was Saturday morning, Doty and his agent wore similar dark blue suits that in the artificial light of Poole's office looked dull black. Poole cursed himself for wearing only a shirt and sport coat; he felt out of uniform. Doty's aide at least drank coffee, for which Poole was grateful, and for once he didn't mind Castro smoking his damn cigarettes.

The young FBI man was quizzing Castro for the second time on the number of people in Parker's group with access to the central computer. The four of them had been going over the events of the last week, detail by detail. Neither agent seemed uncomfortable with the procedure. Only the younger man, perhaps thirty-five, displayed a small nervous habit: from time to time he forced air out with his tongue between two teeth like he was removing a stubborn piece of food. As far as Poole could tell, it was always the same two teeth.

"Most of the individuals check out," said the young agent.

"That is, their backgrounds and activities for the last month or so clear them."

"And the rest?" asked Poole.

"I think we look at them real close," replied Doty. He pointed to the blackboard where five names in a list of sixteen were circled. Poole noticed that the last name was Parker's. "Schneider, Goldman, Kronkosky, Dixon, and Parker," he said, reading the names. "Goldman has a history of political involvement, especially in college in the seventies; the others have periods of time unaccounted for or had unusual access to Berriman and his computer terminal."

Poole studied the names for a moment; they were essentially the same names he had identified. "What about Rollins? He has a terminal too." His name was on Poole's list but not on Doty's.

"We consider him a secondary possibility," said the young agent.

"All of the primary suspects have strong psychological profiles as well," added Doty. "The Bureau has a sophisticated computer model it uses to analyze what we know about a given individual's past, work and play patterns, emotional condition, and so forth."

"I don't see how Parker fits a pattern for espionage," said Poole, "and his past is clean. He even has money, for God's sake."

"It's his wife's money," added Doty. "But we have other information."

"Like what?"

"Disillusionment with his work, for one thing. A disrespect for security, for another."

"I'm not convinced that the 'list' of combination numbers was anything more than carelessness," said Poole.

"Perhaps." Doty looked through his files. Poole took it as a subtle sign that the meeting was almost over.

"His wife is an archaeologist, you know," said the young agent. "She also has a collection of expensive Indian art. No one else in this list has such a collection." He looked at his notes. "We're checking her out as quietly as we can."

"It's just hard to imagine Parker or any of the others working with Berriman to steal weapons secrets." Poole couldn't find himself as enthusiastic as Doty about their list of suspects.

"Perhaps," said Doty dryly, "Parker wasn't working with Berriman. Perhaps the man is being blamed for something he didn't do. But

Parker—or any of these men, for that matter—was in an excellent position to make Berriman the fall guy."

That was true, thought Poole, but still... "And what do you need from us?"

"Cover them as closely as you can inside the laboratory; monitor telephone calls, travel, conversations, you know the things, Ed. But discreetly. We need to know if there's more than one person at work here."

"And outside the lab?"

"Leave that to us; we have special coverage on all of them." Doty closed his file. "And, Ed, all of this is confidential. Nothing outside of you and Castro here, okay?"

chapter

13

MONDAY MORNING

Reyes drove down the pitted dirt road to Jenny's. It was only seven-thirty, but he was following her advice and getting to the house early.

She had called yesterday to say that her brother was planning to spend the night. If Reyes wanted to talk to him, she said, he needed to catch Johnny before he left again. She had no idea of his plans.

"You give me your word you only want to talk to him?" she asked. He promised her that was the case.

Legally, he had no jurisdiction at Santa Clara. Given the information he had from White in Santa Fe, he could officially approach the Santa Clara tribal offices and ask them to arrange for him to talk to Johnny Vargas. That might or might not work. For the moment, this direct, informal approach presented the best chance of getting information. Maybe.

He dodged another large hole in the road and pulled in front of the strange house that was half-new and half-old. He honked politely to give a warning of his arrival. He waited a moment and then walked slowly to the door, wearing his coat loosely to show that he had no gun.

After a moment the door opened and Jenny stuck her head out.

"He's here," she said softly. "I'll talk to him." She turned around and gently closed the door.

Reyes waited maybe five minutes before the door opened again. From inside the house he could hear voices, first one, then another, getting louder. It sounded to him like an argument and for a moment Reyes wondered if he should be carrying his gun.

Just as he decided to knock again, the door opened and Jenny reappeared.

"He doesn't want to talk. He says he doesn't have to talk."

Reyes thought for a moment. "Tell him I know that. Tell him that I know I can't force him to do anything here." He paused for a moment. "But tell him that I could make it difficult for him by going to the tribal council and alerting the state and federal police. I don't want to do that, but I will if I have to."

He said nothing else, hoping that Johnny was near enough to hear the message himself.

"I'll try again," she said.

A few minutes passed before the door opened and a sullen young man of maybe twenty appeared at the doorway. At first, he opened the door only partway, one hand holding the edge of the door, the other half hidden by the wall. Reyes rapidly considered what Vargas might be holding in the hidden hand. A gun? A knife?

"Yeah?" the young man finally said.

Reyes stared at him for a moment. Johnny was shorter than himself and stocky. He wore no shirt and only a pair of old faded jeans. Below his right nipple, too high to have come from an appendectomy, was a line of heavy scar tissue.

"I want you to know," Reyes began slowly, "that I'm only here to talk." The kid gave no expression.

"I'm told that someone approached a dealer in Santa Fe with certain objects. Religious things we people use in our private ceremonies." He hoped that the "we" would suggest to Johnny a link between them. "You know about these objects from your childhood."

Again, there was no comment, but this time Johnny smirked. Reyes suddenly wondered if Johnny had ever been a part of the community at Santa Clara.

"Not only is this against our people's code, to sell these things, but it is against the law."

"So what's it to me, man?"

"So I'm told that you could be the one who approached this dealer in Santa Fe."

Vargas laughed. "Shit, man, you don't know it was me."

"Maybe. Maybe I do. But if it was, you would be in great trouble." Reyes shifted and put his hands in his pockets to further put Johnny at ease. "But I'm not interested in you, but in the people who deal in this trade. Especially if they're white people." Reyes wasn't sure that any whites were involved, but he thought it a good bet. An Anglo would have less compunction about putting a religious object in a collection.

Between Vargas and the doorjamb, Reyes could see Jenny standing and listening intently. There was a moment of silence until Vargas moved the hand that was still half-hidden by the wall; to Reyes it seemed that the boy put something down on a nearby table. Vargas opened the door completely and stood in the doorway with both hands in view. On the one fist Reyes could see clearly, he saw the tattooed letters M A D.

"You got the wrong Indian," he said finally.

"You could help me find the people who are doing this. It would be a good thing."

The same evil smile appeared on Johnny's face. "I don't know nothing, man."

Reyes shrugged. "Have it your way. But I promise you, there'll be more trouble. It's not worth it for you." Reyes knew he was using a white man's logic on this kid. The expectation of trouble probably wasn't the kind of warning that Vargas would listen to. But appealing to his sense of loyalty to his people hadn't seemed to work either.

"Think about it. If you can help me, then call me." He held up his card. For a moment he wasn't sure Vargas would take it. Finally the man flipped the latch on the screen door and took it.

"Don't hold your breath," he said, and closed the door.

Reyes stood motionless for a moment, half expecting the door to open again. After a while, he slowly walked back to his truck.

There really wasn't much he could do now. He couldn't arrest the kid and he couldn't beat anything out of him, although he knew policemen who would try. At least he was fairly certain that it was

Johnny who approached the gallery in Santa Fe. Reyes would have to wait. And watch.

He backed his truck up, forgetting the pothole and bounced heavily as he hit it. There was no sign of movement at the door or windows as he drove away. Now he was worried about Jenny. Would her brother do something to her? The best he could do was check with her later and be sure she was okay.

He wasn't back in his office ten minutes when the telephone rang and the secretary called his name. "Some girl named Jenny."

His heart beat faster; he picked up the phone as quickly as he could. "Are you all right?"

"I'm fine. He was mad, of course, but he didn't do anything except curse."

"Good." He was relieved.

"He's gone somewhere, I don't know where, but he made a call before he left."

"Do you know whom he called?"

"No. He mentioned no name. But it was a call in the area. It wasn't long distance. I watched him dial, and he didn't use enough numbers to make it long distance."

A call in the area, thought Reyes, could mean the whole state since all of New Mexico had the same area code. That could mean a million telephones.

"I think—but I'm not sure—that it was a number in Los Alamos."

"How do you know?"

"Well, he dialed a one, then two sixes, and then some other numbers. But not enough for a different area code and a telephone number."

"Did you hear what he said?"

"Only part of it. He gave his name and then said he had to meet. Apparently the other person agreed and gave a location. He never said where he was going."

"How long ago did he leave?"

"Maybe five minutes. I'm worried that your visit may cause him to do something."

Reyes was worried too. There was no way of tailing him; he couldn't get back to Santa Clara in less than thirty minutes.

"I don't think you need to worry. His call may have nothing to do with our talk." At least he hoped that was the case. "Will you promise to call me if you learn something?"

"Yes."

"But be careful. Don't let him know you're talking with me, okay?" He knew he was asking a hell of a lot from her.

"Okay."

"I'll check back with you later."

He hung up and sat back in his chair. Could it be that someone from Los Alamos was involved with Vargas? The telephone company would have a record of the call, but by the time he obtained the information, Johnny would be long gone.

Thinking of Los Alamos reminded Reyes of something. Maybe another way of learning about the black market in Indian art was to talk to collectors. Those who would talk, he thought. Reyes tried to remember the man in Los Alamos, the expert on Indian antiquities who once worked with Berriman. He pulled out his black notebook and flipped through the pages. Then he saw the name: Gerald Sandys, with a note indicating he was Berriman's boss for years and that he was an expert on Indian arts.

Reyes pulled out the Los Alamos telephone directory and found Sandys's name and number. He wrote them, plus the address, in his notebook, and then dialed the number. It rang four times before a woman answered.

"Hello?"

"Dr. Sandys, please."

"Who's calling?" The voice seemed protective.

"Officer Reyes from San Ildefonso police."

"Just a moment."

There was a pause and Reyes could hear an exchange of voices in the background. After a while he heard the receiver being picked up and then an elderly voice with a British accent.

"Yes?"

"Dr. Sandys?"

"Yes."

"This is Officer Reyes with the San Ildefonso police. Have you a moment to talk?"

"Of course, Officer."

"I wonder if you would have time to meet with me this week. I'm looking into the theft of religious objects from my pueblo."

There was a long silence.

"Dr. Sandys?"

"Yes, I'm here. I'm just not certain that I can be of help to you in this matter."

Reyes thought this might happen. He was prepared. "You could be very helpful if you would tell me what black-market collectors look for and how they buy and sell these kinds of items."

"I just don't know much about this sort of thing, Officer," said Sandys slowly, "perhaps there's someone in Santa Fe who could be more helpful."

"I understand you are considered an expert, Dr. Sandys," replied Reyes.

"An expert in some areas of collection, Officer, not in stolen goods."

Reyes decided to use another approach. "I read the police report on your investigation of Isaac Berriman's collection."

"Yes?"

"You were of considerable help to them, and I think you could help me. I would take no more than thirty minutes of your time."

"Oh, very well," said Sandys. Reyes detected a weariness in the man's voice. "I'm rather busy at the moment. What about Wednesday or Thursday?"

"Wednesday morning would be fine. Say nine-thirty?"

"All right." The voice sounded resigned.

"Good. I'll come to your house at nine-thirty."

"No. I would rather you wouldn't. My wife, you see, is rather upset over Dr. Berriman's death; she knew him well, and I think it would be rather better if we met somewhere else."

"The restaurant at the Los Alamos Inn?"

"Fine. I'll meet you there."

Reyes hung up the telephone. Sandys seemed a bit odd, but then, Reyes found a lot of people in Los Alamos odd.

Poole sat in the director's office with a cup of coffee in his hand. His telephone call to Alan Merritt over the weekend had produced a Monday morning meeting at seven-thirty. The only other participant was Dawes, the young FBI agent on Doty's staff. He could tell Merritt was unhappy with the news and the proposed surveillance.

"You really think all this is necessary?" For the first time Poole could see a small flicker of discomfort in the director's normally expressionless eyes.

"We think it very important, Dr. Merritt," said the agent. "This is one method of determining if Dr. Berriman worked with someone else in the laboratory."

"It won't be obvious," added Poole. He referred to a tap on all calls in and out of Parker's group.

"And these other individuals?" asked Merritt, referring to the list of names mentioned by Poole. "Goldman? Schneider? And even Parker? These are some of my most important staff members."

"Yes, sir, I know, and I personally expect to see them cleared. It's just that we must consider *all* the possibilities." Poole searched for something to soften the news. "We have to consider the possibility that one or some of these individuals could become targets."

"What do you mean?"

"Someone could be harmed, or killed, if they accidentally stumbled on the murderer." Merritt's eyes widened behind his glasses.

"Do you really have reason to suspect these men?" asked Merritt. He pointed to the list of names selected by the FBI.

Poole really didn't know what to say. "We have to look at the possibilities," he said finally. He also suspected that the FBI were considering more than the five names suggested to Merritt.

"There are other reasons, as well," said Dawes. "The nature of Dr. Berriman's death was particularly violent; we may be dealing with an individual or group who will stop at nothing." He subtly emphasized the word "nothing."

"Good God!" exclaimed Merritt.

"This is precautionary, you understand," said Poole. "There may be no one else. Berriman may have acted on his own, stealing classified information to support his art collection and the attempt to enter the computer last week may be unrelated. On the other hand—and this has to be considered—he may have others here at Los Alamos with whom he worked. If that's the case, we must find them before they can do any further damage to national security."

The young FBI agent nodded in agreement.

"The FBI has asked that we have Dawes located here at Los Alamos to act as liaison with the Bureau. He'll be based in my office."

Merritt frowned and nodded. "I want to be kept informed of what you're doing."

Poole nodded. "Of course," he said. He never did like to be the bearer of bad news.

The director of the computer center was on the telephone to Maintenance when his young staff member knocked excitedly at the door. The temperature in the bunker was off by two degrees, a dangerous margin when so much sensitive electronic equipment was involved.

"Get on it, George, will you?" He put the receiver down and looked at the thin man in the plaid shirt.

"We got it!" he said.

The director rose from his chair and grabbed the printout from the young man's hand. "This ID number, whose terminal is it?" he asked.

"A man named Parker. David Parker."

"I'm sure it was him," she said, turning around from the kitchen counter. Her face appeared without expression, although Rollins noticed she had made a fist with one hand.

"Gerald Sandys?"

"Yes. That's the name I was given."

"And you're sure that he was the one you saw in Ojo Caliente?"

"I'm sure now. I knew I had seen him somewhere. It was obviously at a party or some dumb affair in Los Alamos." Angela began to pace the kitchen floor. "The man I saw was older, you know, white hair, probably in his sixties."

At first, Rollins couldn't imagine whom Angela referred to. Bit by bit, she came up with other pieces of a description. "I didn't see all of him, just his face. It was very lined, and he had white, white hair. I'd seen him before, I knew it."

"And this is the same man who's been asking questions about you?"

"I'm certain of it. I remember him because he collects Indian art. Good stuff. I think he even has a book out on the subject and does appraisals."

Angela referred to a call she had received late yesterday evening from someone she only characterized as "in the business." Sandys—if it was him, thought Rollins—had been visiting art galleries and announcing he was in the market for some choice objects. More important, he told at least one dealer that he knew a young woman was selling. The "young woman," Angela said, could only mean herself!

"So what if this old guy is interested in buying something and he knows that a 'woman' has something to sell?"

Instantly he felt her turn cold. "So he could make a connection between me and the stuff I sell." She stared at him. "And *that* could lead to you."

Rollins was leaning against the pantry doors waiting for the moment when he could go to work. He was already late for an eight-thirty meeting. He wasn't making Angela feel any better about the call, so he decided now was the time to leave.

"I've got to go. I'm late." He turned and walked out the door.

Rollins smiled to himself as he gunned the motorcycle away from the house. He still had the most valuable information hidden behind the paint cans in the garage, something she would be able to get a lot of money for. She would be very pleased when he told her what the report contained. He was sure of that.

Angela watched Rollins for a moment through the kitchen window before she turned back inside. She grabbed her cup of tea and walked into the living room and sat down. Last night's fire was nothing more than cold embers now.

She felt a curious mixture of anger and acceptance. Anger that Rollins seemed not to understand the dangers they faced, and acceptance of the fact that what was done was done. The question for her now was: How safe was she? Rollins didn't appear to understand the implications of running into Sandys at Ojo Caliente. Nor, she thought, of the fact that Sandys was now actively visiting local galleries and dropping information that someone, a "young woman," had something to sell.

Rollins could be so goddamn dense sometimes. He didn't even

understand what might happen at the lab unless he was very, very careful.

She got up and went to the spare bedroom that she used as an office. From a shelf, behind a row of dusty-looking books, she pulled a fat plastic bag with a zipper. It was the kind you got from banks to hold money in. From another shelf she retrieved a similiar bag. Extracting the contents from both she began to count the bills. When she was through, she had slightly over eighty thousand in mostly one-hundred-dollars bills. She also knew that in a special account in Los Angeles she had another sixty thousand. She divided the money between the two bags and rehid them behind the books.

Most of this money was hers, she figured, since she had made it from selling goods to special, "no questions asked" clients. So far, she had made less than forty-five thousand on the information Rollins brought from the laboratory, and some of that had gone into the new greenhouse.

Angela stared at the shelves of books, many of them hers on Southwest archaeology. She sensed that business was going to close down here. She hoped that Rollins would follow her instructions perfectly: do nothing to draw attention.

She had to smile at herself. Never when she was growing up did she think she would be dealing in antiquities and government secrets! Certainly she never imagined herself a courier for agents anxious for bomb secrets. But it had come about from a comment a year ago from her friend Zach, an older lover from college days, when she had been part of an undergound political group. He had heard about Rollins's work and had suggested that money could be made if a secret or two could be pinched. Zach had used that word, "pinch," and even now the conversation lingered in her mind.

Rollins's initial reluctance had been no surprise, but it had taken almost a month to talk him into doing something. She smiled to herself at the thought of her boyfriend's teenage secret and the subsequent sexual insecurity he still carried after all these years.

When he finally agreed—partly, she knew, out of fear of losing her—she contacted Zach, who made the necessary connections. Within a week, a dour little man made contact with her by telephone and requested a meeting in Los Angeles. Over terrible Mexican food in a greasy spoon on the east side, she was asked a series of questions, only some of which she could answer. The man spoke with a foreign accent and seemed to know a lot about her and about Rollins, although Bob's name was never mentioned. A system was arranged: telephone numbers, code words and drops, and very specific instructions on transferring information. Only then, the little man with the accent said, would cash remuneration be made.

Apparently they liked what they got, since three times now she'd received a call to be somewhere and money was left in an envelope or wrapped in a newspaper, waiting for her. It was all too comical! Like the movies, or bad television. What would her father have to say about it all?

Now it would have to end, along with her lucrative business, at least in this part of the world. From her wallet she pulled a small piece of paper with a telephone number on it. As far as she could tell, it was a number in Albuquerque.

She dialed the number and let it ring four times and then hung up. She redialed the number and heard it picked up on the second ring.

"Yes?" said the thick voice. Was it Hispanic? Angela couldn't be sure.

"I have a message from Mr. Smith for Mr. Jones."

There was only silence on the other end. Finally, the same voice repeated the awkward word. "Yes?"

"I don't have any more fresh flowers," she said, trying to remember the words she had been taught.

"Would you like some help is selecting new ones?" the voice asked.

"No," she said. "Not just yet."

She hung up the phone and stared out of the window for a moment, into the trees behind the fence. She knew that Rollins liked this house a lot and she wondered if he would be willing to give it up.

Probably not, she guessed, and walked into the bathroom for a shower.

"Do you like the drawing or not?" The short man looked to be at the end of his rope. His face was red and he frowned at the man with the faded plaid shirt across the table. In his hand was a large watercolor of huge lasers floating in space and firing long, thin lines of red light at approaching warheads with small hammers and sickles on them.

"Take it easy, Adam, the art is great." Parker leaned back in his chair and stretched. "Our only question is whether you have given the viewer classified information." He paused. "Or maybe you've stretched a scientific point or two." Sitting around the table in his office were three of his senior staff members, each with a major role in developing the laboratory's laser program. On the table were a dozen sheets of stiff posterboard, each with the artist's personal interpretation of Star Wars.

Parker sifted through the watercolors. One print was a particularly vivid interpretation of a small nuclear explosion transforming small bundles of metal rods into great shafts of destructive light. Another image showed American and Soviet space stations battling it out with a combination of lasers and mechanical weapons. Parker had to smile to himself. It was the stuff of science fiction. Or maybe the storyboards from a George Lucas movie.

"I think this stuff overdramatizes the laser's capabilities. Who's going to see this stuff, anyway?" It was the man with the faded shirt.

"Merritt wants them for a briefing before the Air Force next month," said Parker. *Overdramatic* was exactly the word he had thought of.

"Well, I don't know," said another. "You have to help the nonscientific mind interpret science. This may be a bit colorful, but it's not inaccurate."

"I based all these drawings on conversations with your staff, Dr. Parker." The artist seemed on the verge of walking out.

Parker wondered how the man could survive in Los Alamos. Short and thin and obviously talented, he had a hairstyle that was moderately punkish. His blue workshirt and expensive tie contrasted with the faded wool and Dacron clothes of Parker's staff. "Is there anything here classified?" he asked.

"The prints of the space-based laser generators have a few details that could be borderline. Particularly the ones showing the power sources."

"Has the space mirror been declassified?"

"Bits and pieces have appeared in the press and some of the journals. You know, *Aviation Week*, that sort of thing."

Someone groaned. "Why don't the Russians have their own version of *Aviation Leak*? It would save us billions of dollars in spies. We could just pick up a copy every week and learn what the hell *they're* doing."

Everyone laughed except the artist, who didn't understand the joke. Magazines like *Aviation Week* were famous for breaking news of new defensive weapons systems—sometimes years before information was declassified for the public.

"You know," said Parker, "all these illustrations make Star Wars look offensive, instead of defensive. Is that a problem?"

"We want accuracy, don't we?" said a staff member smiling. "What the drawings also suggest is that every single Russian warhead is being destroyed. Isn't that stretching the point?"

"How do you illustrate a ten-percent failure rate?" asked Parker. He referred to the accepted belief that even in the best of systems, almost ten percent of all incoming Soviet warheads were expected to get through and hit the U.S.

"Okay," said Parker, "let's take a break."

He glanced down at the sketch that lay on the top of the table. It was the one of the space-bound laser shooting a thin beam of yellow-red light at a Soviet satellite. On one side of the metallic-gray object Adam had drawn a small American flag. Parker wondered who the hell would notice that in space.

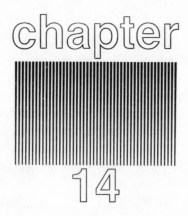

chapter 14

TUESDAY AFTERNOON

"How many of these you gonna make?" Reyes looked over at the makeshift table made from an old door and cement blocks. He counted eleven mud-colored bowls of different shapes and sizes.

"I'll do four more. With breakage and firing defects, I'll end up with maybe a dozen good ones for sale." Jenny Vargas carried on the conversation with Reyes but never took her eyes off of the clay bowl in front of her.

He had been watching her for fifteen minutes now, first forming the general shape of the bowl with long coils of putty-colored clay twisted around and around in circles. Then with her fingers she smoothed the individual rolls of clay into a single mass and smoothed it even further with a small stone slip.

"I'll paint these before I fire them," Jenny said. She studied the bowl for a moment. "Maybe a simple feather design around the lip."

"They're beautiful," said Reyes.

"Thanks." Jenny kept on working the clay, stroking it softly with movements that displayed a unique sensitivity of the hand and eye for the medium.

"Earth and water," he said.

"Earth, fire, water, air," she said laughingly. "Doesn't that describe everything?"

"Maybe."

"Are you still thinking about my brother?"

"Yes."

"He hasn't been back."

"I believe you. That isn't it, though." Reyes shifted his position on the old wooden crate. "He knows something he's not talking about."

"You're probably right, Tomás, but no one can force him to talk. I know that much."

It struck Reyes like a sudden breeze on a still day. She had used his first name. Except for his old aunt, no one around here called him Tomás. In the Marines, to most, it was always an anglicized "Tom."

"Have you got a photograph of him I can borrow?"

She thought for a moment. "I think so. It might be a year or two old."

"That's all right; anything that recent will do. Can you remember anything else about the red-haired woman who picked Johnny up?"

Jenny shook her head. "Not really. She's called a couple of times for Johnny. Or at least I think it was her. She seemed businesslike."

"What do you mean?"

"Well, you know, no chitchat. 'Is Johnny there?' 'When will he be back?' Click. All business. No message."

"Local call?"

"I guess so. I don't remember any static or anything like that on the line."

Reyes watched her for a moment in silence, marveling how someone could work with something so formless as clay and still mold it into a nearly perfect shape.

"Wait a minute. There was something." For the first time Jenny looked up from her clay.

"What?"

"She had California plates."

"Her car?"

"It was a van, with four doors. And her license plates were from California." She wiped her brow with the back of her hand.

This was something, thought Reyes. Maybe there was some luck after all.

"Can you remember anything else? The color of the van maybe?"

"Tan, I think. Maybe white. It wasn't a dark color."

"Old? New?"

"Something in between. I don't know, really."

"That's okay. This has been very helpful."

"I don't know much about the woman. Red hair. Tall, I think, from the way she rode in the cab. I've never seen her up close."

"Is it possible," began Reyes slowly, "that she and your brother have something going between them?"

Vargas looked up from her clay and stared at Reyes. He wasn't sure if he had touched a sensitive area or not. Finally she smiled, very faintly, with the edges of her mouth.

"I don't think so." Then she laughed out loud. "But who knows? Is it the Indian boy that's in love with the forbidden white girl? Or the redheaded Anglo that's in love with the erotic Indian stud?"

Reyes laughed too. He liked this girl. She had a sense of humor as well as a heart.

Twenty minutes later, on the road to Los Alamos, Reyes wondered what to do next. Call her for a date? Dinner, maybe in Santa Fe? Or just drop it and see what happened? He decided to hold off. After all, he had damn little reason to believe she'd be interested in having dinner with him, or anything else for that matter.

Her image still occupied his mind as he drove into the parking lot of the Los Alamos County Police Building.

Suddenly it hit him what a wild-goose chase he was on today. First with Jenny Vargas and her mysterious brother. And now with the sheriff and hopes for information on black market Indian antiquities. He wasn't ten feet inside the building when he saw Smith's deputy walk out of a room. The man took one look at Reyes and kept walking.

What the hell? He quickened his pace and caught up with the heavyset deputy. "What's going on?" he asked, keeping pace.

"Nothing."

"I do something bad?"

The deputy stopped and looked around, making a strange gooselike movement with his neck.

"Step in here." Both men moved into the men's restroom.

"Something happening I don't know about?"

"You could say that," the other man said, poking his head low to see if anyone occupied the single stall in the room. "I caught holy shit talking to you last week."

"Why?" Reyes was genuinely baffled.

"The word's come down from on high. No talking about the dead guy." The harsh light from the ceiling accentuated the deputy's pockmarked face.

"What's that got to do with me?"

"*I* told you more than you were supposed to know. And besides, you got into the dead guy's house. Apparently, the FBI don't want no one screwing with their case."

"Shit," said Reyes, almost in a whistle.

"Word is, not to talk to anyone about anything. And your name came up specifically."

Reyes shook his head. "I don't know what I've done but ask a few questions."

"It ain't personal, Reyes. Apparently something big is coming down. You know, FBI and all. They don't want any of us talking out of house. They don't know you seen the file."

"Okay. This conversation didn't take place." Reyes let the deputy go out first and waited almost five minutes before he followed.

Something big was happening, just as he suspected. But for him, the question was still the connection between Berriman and the valuable objects in his house. Reyes sat in the stall, with the door closed and the toilet-seat cover down, wondering what to do next.

He decided to go directly to Smith and pretend that nothing had happened. He would ask for assistance in scanning their files for any record of art thefts in Los Alamos in the last twelve months.

Once again he found the sheriff's office and introduced himself and asked for Smith. The same spacey woman asked him to wait on a small sofa at the end of the room. He could see her dial something and talk into the telephone. Once or twice she looked up from her desk at him and then said something back into the phone.

"Sheriff Smith asked for you to wait for a few minutes. Then he can see you." Reyes watched her lick the end of her pencil and stick it in her hair.

He nodded and picked up an old, worn issue of *Field and Stream*. Reyes studied the ads and then forced himself to read a lengthy article on hunting Alaskan black bears. A few minutes later a tall, young man in his thirties walked briskly into the waiting area, nodded at the secretary, and walked into Smith's office. Reyes was calculating the odds on this being FBI when Sheriff Smith opened the door and invited him in.

"I'm glad you stopped by, Reyes. We could use your help on something." He motioned Reyes over to a stiff-looking metal framed chair. Standing by a similar chair was the tall young man.

"Do you know Dawes from FBI?"

Reyes shook his head and saw a packaged smile break out on the agent's clear-skinned face. At the same time, the man's hand pushed out toward Reyes, ready to be shaken. Reyes took it—and felt the extrafirm grip of a man who prided himself on his handshakes.

"Good to meet you," Dawes said.

"Thanks."

Smith cleared his throat and then plopped down in his plush leather chair behind the metal desk.

"Reyes, we got a problem and we want to ask your help."

Reyes felt he knew what was coming. "Sure. What can I do?"

"You know about Berriman, the scientist who was murdered last week?"

"I know he was killed, but that's about it."

"There's more to it, Mr. Reyes," said Dawes. "He may have been involved in a serious breach of security. We are in the middle of an intense investigation."

I'll bet, thought Reyes. He remembered what Smith's deputy told him earlier in the week. "What does this have to do with me?"

"You were asking questions about Berriman," snorted Smith, who lacked the younger agent's sense of finesse. "You even went to his home and poked around. You talked with one of my men here."

"That's true, Sheriff, but not as part of any investigation of Dr. Berriman."

"What sort of interests do you have, Mr. Reyes?" asked Dawes.

"I'm interested in stolen Indian antiquities, Mr. Dawes, the sort of things that are part of my people's religious customs."

"I see," he said.

"Well, damnit, you've horned in on this investigation." Smith slumped back in his chair.

"I'm sorry about that," said Reyes, suddenly realizing that he wasn't going to get any more help from Los Alamos. It sounded to him that the FBI was putting pressure on Smith for his behavior.

"I can appreciate your work," began Dawes diplomatically, "but you see, at the moment we would like to ask you to refrain from any activities that might compromise our own investigation. Or at least hold off until we can clear you to proceed."

"Let me understand this," began Reyes, "you want me to stop doing anything that will draw attention to Berriman's murder, even if it might be of some help in its solution?"

"Let us be the judge of that," said Dawes.

"Just lay off Berriman, Reyes," said Smith, wiping the sweat from his forehead with a dirty handkerchief. "Or anything relating to Berriman."

"We would greatly appreciate your cooperation in this." Dawes smiled again, revealing a set of perfectly white teeth.

Reyes nodded. What a son of a bitch. "Well, of course, I don't want to jeopardize your work in any way." He produced his own smile, which he knew couldn't match Dawes for whiteness or orthodontics.

Both men got up and shook hands. Smith stayed in his chair and played with a letter opener. "We'll keep in touch," he said.

Reyes heard their voices behind the closed door as he walked away. He was on his own, and he'd be damned if he'd stop watching Vargas.

The phone rang twice before she answered it. She was hesitant because of what had happened in the last few days.

"Hello?"

"It's Johnny." She realized it was Johnny Vargas, although he sounded terribly hung over.

"Where've you been?"

"With friends." He coughed loudly into the phone. "You called?"

"Two days ago."

"Yeah, well, I've been with friends."

"I got a job for you. I need some things taken to Arizona. You interested?"

"When?"

"As soon as possible."

Vargas whistled. "I don't know, I just got here."

Angela controlled her anger. "There's some extra money in it for you. I just need some stuff delivered soon. Can you do it?"

"Yeah, I guess so," he said, coughing again. To Angela it sounded like a mixture of alcohol and dope.

"There's something else. Another job here."

"Yeah?"

"Can you meet me in two hours? The job will be tonight."

"What is it?"

"I'll tell you when I see you. Where are you?"

"A friend's house in Española."

"I'll meet you at the Big Burger on Highway 84 in Española in two hours."

"Okay." Vargas coughed violently again. "There's something I gotta tell you."

"What?"

"A man's been around here. A cop. Wants to know something about stolen Indian stuff."

"What kind of cop?" Angela immediately thought of the FBI or someone from the laboratory.

"An Indian cop. From San Ildefonso."

"How'd he learn about you?"

"Don't know. I didn't tell him nothing."

Angela was quiet for a moment. "Okay. We'll talk about it later," she said and paused. "And come alone."

She hung up. She realized that after tonight Vargas wouldn't be of help anymore. In fact, he was a liability. The cop had looked him up for a reason. She wondered if Vargas was selling the stuff on the side.

Suddenly, her thoughts jelled into a plan, a way of taking care of Sandys and Parker at the same time. But there was a lot to do between now and then, and she needed Rollins's help.

She started to dial his number and then realized that she had never called his office before. She had no idea what his extension was. She found the general information number for the laboratory and dialed it, asking to be connected to Dr. Robert Rollins.

Here was a chance to kill a couple of birds, she thought, but she needed to act quickly.

He was a little nervous. All day he had been carrying around the cover sheet marked TOP SECRET, waiting for the right moment to plant it in David Parker's office. Now, after a telephone call from Angela, he was cryptically told to hold on to it, that something else was in the works. His instructions were to meet Angela at the nearby Safeway promptly at five o'clock.

The last few days had been tense between them. Really, he thought, nothing had been the same since Angela got back from the West Coast. She seemed distant, preoccupied, even a little put out with him. She kept talking about "moving on," and "clearing out." He wasn't sure what she meant by that, except that it seemed to mean leaving Los Alamos.

They were of two minds about the situation. Rollins felt that the Berriman business would eventually blow over, especially if they were successful in framing Parker. Maybe he couldn't bring out any more weapons information, but there seemed no reason to give up his job, which was a good one, simply to run off somewhere to hide. Besides, what would he do somewhere else? All things considered, he liked his work at Los Alamos.

Angela, on the other hand, appeared to think her underground network was compromised and that Berriman's murder meant the end of the connection in California. Anyway, Angela was edgy. Even their sex life was off, something he had never experienced before with her. She seemed disinterested in making love, giving in to him last night in a detached sort of way.

Rollins got up from his desk and paced his small office. He could see that Theresa was away from her desk. He got up and walked across the hall, looking at the hall clock as he did so: it was nearly four-thirty.

He stepped into Theresa's office. Even her assistant, Veronica, was gone. He peered into Parker's office; he was out as well. This might have been the perfect moment to plant the cover sheet. Suddenly, behind him, he heard Theresa's voice.

"Hello, Bob," she said.

"Yeah, hi. Parker in?"

"No, he's in a meeting, but he said he'll be here late this evening. Want to catch him later?"

He shook his head and walked back across the hall to his office. In a few minutes he would leave to meet Angela. Maybe then she would explain what all this was about.

Poole looked at his watch and realized that it was time to leave. He gathered up his notes on the Berriman matter and put them into his safe, spinning the dial a couple of times.

He was just ready to collect his coat and leave when there was a knock on the door. The door opened and Farrell Doty stood in the doorway; behind him was Dawes.

"Good, you're here."

"Farrell. This is unexpected." When in the hell had he arrived? thought Poole.

"Have just a minute?"

"Sure." Poole sat back down and motioned to Doty and Dawes to take the chairs.

"Dawes has been briefing me on his activities here."

Poole said nothing, waiting for Doty to take the lead. He could guess what was on Doty's mind.

"We consider the identification of Parker's computer terminal an important breakthrough."

"I thought the computer people said the intrusion could have been done from any similar terminal in the lab. It was that sophisticated."

"That's true," said Doty, "but then, there are only a few individuals with circumstances as, uh, questionable as those surrounding Parker."

"I'm not convinced..."

"Ed, I appreciate your concerns, but believe me, we've considered everything."

"What now, then?"

"We're watching him twenty-four hours a day and tapping his home."

"Why not call him in and talk with him?"

"That's premature, Ed. If he's working with someone, we want to give him a chance to make contact."

"And my office?"

"Continue with everything. But discreetly, of course."

"And the others?" Poole thought of the list of names of primary suspects.

"We're watching them as well. We just want some time."

Poole nodded and sat back in his chair. "Does Parker even know his terminal was identified?"

"No, and it's important that he doesn't."

"What about Merritt?" Poole wondered how the laboratory's director would react to one of his brightest and most promising staff members becoming the center of the investigation.

"We'll talk to him."

Well, this was the FBI's call, he thought, but knowing that didn't make him feel any more comfortable.

Work traffic had just begun to thin on Highway 84.

They had been waiting ten minutes, sipping iced tea and parked off to one side of the Big Burger where they had a good view of the parking lot. Rollins was content to watch the "low riders" poking along the highway, their cars tying up traffic behind him. As far as he could tell, each car was ten or fifteen years old but had been meticulously rebuilt and rode no higher than four or five inches off the ground.

Angela leaned her head back against the rest, one hand lightly holding the steering wheel, the other clutching an envelope containing the cardboard sheet marked TOP SECRET and five thousand dollars in cash. In her pocket was a 9mm pistol with a silencer, wrapped in a plastic food bag.

She was just about to close her eyes when she saw an old brown pickup pull into the lot from the highway. The sun hit the windshield and prevented her from seeing the driver clearly, but the cab seemed to have only one person in it. For a moment she sat perfectly still, almost afraid to move and draw attention to herself. Finally she saw the driver's door open and a young man step out and look her way. It was Vargas.

"Wait here," she said to Rollins. "I'll be back in a few minutes." Rollins nodded, relieved to be in the car. He didn't care for all the subterfuge that seemed to be part of Angela's life. He watched her walk over to the ancient pickup, talk across the hood for a moment, and then get inside the cab, where she and the young Indian disappeared behind the wall of reflected sunlight.

He didn't feel comfortable with her latest plan, but Angela was insistent. She had asked for the cover sheet and explained that it was going to be planted on Gerald Sandys as part of a plan to connect him to Parker. She wouldn't say more than that and insisted he trust her.

Rollins looked at his watch; she had been in the truck for almost ten minutes. Suddenly he saw the passenger's door open halfway and linger that way for a few moments. Then Angela stepped down and walked quickly back to their truck.

"He'll do it," she said softly when she had closed the door.

"He'll do what?" he asked.

"Plant the cover sheet on Sandys after he kills him," she said.

Rollins felt a new wave of uneasiness wash over him at the mention of another murder. But it was more than that: he didn't feel comfortable with a third party involved. Somehow they seemed to be losing control of events.

"Why don't we just get Sandys ourselves?" he asked.

"Too risky. Besides, if things get too hot for us, we can always deliver Vargas to the police."

"Deliver?" Rollins looked dumbly at Angela.

"Dead, of course."

"Well, what do we do now?"

"We watch Vargas to be sure he doesn't screw up."

Johnny Vargas wasn't keen on killing an old man, especially a white guy in Los Alamos. But right now he was pretty high from the dope and five thousand dollars richer. For that, he could accommodate the red-haired Anglo woman. Man, he thought, what a bitch she must be to live with.

He pulled the sheet of stiff paper out of his pocket again and studied it. There was no telling what the hell the paper meant, but he guessed it must be important; all around the edges were bright red stripes. The words TOP SECRET were stamped across the top in big letters. But that was it; there was only the single sheet of paper, nothing else. He could only guess it meant something to the woman and her crazy man in the truck; they were paying him a lot of money to be sure that this piece of paper ended up in the pocket of a dead man.

Vargas thought about the six-pack of beer sitting on the floor-board of his truck a block away. That's what he really wanted right now. Instead, he was standing in the cold in the shadows of the old dude's house waiting for him to come out to his car. He had already put the wooden prayer stick from Angela on the seat like he'd been told.

The Anglo bitch had taught him one thing, however. There was money in the kind of things the Pueblos used in their ceremonies. Old stuff especially. His friend Juan in Española had some things that with a little luck he'd sell to a gallery somewhere. With the cop around, he'd have to forget about the store in Santa Fe.

He felt good, even if he was cold and bored, and wondered how he would spend his money. Maybe he would buy a newer truck, trade this old piece of shit in and get a Ford maybe two, three years old.

In the pocket of his denim jacket was the gun the woman had given him. He had never seen a pistol with a silencer on it and he was fascinated. It was good to have it, he thought, because you never knew when some *pendejo* might come at you. He could tell it was new, but tonight he would break it in. The Anglo woman wanted it back, but he would just have to see about that.

He had almost dozed off reading the latest physics journal when the telephone rang on the small table next to his chair. He jumped a little when he first heard it, and it took him a moment to identify the sound. For a moment, he thought he might let his wife get it—it was usually for her at night—but then he realized she was probably asleep watching television. He could hear the set going in the next room.

"Hello?" he said, still a little groggy. He didn't hear anything on the other end. "Hello?"

"Dr. Sandys?" asked a woman's voice.

"Yes," he said.

"You don't know me, but I have something that I think will interest you."

"Who is this?"

"It doesn't matter who this is. What matters is that I have some very special things."

"What kind of things?" Sandys was fully awake now, and he could feel the anxiety rising in him.

"I have some objects you will like," the voice said. Sandys wasn't sure, but he had the feeling that some effort was being made to disguise the voice. It sounded somewhat muffled, and there was background automobile noise.

"I have some nineteenth-century Hopi and Zuni masks, as well as some prayer sticks. Only the finest items, absolutely exquisite."

"Well, I don't buy from people I don't know," Sandys said, half meaning it. "I'm not interested."

"You should be," the voice said. "Arthur sent me to you."

Arthur! What the hell was he doing sending some crazy woman to him in the middle of the night? Was this the woman he had seen in the truck?

"I'm still not interested," he said, now fully awake.

"I know you're a cautious man, Dr. Sandys, but you really should see these items. There's nothing like them on the market."

"Where did you get them?" asked Sandys, knowing the answer.

"It doesn't matter, but they're clean if that's what you mean."

Sandys snorted. This was crazy. For all he knew, this was some pathetic policewoman trying to entrap him.

"Young lady, I have to go. I'm not interested in anything you have. Good night." He started to hang up when she spoke up again, this time with more animation.

"I understand your concerns but listen to me!" The woman paused, then continued calmly. "Go to your car, the Buick, and check the front seat. You'll find an example of what I'm talking about. Check it out and then make up your mind."

"What?" Sandys shouted. "You put something in my car?"

"Something special. An act of good faith on my part."

"What is it?"

"Check it out for yourself. I'll call back tomorrow. If you like what you see, then we'll talk business. Believe me, it's worth your time."

"How do I know this isn't some sort of trick?"

"My 'gift' is worth a lot of money. You'll see for yourself." The receiver clicked on the other end.

What in the hell was all this about? Sandys wondered. Was the call for real?

He got up and walked into the den and saw his wife asleep on the couch, the television on. She never even heard the telephone ring.

Sandys walked to the hallway and put on his jacket; it would be chilly this time of night. On his way to the kitchen and to the door to the carport, he stopped again in the den. His wife hadn't moved since he last checked on her.

From the wall by the door, he started to flip a switch that would flood the carport with light. Then he hesitated. Perhaps it would be a good idea not to draw attention to himself. Instead, he peeked outside the window. He saw nothing.

Cautiously, Sandys opened the door and peered out; again, there was nothing but the dark form of the car in front of him. He hurried down the small steps and over to the car. When he opened the heavy door he saw a small object, like a carved figure on a stick, lying on the front seat, in the indentation that separated the two electrically controlled front seats.

So it wasn't a joke, he thought. He had just climbed into the car and was reaching over for the object when he heard a noise. It was more of a shuffle really. He turned just in time to see the face of a young Indian he didn't recognize. Almost at the same moment he heard a muffled pop and then everything went black.

Vargas stood immobilized for a moment. He had never heard a gun with a silencer go off before except in the movies. The noise wasn't what he expected, but then he didn't know what to expect.

Amazingly enough, he had hit the old guy in the head, somewhere to the left of his temple. He pulled the folded sheet with the red edges out of his jacket with a handkerchief just like he had been told. It wasn't until he reached over the slumped body to find a pocket that he realized there was a great deal of blood and pulpy matter in the car. Although it was half-hidden by the shadows, he could tell that the object he had placed on the seat had little splotches of dark red blood on it.

Suddenly Vargas knew he had to get out of the car and away from the house. He stuffed the stiff sheet clumsily into the shirt pocket of the dead man and then wet the tip of one finger with some of the man's blood. Pushing the car door closed with his knee, Vargas drew a jagged line on the side window and studied it for a moment.

Just to be sure the old man was dead, he opened the door, lifted the gun again and pumped two more shots into the still body. As far as he could tell, the bullets hit somewhere in the chest, but he was no longer concerned. His job was done.

Now all he had to do was hike down the street, hiding in the shadows, and find his truck and drive away. The five thousand was still stuffed into the pocket of his jacket. He could feel it there, burning a hole and waiting to be spent.

Vargas shut the heavy door to his truck and once again fell into darkness. The nearest street lamp was a good block away and the night clouds obscured whatever moon there was tonight. With luck, he would be back in Española with Lupita in thirty minutes.

He figured the only thing he needed now was another beer and another joint. He could have both in less than an hour.

chapter 15

WEDNESDAY MORNING

Reyes sipped his third cup of coffee and looked at his watch again: it was ten o'clock and Gerald Sandys was thirty minutes late.

He looked around the dining room of the Los Alamos motel: the breakfast crowd had thinned and only a few tables with elderly couples remained. With their baseball caps and cameras, Reyes pegged them for tourists.

He wasn't sure what to do. Sandys didn't appear to be the sort who was late for meetings, even one with a policeman from San Ildefonso. The waitress came by with the coffeepot, but Reyes smiled and waved her away. Perhaps he should call Sandys and see if there was a problem.

Reyes got up and went to the pay phone in the lobby. He dialed Sandys's number. It rang five or six times before someone answered and a woman's strained voice came over the line.

"This is Officer Reyes. Is Dr. Sandys in?"

There was a gasp on the other end of the line. Reyes sensed something was wrong. "I had an appointment with Dr. Sandys this morning, but he's late."

"Who is this?" asked the other voice.

"This is Officer Reyes from San Ildefonso."

"Well, I'm sorry, but Dr. Sandys is dead."

"What?" asked Reyes.

"This morning. Murdered. This is a neighbor."

"Oh my God," he managed to say. "I'm very sorry." He hung up.

Stunned, Reyes walked back into the restaurant to get his hat and jacket and paid the check.

"You're friend's not joining you?" asked the waitress.

Reyes shook his head.

The murders of Sandys and Berriman had to be more than coincidence. He looked up the address in his black notebook and drove there. In front of the house were two Los Alamos police cars and a small group of onlookers in a neighbor's yard. Reyes suddenly realized that the neighborhood was more expensive than Berriman's; it was more like the one the Parkers lived in.

Reyes pulled up amid stares and parked his car. He couldn't see Smith, but he saw the big deputy. He decided to risk asking a few questions.

"How the hell did you find out about this?" asked the tall man.

"You won't believe this, but I had an appointment with Sandys this morning." Reyes looked around for Smith.

"He's inside," said the deputy as he uncoiled some bright yellow ribbon and began stringing it around the entrance to the carport. "I thought you'd been told to keep your ass out?"

"More or less. But I arranged an appointment with Sandys before my little talk with the men from the Bureau." He looked around. "What happened?" Reyes made way for the deputy to staple one end of the tape to a wooden post.

"Shot a couple of times. Head and chest. Close range." He moved to the next post and shot a staple into it. "They just hauled the stiff away. Take a look inside."

"Has it been dusted?" asked Reyes, peering through the open door on the passenger's side. Then he saw the streaks of dark powder.

"Yeah. Didn't get much. Prints on prints."

Reyes carefully stuck his head partially inside. At the same moment he caught the smell and saw the pools of dark blood and bits of skull and brain tissue.

"Jesus!" he cried. The smell was more sour than anything else, just on the edge of turning rotten. Bits of human tissue and blood were stuck to the inside of the passenger's window.

"Killer must have been no more than two, three feet away. Small caliber," said the deputy.

Reyes staggered backward. "Why?"

The deputy shook his head; he leaned against a post and lit a cigarette. "Don't know much. Apparently happened late last night, although he wasn't discovered until this morning. No apparent motive."

"Who found him?"

"His wife."

"Christ!"

"She was hysterical. Woke up last night and found the old guy gone and assumed he was out taking a walk, which he sometimes did. Then she went back to sleep and didn't look for him until this morning around eight. She found him in the car, slumped over like he had passed out." The deputy took a deep drag on his cigarette. His tone of voice struck Reyes as the one you would use to describe a bicycle robbery.

"You sure it wasn't suicide?"

"Coroner says no. Angle of bullet wasn't right, or something."

"Any evidence? Robbery, maybe?"

"Nope. None that we could tell. Nothing touched inside the house as far as the wife can tell. Anyway, there was something on the seat of the car next to the body that was worth a few bucks."

"What?"

"I don't know. Some Indian thing."

Reyes felt his heart race. "What kind of Indian 'thing'?"

"Some wooden deal. Painted. You know, it looked old. And there was this," he said, pointing to a dark red smear on the driver's window.

Reyes looked closely at what he had missed earlier: it was a wavy line of dried blood maybe six inches long, with a smaller streak flowing out of one end. There was no doubt in Reyes's mind: it was a plumed serpent similar to the one on Berriman's forehead.

Reyes's mind raced. "Any chance of seeing the object?"

The deputy laughed. "Smith's got it inside. The boys from the Bureau are with him."

Reyes felt the odds drop. He didn't know how much he could push his luck.

"Anybody see anything? Hear anything?"

"Nope. The killer could have used a silencer, though."

Reyes nodded. That made sense, all right. Whoever killed Sandys wanted to do it quickly. Quickly enough to take the risk of shooting him at his house and in an open carport.

"What time did you say this happened?" he asked.

"Won't know for sure until the autopsy. But the coroner thinks it happened around nine, maybe ten last night."

It would have been dark at that time, but still early in the evening. Had Sandys simply walked outside to check something and stumbled into the murderer, or had he been lured to the car?

"How was he dressed?"

"What?" asked the deputy.

"What was he wearing when they found him?"

The deputy appeared to think for a moment. "Just regular clothes. Why?"

"Well, was he wearing pajamas or something like that?"

"No. Just regular clothes." He thought for a moment. "He was wearing slippers, I think."

At that moment Reyes saw Smith walk around the corner of the house.

"I thought we had an understanding, Reyes," he said coldly. The edges of his mouth formed a frown.

"I had an appointment with Sandys this morning. He didn't make it," he added, almost as an afterthought.

"What the hell you want?" Smith was openly hostile now.

"He and I had agreed several days ago to meet this morning. When he didn't show up, I called and found out he had been murdered." Reyes paused, but Smith remained angry.

"Sandys and I were going to talk about the market in Indian artifacts. That's it. Nothing to do with Los Alamos."

"Well, he's not talking now, Reyes. This ain't your game."

Reyes forced a smile. "I'm on my way, Sheriff. But there's one thing."

The bulky sheriff sighed and shook his head. "What?"

"Apparently you found something in the car. Something next to the body."

"Yeah?"

"I understand it was an Indian object. Something old."

The sheriff looked at his deputy and then at Reyes. "Right. I don't know what it is, but it looks old. It's kinda like a wooden paddle, a figure on a stick." Smith made a gesture with his hands that Reyes took to mean ten or twelve inches long. "The paint's worn off. Is that all?"

"Any chance of seeing it?"

"Look, Reyes, I've got the goddamn FBI breathing down my neck on this."

Reyes forced another smile, a weak one. "I know that, but I've got evidence that someone around here is dealing in Indian religious works, probably stolen. And there might be a connection between what's happening here and down at my pueblo."

"Reyes," said Smith, a weariness creeping into his voice, "I don't have time for this goddamn conversation. You heard the FBI man: stay the hell out of this."

Smith walked away taking the deputy with him. There was no way Reyes was going to see the object found in Sandys's car.

As he drove away, he tried to imagine something from his own experience that looked like a paddle. At first, he couldn't think of anything. It wasn't until he was well on the road to San Ildefonso, winding his way down from Los Alamos, that an image hit him. It could be a prayer stick, or *paho,* he thought, remembering the Indian word for the religious article. It would have a handle and could easily have been painted at one time. There was no way of checking it out, at least at the moment, but his conjecture made sense.

Now, more than ever, he needed to find Johnny Vargas and the redheaded woman.

"His wife found him?" Poole asked, turning to Castro and Dawes.

"Unfortunately. It was a hell of a mess in the car."

"Poor woman," Poole said, mostly to himself. "She found him this morning?"

"Around eight. Apparently she fell asleep last night watching television. When she woke up, she realized her husband wasn't home and thought he'd gone for a walk. Apparently he'd do that sometimes when he had something on his mind."

"He had problems?"

"Mrs. Sandys doesn't know what. She was really shaken up, but she said he had been getting an unusual number of calls this last week and seemed preoccupied."

"I wonder what about?" mused Poole.

"She went to lie down and didn't wake up until this morning. When she realized her husband hadn't been home all night, she got frightened and called a neighbor. Both of them discovered the body in the car."

"Shot in the head and chest," added Dawes.

"Any apparent motive?"

"Nothing obvious, like theft or something." Castro seemed to know the details. He had taken the call this morning from the police.

"What's this object they found in the car?"

"Something Indian. We're not sure, but we're checking it out."

"And the blood on the left window?"

"Looked like someone ran his finger on the glass."

Poole nodded. "Any witnesses? Suspects?" Something was nagging him in the back of his mind.

"None," said Dawes. "It's a good bet, however, that it's related to the Berriman murder. Our list is being checked out."

Poole sat back in his chair. As with Berriman, none of the individuals seemed candidates for this type of brutality. "Even Parker?" he asked.

"Of course."

"The cop from San Ildefonso was there this morning," said Castro.

"Reyes?"

"Yeah. Claims he had a meeting arranged with Sandys."

That was it! thought Poole. That was what he was trying to remember. The conversation about stolen antiquities came back to him.

"I'd like to talk to him," said Poole.

"We'd rather you wouldn't." Dawes leaned closer to Poole's desk. "We've asked him not to do anything that might compromise our work. We certainly don't want to encourage him in any way."

Poole nodded. "What next?"

"We want to do a search of offices; everyone in Parker's group."

"Formally?" Poole could predict the outcry if they did.

"No. Quietly. At night."

The telephone rang in the outer office. Parker heard his secretary's voice and then the intercom buzzer went off on his telephone.

"It's Greenberg," Theresa said. "He sounds unhappy."

"Can you come to my office, David? Right away? It's important."

"What's up?"

"We'd better talk here." The voice wasn't angry, just tired.

"Of course. I'll be right there."

Parker got up and grabbed his coat. What now? he wondered. "I'm off to Greenberg's. I don't know when I'll be back."

"Your plane for Vegas leaves this afternoon," Theresa said.

"I know. But Greenberg sounds upset. I'll be back as soon as I can."

Theresa nodded and watched him hurry out the door and down the hall.

Greenberg's office was only a few doors down the marble hallway. Parker walked briskly in and nodded to the secretary.

"He's expecting you," she said.

Parker was surprised to see the young FBI agent named Dawes sitting in one of Greenberg's chairs. He knew this conversation wasn't going to be about lasers.

"You know Dawes from the FBI?" asked Greenberg.

Parker nodded.

"Something terrible has happened, David," he began. "Something *else*, I should say." Greenberg looked wearily away toward the bookcase against the wall. "Gerald Sandys has been murdered."

"What?"

"Dr. Sandys was murdered, apparently last evening," said Dawes. "His body was discovered only this morning."

"Oh, good God!" mumbled Parker. "I don't believe it."

"Believe it," said Greenberg.

"We think there's a connection between this event and Dr. Berriman's murder two weeks ago."

"How?"

"A very expensive Indian relic was found next to the victim's body."

"Relic?" asked Parker.

"A ceremonial object of some kind. We're not exactly sure, but Dr. Sandys's wife indicated it looked like something from one of the nearby pueblos."

Parker suddenly thought of Elisha. Like Sandys, she was an expert on pueblo religious objects. Was there a chance, a bizarre one, that she was in danger?

"He was shot in the head," said Greenberg suddenly. "Shot in the goddamn head sitting in his own car." The man slowly shook his big head. "This isn't good," he said. "Washington is going to think we're a den of spies down here. And God knows what the press will say!"

Parker was silent. There was no doubt that there would be repercussions from this.

"Dr. Parker, I hope you won't misinterpret this inquiry, but there's something I'd like to ask you."

Parker looked at Dawes. "What?"

"Just as part of standard procedure, I wonder if you could tell me where you were last night?"

Parker was incredulous. "Are you suggesting that I had something to do with this?" he asked, his voice rising.

"No, sir, we're only interested in accounting for individuals connected with this case."

"*Connected* with this case?" asked Parker. "What do you mean by *connected*?"

"Well, your association with Dr. Berriman, of course."

Parker felt energy draining from him.

"Just tell him where you were, David. He asked me the same thing. All of us could be the potential victims of this madman."

Greenberg was missing the point, he thought. Perhaps they *were* in danger, but the question from Dawes had a more ominous edge. All of them, Parker now knew, were suspects.

"I worked here last night, in my office, until maybe ten-thirty, eleven."

"You were here the entire time?" asked Dawes.

"Yes. Well, no, not all the time. Elisha—my wife—came by around nine and we had a hamburger together."

Dawes made a note on a small pad he had in his lap; they had already pulled the evening building roster. Parker's statement checked out with the record; theoretically, there was time for him to drive to Sandys's house and back.

"Do you remember where you had dinner?"

Parker sighed. "Nearby. At the Hamburger House."

"Have you had any contact with Sandys in the last few weeks?"

"No. In fact, I don't know when I last saw him."

"You had no contact with Sandys?"

"I said no." Parker felt irritation rising within him.

"I don't think it'll be necessary, but it is possible that we'll want to talk to you. Will you be in town?"

Greenberg nodded.

"I'm leaving for Las Vegas this afternoon. The Nemesis test is day after tomorrow."

"Nemesis?"

"It's the code name for our underground nuclear test," said Greenberg. "Nemesis is the Greek goddess of retribution."

Ten minutes later, Parker was left alone with Greenberg.

"This isn't good, David. Not good at all." Greenberg looked drained too. "Damn it, there's a lot at stake! The success of the project. Your nomination. A goddamn lot."

"I think the project will survive, Francis. My future with Los Alamos may not." Parker tried to smile.

"Don't joke about it, David, there's too much at stake. Let's pray this is the end of it."

"God, I hope so." Inside, a voice told him not to count on it.

Angela sat on the hearth of the fireplace, the flames from the fire turning her hair a golden red. One by one she looked through a stack of papers, throwing each one of them into the fire. From the couch where he sat, Rollins was certain he could make out the shapes of her breasts through the robe she wore.

"We need the gun back," she said.

"Is there a problem?"

"Maybe."

"What would he do with it?" he asked. But as soon as he did, he regretted it.

She stopped, one hand in midair, and looked up from her papers. "A junkie with a nine millimeter pistol? What the hell do you think he'll do with it?" She shook her head.

"How can we plant it on Parker?"

"Not we. You." She resumed throwing papers into the fireplace. She was cleaning house, she told him. "You did it once. What the hell?"

"Yeah," he said finally, not even sure what he was acknowledging.

Rollins looked at his watch. He was several hours late for work. He had called in, of course, saying he would be an hour or two late, but now he was feeling anxious. Surely Sandys would have been found by now and the word would be all over the lab. Unless, of course, Vargas had screwed up. He told himself he needed to be careful. But somehow, this morning, he wanted to stay with Angela. At least for a while.

"You say Parker stayed late last night?"

"He said he was trying to finish some work before he left town."

"Good," she said, throwing a batch of credit card receipts into the fire. "That might help."

"When can you get the gun?"

"Today. Maybe tomorrow."

"Parker leaves this afternoon for Nevada. That's one less person in the house tomorrow."

"I'll get it." She looked back at Rollins. "You scared?"

He just stared at her. He wasn't sure how he felt. He wasn't even sure what was going to happen tomorrow. Right now he needed to leave for work, but what he really wanted was to stay and make love.

chapter

16

THURSDAY

Tevis had a funny feeling inside. Suddenly he wasn't hungry anymore. Instead, he just stared at the newspaper and the photograph of the elderly man who had been murdered.

He had no idea who Gerald Sandys was, and under normal circumstances Tevis wouldn't especially care about someone he didn't know being shot in the head. But what had caught his attention was the fact that Sandys had been Isaac Berriman's boss for years and that he was a major collector of Indian art. Even more significant, the newspaper reported that a small Pueblo "prayer stick" dating from the last century was found next to Sandys's body by the police. *That* fact hit Tevis like a punch in the stomach as the image of the Shadow Man came into his head.

Tevis got up from the table and poured what was left of his Cheerios into the sink. Then he went to his room and pulled open the drawer of his chest containing the two prayer sticks from Tsankawi. They were still hidden in the rear of the drawer, each covered by a T-shirt.

For the moment, Tevis didn't dare look at the flat, wooden images. The question now was what to do with them. The bad feeling in his stomach came back, and he wondered if even having them in the house might bring the Shadow Man back.

He closed the drawer slowly, almost reverently, and sat down on his bed until he heard his mother telling him he would miss the bus for school. He had to do something. He quickly opened the drawer of his desk and rummaged around until he found the small white card. As soon as he could, from a phone near school, he would call the policeman at San Ildefonso.

"You canceled my airline reservation?" asked Parker.

Theresa nodded. "And the rental car and the motel."

"Good." It had been on the spur of the moment, but he had decided yesterday afternoon to cancel his trip to Las Vegas. He feigned a heavy work load, but really, with Sandys's death, Parker felt uneasy and even unwilling to be away from home. Besides, he had hardly slept last night, tossing and turning, and trying to imagine what it meant to be suspected by the FBI.

He got up to get another cup of coffee from the machine in Theresa's office and ran into Rollins.

The tall man looked startled. "I thought you were in Nevada."

"Too much to do here. I decided to stay." There was no way he could explain to Rollins the uncomfortable feeling he had about the events at the laboratory.

Rollins stood at the doorway, looking a little confused. "You're not leaving?"

Parker just looked at him. "I said no."

Rollins shrugged and walked across the hall to his office and shut the door. Parker watched the light go on behind the frosted glass door. What a strange man, he thought. Behind him, he heard the telephone ring.

"It's someone named Dick Lawton calling from Washington," Theresa said.

"Good," said Parker, "I'll take it in my office."

He went in and closed the door. "Dick, good morning."

"What the hell's going on down there?" The voice on the other end wasn't friendly.

"What do you mean?"

"I mean what the hell's going on? Two murders in two weeks?"

"You heard already?"

"I just got a call from someone at Energy."

"Good news travels fast."

"This isn't funny, David. There's a lot going on that could be jeopardized by the events at Los Alamos."

"Look, Dick, I don't know the details. A former scientist was murdered the other night. The FBI thinks there's a connection between his death and Berriman's death a few weeks ago. As far as I know, nothing has happened to compromise the work of the laboratory."

"I thought this guy worked for Berriman."

"Other way around. Berriman worked for Sandys for years."

"What about you?"

"What do you mean 'me'?"

"I understand you've had some trouble."

"Where are you getting this crap?" Parker felt the same uneasy sensation as yesterday when he talked with the FBI. There was an undertone in the conversation that he didn't like.

"It doesn't matter where I got it. I know that the FBI is deeply involved."

Parker thought about the list of missing combinations and the fact that the FBI was investigating his group. He decided to say nothing.

"When the senator hears about this, he won't like it. He feels that the hysteria over Soviet spying can't do anything but harm the SDI program."

"The work isn't compromised, Dick."

"But you might be."

"Oh hell, Dick, come on. The work's going well here. There's an underground test this afternoon in Nevada that could confirm a lot of theoretical work. The senator will like that."

"The point is, you and your lab may be a political liability, David. I don't know what's going to happen to your nomination."

Parker hung up. His ticket out of Los Alamos looked slimmer than ever.

It was the sort of thing she could do even as a child: make a list in her head, add to it, eliminate, keep it up to date all the time. She always knew where she was by the list in her head.

Now, reviewing that list, she knew that not a lot remained to be done. The most important item was to finish the business with

Vargas. Then she needed to withdraw most of the money she kept in her checking account in Los Alamos. Not all, of course, but most of it. She had half a dozen good Indian pieces left, but she could take them with her to California. They might fetch four or five thousand. That was about it.

She couldn't quite decide what to do about Rollins. She had to leave, of course, and he couldn't. Or wouldn't. But the last thing she wanted was a big scene before she left and Rollins moping all over Los Alamos. The best thing all around was for her to just pull out. Later she could try to explain that it was important to separate for a while, to test the relationship. They could always get back together later, when things settled down.

She caught herself smiling. It wasn't likely that they would get back together, but then, who knew for sure what was going to happen. California was more her speed anyway.

The telephone rang. It was probably Rollins. He had taken to checking on her with telephone calls once or twice a day. Somehow, she figured, he sensed she was going to leave. She hated it, but then, that only made it easier for her.

"This is Vargas."

"Good. We need to talk."

"What about Arizona?"

"That won't be necessary now."

"What the hell, woman? I need the money." Vargas's voice suddenly turned surly.

"Look, I've made other arrangements. What I need is the item I loaned you the other night."

Vargas said nothing. Then she realized there was something else she had to do.

"But I have another job for you, if you want it."

Vargas waited a moment before responding. "What kind of job?"

"Something local. A man in Santa Fe needs a favor. It'll pay a thousand."

"What is it?"

"We'll talk about it this afternoon."

"Where?"

"You know the mineral baths in Ojo Caliente? The old hotel?"

"That dump closed down a long time ago."

"I know. But meet me there. Four-thirty."

"Española."

"No. We can't be seen together right now. Everything's too hot. The old hotel at four-thirty."

He hung up without a word.

Angela thought for a moment. There was no way she could trust Rollins to do this. He was edgy, she thought, too edgy to do something carefully. She would have to go herself.

Reyes watched through the window as White drove away; the man had been kind enough to stop at San Ildefonso on his way to Taos.

He picked up the creased photograph that Jenny had loaned him. The image hadn't changed, although something inside of Reyes wanted it not to be there: Jenny sat working her pottery as her brother stood nearby. It wasn't the best photo of Johnny Vargas, but it had been enough for White. It was the same young man who had approached him a week ago in Santa Fe with something to sell.

Reyes felt sad; he had really hoped that Johnny wouldn't be the one, for Jenny and her mother, of course, but also for himself. It was never pleasant go after a member of one's own people.

The sky was unusually bright, and Doty was forced to put on his pair of prescription sunglasses. He had had them for years but didn't like to wear them since they pinched the bridge of his nose.

He sat in the back of the car with Whitewater, his senior agent; another agent drove the Bureau's unmarked Albuquerque car. Whitewater handed him a package of papers and photographs. Outside, he saw they were passing a private airfield at the north end of Albuquerque.

Doty briefly scanned the court document he had just been handed.

"Any problems?"

"None," replied Whitewater.

"Good. When can the technical coverage start?"

"I need to talk with Dawes and check the family's daily pattern.

We should be able to hit Parker's car in the parking lot, but wiring the house may take some time."

Doty shifted in his seat. The murder in Los Alamos had forced his hand sooner than he had anticipated. But there was a lot at stake, and the pressure from Washington was intense. The circumstantial evidence on Parker was too strong to ignore.

"The tap on the family telephone is already live."

"Good," said Doty. "I think we're going to have some visitors from Home in the next day or two, and I want us to look good." Home meant Washington.

"No problem."

"Anything from the taps on the laboratory lines?"

"Nothing. We check the log summaries regularly."

"Do we have anything on Gerald Sandys?"

"Nothing provocative. Bank records show nothing out of line. Employment history is nothing but exemplary. He retired just six months ago, you know." The agent flipped through a folder.

"I heard. What about his art collection?"

"Reputedly one of the best of its kind. He's been collecting for thirty or forty years and his wife claims he was a national expert."

"What was the object they found in his car?"

"Something used in religious ceremonies." The agent flipped another page. "Old. Worth maybe three, four thousand dollars."

Doty shook his head. "Incredible. Was it part of his collection?"

"We don't know for sure. His wife doesn't recognize the piece, but then she never paid much attention to her husband's collection."

"Any prints?"

"Mixed on the car. Smudged in some places. It appears that the murderer wore gloves of some kind."

"What about the Indian thing?"

"Nothing."

"Anything on the cover sheet?" Doty picked up several eight-by-ten photographs. One was a copy of the cover sheet containing Berriman's name. The photo revealed that the paper had been folded over twice.

Whitewater saw Doty thumb through the photographs.

"No prints, but we're running the cover sheet through the lab right now for chemicals, fibers, anything out of the ordinary."

"What about the other names on here? The ones before Berriman's?"

"We're checking them out now, but the library confirmed they were legitimate users."

"Naturally. Anything else?"

"Not yet. I'll confirm the taps on Parker as soon as they're in."

"What about the others?" He referred to the other four suspects on their primary list.

"All covered. We'll move in with taps when you give the signal."

Doty shuffled through the rest of the photographs and winced when he came to one of Sandys. It was a shot taken from the victim's side of the car, revealing the body slumped over. Clearly visible was the huge stain of dried blood on the velour upholstery.

"Nine millimeter?" asked Doty.

"Yes, sir. Used at close range with a silencer."

"Still powerful enough to exit, right?"

"Look at the next shot."

Doty flipped to the next one and saw a photograph taken from the passenger's side. The body's position was reversed but now he could see bits and pieces of skull and tissue plastered to the seat. A third photograph showed additional matter stuck to the door panel and window.

"This is something more than espionage," said Doty. He thought about Berriman and the slashed throat. Both murders seemed to have a violence associated with them that was more than simply murder. "The man who did this is sick. There's no telling what he'll do next."

He gathered up the photographs and handed them back to Whitewater. Through the window he saw the small community of Bernalillo, which stretched for two or three miles along the Rio Grande. With spring, the trees along the river ran a spectrum of greens.

There were five of them, although Parker was their strongest shot. Doty had a gut reaction on this man. And if Parker was their man, he was violent and dangerous. "We need to move on this as fast as we can," he said. "Before something else happens."

Angela took the back way to Ojo Caliente. Just in case.

That meant taking Highway 75 to Pilar, cutting west to High-

way 285, and then heading down to the small village of Ojo
Caliente. The place had been popular earlier in the century with its
mineral mud baths that survived today in the form of health spas.
She had never been to them, although she was tempted by the claims
of natural healing. Rollins had always dissuaded her, citing the fact
that no scientific evidence existed for the therapeutic qualities of
mud.

The hotel she was looking for had been abandoned sometime
before the last war. She had driven by it often enough, wondering
what sort of people had once come there to be treated. Now she was
coming to perform a cure of her own. She hoped that Vargas had
had the sense to park behind the abandoned building, not in front
where his truck could be seen from the road.

From the slight rise she could see the rooftops of several
buildings. Off to one side were the hulking remains of the old
hotel on the edge of town. Angela looked at her watch: it was
4:35.

Pulling off the main road, she looked for tire tracks but saw
nothing. Damnit! she thought, he'd better show up.

Not until she was nearly at the edge of what once had been a
paved driveway did she see the tail end of a pickup. That was good:
they couldn't be seen from the road.

As she pulled up next to his truck, she realized Vargas wasn't in
it. She parked and for a moment considered leaving the motor
running. That, she reasoned, might put Vargas off.

Cautiously, but conscious of appearing confident, she walked
toward the wall of the dilapidated building. She was considering
whether she should enter when she heard a shuffling sound behind
her and then a hand came around her breasts. At the same moment
she smelled alcohol.

For a moment she did nothing. The hand stayed where it was
and didn't tighten. Then, as smoothly as she could, she pushed
backward and then whirled around to see Vargas looking drunk and
mean. He was drunk and maybe stoned, she couldn't tell. He just
stood there for a moment without saying anything.

"Do you always do that?" she asked.

Vargas produced something like a snort. "You got the money?"

"Of course. You got the gun?"

Vargas laughed and leaned back against his truck. "Right here," he said, patting the pocket of his coat. "That's not all I got," he said, moving his hand to his crotch.

"I'll bet," she said, "but what about the job in Santa Fe?"

"What I gotta do?"

"A man I know is having trouble with a business partner. A disagreement over funds, you could say. He thinks a little scare by someone might just bring the partner around."

Vargas eyed her for a moment, then seemed to drift off.

"What do you say? It's worth a thousand." Angela smiled. "You get five hundred now, and five hundred after you pay a visit."

"All right," he said. Vargas put his hand in his coat pocket and pulled out the gun. "I might need this for the job."

"You're supposed to scare the guy, not kill him." She realized she had to conclude this quickly; there was no telling what was on his mind.

Vargas shrugged. "I think I like it." He kept the gun in one hand, running the other over the blue gray barrel.

She had to be quick, she thought. Why in the hell had she put her own gun inside the bag instead of her jacket?

"Okay. Keep the goddamn gun. Here's the name and address in Santa Fe," she began, lifting the bag from her side. At the very edge of her vision she saw Vargas raise his gun. "Here," she said, holding the bag out, "take it. The money's there."

Momentarily, she locked eyes with Vargas. His were crazy, like they were wired electrically.

With all the calm she could muster, she held the bag and forced a smile. "You got something else on your mind?" she asked, widening her smile.

For a long moment she wasn't sure it had worked. Only after many seconds did Vargas lower the gun. Making his snorting sound again, he started toward her and grabbed the bag from her hand. This is it, she thought.

Just as he lowered his eyes to study the bag, she kicked Vargas in the groin with all her strength. Vargas let out a loud gasp, as if all the air had been knocked from him, and began to fall forward, grabbing his crotch, his hands still on the gun and bag.

As he fell forward, stunned, she quickly positioned herself and kicked him again, this time in the head. Her boot made an odd sound as it hit his skull and knocked him slightly to one side. Angela grabbed at the gun in his hand and, after a short struggle, managed to wrench it free. Just as she was about to use it, she realized she needed to use her own pistol.

Vargas, conscious but obviously dazed and in pain, stared up at her from the ground. He still clutched the bag to his body, one hand holding tightly to the leather strap.

Angela couldn't get the bag away from him. It wasn't until she had kicked him again, this time in the left side, that he emitted a loud cry and let go.

Shaken, she fumbled with the zipper and nearly tore the bag open. With Vargas still on the ground, groaning and wrapped in a fetal position, she pulled out her .38 snub-nose. She knew enough about it from her friends in California to remember that it was effective only at close range. If she shot Vargas, she needed to be damn sure that she killed him; she didn't need a witness.

Looking around, she bent down and studied Vargas for a moment. He appeared only vaguely aware of what was happening. From the bag she pulled an old towel and wrapped her hand and gun with it. Very carefully she put the muzzle against his head and pressed down.

At that very moment Vargas turned and looked up. Angela quickly repositioned the gun against his forehead. Just as his eyes widened, maybe with an understanding of what was happening to him, she pulled the trigger.

Even with the towel, the sound was deafening. Angela pulled back quickly, struggling to keep her balance. As quickly as she could, she bent down again and fired another shot into Vargas's chest. The body shot back into the ground and up again like it had been jolted by an electric shock. Then the body was perfectly still, blood rapidly forming a pool under the head.

Angela started to leave and then crouched again. Pressing the gun against the body, she fired a third shot into the dead man's groin. Pushing the body with her foot, she pulled out his wallet; there was no sign of the five thousand. Stuffing the wallet and both guns into her bag, she made a quick visual search of the immediate area and hurried to her van, throwing the bag onto the front seat.

It was odd, she thought, but she had the sensation that her hand was still warm from the gun.

chapter 17

FRIDAY MORNING

Merritt nervously adjusted his glasses with the finger of one hand. "I don't believe it. Are you sure?" He knew when he got the call at home this morning at six that it had to be more bad news. Now, at five minutes past seven, he knew he had been right.

Doty pushed three plastic folders across the table to Merritt. Each one contained a report and a "top secret" cover sheet; on both sheets the name "Isaac Berriman" was the last name in the checkout column.

"And you found them in Parker's office?"

Doty nodded. "Last night. In a sweep of his offices."

Merritt was dumbfounded. "I find it hard to believe." He gingerly picked up one of the reports. Encapsulated in plastic, they looked unsanitary, even ominous. "Where were they?"

"On a shelf, carefully hidden behind some books."

"Could someone else have planted them there?" Merritt looked around the table: Doty and Dawes sat on one side of his conference table, Poole and Walthers, Merritt's deputy, on the other.

"Who?" asked Doty.

"Well, isn't that what you're investigating?" replied Merritt. He pushed his glasses up again.

"The point, Dr. Merritt, is that this is the first major break we've had; David Parker has to be considered carefully in light of this development. If someone else planted the documents in his office, we need to know who." He leaned forward slightly. "And if more than one individual is involved."

"What do we do in the meantime?" It was Merritt's deputy.

"We take every precaution we can and see where he leads us."

"What kind of precautions?" asked Poole. He had said nothing up to now, trying to understand how a man like Parker would be stupid enough to hide stolen weapons data on a bookshelf. If it wasn't deliberate, it was goddamn careless! One of the lab's holiest rules was to protect classified information. People just didn't leave documents lying around, especially after the events of the last few weeks. Even more puzzling was the fact that the classified reports were the ones checked out to Berriman! Why leave those where they could be found?

"Cut his access to the computer; pull him inconspicuously away from important work. We'll do the rest."

Merritt turned to Walthers, his deputy. "But isn't Parker scheduled to participate in the big program review on Monday."

"Of course."

"Hold him off," said Doty. "Can he be given another assignment? Something that will keep him busy for a day or two? That's about as much time as we can hope for." Doty needed the delay. Washington was sending down its most experienced espionage man over the weekend to coordinate the wrap-up, and he hoped to keep the investigation open until then.

"What about these documents? Won't he know they're missing?" Walthers held one of the plastic folders up.

"We propose putting them back where we found them. Just for the day."

"Won't he know you've been looking around?"

"Maybe. But if he does, he might feel forced to act. If there are others, he may contact them. Or he may contact his Soviet connection."

"Assuming he's the one," said Poole dryly.

Doty ignored the comment.

"Well, I feel that I have no choice but to involve Greenberg in this. After all, it's his division that's the victim in this business. And he certainly needs to know about Parker. It's crucial." Merritt rapped his finger on the table to emphasize the point.

"Of course, we'll yield to your judgment in this, Dr. Merritt, but I would like to ask you to hold off talking with Dr. Greenberg for a day or two. I think that the fewer people who know about this, the better."

Merritt suddenly thought of something else. "Is anyone else in danger?"

"That's impossible to say," replied Doty. "We'll be as careful as we can."

"Is that enough?" Walthers asked. "How can we guarantee no one else will be murdered?"

"There are no guarantees, gentlemen," said Doty, "but we have the nation's security to think about." He cleared his throat and leaned forward again, as if to confide something very special. "National defense has been compromised by this man. We don't know who he's working with, or what methods he's using to pass defense secrets along. But we have to stop it. Now."

Merritt thought about it for a moment. He felt very uncomfortable with the thought that someone else might be killed. There was no telling what the press would say, or what kind of legal trouble might arise from such a situation. There was even the question of his own liability. "Why don't we just ask Parker in here and give him a chance to explain? Perhaps there's an explanation."

Doty gave Merritt a small smile. "He'll have his chance, Dr. Merritt."

"All right, but, ah, I'll have to speak to Greenberg sometime over the weekend. Or Monday morning at the latest," said Merritt.

"Of course."

"Do you plan to search Parker's house?" asked Poole. At least, he wanted to know what else the Bureau planned.

"We're obtaining a warrant to do that, but again, we want to hold off for a few days."

Doty prepared to leave. "I'm sorry about this, Dr. Merritt. I know that it's unpleasant. But we may have contained the damage."

It was a quarter to eight when Theresa flipped on the lights in her office. Arriving fifteen minutes early gave her just enough time to make coffee, open his safe, and make a quick check of Parker's schedule for the day. At eight o'clock, she would start counting the minutes before Veronica, her assistant, arrived, always late.

She was just about to walk down to the women's bathroom and fill the coffeepot with water when she tried opening the top drawer of her desk. It moved only a quarter of an inch and then jammed. After pushing and pulling on it several times, she popped it open. It was then that she realized someone had been in her desk.

As far as she could tell, nothing had been taken, but items had been rearranged. Her desk was always organized, something she had done since childhood. She opened the lower drawer, the one containing nonclassified files in manila folders, and saw that they were bunched irregularly together, very different from the way she had left them last night. As she got up and looked around the room, she noticed a number of small things out of order, like the books rearranged slightly on the bookshelf. The night cleaning crew hardly ever dusted, she thought.

She walked into her boss's office, hesitating for a moment at the doorway and peered in. Nothing looked changed until she looked at the bookcase and saw that, like hers, the books had been slightly realigned. Parker's large Hopi pot on the top shelf had been moved as well. Nothing was moved more than an inch or two, but it was just enough for her practiced eye to catch.

"No coffee yet?" a voice said behind her.

She gasped slightly and turned around. Parker was standing outside his office looking at the small table that held the coffeepot and utensils for making tea.

"Running late?" he said, looking at her.

"I haven't made it yet." She felt her heart pumping quickly.

Parker laughed. "I can see that." Then he noticed the look on her face.

"Are you all right?"

"Someone has been through our offices, David."

"What?"

"I'm sure of it. Things are rearranged."

"Why?"

"I don't know, but someone went through my desk and poked around the office. They were in your office too."

"How can you tell?"

"The books." She pointed to the bookcase and then to the Hopi pot. "See. It's not centered like it was."

Parker studied his desk then opened a drawer. "I can't tell anything." He looked around the room. "Are you sure it wasn't the cleaning crew?"

"I don't think so. They've never touched the bookcases and never gone through my file drawer before. Why would they do it?"

Parker shook his head. "I'll report it. Why don't you make some coffee now?"

Parker sat down at his desk without taking his coat off. Theresa was right. Someone had been in the office. He couldn't say what had been changed, but he could sense it.

Suddenly he remembered an incident from last night. When he arrived at his house there was a car parked at the edge of their cul-de-sac with a man in it. It was a nondescript car—blue, he thought—and it sat there until Parker pulled into the carport and parked. Then the car drove away.

Was he being watched? he wondered. He looked around his office. If it was Security, what were they looking for?

Then another thought hit him. Was he the only one they were after? He decided this was something he should talk to Greenberg about.

By ten minutes to eleven, several dozen people had gathered in the warehouse next to the laser facility. A television monitor sat on a metal dolly at one end of the room with an image that never changed: an open expanse of desert empty except for a few mobile trailers at the bottom edge of the screen. A voice from the monitor counted down by the minute. Parker stood with his hands in his pockets talking with members of his staff. Greenberg wasn't far away.

In their jeans and Nike shoes and with security badges hanging from open collars or belt loops, his staff had the peculiar Los Alamos look. A few had beards and long sideburns that seemed more typical of the seventies than the eighties. The conversation was animated although everyone kept an expectant eye on the TV screen as the clock neared eleven.

They were watching a live image by cable of the underground

Nemesis test in Nevada, a hundred miles or so from Las Vegas. The camera stood on a tower half a mile away, its image fixed on a single point on the surface. Fifteen hundred feet below that point, at the end of a large tunnel, was the nuclear weapon that had been so carefully assembled at Los Alamos the week before. On Thursday, it had been reassembled again underground, surrounded by an army of metal pipes, electronic equipment, and the laser that Parker's group had labored on for over a year.

Parker moved over next to Greenberg. The voice from the monitor called three minutes. Parker knew that a phalanx of electronics had now taken over and that, short of some emergency, nothing would stop the test. He imagined someone in the Nevada control center, in a room in the center of a concrete building, with his finger on a red button, ready to sever the connection on command. What if the finger slipped? How would they explain the loss of an eight-million-dollar test?

"I hope this goddamn thing works, David," said Greenberg. "We need a success."

"Well, it isn't our weapon, only our laser."

"I mean our laser, of course. This division needs a morale boost after the last few weeks."

"We've done our best."

"Hopefully."

The voice called out, "One minute," and the animated conversation died down. Everyone stared at the twenty-seven-inch screen.

At ten seconds, the voice from Nevada Control started counting down second by second and stopped at three. Then the voice said simply, "Detonation."

The next image was anticlimactic. The ground shook in the center of the screen and a cloud of dust rushed outward across the desert in concentric circles, and then back again in seconds, like waves on water. Then, as the aftershock hit the camera mast, the image rocked back and forth for a few moments and the desert was perfectly still again. Sometime in the next twenty-four hours—scientists never knew exactly when—the ground would drop out and a large crater would form.

The room broke out in cheers. At least, the nuclear device had detonated. The question now was whether the experimental laser had worked.

Some of the tension seemed gone from Greenberg's face. Parker knew it would take a few minutes for members of their staff stationed in Nevada to scan the preliminary test data and tentatively announce the laser experiment a success or not. Everyone's spirits were up; they talked in whispers, hanging around for the telephone call to come.

"What are the odds?" asked someone.

"Good," said Parker, hoping that it was true.

Finally, the telephone rang. Parker's assistant picked it up and listened for a moment. Then his face broke out in a smile and he gave a thumbs-up. The room broke into cheers. The man covered the other ear with his hand and turned toward the wall, straining to hear the voice at the other end. Then he hung up.

"Only preliminary, but it looks good. We don't know how much, but there was activation."

Greenberg slapped Parker on the back. "Thank God!"

Parker nodded. Thank God for something.

Someone finally turned off the monitor and individuals began to drift back to their offices and laboratories. Parker leaned over to Greenberg and said, "I need to see you for a few minutes." Greenberg nodded and drifted toward the wall.

"Someone went through our offices last night," he said. "I presume it was Security, but I don't know."

"They looked at several, or so I've been told."

"You knew about this?" Parker was incredulous.

"Not until people started complaining this morning."

"Was it Poole?"

"I assume. Maybe the FBI."

Parker found it hard to say what he felt. "Well, what the hell are they doing? Do they suspect us all?"

Greenberg's jaw tightened. "Well, I don't know anything more about it. But you can hardly be surprised, given the events in your group."

Parker felt stunned. It wasn't the reaction he expected from Greenberg. "I don't like the feeling that I'm not trusted, Francis. They came in the middle of the night."

"Look, David, the whole division, not just your group, has got to be under scrutiny right now. Berriman, the missing reports, the computer taps, they're all bad news for the laboratory. I told you, there's a lot at stake here."

"What the hell do I do?" asked Parker.

"Stick it out. Hopefully, they'll find out who's behind this soon. Until then, don't give anyone any reason to believe that something else is going to happen."

Parker didn't know what to say. None of this seemed real to him.

"You've got one thing going for you now that you didn't have before," said Greenberg.

"What?"

"This test. If it's as good as we think, you'll be hot shit again."

Parker shrugged.

"One thing, though," said Greenberg.

"What's that?"

"The report that Berriman pulled off the central computer. The one he printed out? It has the critical configuration for this test."

Parker suddenly knew what Greenberg meant.

"It's a hell of a lot more valuable now than before."

chapter 18

FRIDAY AFTERNOON

He was just walking out when the telephone rang. He heard the secretary pick up the phone and call his name. He started to walk out anyway but then changed his mind. All of his life he could never resist answering the phone when it rang; he always wanted to know who was on the other end.

"It's some kid named Teddy," the young girl said. She didn't look up from her teen magazine.

"This is Reyes." In the background he could hear children playing.

"It's Tevis Parker, Mr. Reyes."

"Yes, Tevis," he said. He hadn't expected this.

"Well, I'm calling, you know, like you said." The boy sounded nervous.

"Sure, Tevis. What can I do for you?" He forced himself to be patient.

"Well, I was thinking about, like, what we talked about."

"What was that?"

"You know, about Tsankawi. And the cave there. I think I remembered something."

Reyes held the phone closer to his ear.

"It's about the cave and the dead man. I think I remember seeing something in the cave with him."

"What was that, Tevis?"

"There was something at his feet. Figures made of wood. I think they're called prayer sticks."

Reyes remembered the two small dimples in the floor of the cave. "What did they look like?"

"They were figures on sticks," Tevis said, and described what he had found. Images of *pahos* formed in Reyes mind; for a moment he saw his uncle holding a pair of prayer sticks in a ceremony in a kiva. Reyes was a teenager then.

"Do you know where they are now, Tevis?"

There was silence for a moment on the other end. "Well, maybe."

So the boy had found something, Reyes thought. All of his conversations with Tevis now made sense, but he had to be careful. Tevis had to be comfortable in admitting he had taken something from the cave.

"Do you think you could help me find them?"

"Maybe. I guess so."

"Good, Tevis. That will help me a lot."

"Mr. Reyes? Tom?" He hesitated briefly. "If we find them, will that make everything all right again?"

"What do you mean?"

"You know, with the kachinas?" Tevis was thinking of the murders and the awful thought that his father might be next.

"It will help, Tevis." Reyes looked at his watch. His meeting with Ed Poole was in less than twenty minutes.

"I tell you what, Tevis, can I come to your house and talk with you this afternoon?"

"No. Not my house." Tevis didn't want his parents to know anything about the stone figures. "Tomorrow at the library. Where we met before. At ten."

"Okay. And, Tevis?"

"Yeah?"

"Thanks." He hung up and walked to his car.

There was no telling what had prompted Tevis to call and talk about the cave. Maybe his conscience bothered him, Reyes thought.

Or judging from the conversation, maybe he was worried about violating some Pueblo taboo. He seemed to take the business of kachinas very seriously.

Poole sat in the dining room of the McDonald's on Trinity Drive. He was sipping on a vanilla shake, something he knew he should never do if he hoped to lose weight. Behind the red tile counter a couple of pimply-faced kids were noisily horsing around.

He was taking a chance meeting with Reyes, but he hadn't been able to put the conversation with the man out of his mind. He looked at his watch; Reyes was several minutes late. Was the man going to show up? He was just about to get up and get a new straw when Reyes walked in.

"Get yourself something," he shouted to Reyes. Poole was surprised at how tall the man was.

Reyes nodded and ordered a soft drink and sat down at the tiny table.

"I think this was built for kids," he said, as his knees hit the underside of the tabletop.

Poole smiled. "Everything going okay?" he asked.

"So-so," he replied.

"Still thinking about Berriman and Sandys?"

"Yeah."

Poole tried to lean back, but the small table kept him sitting upright. The back of the small chair dug into his back. "You said something earlier about stolen artifacts. What did you mean?"

Reyes told him what he could remember, beginning with the cornmeal in the cave and the information he had about the extensive, and lucrative, underground market. He mentioned Johnny Vargas but didn't give his name. Poole never pressed him.

"There may be a connection here in Los Alamos," Reyes said.

"What kind?"

"The young Indian apparently works for a woman, or helps her in some way. Apparently she lives in the area. I think she has a Los Alamos telephone number."

"And she's the conduit for the stuff?"

Reyes nodded. "She may also be involved in stealing it."

"Do you think there's a connection between this business and the murders?"

"I'm not sure, but the objects in Berriman's house—the expensive ones—were the sort of thing that the black market deals in. Especially the stone object, the deity stick. What struck me about those objects, however, is that they were in a closet and not displayed."

"That would suggest Berriman didn't want anyone to know about them," said Poole.

"Yes. Or it could mean that someone put them there to make it look like Berriman was hiding them. If that was the case, they were in a hurry; clothes and ski equipment were all thrown on the floor of the closet while everything else was neat and orderly."

Reyes leaned forward a little, concerned that they might be overheard. "In both murders, the killer left a streak of blood, like a symbol."

"Do you know what it means?"

"The symbol could be that of a serpent, a figure in Pueblo mythology called Avanyu. The image itself may not mean much, but the fact that someone left it in both murders suggests that it was the same man."

Poole nodded his agreement. "An Indian?"

"I don't know. Maybe an Indian, maybe an Anglo who knows about these things."

"You know the FBI's involved?" asked Poole. "I can't tell you much more than that, but they don't seem to think this line of investigation is important."

"There's something else," said Reyes. "I've talked with the Parker boy again, and he thinks there were several religious objects on the floor of the cave with Berriman." He didn't try to explain what the objects were or to clarify what had happened to them.

Poole lifted his eyebrows. "What does that mean?"

"If it's true, someone put them there to be found. Maybe to make it look like an Indian was involved. Only they got lost or misplaced in the shuffle, and the investigation took a different direction. Whoever put them there knew something about Indian customs."

"That could be Mrs. Parker."

"Yes. But there are a lot of other people around here who know something about Pueblo customs." He thought of Tevis and the kachinas the boy imagined. "They could be the same as the thing left in Sandys's car."

Poole nodded. "I understand the boys from the Bureau asked you to keep out of their investigation." Poole said it kindly.

"We had a talk," said Reyes.

"I'll bet." He looked at Reyes; he knew that the man wasn't going to let go of this, no matter what. He also knew that Doty would be furious that he was meeting with Reyes. "Do you know anything about this woman in Los Alamos?"

"Only that she has red hair and drives a van with California license plates."

"Let me see if I can find out anything." Poole looked at his watch. "I need to get back to my office." He took out a card and wrote a number on the back of it. "That's my direct line. Okay?"

Rollins hoped this would be the last thing he would ever have to do with Parker and with the whole goddamn business.

He stood in a phone booth half a mile from Parker's house looking for the telephone number. He sure as hell didn't want to run into Parker or his wife at their home just as he was trying to break in. Jesus! he thought, this had to be it. No more, no matter what Angela wanted.

His whole world was upside down. Angela was in a bad mood all of the time now. She kept talking about separating, something about it being good for them. Then she wanted to make love. Then she wanted to be by herself. She didn't know what the hell she wanted.

At work, however, everything seemed the same. People were still talking about the murders and the latest rumors, but there was no mention of Parker in all of this. He was still in his office and still in charge of the group. There were rumors that their offices had been searched, even gossip about some staff being arrested. Maybe Angela was right; it was going to take this gun and the last report from Berriman's safe to finally nail Parker.

Rollins dialed the number. There was a click and he heard a woman's recorded voice: "Hello, this is Elisha Parker. I can't come to the phone right now, but—" He hung up. Hopefully, this meant no one was home. There was, however, the car he had spotted earlier a half-block away with a strange man sitting in it. It was parked facing the street where the Parkers' house was located.

What frightened him was being seen breaking into Parker's house. It sat at the bottom of a cul-de-sac where it would be very easy to be spotted. The car with the man could be police. Or maybe FBI. The last thing he wanted was to be caught with the gun that killed Sandys and a classified report belonging to Berriman. The only chance, he figured, was to come up from the canyon to the back of the house. From what little he had seen last week, the Parkers' house sat on the rim of a canyon with trees between the house and the rim.

Rollins left his car parked on the street about a block away and found the path that wound down to the valley. It would take him maybe twenty minutes, he figured, to wind his way around the edge of the canyon wall to a point where he could climb up into the backyard.

When he finally pulled himself over the edge, he was dirty and sweaty and he had banged his leg on a tree trunk.

He was in luck, though, because the house looked empty. As carefully as he could, he stalked his way from tree to tree to the back door and tried the doorknob. It was locked. Rollins studied it for a moment; like many people he knew, the Parkers had never replaced their door locks with newer, more sophisticated equipment. They didn't even have a deadbolt. This one was maybe ten years old.

He pulled a screwdriver from his back pocket and carefully worked it on the bolt between the door and the frame. In a few seconds the door pulled free.

The house was perfectly still, giving it an eerie, queer feeling that Rollins found strangely exciting. He worked his way up the stairs to the main floor and found the study. It was just as he had seen it last week: the expensive rugs on the floor, the pots on the shelves, and the desks back to back. For the first time, it struck Rollins as ironic that Berriman, Sandys, and now Parker, were all connected by their collections of Indian art.

Now he had to decide where to leave the gun and report. He ruled out the desk; Parker himself might find it and dispose of it. Putting it behind some books was no good; it might never be found.

He finally chose a large Hopi pot, almost two feet in diameter, that rested on a hip-high cabinet. Very carefully, he removed the gun from its plastic zip-lock bag and, holding it with a handkerchief, laid it at the bottom of the pot. Then he put the twenty-page report on top.

For a brief moment, he considered checking out the rest of the house. He wondered what Parker's bedroom was like. Maybe they had a collection of pornographic tapes? Then Rollins remembered something.

He walked over to Parker's desk, the one Parker had sat at the night they talked, and ran his hand over the smooth redwood finish. Parker's was the neater, the folders and papers stacked carefully; his wife's was messy, with groups of papers stuck in with magazines and shopping receipts and most of the surface taken up with a computer. What he was looking for wasn't on the desk top anymore.

Rollins started to reach for the center drawer and stopped. He pulled out the handkerchief again and grabbed the drawer pull. There, right in front, was the old brass compass, the one with the initials BSA on the lid. He stuffed it in his pocket and hurried out.

With any luck, Parker wouldn't need it anymore. And if not, well, he wasn't likely to miss it.

The magazine's cover featured a shirtless young man, next to whose androgynous face was a cutline that read: "Todd Tells All." Elena, the secretary, scarcely looked up as she handed Reyes the pile of small pink telephone slips. The first was from Ed Poole; the second from Jenny.

"Poole say what he wanted?" He had called less than ten minutes ago.

Elena kept her eyes on the magazine. "Nope."

Reyes dialed the Los Alamos number and asked for Poole. "It's Reyes," he said.

"Look, this isn't much. We've run a computer check on laboratory parking permits; no vans with California plates. We're gonna try local insurance companies, but that'll take time." Poole shuffled his notes. "But a woman here in the office lives in White Rock. She claims she's seen a light-colored van with California plates lots of times."

Reyes felt a rush of excitement. "Thanks," he said. It wasn't anything concrete, but it was a lead.

He looked across his desk at an old portrait of him and his grandfather taken in the forties when Reyes was eight or nine years old. His grandfather wore his overalls, the only thing Reyes could really remember the old man wearing. Somehow he could imagine his grandfather pointing him toward White Rock and telling him to go as a hunter, a man with all his senses able to see the subtle, almost invisible clues left by the quarry.

Then he thought of Jenny. He dialed her number and let it ring six times before someone answered.

"Hello?" the voice said. It wasn't Jenny; it was an older woman's voice.

"Is Jenny Vargas there?"

"Uh, wait," the woman said, and put the phone down on something. In the background, Reyes could hear voices. He couldn't hear what they were saying, but it was several different people.

"Hello?"

"Jenny? It's Reyes."

"Oh, thank God." Her voice was distraught.

"What happened?" he asked. Her voice told him something wasn't right.

"It's Johnny."

"What about Johnny?"

"He's dead." She paused. "He's been murdered."

"What?" Reyes felt sick to his stomach. Something told him it wasn't just a fight between drunk Indians.

"He was shot. The police think yesterday sometime." She fought back her emotions. "They didn't even find him until this morning. Some kids."

"Where was he?"

"Ojo Caliente. Behind an old hotel or something."

Reyes searched for words. "Jenny, I'm sorry, I really am. Are you all right?"

"I'm okay."

"What about your mother?"

"She's broken up. My aunt and uncle are here now. No one knows what to think."

Reyes didn't know what to say. This wasn't the time to ask questions about the murder itself. "Will she be okay?"

"I think so. They want her to rest now. The police have his body and we can't do anything until tomorrow. There's nothing to do but wait."

"I know it's hard, Jenny, but the police need to learn as much as they can. It may mean finding the person who did this."

"Do you think it's connected to the thing you're investigating?"

"Maybe. But I don't know what to think right now." It was quite likely that Vargas had been killed for what he knew, or had done, including the murders of Berriman and Sandys. Somehow, he didn't feel he should say that to Jenny.

"Tomás?"

"Yes?"

"Can you come by later, in a couple of hours? I really need to talk to someone."

"Of course. I'll see you then." He hung up. This wasn't how he had planned to see Jenny again. There was no telling what was involved, but his instincts told him that Jenny was right. Johnny's death was connected to the black market, and maybe to the strange business on Tsankawi.

chapter

19

FRIDAY EVENING

The old truck hit the deep cut in the road and bounced violently, throwing Reyes against the roof of the cabin. He cursed as his head struck the hard metal.

It was almost dark, and he was surprised to see that there were no cars in front of the house. From the conversation earlier, he had assumed there would be lots of family and friends around. For a moment, he wondered if Jenny was even home.

There was only the single light burning on the porch. From the front, it looked as if the house was deserted. He pulled up in front and cut the engine. Somehow it didn't seem necessary—or appropriate—to honk.

He knocked on the door and waited. Through the small glass window he could see a soft glow coming from inside; a dark form approached and grew larger.

Jenny opened the door. "Thanks for coming," she said.

Reyes stepped inside and instinctively hugged her. She seemed to soften into him, wordlessly putting her head against his chest. For the first time, Reyes noticed how much shorter she was than he; something had given him the impression she was taller. Against the rear wall, curved in the traditional form of the kiva, was a fireplace whose softly burning embers cast the room's only light. From a doorway he could see part of the kitchen harshly lit by a single overhead bulb.

"I'm very sorry," he whispered, stroking her shoulder.

"I know," she said. After a while she pulled away and wiped her eyes. "Would you like some coffee?"

"Yes, thanks."

"Sit down. I'll be just a minute."

Reyes took off his leather jacket and sat down on the couch and looked around. The room looked like a hundred others he had seen in his life. The couch was old and frayed at the edges, with a bright Navajo blanket hanging over the back cushions. The two other odd chairs didn't match. On the wall were an assortment of religious pictures—Jesus smiling, Jesus with a burning heart—and photographs of young children and family. Scattered around were beautiful pots, probably made by Jenny or her mother, he thought, and photographs of an older woman holding ribbons and other awards. One photograph, in a cheap gold frame, was a man in an Army uniform.

The room smelled of burning wood and years of people coming and going, and aging. To Reyes, it smelled like his grandparents' house.

Jenny came back with two mugs. "Black, right?" she asked.

"Right."

She threw two small logs on the fire and sat down in one of the chairs.

"You don't have to talk about it if you don't want to," said Reyes.

"I want to," she said, blowing on her coffee. "Be careful, it's hot."

Reyes held the cup, letting it warm his hands. "Where's your mother?"

"She went to my aunt's."

"Did you tell them I was coming?" he asked.

"Yes. I said you might be able to help find Johnny's killer."

"I don't know that," began Reyes, wondering if somehow their relationship would turn on his finding the murderer.

"I told them Johnny was mixed up in something, something bad. They understand. They think it's drugs."

"Maybe it is."

"Maybe."

"What happened to Johnny?"

"He was shot. Three times. Once in the head." She took a sip of coffee and was quiet for a moment. This couldn't be easy for her, Reyes thought.

"The highway patrol said that he had been kicked a few times. They have no idea of who did it, of course. I'm not sure they even care."

Reyes knew what she meant. A dead Indian wasn't news around here.

"Some kids found him this morning. They were playing hooky from school and wandered behind an abandoned hotel in Ojo Caliente. Johnny's body was next to his truck."

Her eyes grew moist again, and she hesitated before she continued talking.

"The police think he'd been killed the day before. The autopsy will tell more." She let out a short, nervous laugh. "He was only twenty-three, you know."

"Did they find anything on him. Was it robbery, maybe?" Reyes was thinking about drugs.

"His wallet was missing, but they don't think it was robbery."

"Why not?"

"They found almost forty-eight hundred dollars on him. It was in his coat." She shook her head slowly. "The keys to his truck were still in his pants pocket."

Forty-eight hundred dollars? wondered Reyes. Where in the hell would he have gotten that?

"Did he have that kind of money?"

"No. In fact, he borrowed a hundred from me last week."

"Do you know where he's been the last couple days?"

Jenny shook her head. "He's been in and out. Sometimes drunk, sometimes high on grass. You could smell it on him. We never knew where he went or who he spent time with. Some days he didn't come home at all." She dabbed her eyes. "My mother always worried about him but never did anything. She never could."

"Did he leave anything here? Clothes, personal effects. Things like that."

"A few things. You want to see them?"

"Yes." He immediately thought of the objects in the photographs given to Richard White in Santa Fe. He followed her into the hallway that led to two small bedrooms and a bathroom. In the hall was a closet.

"He kept some clothes there. When he stayed here, he slept on the couch in the living room."

Reyes looked through the clothes hanging haphazardly on wire hangers. There were a few shirts, thin and well worn, and a denim coat and a heavy sheepskin coat with a fur lining. On the floor was a dirty duffel bag that Johnny must have used as a suitcase. Reyes searched the heavy coat. In one pocket was a stained coaster with Budweiser printed on one side. On the other, scribbled in a childish hand, were the words "Indian Lover." In the other pocket was a matchbook from a Los Angeles bar called the Beaver Club.

In the duffel bag Reyes found only dirty underwear, some loose change, and small personal items, nothing that would give a clue to how he lived in California.

"He kept some things in his truck," said Jenny. "The police have all that until they finish their investigation. But I don't think they found anything important."

Reyes stood up and stared at the closet. Twenty-three years old and this was all Johnny Vargas had to show for his life. And forty-eight hundred dollars and three bullet holes. What a waste, he thought.

"There's nothing here, Jenny. Maybe the truck will have something."

She shook her head. "He didn't have much. I remember when he first left home—he was fifteen, I think—he didn't even take a toothbrush."

"It's over now, Jenny. You have to put it behind you."

They walked back to the living room. The small logs were embers now, giving out little heat but burning with a warm, incandescent glow.

"Did he say anything about what he was doing?" asked Reyes.

"Not really, he just came and went." She carefully put another small log upright in the fireplace. "He did say something about going to Arizona. Something about making a 'run' there."

"Did he say for whom?"

"No. Just about going sometime soon. I heard him tell someone over the phone."

"Do you know who he was talking to?"

"No. I gave the highway patrol a list of what friends of his I could remember. But I don't think that will help."

"Will you make a list for me as well?"

"Sure. But I think he was hanging out with different people this last year. I never saw them. He never brought them by, either—I think because of Mother."

Reyes didn't know what else to say. He just stared at the fireplace and then at Jenny. She seemed lost in her thoughts, looking very sad and very tired.

"Are you staying here by yourself tonight?"

"I'll go to my aunt's, I guess. I thought someone should stay here in case the police called or something."

The fire briefly crackled and tiny sparks shot off of the burning log.

"Well," he began.

"Please stay," she said and looked up at him. Her eyes reflected the dancing light of the fireplace. Still, he thought, they were sad.

He got up as she did and took her again in his arms. She hugged him first and then lifted her head and kissed him. It was then that he knew that it wasn't only her sadness and sense of loss that drove her now. She led him by the hand to her bedroom and slowly, but without awkwardness, peeled back the covers on the bed, and then began to take off her clothes. Watching her watching him, Reyes did the same and lay down first.

The room was small but very unlike the rest of the house. The curtains were simple and white and very sheer, and the moonlight tumbled easily inside, giving the room and the naked walls a soft, caressed feeling. The only other furniture in the room was an antique chest and a chair with an elaborately carved back.

Jenny laid the last piece of clothing on the chair and turned back toward the bed. She was so beautiful, he thought, and suddenly he worried that he might seem too old to her. But she only lay down and quickly melted into him, kissing him again and stroking his chest.

For a moment he lay there without moving, letting her touch

him. Then slowly he brought one arm up and around her, and then the other, feeling her and breathing her in.

"I think you should talk to him, too," said Elisha. "I think we both need to reassure him that everything is all right."

"Where is he?"

"In his room, I think."

"You think something's wrong?"

"I don't know." Elisha shrugged. "He's probably taking everything too hard. The psychologist said this might happen."

"Has he said anything?"

Elisha thought for a moment. "He talked about Sandys; that seems to have bothered him."

"Why?" Parker was confused.

"I think he sees a connection between that man's death and Berriman's."

"Oh, Jesus," said Parker. He had made the connection too.

He found Tevis lying on his bed reading a book.

"Tev?"

The boy looked up.

"You feeling okay?" Parker walked over and sat down on the edge of the bed.

"Sure, Dad."

"You've been awfully quiet the last couple of days." He reached over and felt Tevis's forehead with the back of his hand. It felt normal.

"I've been thinking."

"What about?"

He shrugged. "Lots of things."

Parker laughed. "Like what?"

"Like about that man that was killed, the old one."

"What about him?"

"I read that he collected Indian things, old things."

"So?"

"So did Berriman." Tevis paused. "Both men were killed."

"That's true, Tevis, but that doesn't necessarily mean anything. Those men could have been murdered for very different reasons. And by different people."

"We collect those things too, Dad."

"So do lots of people, Tevis, and they aren't in any danger because of it."

Tevis thought for a while. He remembered the prayer sticks from the cave now hiding in his drawer. And he remembered the newspaper article about Sandys which said something was found in the dead man's car.

"Dad, what if someone knew something about those murders but didn't say anything? And maybe it happened again. I mean, someone else might be murdered."

Parker ruffled his son's hair. "Well, if someone knew something important, he should say something about it. But you shouldn't become too concerned about this. I don't think anything else will happen."

"But, Dad, the police haven't caught anybody yet. It could happen again."

"Tevis, look, the police are just as worried about him as you are and much better able to do something about it. Believe me, they're doing everything they can to see that no one else is hurt. Don't worry, they'll catch the man."

"But what if it isn't a man?"

"Well, what could it be? A ghost?" Parker smiled, but his son's face was serious.

"Yeah, maybe a ghost. Or a spirit, the kind the Indians believe in." Tevis thought of the voices he had heard at Tsankawi, and the shadow figures that seemed to be all around him.

"I think those spirits are in your head, son."

"But what if someone was being forced to do these things, by the spirits? I mean, like they were possessed or something."

"Tevis, you'll just have to trust me. There aren't any evil spirits at work. It's some bad men, but they're human beings like you and me." He took his son's hand and held it for a while—remembering how, when his son was first born, he had marveled at the infant's perfectly formed hand.

"Come on, it's time to eat." Parker leaned down and kissed Tevis on the forehead. Please, God, he prayed, please protect my son.

Later that night, when he and Elisha were both in bed, they

talked in whispers even though the door was shut and Tevis had been asleep for several hours.

"You were right," Parker said. "He is worried about the murders. He thinks that some Indian spirit may be behind it all."

Elisha ran her hand slowly over his chest. "He's so young to have to deal with things like this. And so imaginative, it makes it all the worse."

"Has he been to the psychologist this week?"

"Yes. That helps, but every time it quiets down, something else happens." Parker could feel her breath on his shoulder.

She pushed closer to him. "What next?" she whispered.

"I wish I knew," said Parker, wishing he could predict the future.

"How's work?" she asked.

"Things are very difficult now. I don't mean with the project—that's fine. The test in Nevada went very well, in fact. It's everything else." For a moment, he debated whether or not to tell Elisha about the FBI's visit and the fact that his office had been searched.

"There's something else, something scary." He felt her hand stop over his heart and tighten.

"What?"

"Some of us at work are suspects in these murders."

"Who? By whom?" she asked.

"Me. Greenberg maybe. Maybe the whole goddamn group. The FBI is swarming all over."

"They must be crazy."

"No. But they have to suspect someone." He laughed quietly. "The FBI always gets its man, you know."

Elisha was quiet for a long while, gently resting her arm across his chest. "I have to tell you something."

Parker gently turned over on his side to face her.

"Someone, I guess the FBI, has been making inquiries about me in Albuquerque."

"What do you mean?

"With the chairman of my department, with a few others."

"How do you know?"

"One of them told me, swore me to secrecy. They said they were checking because of your work." She tried to remember everything she had been told. "But mostly they wanted to know what I did and if I bought or sold Indian art. They were very circumspect."

"Oh Christ, join the club." He tried to play it down but he knew she was worried.

"I think the chances for my nomination to the presidential commission are pretty low right now. At least I won't be traveling to Washington very much."

"What will it mean at the lab? Will they do anything to you?"

"I don't know what they can do. I haven't done anything, of course, except maybe be careless about security. I guess Merritt could kill any promotion within the lab."

"But what about Greenberg? Won't he help?"

What about Greenberg? he thought. The man seemed to have changed a lot under the pressure of the last few weeks. There was no telling where he stood right now, except that he was damned worried about the project.

"I think so. But this has been hard for him too. He must see everything that's happened as a threat to his last, great success in the 'business.'" Parker emphasized the word for effect. For once, he was sympathetic to Elisha's dislike for weapons research.

"Maybe it's time to get out, David. Accept one of the offers you have from a university to teach. You'd make a good teacher, you know."

Parker smiled and leaned over and kissed her.

"I can't leave, not just yet, anyway. What would the FBI think?"

"I don't mean tomorrow. But when this business is over?"

"What about the project?"

"Who gives a damn about that? Do you? Really?"

He couldn't answer. Not with certainty, anyway.

"I think I do. I think I owe it to my group to stay with it long enough for someone else to take over. Some of the technical achievements have value outside of making bombs, you know."

"Does that make it worth staying?" she asked.

He couldn't answer.

"Well then, don't take too long, my love."

"Or what?"

"Or you may find yourself burned out for good." She leaned softly over and kissed his ear. "And I wouldn't like that at all."

chapter 20

SUNDAY AFTERNOON

Greenberg grumpily rummaged around in his pocket for his security badge and flashed it for the guard to see. The Hispanic man wordlessly pointed to the weekend roster to sign and then complaisantly waved him on. Greenberg headed for the fourth floor and an emergency Sunday meeting with Alan Merritt. The only good thing so far was that he found a parking space in the visitor's area immediately outside the building entrance.

His fervent hope was that nothing else was wrong, that someone else hadn't been killed. Most of all, he hoped nothing had happened in his division. Merritt didn't sound upset over the telephone, although he rarely displayed anything more than mild annoyance. But then, he had never called a Sunday afternoon meeting before.

As he walked into Merritt's suite of offices, Greenberg saw a young man with a familiar face sitting calmly on the couch. Then he realized the man was from the FBI.

"Good afternoon, Dr. Greenberg," said the agent.

"Uh, hello, is Alan in?"

"Come in, Francis," called Merritt from the inner office.

Greenberg walked in and was surprised to see no one else in the room. This wasn't good, he thought.

"Sit down, please," said Merritt, pointing to the couch and chairs on one side of the room.

"What's the FBI guy doing in the next room?" asked Greenberg.

"I'll explain in a minute. But I have some news, ah, to share with you first." Both men sat down. Merritt crossed his legs and his hands.

"This is very difficult for me," began Merritt, "especially because I know you're very fond of him."

Oh God! thought Greenberg, it *was* someone on his staff.

"But the FBI has assembled a rather strong case against David Parker."

"Parker? That's crazy!" Greenberg felt his blood pressure soar.

"Unfortunately, it's not, Francis," he said calmly. "They haven't linked him directly to the murders, but he appears to be involved in the theft of secret weapons data."

"Alan, that business with safe combinations, that could have been an accident." Greenberg floundered around for explanations. "Or someone else could have taken it."

"That's only one incident, Francis, there are others, far more damaging." Merritt carefully outlined the FBI's evidence, beginning with the events surrounding Berriman's death and ending with the discovery last week of Berriman's documents in Parker's office.

Greenberg shook his large head. "I just can't believe it. I can't."

"None of us want to believe that a trusted member of our staff is involved in something as shocking as this, but if it's true, we must act."

"Why don't we just call him in and ask him to explain?"

"I asked that too. But the Bureau believes that there is a chance he might lead us to others."

Greenberg's eyes grew large. "How many are there?" He wondered how many were in his division.

"I don't think anyone knows. Maybe Parker is working by himself; he doesn't seem the type to actually commit murder, though. But someone is."

Greenberg slumped back in the couch then sat up again. Suddenly he realized there were other implications.

"Do you mean to say, that some of us have been suspects all along? I mean, have I been a suspect in this goddamn business?"

Merritt tensed slightly and moved toward the edge of his chair.

"You have to understand, Francis, that initially everyone had to be considered a suspect, even myself."

Greenberg knew damn good and well that Merritt was never considered.

"It's only in the last week that the evidence has accumulated sufficiently to narrow the focus on Parker. The documents in his office were the breaking point."

Greenberg didn't know what to say. "All of these things are circumstantial, Alan."

"Maybe, but I'd like to ask Mr. Dawes, from the FBI, to step in for a moment. I just wanted you to hear about David from me personally." Merritt got up and walked over to the door and asked Dawes to come in.

"Dr. Greenberg is understandably upset, Mr. Dawes, but I've shared with him the events and circumstances of the last few days."

"I'm sorry that it's a member of your staff, Dr. Greenberg."

Greenberg just stared at the floor. "Not as sorry as I am."

"What's important now is that we give Dr. Parker an opportunity to contact anyone else he may be working with."

"Well, I damn well hope so. Maybe he's a spy, but I just can't believe that he's a killer too!"

"We want you to act as if nothing is wrong, at least for the next day or two. We think that's all the time we can afford."

"Then what?" asked Merritt.

"We'll close in. Arrest him." The young agent paused. "Of course, at that time, he'll have a chance to clear himself, if he can."

Greenberg wondered if that was the case. Once charged, would he really be able to clear himself? And what would happen to his career at Los Alamos?

"What about the briefing tomorrow, Alan? Parker's planning to attend."

"I don't think he should. The information is too valuable, and if he's still in a position to pass further data to the Russians, then he'd have even more after tomorrow's meeting." Merritt cleared his throat. "Can't you, ah, find some excuse to keep him away from the meeting. Something that wouldn't be too obvious?"

"He's going to suspect something. What can I say?"

"I think that's a chance we'll have to take, Dr. Greenberg." As Dawes left, Merritt signaled Greenberg to stay behind.

Greenberg moved to the edge of the chair and stared at the mauve-colored carpet Merritt's wife had chosen for the office. "If David is the one, if he's guilty, what will happen to the project?"

"Nothing. Unless we lose the funding from Washington, of course. Defense could give it to Livermore, you know. If we keep it, however, we may well have to make administrative changes."

"Changes?"

"New leadership, of course. It's nothing personal, Francis, but for morale purposes I think we have to consider putting the project somewhere else."

So that was it, thought Greenberg. Merritt would take the project away from him.

"This isn't a happy situation," Merritt continued, "and when it's over, we can reassess the situation and make decisions then. Right now, let's just get it over with and minimize the damage."

Greenberg was dumbfounded; he didn't know what to say. He had worked for four different directors at Los Alamos and had never been intimidated by any of them. Now, for the first time, he felt powerless. There must be *something* he could do, he thought.

"Yes," said Greenberg. It was all he could say.

Reyes hung up. The pay phone clicked and deposited his quarter somewhere inside with a hollow sound. He turned and stared one more time at the van sitting at the other end of the parking lot. It was tan, four doors, and had California license plates.

He had just talked with Poole, who had a friend run the plate numbers through the computer. Running them through his office at San Ildefonso would have meant contacting the highway patrol and waiting maybe an hour. He looked at the notes he had scribbled on the back of a gasoline receipt: another cross-check gave the name and address of a woman living in White Rock, New Mexico, by the name of Angela Olmstead. The same woman co-owned a home with a Los Alamos employee named Robert Rollins.

It had taken him seven hours, since ten this morning, and a full tank of gas to locate the van. Even then, it was mostly luck that he found it. Twice he had driven through all of White Rock, street by street, looking for any van with California plates. In the end, it was sitting in the parking lot of a shopping center.

Reyes felt his grandfather would be pleased that the hunt had gone so well, although he wondered how the old man would explain the sheer luck involved. It didn't really matter anyway.

Now he waited. He wanted to see if the owner was a redheaded woman. If so, he wanted to see her face.

"I saw Greenberg come into the building," said Castro. "Must be important."

"Maybe." Poole was only half-listening. He had other things on his mind and he was angry. "Goddamnit, they won't return my phone calls." He waved his hand at the telephone. He had been trying to get through to Doty for almost an hour now. It was nearly dark, and he knew the chances of talking with the FBI before tomorrow were growing thin. They obviously didn't put a lot of value on what he might have to tell them.

"What about Dawes?"

"I tried him. He's out too."

"Do you think it's that important?" asked Castro. He was searching his pockets for a match.

Poole just stared at him. There was a connection now that had not existed before: a member of Parker's staff—Rollins—was tied in with a woman who very likely was dealing in stolen antiques, the sort of objects that both Berriman and Sandys had in their collections. *Goddamnit!* He felt it in his gut; it meant *something*.

"Yes, I do," he said quietly. "Don't you see? This man works for Parker. He knew Berriman, and he was one of the names on *our* list."

Castro nodded and snuffed out his cigarette. "The FBI's had his name as well."

"Shit!" said Poole. "Get me Rollins's personnel file again."

"It's gonna take a while; it's locked up."

"Just get it."

Poole sat quietly in his chair for a moment. He tried to piece together what he knew about Parker, the murders, the computer break-ins, and now the news about Rollins and his girlfriend. Something told him that all of this tied together.

Castro returned with two folders in his hand. "I brought you

Parker's too." Poole took them both and said good night to Castro.

He started to look at them and then stopped. He needed to be fresh when he did this. He would start first thing tomorrow morning.

The sun was down, and a thin line of yellow along the horizon seemed to divide all of the world between dusk and night.

The four of them were on the outskirts of Santa Fe, on a high point just before the road descended into the city. All over Santa Fe, in a sea of dark, tiny lights flickered on and shone like those on Christmas trees.

Parker turned south on Cerrillos Road. Toward the edge of town, he pulled into a parking lot jammed with cars and pickups. Next to the huge, prefabricated building was a tall electric sign that read MR. R'S.

"You said you wanted to dance," said Parker. "Well, this is *the* place." Tom and Linda, their friends from Stanford, stared out into the noisy lot.

"Will we be safe here?" Linda asked. Six cars away, two pickups were gunning their engines while the occupants shouted obscenities at each other.

Elisha took her hand and laughed. "Of course. This is a family place."

The band was already playing when they walked in, a slow, soulful piece about a farming man who had lost his wife to a truck driver.

"Oh my," said Linda, looking at the auditorium-sized room. The band played up front, on a small stage, and tables ran on either side of the huge dance floor to the rear of the room, where the bar stood.

"I've never seen so many cowboy hats," said Tom.

They found a table halfway back from the stage and ordered beer. The waitress wrote nothing down and danced by herself to the music.

"Come on!" yelled Tom to his wife, "let's get going!" Both of them rushed to the wood floor and disappeared among the couples.

"Thanks for coming, David," said Elisha. "This is what they wanted to do." She reached over and touched his arm.

"It's all right," he said, "I needed something like this after last week." He patted her hand and then paid for the beer when it came.

All weekend, he had busied himself with small tasks around the house: stacking the firewood, washing the truck, sorting through the stack of papers left over from income tax. Anything to keep from thinking about the lab.

Elisha leaned over and kissed him gently on the cheek. "Wanna dance, stranger?" she whispered.

He nodded and they joined the crowd. The band was playing a song called "The Lights of Albuquerque."

Later, when all four of them were sitting back at the small table, Tom tried to signal the waitress again. "Another round!" he shouted.

"Look!" said Elisha. She pointed to friends of theirs from Santa Fe. Maurice and Joan glided elegantly among the couples, the silver from their belts and jewelry occasionally catching the rotating ceiling lights and playing them back like bursts from a flash gun.

"Everyone looks like they're having a wonderful time," cooed Linda.

"Except for that guy," said Tom.

"Where?"

"Over there, sitting by himself." He pointed to a small table across the room. A man with a face lost in the darkness sat by himself nursing a beer. He was wearing a dark blue blazer.

"I've been watching him," said Tom. "Several women have asked him to dance, but he just sits there."

Parker stared across the room. He couldn't do much more than make out the man's general shape and the fact that he wore a sport coat in a dance hall in which everyone wore jeans and cowboy boots. Was he an FBI agent? he wondered.

Parker leaned over to Elisha. "Do something for me, will you?"

"What?"

"That man in the coat may be watching me."

Elisha looked back across the room. "Oh, David, come on."

"Let's dance," he said, taking her hand and pulling her up from the table.

"When we get by the band," he said in her ear, "I'm going to leave you and get around in back of the guy. You go back to the table and see what he does."

"I don't like this," she said.

"Please," he whispered. He gave her a squeeze and broke away. From the dark end of the room he moved behind the man, clinging to the shadows until he found a table out of the man's view. A waitress quickly appeared at his table.

"A Coors Light," he said to the waitress, and handed her two dollars.

Across the dance floor, Parker saw Elisha walk back to the table and sit down. The three of them started talking. To his left, the man in the coat sat up stiffly and began scanning the dance floor as it emptied with the end of the song. From the stage, the band announced a ten-minute break and the colored lights dimmed on the stage.

With no one else on the floor, the man in the dark coat sat rigidly straight and methodically studied the room. Parker sat hidden in the shadows.

Parker got up and walked back to Elisha and his friends.

"Where've you been?" asked Linda.

"Restroom," he replied.

He leaned over to Elisha. "Well?"

"I think you're right. He was very nervous until you sat down, then he relaxed."

"Well, we've had enough," said Tom, "what about you two?"

"Let's go," said Parker. "How about something to eat? New Mexican food at La Tertulia?"

On their way out, he paused at the exit and looked back into the huge room. Cigarette smoke hung like a cloud over the dance floor. The man in the dark coat was gone; only his half-consumed beer at the table was left.

chapter 21

MONDAY MORNING

Parker arrived at his office at a quarter after eight, tired and edgy. He had slept little last night, exhausted from forcing an interest in entertaining his friends, while in the back of his mind, running over and over, were the events at the laboratory. What distressed him most was the innuendo, the failure of anyone to confront either him or his staff directly. Even Greenberg was guilty of that.

He could tell that Elisha was worried too, although she was trying not to show it. This morning she asked if maybe their house was bugged, if someone somewhere was listening to their conversations. He said he didn't think so. Inside, he wasn't sure.

The damn thing was, there was nothing he could do. He had no explanations for the events in his office, the mysterious computer entries that even Greenberg implied stemmed from someone on his staff. He had absolutely no idea who killed Berriman and Sandys, or why. None of the people around him appeared to be the type to do this sort of thing, so who was it? He wasn't even convinced that Berriman had done any more than be in the wrong place at the wrong time. His head swam with unanswered questions.

Outside his office he heard Greenberg's voice. Francis rarely visited unless it was bad news. It was a curious thing about the man, but he seemed more at ease with difficult matters in someone else's office.

Greenberg stood in the doorway, his bulky shape dominating the frame.

"I need for you to do something for me, David," he said without any greeting.

"Sure. What?"

"I need an up-to-date status report on your group's work. I promised it to Merritt by the end of the day."

"What? I can't do that and make the program review this afternoon."

"Skip the review. This is more important. Merritt promised it to Energy in Washington. It's something urgent. For their annual appropriations request, I think."

"Francis, it could take a couple of days. I've got half a dozen major activities going on and status reports due from their coordinators over the next few weeks. I don't even have the full results in from the test in Nevada. You know that."

"I know, and I told Merritt. He says do what you can. Nothing long; you know what to do."

"What about the program review? I need to know what's going on in other divisions. Who'll present from my group?"

"Sorry. But this has priority."

Parker studied Greenberg. This wasn't like him. In fact, it wasn't like Merritt either. He felt his anxiety rising; it had to be something to do with Berriman.

"What's going on, Francis?"

Greenberg said nothing and started to leave. Parker jumped in front of Greenberg and blocked his exit. He grabbed his arm.

"Francis, you owe me an explanation. We've worked together too long for me not to know that something's going on."

Greenberg let out a sigh. "Just do the report, David, and get it to me as soon as you can." He started out, but Parker blocked his way again.

"It's this goddamn spy business, isn't it?"

Greenberg said nothing and stared at the floor.

"Isn't it?"

"You're in trouble, David, and I just hope to God that you can clear yourself."

"In trouble for what?" David asked. "With whom? The FBI?" Greenberg reached over and shut the door.

"Keep your voice down! You're in trouble with everyone." He said the last word in a fierce whisper. "You're the main suspect in all of this, David."

"You're telling me. I was even followed last night in Santa Fe. But why? I told you the truth: I don't know anything about Berriman or his goddamn missing reports—and this computer business! Someone else had to do it!" Parker let go of the older man's arm. "You *know* me. You know I wouldn't do anything like this. You know that." He was pleading. Almost certainly Theresa could hear their conversation.

"I thought I knew that," he said sadly. "But what about the stuff in your office?"

"What stuff?" Parker's heart was racing.

"Berriman's reports. They found them hidden on your bookshelf."

"Oh my God! I don't even know what you're talking about!" Parker felt weak all over. He sat down limply in one of the chairs by his desk.

"The FBI found something here?" He waved his hand around the room.

"Yes." Greenberg straightened his body. He had broken his word with Merritt, but somehow he figured Parker deserved to know. "There's something else. It was your terminal that pulled data from the central computer. Sigma data."

Parker struggled to regain his composure. "Well," he choked for words, "I don't know anything about it." He suddenly got up again. "I'm going to the FBI right now and talk to them. What's that guy's name? Dawes?"

"I think you should," said Greenberg.

As Parker reached for his coat, Greenberg caught his arm. "I hope you're telling me the truth, David. I really hope so."

Parker just stared at him. "Even you?" he said and walked out.

"Are you leaving, David?" asked Theresa. Her voice was trembling. She was frightened; she had heard only Parker talking, but it was enough. "You have a meeting in ten minutes, remember?"

"Cancel it. I'll be back as soon as I can."

Parker hurried down the hall and took the stairwell to the

second floor. He had heard that Dawes was using Poole's office during the FBI's investigation.

His mind was racing. Damn right he would speak to Dawes! At least, it couldn't make things any worse.

"Does Dawes have an office here?" he asked the startled secretary.

"He can be reached through this office, but he's not in at the moment."

"When will he be back?" Parker tried to calm himself down. He could feel himself shaking.

"Sometime later in the morning. I believe he and Mr. Doty are in conference."

"Doty?"

"The senior agent from Albuquerque."

"Well, I want to see Dawes or Doty as soon as possible. You tell them it's important." He left his name and office number.

But now what? He needed time to think, to sort all this out. For the first time, an awful clarity was coming to him: someone was setting him up. If only he had been told earlier, he could have explained. The bastards! he thought.

His hands were trembling, and for a moment he wasn't sure that he could make it back to his office. From his stomach he felt a wave of nausea creeping up his chest and throat. He quickly turned into the men's room and rushed into a stall. Twice he vomited into the toilet, each time with a racking, heaving spasm. When it seemed to ease, he wiped his mouth and flushed the toilet. God! he hoped no one had seen him come in.

He stood there for a moment, chilled and shaking badly. He put the toilet seat down and sat on it, trying to regain his composure. He was exhausted and wrung out. Suddenly, despite all the will he mustered, he began to cry, quietly but with tears flowing down his cheeks.

For several minutes he thought of nothing until, with a sigh, the conversation with Greenberg came rushing back to him. He tried to figure out why the FBI hadn't come to him as soon as they found Berriman's reports in his office. When had they found them? Yesterday? Last week? Then he remembered the conversation with Greenberg on Friday. Had he known about Parker's computer terminal then?

Everything was a jumble in his head and it was impossible to think clearly. A few feet away he heard somebody enter a stall, close the door, and begin to urinate. The sound echoed weirdly throughout the small room. He needed to get out, to get away from the laboratory for a while and think this through.

Then it hit him. They would be watching him, aware of every move he made; certainly they knew what he drove. He wiped his eyes and walked to the office of a friend on the third floor.

"Fred," he said, trying desperately to sound in control, "I need a favor."

"Sure. What?" said the pleasant-looking man. He was studying a computer printout.

"Lend me your car for a while?"

"What's wrong with yours?"

"Nothing. I need to go into town and buy a gift for Elisha. I'm afraid she'll see my truck. It needs to be a surprise." He winked. "Take my keys if you need a car for something."

Fred laughed. "I know what you mean. Here," he said, handing Parker a set of keys. "You know which one it is?"

"Yeah. Thanks."

"Yours is a brown Blazer, right?"

"Right. Thanks."

Maybe, just maybe, he had bought some time. Just enough to think through his options. If—and it was a big if, he thought—he had any options left.

"Where can we set up operations?" asked the large man.

"The Department of Energy's regional office has agreed to lend us a suite. It's only a few blocks from the main building," replied Doty.

"Secure?"

"Absolutely. We've checked it out," said Dawes.

"When can the telephone lines go Home?"

"A few hours at most. They already have secure connections with Washington."

"Good," said Al Borne, "bring me up to date." Doty passed the thick case file to his superior. Borne had just arrived from FBI headquarters in Washington to command the final stages of the investigation.

He took the folder and sat back in his chair. He was a large man, almost six-five, and a solid 250 pounds. He liked to joke that his size made his large nose less conspicuous. He flipped open the folder and scanned the first sheet.

"Poole? Wasn't he one of us?"

"Yes, sir," said Doty, "got a medical out on a bad heart. He's been here at Los Alamos since then."

"What does he know?"

"Most of this. We've withheld certain aspects of the investigation, of course, as well as the background information provided from Washington."

"He's no problem?" Borne sifted through the pages.

"No problem."

"Good. Continue."

Doty tried to be brief but thorough. Borne had a reputation for being the Bureau's best espionage man, but one with a short attention span in meetings. Doty highlighted the discovery of the classified report in Parker's office and the procedure used to identify his computer terminal.

"Anything from the technical coverage?" interrupted Borne. He referred to the taps in Parker's house and office.

"Nothing out of the ordinary. The man is extraordinarily careful. He did, however, receive a telephone call from a member of Senator Kearney's staff, a Richard Lawton, advising him he was in trouble."

"You think the man is involved?"

"No. The Washington office checked Lawton out. His source was Defense Intelligence. Lawton is cleared for that sort of information because of his administrative position on the subcommittee. He and Parker are friends from college. The call was apparently to let Parker know that the subcommittee knew of the situation here in Los Alamos."

Borne said nothing and continued to flip through the file. "What about the others?"

"You have a summary in the file. Four others are also under surveillance." He directed Borne's attention to the right report and the names of Schneider, Goldman, Kronkosky, and Dixon. "They remain suspects for different reasons." He outlined the report, emphasizing what his men had learned about their backgrounds, activities, and profiles. "None of them," he added, "as far as we can tell, have the sort of expertise to develop a computer program capable of violating the security system of the central unit."

"You don't think that the reports in Parker's office are too obvious?" asked Borne.

"We think not. It's consistent with the incidents involving Parker's attitude toward security. His behavior also suggests, well, a man under pressure. He has been quoted as opposing the laboratory's advanced weapons program. And while we can't link him directly with the murders, there is reason to believe that he had time to do them."

"How so?"

"On both occasions, there were periods of time when he was unobserved. It would have been close, but possible."

"It says here that he and his family discovered Isaac Berriman's body in a cave."

"That's true, but our investigation suggests that there was enough time between leaving his office at the laboratory and arriving at the cave for him to have killed the man and then wait for his family."

"Of course," said Dawes, "his family, or at least his wife, could be involved."

"What's her background?"

"She met Parker at Stanford, where she obtained a doctorate in anthropology. She has a sizable family trust fund that makes annual payments. She has no political or criminal record that we know of."

"She hardly seems the type, then," said Borne.

Doty was silent. There were many "ifs," he knew, although the events of the last two weeks were undeniable. And all of them implicated Parker.

"Why didn't you bring him in earlier?"

"We've questioned him on several occasions—when, by the way, he has been less than cooperative—and we've had him under twenty-four-hour surveillance for almost a week now. If he was working with others or had a contact here, we hoped to learn about it." Doty knew everything he'd said reflected standard practice. Borne could hardly find fault with the procedure.

"Anything from surveillance?"

"Very little. He was observed last night at a dance hall in Santa Fe where he disappeared for a short period, although we know he didn't actually leave the building. All of his contacts with individuals out of the laboratory have been normal."

"What about his house? Can we search it?"

"We're ready to move on the legal end as soon as we want."

Borne flipped through the last of the file and closed it. "I think we should bring him in during the next twenty-four hours. Where is he now?"

"As of this morning, in his office," said Dawes.

"Let's move on the search and then bring him in."

Dawes nodded and left the room.

"I think we need to have a long talk with Dr. Parker. But for the moment, Farrell, I'd like to keep it as quiet as possible. We're short on time, but if there's any chance of expanding the net, then we need to do it. Maybe a little extra rope won't hurt at this point."

Doty nodded.

"Let's get the office set up as soon as possible. I have a few more men coming later in the day from the Los Angeles office. They've worked with me before."

"Right away," said Doty.

Dawes stepped back into the room looking shaken. "Something's happened," he said.

Borne and Doty looked at him.

"Parker's gone. Out of the building, we think."

"What happened?" asked Doty.

"Apparently he had a talk this morning with Dr. Greenberg, his division director. They had words, according to the secretary, and Parker came down to Poole's office looking for me, rather distraught."

"Shit!" said Borne. Doty frowned; he disliked what he called gutter language from anyone, but especially from a senior man like Borne.

"Call Greenberg," ordered Doty. "Find out what happened. I wonder if Greenberg told Parker that we wanted him?"

"What do you mean?" asked Borne.

"Merritt insisted on telling Greenberg about Parker over the weekend. Mostly to prevent Parker from attending a high-level review of major weapons work at Los Alamos. Greenberg was sworn to secrecy."

Borne snorted. "These places are like sieves," he said. "That's our problem."

"Alert the boys outside. If Parker has left, we'll want to know where he goes."

"Do you think he'll make contact now?" asked Dawes.

"Well," said Borne, "if there's anyone around, this would be the time."

Doty was silent. This wasn't what he planned for Borne's arrival.

"Let's bring him in," said Borne, "but quietly." He lifted his huge frame out of the chair. He was a good six inches taller than Doty. "No fuss," he added.

Tevis sat by himself on a bench at the edge of the playground. His friends were playing a version of soccer, kicking the ball into a group of young girls who stood off to one side talking among themselves.

He had thought about it all weekend, especially since Reyes failed to show up Saturday. He wasn't sure why the policeman hadn't come, and it only made him feel worse. Tevis felt that somehow the older man understood about the caves and the power of the spirits that lived there.

Now he didn't know what to do with the two objects he had in his drawer at home. He couldn't keep them because they seemed to bring only trouble, and if he read his parents right, they were having some sort of problem between them.

He was certain that the prayer sticks had been placed next to Berriman's body for a purpose, and somehow Tevis had violated that purpose by taking them. Now his father and mother could be in danger.

The objects seemed to have some power in them, sufficient to bring even death. Tevis couldn't quite shake the notion that the murder of the two men was related to the objects and maybe even a result of them. He had to take them back. That was the only real solution.

But when? He had chores at home this afternoon, but he could go tomorrow right after school.

It wouldn't take long. Just enough time to put the two wooden figures back into the heart of the cave where the spirits of the Underworld could easily reach them.

chapter

22

MONDAY AFTERNOON
AND EVENING

Elisha hit the "save text" key on the computer and waited while the disk drive spun around to capture what she had typed. The computer made a whirring sound and then stopped.

From the hallway she heard the doorbell ring.

"Maria!" she shouted. "Can you get that?"

She went back to her notes and the doorbell chimed again.

"Maria?" She waited a moment then got up. "Damn," she said.

She opened the door and saw a man in a suit staring at her. In the driveway were two cars with other men in dark suits stepping out.

"Yes?" she said, alarmed; there was a threatening, cold quality to the man despite his well-groomed appearance.

"Are you Mrs. Elisha Parker?" the man said without any trace of emotion.

"Yes."

"My name is Dawes, and I'm with the Federal Bureau of Investigation. I'd like to talk to you." In his hand was a small black wallet with an identification card.

Elisha was nearly speechless. "Of course, come in."

"These are my associates," he said and waved to them. One of them, she saw, walked over to the side of the house and disappeared.

"This is difficult, Mrs. Parker, but we're looking for your husband. He could be in a great deal of trouble."

"I know he hasn't done anything," she said.

"We have reason to believe he has. Do you know where he is right now?" The pitch of Dawes's voice hardly changed.

"Well, at his office."

"He's left the lab."

"Well, I don't know where he is. What's all this about?"

Dawes handed her a folded paper. "This is a search warrant, Mrs. Parker, giving us permission to search your house. We'd like your cooperation, of course, but we're prepared to act without it."

Dumbfounded, she stepped back away from the door.

Dawes turned around and nodded to the other men, who one by one came in and fanned out into the house.

"Do you or your husband have a gun?"

Elisha had to think for a moment. "No. My husband doesn't approve of weapons. Never in the house. We have a young son."

From another room there was a loud shriek. Elisha jumped.

"Señora!" It was Maria.

Dawes quickly moved his hand to the lapel of his coat and held it there.

Elisha caught the movement. "She's our maid," she quickly said. "In the living room, Maria!"

Maria came running in, frightened and talking in Tewa to herself. "It's all right, Maria, these men are with the FBI." The older woman looked confused. "They are the police, Maria."

"*Dios Mío,*" she whispered.

"Is there anyone else in the house, Mrs. Parker?"

"No." She led Maria over to the dining room and sat her down at the table. "It's okay," she repeated, taking Maria's arm in hers.

"What kind of trouble is my husband in?"

"We believe he may be involved in espionage."

Elisha remembered the conversation last night and shook her head. "It can't be true."

From the other rooms, Elisha could hear objects and furniture being moved. A walkie-talkie blurted out words she couldn't understand.

"Does your husband keep an office here?"

She nodded.

"Could you show me?" Dawes's voice was seductively calm. Elisha wondered if all FBI agents were taught to talk like that, in a low-key, almost melodic voice.

"This way."

Both of them walked into the spacious office followed by another agent. The computer monitor was still on, its green face filled with Elisha's text on ancient Pueblo animal motifs.

"You may want to wait in the living room," said Dawes. Dazed, Elisha nodded and walked out.

The two men began to open desk drawers, quickly but thoroughly looking through papers, checking for unusual construction that might suggest a hiding place. "Start on the books," ordered Dawes.

"Let's make some coffee, Maria," suggested Elisha. It would give them something to do. Maria clung close to Elisha, jumping nervously and clutching her arm when an agent walked through the room. Elisha tried to fight back the fear and choking feeling she felt inside. What was happening to them?

In the study, Dawes's assistant was lifting pictures on the wall and checking behind them.

"Check the pottery," said Dawes.

The other man nodded. He started to roll one over and caught it before it fell off the shelf.

"Careful!"

Gingerly, the man righted the pot and checked inside. He moved to the next one.

"Bingo!" said the man. "Look."

Dawes walked over and peered inside the large Hopi pot. Clearly visible was a red-bordered report cover with the words TOP SECRET. Using his handkerchief, he carefully lifted it out by its edge. Resting underneath was a pistol. The agent whistled. Handing the report to Dawes, he used a pen to pick the weapon up.

"Nine millimeter," he said. "I think we have the son of a bitch."

The agents spent another hour before they left, taking photographs and carting away a box of papers from Parker's files. Elisha could tell they weren't important, but it seemed ridiculous to argue.

"Maria," she said, "go home."

"Oh no, no," the woman protested.

"Yes, go home. I'm okay and David will be home soon. You had more than enough excitement today."

She almost pushed her out of the door and waved good-bye. Across the street, she could see one of her neighbors staring from her carport. It was only a matter of time before the woman would come by to ask what was going on.

She walked back inside and wandered through the house. In her study, the green-faced monitor was on, the same page of text still visible. The agents had been careful, but she could tell that things had been rearranged in every room. And then, for the first time in a long time, she sat down in her chair and cried.

Castro knocked on the open door and waited politely. Poole looked up from his desk and waved him in.

"Parker's gone," he said.

"What do you mean?"

"He left the building and hasn't returned. His car is still in the lot."

"So?"

"Apparently Greenberg spoke with him this morning and told him he was the FBI's primary suspect."

Somehow, Poole didn't find any of this surprising. "Have you checked with Building Security?" There were five guard stations through which individuals had to pass going in or out of the administration building.

"Yes. A guard on duty this morning thinks he saw Parker leave the building around eight-thirty. We can't be sure."

Poole looked at his watch. "If he was in the building, we'd know it."

"The FBI's going to bring him in."

"Right." But if they were wrong, he thought, if Parker wasn't the one, the real person they were all looking for would get away.

"Did you tell them about Rollins?"

"Yeah. Dawes took it all down and said he'd pass it along to Doty." He looked at the stack of reports on his desk. "Keep me posted."

Poole went back to the credit report from Santa Fe. The house in White Rock was jointly owned by Robert Deever Rollins and Angela Olmstead. They paid exactly $1,037.56 a month in mortgage payments, and a search of their credit revealed no outstanding debts of any importance. Olmstead listed herself as self-employed and a "natural foods consultant"; Rollins made $46,250 a year at Los Alamos. Both were single.

The van she drove was a late model and had been purchased from Jack Olmstead Ford in Los Angeles; Poole assumed the man was related to Angela. Neither of them had a police record.

Poole shifted over to his department's internal report on Rollins. He was a mathematician with access to classified weapons data and had a computer assigned to his office for his use. According to both Rollins and Parker, he had been assigned to work with Berriman in preparing advanced theoretical calculations for the laboratory's free-electron laser.

Poole put the report down and thought for a moment. Rollins had been part of his original list, although he hadn't been considered a primary suspect by the FBI. Poole went back to the chart that he'd prepared last week of times and places; Rollins was at work on the Sunday that Berriman was killed and that had been verified by checking the weekend security log. There was no record of where Rollins was on the Tuesday that Sandys was killed.

He thought of the small piece of paper found in Berriman's desk the day after the man's murder; it was the one with the dates and times written by hand. By sifting through several reports, Poole was able to confirm that Rollins was in the administration building during each of the dates and times listed on Berriman's note. Parker was there on all occasions but one.

Poole dug around in his notes and finally found Castro's research on the whereabouts of Parker, Rollins, and the others on Sunday. The weekend security log showed Rollins checked in to the administration building at 12:35. That, thought Poole, wouldn't have given Rollins time to go to Tsankawi, kill Berriman, and make the drive up to Los Alamos. But that was based on the assumption that the murder occurred around noon. As far as Poole could remember, that was the time the police gave when they first examined the body. But what, wondered Poole, was the coroner's official estimate of time of death?

Jesus! he thought, why hadn't he seen this before? He quickly looked through the pile of papers and gave up; he couldn't find the coroner's report. It dawned on him that no one had bothered to match the coroner's official time of death for Berriman with Rollins's check-in at the lab. If it was before noon, even by thirty minutes, then Rollins could have killed Berriman and made it to the lab by twelve-thirty. It would have been close, but possible.

He called Castro on the phone and told him to find out what the autopsy report gave as the time of death for Berriman. He knew that Parker's checkout time from the lab that Sunday permitted him to go to Tsankawi as much as an hour before he met his family. But that could be coincidence, just as Parker had said.

He then picked up Rollins's personnel file and thumbed through it. For a moment, he studied the man's résumé, submitted five years ago when Rollins applied for work at the lab. The entry under "Publications" leaped out at him: "Programming Considerations for Advanced Computer Security." It hit him like a blow to the stomach: under their noses all this time was a man with skills that never appeared on record anywhere else. The computer-generated bio on Rollins contained no mention of his publications except those under the aegis of the laboratory. The man very possibly had the advanced knowledge to manipulate the security system of a highly classified computer. *That* might explain the computer break-ins and the fact that Parker's terminal had been used.

He slowly put the file down and sat back in his chair. Rollins had been in a position to manipulate the events around Parker. There was no evidence yet that he had killed Berriman—or Sandys, for that matter—but suddenly, as far as Poole was concerned, Parker wasn't the only one out front.

Doty had not bothered to call. It was just possible, he decided, that he would have to act on his own.

"Damnit," he said out loud.

Where in the hell was Doty?

At first she was tempted not to answer. Neighbors had come by all afternoon, and Elisha was tired of lying to them. She didn't even have the energy to explain that they were from the FBI. And during all this time she hadn't heard one word from David.

At last she gave in and went to the door. It was Francis Greenberg.

"Can I come in, Elisha?"

She nodded and opened the door. "This is about David, isn't it?"

Greenberg nodded. She had never seen him so quiet before, so depleted, as if all of his energy had been bled out of him. Both of them sat down in the quiet living room. The sun broke calmly into the large room as if nothing were wrong.

"I don't suppose David's here, is he?"

"No. I haven't heard from him since this morning." She might have resented the question, but she was tired and Greenberg seemed genuinely concerned.

"Does the FBI know you're here?"

Greenberg nodded. "I told them I wanted to come." He searched for words. "I told them that David was my staff member and friend." He looked plaintively at Elisha. "This is terrible."

She sat quietly on the couch cupping her hands.

"The FBI thinks David has been stealing weapons information from the laboratory. Frankly, I don't know if it's true or not, but they have a lot of evidence."

"Do you believe it, Francis?"

"I don't know what to think. Some things have happened at the lab, in David's office, that are very bad."

"Like what?" She almost spat it out; her head seemed to spin. Oh God, she thought, David isn't here, and Tevis is coming home soon. She tried to calm herself down. "What has he done?"

"Classified data, very important stuff, was found in his office; it belonged to a man named Berriman." Then he remembered she had been at Tsankawi the day the body had been found. He looked at her and realized for the first time just how much stress she was under. Her face, which he always thought so lovely, looked exhausted.

"They found a gun today, Francis. David hates guns; he's always made a scene about them and about people having them in their homes." She fought back tears. "And I don't know how that paper got here either."

Greenberg said nothing.

Elisha sighed. "I know David, he hasn't done anything. Someone else has to be doing this to him!"

"Who, Elisha? If that's true, we all want to know."

"I *don't* know. Someone who knows David and knew how to implicate him."

"He's got to come in, Elisha. He has to talk to the FBI and explain everything. It's his only chance." Greenberg didn't know what to think anymore. David had worked for him for nearly eight years, and none of what was happening made any sense. Goddamnit! he thought, Parker was *his man!*

"I know. I think he just wants some time to figure out what's happened to him. That's all."

"The sooner the better. Hiding somewhere only makes it look worse."

She nodded. It was true, she thought, he couldn't help himself by running away. But when he came in—what would be his chances then?

"If he comes home or calls, will you talk to him? Tell him that he has to come in?"

"Of course I will."

"Tell him I'll help him however I can. If he's innocent, then we can clear this crap up." He walked back to the door, with Elisha following wordlessly behind him. He stopped and turned around. "Elisha? You might want to contact an attorney."

She walked Greenberg out to his car and watched him drive away. Although she couldn't see anyone, she knew they were watching: the FBI, the laboratory, even the neighbors.

Walking down the sidewalk from the street was Tevis. She waved and he started running.

"Hi, Mom," he said.

"Hi, yourself. Come in, I've got something to tell you."

They both sat down in the living room by the big picture window that looked out through the trees to the canyon.

"Something has happened to your father," she began.

A look of horror shot into his face. "Is he dead?" he cried.

"No, nothing like that. But he could be in trouble and he needs our help." She took his hands and held them in hers. "Some people think he's done something wrong, some people at the place where he works. It's not true, but your father has to prove it."

"What's he done?" Tevis's blue eyes were wide and frightened.

"Some people say he's stolen something from the laboratory. They say they have evidence to prove it. But they're wrong, Tevis, they're wrong."

"Where's Daddy now?"

"He's away, trying to prove he's innocent. He may be gone for a little while, and we have to be patient."

"Will he be back tonight?"

"I don't know, Tevis, we'll just have to wait."

Tevis's head began to swim. Just like he feared, something else bad had happened, this time to his dad. The more he thought about it, the more he knew he had caused it with the wood figures from the cave. If only he had talked with Reyes, maybe all this could have been avoided.

"Sure, Mom."

"One other thing. People may come up to you at school or call on the phone and ask you questions about your father. Just say you don't know anything about it and leave. Or hang up. Okay?"

"Okay."

"Now, why don't you get cleaned up for dinner."

The convenience store had a full rack of candy and another row of cookies and flattened pastries wrapped in cellophane. Parker picked out a candy bar and a package of small doughnuts.

He had been driving around all day, trying to sort out what had happened to him. Now he was in Española, trying to decide whether to drive back to Los Alamos. He pulled the tab on the Cherry Coke and settled back in the seat of Fred's Nissan. It was the first food he had had since breakfast.

Someone was framing him, someone close enough to know what to do to make it look like he was guilty. In all likelihood, it was someone from the laboratory, probably someone from his own group. Berriman might have been involved in the beginning, but he had been dead for two weeks and a lot had happened since then. No one outside of the computer center would have had access to his special terminal. Someone had to know when he came and went in order to put Berriman's documents in his office. That meant some-one around him. That much he had figured out.

The problem was, it wasn't enough to go to the FBI with. Saying he was innocent was hardly proof.

For most of the afternoon he had considered his staff one by one. Even Greenberg was a candidate. Theresa could have planted the documents in his office, but she was incapable of murder. She would have to be working with someone else. He had to consider her a possibility, though his gut feeling was that she was as much a victim as he.

Members of his staff located outside of the administration building had to be eliminated because of their lack of access. If it was a member of his staff, it had to be someone in the administration building. But who?

None of them seemed to have a motive. None were in financial difficulty, at least as far as he knew, and everyone appeared to live within their means. Nothing in their background or daily lives suggested political motivations, although he had seen enough spy movies to believe that motives were not always worn on the surface like clothes.

Of the possible candidates, they ran the gamut in personality from individuals like Rollins, who was abrasive and crude, to men like Kronkosky and Travis, who observed birds and never spoke above a whisper. Was there a clue there? If there was, he couldn't see it.

Still, if he had any hope, there had to be someone. Something had eluded his analysis, he thought, or was he acting out an old "B" movie?

Parker got back on the highway again, thankful when a highway patrol car passed by him without interest. He couldn't stay in Fred's car much longer. Sooner or later, Fred would call his house and ask for him. Then he would learn he wasn't home and report his car—and Parker—as missing. Then the FBI would know what kind and color of car to look for.

He had an idea. Santa Clara wasn't too far from here on the road to Los Alamos. He pulled into the pueblo and looked for Maria's house. Fred's Nissan bumped violently up and down.

He found it only when he recognized her beat-up green Beetle parked next to a neatly kept adobe house. There didn't seem to be anyone else around.

Maria was startled to see him when she answered the door and found him standing outside.

"Aye, holy mother," she said. "Dr. Parker."

"Can I come in, Maria?"

"*Sí*, of course, come in."

She made coffee for him before she sat down and let him talk.

"But what is wrong with your car, Dr. Parker?"

"Nothing, Maria. I just need a car that no one will know is mine."

He debated how much he could tell her.

"Maria, I'm in trouble. I'm not guilty, but the police in Los Alamos think I am."

Maria nodded and told about the men who came into his house earlier in the day.

Parker wasn't surprised. "They think I've done something wrong, but I haven't. And now I need some time, another day only, to try to prove that I'm innocent." Then he asked to borrow her car.

"Yes," she said.

He was so relieved when she said yes that he got up from the couch and kissed her.

"Tomorrow's your day off?"

She nodded.

"Good. Don't call the house. I'm going to leave the other car here, just for tonight. If any of your friends ask whose it is, tell them it belongs to a friend." He paused. "But don't lie to the police. If they ask you, tell them it belongs to me and that I asked you to keep it for a few days. Okay?"

"*Sí*, I understand." Parker wondered just what she understood, but her loyalty was worth more than he could ever acknowledge.

"You'll get your car back tomorrow," he said and waved good-bye.

Now he would go back to Española and call Elisha. Just to tell her he was all right. And he needed money. He knew there would be a bank machine somewhere, and he could get at least two hundred dollars in cash. There were plenty of small motels around that asked no questions—but what if the FBI was watching his credit card account? He would have to do something else.

The way he saw it, he had tonight to figure out what to do. Tomorrow would be it.

On the television, the tall, suave detective with the British accent ducked at the last second to avoid the gunfire. He was saved by some other character from the movie, although Elisha wasn't sure who the woman was.

The television provided most of the light in the darkened room. It was hard for her to pay attention to the program. She hadn't heard from David since morning, and all day she had jumped with every ring of the telephone.

She hadn't called an attorney; she hadn't called her parents. Right now, she felt paralyzed until she could talk things over with her husband. She hoped that it was somehow all a mistake and that it would be cleared up as soon as everyone sat down and talked. Her husband was brilliant, after all, everyone liked him.

The phone rang, jarring her from her thoughts. God, she hoped it was David.

"Uh, hello. This is Rollins. Is Parker, uh, David, there?"

She tried to calm down. Was it possible that one of David's staff didn't know what had happened?

"Bob? This is Elisha. David's not in right now; can I take a message?" She struggled to remain composed.

"Will he be back later?"

Elisha looked at her watch. It was after nine. "I don't know when he'll be back. I'll have him call you." What the hell was he calling for, anyway? she wondered.

She hung up and started to walk back to the living room when the phone rang again.

"It's me," the voice said.

"Oh, David, thank God! Are you all right?" Tears sprang to her eyes.

"I'm fine, really."

"Where are you? The FBI's been here and searched the house. They all want you to come in."

"I'm okay. I'm sure the phone is tapped, so I can't say a lot. But I'm okay. How about you and Tevis?"

"We're both pretty shaken, but we'll be all right."

"Good."

"David? They found a gun in the house."

"What?"

"Yes, in the study. In one of the large Hopi bowls. I've never seen it before. And they found a paper. A classified one."

There was a brief silence on the other end. "I don't know how it got there, Elisha, but I'm not surprised. Someone has set me up."

"Oh, David, come in and talk to them. Greenberg wants you to turn yourself in."

"I'm sure he does," said Parker. So does everyone else, he thought.

"I still need some time to figure this out. When I come in, I'll be in their hands and won't be able to do anything. But I'll come in tomorrow. Tell them that if they ask." Then he remembered that they already knew what he had said.

"I can't talk much longer. Will you and Tevis be okay?"

"Yes. Everyone wants to help, although they don't know what's going on. They call and they visit."

"Who?"

"The neighbors. Greenberg. Even Bob Rollins called."

"Rollins? Why?"

"He wanted to talk to you. He just called a few minutes ago."

"Elisha, I have to go. I'll see you tomorrow." Reluctantly he hung up.

Elisha fought back the tears. From behind her, she heard a small, sleepy voice.

"Who was it, Mom?"

"It was your father. He's all right." She knelt down and hugged him.

"When will he be back?"

"Tomorrow, Tevis. It'll be all right." She ruffled his hair. "Go back to sleep."

Rollins hung up the phone and smiled. It was true! he thought, Parker was on the run. All day he had heard rumors that the FBI was looking for Parker, that the man was in trouble and had skipped out. Where else would he be at 9:20 in the evening but hiding somewhere?

God, how he wanted to talk with Angela! Where in the hell was she? She hadn't answered the phone this afternoon, and she wasn't here when he came home from work. Nothing in the house had changed; everything was in its place, only she was gone.

When she did come home, he would present her with the one classified report he had left, the one he had hidden in the garage. She would be pleased because it was by far the most valuable data he had taken from the lab.

Parker shifted on the floor, trying to find a comfortable position. He tried using an arm as a pillow until it went numb and he had to move it. In all of his life, he couldn't remember a more miserable night.

When he couldn't take it anymore, he sat up and propped himself against the damp wall of the cave. It was cold and dank in the small chamber, and his only cover was a torn wool blanket he had found in the trunk of Maria's car. He sat there for a while, trying not to move and hoping that he might be able to go back to sleep. But running through his mind was what awaited him in Los Alamos in the morning.

He lit a match and looked at his watch: it was only four-thirty. It would be another two hours before it was light. Hours ago, he had resolved to go home first thing in the morning. Undoubtedly they would be waiting for him there.

Maria's car was parked about a mile away in the parking lot of a shopping center in White Rock. He had hiked to the cave, stumbling around in the dark wearing only his office clothes. He had seen two highway patrol cars sitting off the side of the road on the drive from Española. Maybe it was paranoia, but he had to assume they were looking for him. He couldn't risk staying at a motel or just pulling off the side of the road. And he wanted at least the night to consider everything that had happened.

Ironically, he thought, not more than half a mile away, was the cave at Tsankawi where all this damn business had begun!

Again, piece by piece, he tried to reconstruct in his mind what he knew. The most puzzling elements were the documents hidden in his office and the use of his computer terminal to access the lab's Sigma files. Anyone could have entered his office and put Berriman's reports there; any of his staff were possibilities. But the special terminal in his office was different.

The terminal operated only during the day, unless special arrangements were made—which couldn't happen without his knowledge. And it was unlikely that someone would have entered his office and used the terminal without being seen.

One by one, he went through the names: Schneider, Goldman, Edwards, Teelittle, Rollins, and a dozen others. None of them had an apparent motive; none that he knew of had a grudge against him personally. But it almost certainly had to be someone close.

His conversation with Elisha last night came back to him, especially her mention of the call from Rollins. Why had Rollins called when word must be all over the lab that he was wanted by the FBI? Perhaps it was innocent, but it also seemed out of character. That made two odd contacts by a man who rarely sought Parker out for anything but business.

Parker sat up and gathered the flimsy blanket around him; the cold seemed to linger in the cave, like an invisible fog. Outside he heard a shuffling sound, a slow careful movement amid the rocks and small branches. He stiffened and looked around for something, a rock, a stick, anything. When the sound got nearer he realized it was too light to be human; he threw a rock as hard as he could out the cave. Four little feet scampered away.

What had Rollins said to him during their conversation the day after Berriman's murder? As best as Parker could remember, it was something about an attempt to help Berriman. Something about programming techniques. Was it possible that the man was able to manipulate Berriman's computer programs in some way? Or more important, was he able to access Parker's high-security terminal? Another thought hit him: Rollins was in a position to know what Berriman was working on and where or how he kept his files. That fact had been obscured by Berriman's obsessive desire to work alone. They had all assumed that everyone else was just as ignorant of Berriman's work. Why hadn't he thought of this before?

Suddenly there was a flood of questions and events in Parker's head. There was the out-of-character, late-night visit from Rollins to Parker's house over some small matter that could have easily waited until the next day. There was Theresa's remark about finding Rollins in his office. There was Rollins's peculiar lack of surprise or remorse at the news of Berriman's death.

None of these were earth-shattering revelations, none of them conclusive evidence that Rollins might be the man behind what was happening. But put together, they both frightened and intrigued Parker. Suddenly there was the possibility of an explanation.

None of this would satisfy the FBI, at least until they could conduct their own investigation. By then, however, Rollins could disappear or contrive to implicate someone else. *If* he was guilty.

Parker found himself shivering in the cold chamber, suddenly very awake and frightened. He felt like a wounded animal, hiding and fearful, trying to make a case out of nothing, just his own fears and suspicions. But he knew he had to check Rollins out.

It would have to wait until morning. He needed to think very carefully about what he should do. He would have only one chance.

chapter 23

TUESDAY MORNING

"He's still out there?" Borne poured himself a second cup of coffee and added two spoonfuls of sugar.

"Yes."

"And he made contact with his wife?"

"Last night, around nine-thirty." Doty pushed a copy of the transcript across the table. Similar transcripts of calls to the Parker house from Bob Rollins, a staff member, and from neighbors were also included.

Outside, it was barely light. The heavy, overcast sky seemed to want to hold the night from day.

"He says he plans to come in today."

"I see that. Could we trace the call?"

"It was a phone booth on the outskirts of Española, a small town about twenty miles from here." Doty stirred his herbal tea.

"Good. He's still in the area. Let's send someone down there to look around."

"Do you want to call the police in on this yet?" asked Dawes. "Los Alamos has only four entry points. It would be easy to establish some control." Dawes pointed to four spots on a map where checkpoints could be set up.

"No, not yet. I don't want to make a fuss and bring the press in. Besides, we don't know that Parker will really come back here."

"What about his contacts here?"

"If he has them, then we can consider roadblocks."

"The word's out here in Los Alamos," said Doty. "Everyone knows we want Parker. They just don't know why."

"Let them guess," said Borne.

"What about an all-points?" asked Dawes.

"That we can do. Notify the local police about Parker and the type of car he's driving. But no fuss. No heavy stuff. We need to talk with Parker." He looked over a two-page memorandum. "What do we know about the guy Parker borrowed the car from?"

"The man works in the same division. They've been friends for the last few years. Parker said he needed it for a few hours and never returned it. The man didn't miss it until last night."

"I wouldn't be surprised if Parker has found something else by now." Borne looked out the window. There seemed to be no break in the clouds.

"Let's put some pressure on Mrs. Parker." He turned to Doty. "Farrell, why don't you visit her this morning. Impress on her the importance of what her husband has done. And the *penalties* for espionage and even murder."

Doty nodded.

"From your profile, Parker seems to be a family man. Arrogant, maybe, but devoted. If he calls home again, it will help to have Mrs. Parker concerned about his future with his family."

"Anything else?" Doty looked calmly across the table.

"Let's alert Parker's friends. His close ones. And maybe his boss here at the lab. He may try to contact them as well. Continue with airports, bus stations; you know the routine."

Borne turned again and looked out the window. "Is it going to rain today?" he asked.

At 7:45, Tevis pushed the bowl of cereal away and took one last bite of toast. Then he walked to his room and put on his jacket and grabbed his backpack.

It contained his notebook all right, but hidden underneath it, still covered by T-shirts, were the two *pahos* from Tsankawi.

He studied the backpack carefully; everything looked normal. There was no way anyone would suspect what he was carrying. From the top drawer of his desk he pulled out an envelope. He withdrew the letter inside and read it one more time. Then he stuffed it back into the envelope and laid it carefully against a book on his desk. Eventually, his mom would find it, he thought, but by that time he would have done what he should have done long ago, before everything bad began to happen. Now all he had to do was get past her.

She was in the kitchen.

"I'm leaving for school, Mom," he said. "I'm taking my bike."

Elisha looked out the kitchen window at the somber morning.

"It looks like it's going to rain, Tevis, why don't you take the bus?"

"Too late. I already missed it."

Elisha looked at the clock. It was nearly eight.

"Want me to drive you?" she asked.

Tevis shook his head. "I want to take my bike."

Elisha sighed. "All right, but don't hang around after school. Come right home." She looked at him. Part of her wanted Tevis to stay home; the other part told her—forced her—to make his life continue as normal.

Tevis nodded. "Sure."

Instead of darting out, as he usually did these days, Tevis walked over and kissed his mother.

"What's that for?" she asked.

"Nothing. I love you."

She smiled. "I love you too. Be careful."

Elisha walked him to the door and watched him put on his backpack and climb his bike. He waved and peddled out of the driveway. Around the corner, she could see the front edge of a car. The FBI, she thought; they weren't even bothering to hide now.

She sat at the dining room table and sipped her coffee, studying the clouds through the window. It had been a long, sleepless night, worrying about David, and Tevis, and even herself. Friends had called, all solicitous but cautious, but she had sent them away with her thanks. She wondered why she was keeping up the front.

Outside the house, Tevis peddled hard to work his way up the hill. He passed first one parked car, then another a little farther up. Both of them had men dressed in dark suits sitting in them. He waved to one but got no response.

Inside the car, there was a crackle as the radio was flipped on.

"Rooster? It's Hen. It's the Parker kid," said the agent, "he's on a bicycle."

"Noted," crackled the other voice. "Make no move."

"Ten-four," said the first agent, cutting the microphone button. "What if the old man tries to contact his kid?" he asked, turning to his colleague in the car.

"Don't worry. Someone's covering the school."

The old car warmed up and hit its stride at forty. Parker cut back to thirty-five, although he wondered if going the speed limit in New Mexico might not attract just as much attention as speeding.

Fortunately, the car was just where he had left it; if someone was watching him, he couldn't tell. Right now he was outside of White Rock heading for the turnoff that led to where Rollins lived. He would be there in less than five minutes.

He had no idea what he was going to do once he got there. All of his plans concocted in the dark of the cave seemed melodramatic in daylight. Parker could no longer decide if Rollins was guilty or innocent, since there was so little evidence and so much conjecture. Still, he felt that he had to confront Rollins, or check him out. It was the only chance he had.

Now he had to decide what to do. Rollins and his girlfriend lived on the outskirts of White Rock, in an expensive subdivision in which each house sat on several acres of land. From what he could remember, Parker knew that most homes were set back from the street. He would have to move in close, probably on foot.

Out of his pocket, Parker pulled the thin page he had torn from the telephone directory. He looked up Rollins's name and street address and drove slowly toward it.

Just as he remembered, the street that Rollins lived on had houses set far back, some hidden by trees or drops in the terrain. When he found Rollins's house, he looked quickly down the gravel driveway and then drove on, deciding to make another drive-by in a few minutes. The house itself was only several hundred feet from the street but seemed to be part of a small complex of buildings. Now the question was where to park without attracting attention.

The answer was less than a block away where a new house was under construction and several pickup trucks were parked by the side of the road. Parker turned and pulled off on the same side of the street and parked, but at a discreet distance behind the last truck. For a moment, he just sat there, working up his courage.

He walked briskly, hoping to be taken for a resident out for early morning exercise. It was chilly in the open air, and damp from an early morning rain. When he came to the edge of Rollins's property, which was marked by a rustic wooden fence, he looked around to see if anyone was coming and then jumped over. As quickly as he could, he headed for the low cedar trees and chamisa bushes. Crouching low, he crisscrossed his way behind the bushes toward the main house several hundred feet away.

From what he could see, the house was a California-style structure with cedar walls and large-paned windows. Next to it was a freestanding garage made of the same material, and in the back, a large, very new greenhouse. Parker had no idea that Rollins had put so much money into the place. Parked in front was a four-wheel van. In the garage, which was open, Parker could see Rollins's motorcycle.

Parker looked at his watch. It was almost seven-thirty. Rollins would be leaving for work soon. Whatever he planned to do, he needed to do quickly. He had moved no more than a dozen feet, however, when the door to the house swung open and a woman came out carrying a large canvas bag. She was talking but he couldn't make out what she was saying. Frightened, Parker jumped behind a clump of chamisa, trembling as he crouched and peered between the branches of the dense bush. He cursed himself for his lack of courage.

The woman walked back in and reappeared shortly with another bag. This time she didn't go back in. Instead, she closed the rear door to the van and walked around to the side. Rollins appeared at the door, dressed for work, but looking stiff and wrung out. The woman walked up to him and started to kiss him when Rollins turned away. Were they having a fight? wondered Parker. Could she be leaving Rollins?

There was a brief exchange, but Parker still couldn't hear what they were saying. There was no shouting, no hysterics, and for a moment the woman only stood there with her back to Parker. Finally she turned and walked to the van and got in. The engine started and revved several times and the van took off, slowly at first, and then faster as the woman negotiated the gravel road. It hit the pavement with a spew of tiny pebbles.

Rollins stood in the doorway and watched the van disappear before he walked back in, leaving the door open. Parker realized that he was going to leave! Frantic, he tried to decide what to do. But he couldn't move; he just stayed there, frozen behind the chamisa bush. Rollins reappeared and locked the door and walked to the garage. Seconds later, the engine of his motorcycle roared to life, and Rollins darted out of the driveway. Parker was left by himself.

Scared, and now chilled, Parker worked his way to the rear of the house hugging the dense line of trees and chamisa. Any moment, he told himself, Rollins could return, or maybe the girlfriend.

He tried the door. It was locked.

Without thinking, he doubled his hand into a fist and smashed the lower glass panel and reached in to open the door. For a long moment he stood there at the entrance, waiting for an alarm, or for someone to appear. Instead, all he heard was the sound of a bird in the trees behind him.

It wasn't until he was in the kitchen that he looked down at his hand and saw that it was bleeding. Jesus Christ! he thought, what have I done? He found a paper towel to wrap his hand and walked through the house still expecting *someone* to suddenly appear. The rooms were sparsely furnished with wood furniture and only a few framed posters on the walls. A fake wagon wheel with electric lights hung from the ceiling over a table and chairs that were stacked with unopened newspapers. In a corner was a polished wood and glass gun case with two rifles standing upright in it.

Cautiously, he walked down a hallway to the bedrooms. In one a double bed stood against the wall with only sheets on it. For a moment, Parker thought of Elisha and her well-bred concern that even guest rooms had to look occupied with furniture, flower arrangements, and things for the wall.

The next room was apparently a study with a desk and metal bookshelves. At first, most of the books seemed to belong to Rollins because they covered mathematics and physics. But then he saw something that surprised him. Several shelves were filled with books on Indians, Pueblo religion, and archaeology. One or two of the books he recognized from Elisha's library at home.

Parker walked to the last room, which he guessed was their bedroom. There was a large waterbed against one wall and some exercise equipment scattered around. Against another wall was a chest and next to it a small desk. On the floor was a large and colorful Navajo rug, which he guessed was worth several thousand dollars. Yet nothing seemed peculiar or out of place.

He walked to the chest and carelessly began pulling out the drawers. Some of them were nearly empty and Parker remembered the scene between Rollins and his girlfriend just a few minutes before. The other drawers were just as uninteresting.

He turned to the desk. The surface was covered with magazines and old letters. For a moment, his hopes soared when he saw the familiar shape of a computer printout. He quickly pulled it out and studied it and then threw it down; it was nothing more than a list of formulas for making lotions and creams out of plants.

The bottom drawer of the desk contained more papers and a small collection of photographs. Parker guessed they were shots from Rollins's childhood, or maybe his girlfriend's, but in none of them did children appear. There were photos of houses, backyards, and a few adults with unsmiling faces. Did Rollins even have a past before Los Alamos? he wondered.

The next drawer startled him. Half hidden in the rear was a gun. With a pencil, Parker pulled it forward and stared at it. He had no idea what gauge it was, or if it was even loaded. To him, it looked big and ugly. For a moment he stared at it, wondering if he should take it. Finally, he shoved it back toward the rear and closed the drawer.

He opened the thin drawer immediately under the desk and rummaged through the contents. He was just ready to close it when something caught his attention. Like the gun, it was half hidden by loose papers, but the dim light in the room reflected off its dull brass surface and caught his eye. When Parker pushed the papers aside, he saw the circular brass case and the letters BSA. It was his father's Boy Scout compass.

Parker was stunned! Somehow Rollins had stolen the compass from the desk in his study in Los Alamos.

Parker sat down on the edge of the waterbed and nearly sank backward. He remembered the evening Rollins was in their study and how he had admired the compass. But then he remembered very deliberately putting it in the desk drawer. There was no way Rollins could have taken it that evening. That meant only one thing: Rollins had gone back to the house and taken it when no one was there!

Oh my God, Parker thought. *Rollins has to be the one!* He must have broken in and hidden the gun in the pot in the study. The same room where he kept his father's compass!

He looked at his watch. By now, Rollins must be in his office. Theresa would be there too, as well as Security, the FBI, and everyone else. There was no way he could talk with Rollins there. But he did have the compass and the gun. Would that be enough to lure Rollins back to White Rock?

He walked over to the telephone and dialed Rollins's direct line at the laboratory. He was going to try something that he hoped to God would work.

"Dr. Rollins's office," the female voice said. Damn! thought Parker.

"Hello?" the voice said.

"Is Dr. Rollins there?" Parker tried to disguise his voice.

"Just a minute." Parker heard the phone being put on hold. Oh God, please let this work, he prayed.

"Yeah?" said the voice.

It was him! "This is Parker."

For a moment, there was only silence.

"Uh, David, where are you?" Rollins cleared his throat.

"Just listen." Parker had no idea if this line was being tapped. He had to hurry and be convincing.

"I'm at your house. I have the compass you took and the gun. And I have other evidence." Parker tried to stifle the fear in his voice. "I want to talk with you."

"The FBI is looking for you, Parker. They want you."

"They'll want both of us before I'm through, Rollins, you can be sure of that."

"What do you want?"

Parker tried to read the other man's voice. Was that fear he sensed? "Just what I told you. To talk. If not, I'll be sure you burn right along with me."

There was a long pause. Rollins's mind raced through the alternatives. He'd have to get rid of Parker, that was certain, but not in Los Alamos. "I'll come down."

"Not to your house." Parker felt everything inside of him tighten even further. Rollins had agreed to come, but that didn't mean the bluff had worked. Rollins could turn around and call the FBI.

"Where?"

"At the parking lot of Smith's Supermarket in White Rock. I'll find you there."

Rollins was silent.

"And Rollins?"

"Yeah?"

"Don't be stupid. I'll be watching from someplace nearby. Don't bring anybody with you, is that clear?"

Again, silence.

"*Is that clear?*" Parker shouted into the phone.

"Yeah, it's clear."

Parker hung up, his hand shaking. Even in the chilly house, he could feel the sweat on his forehead. He had maybe twenty or thirty minutes before Rollins showed up, *if* he showed up.

He felt his hand throbbing. Blood had seeped through the paper towel staining it a dull red. He hadn't eaten anything since last night and he wanted a cup of coffee very badly.

In the kitchen, Parker looked at his hand; the cuts were minor but they hurt. He rewrapped his hand with fresh towels and started out the door before anyone showed up.

Then he remembered the gun. He went back to the bedroom and to the desk. Parker opened the drawer and picked up the pistol and examined it; it was loaded. He stuffed it in his pocket, and for the first time in his life, he was glad to have a gun with him.

It took almost a minute for the morning traffic to clear before Reyes could turn off the pueblo road and onto the highway. He sat watching the cars head toward Los Alamos, amazed at the number of people who were willing to commute.

He was on his way to Santa Fe to talk with White at the Dewey Galleries. One thing he could do, he thought, was see if anyone had heard of Angela Olmstead. Any kind of connection with Angela could help make a case of what was now only coincidence and his conjecture.

When he was through, he planned to drive to Santa Clara and visit with Jenny. When he left her house Saturday morning, he asked her if he could see her again. She had said yes.

The other person he would try to see was Tevis. He had missed him on Saturday because of Jenny, and he was reluctant to confront him at the boy's house on Sunday. The only way to protect Tevis was to talk to him at school. Whatever the boy knew about the cave could be the link between the red-haired woman and the murders of Berriman and Sandys.

Reyes felt bad about missing the appointment, but finding the woman had seemed more important. There was something about Tevis and his insistence on kachinas and spirits that made Reyes worry for the boy's safety. Reyes could imagine his grandfather warning him to take care.

He was barely on the highway when the police radio blurted out an all points bulletin. All police in the area were asked to assist in locating a blue Nissan driven by a David Parker of Los Alamos.

Reyes quickly turned the volume up. The request asked for no action to be taken other than reporting the car immediately and observing if at all possible. To Reyes's surprise, Parker was considered dangerous.

What the hell was going on in Los Alamos? he wondered. He pulled over to the side of the road and parked for a moment. Out of his window, he noticed cars hit their brakes and slow down when they saw him. Was Parker on the run for something? Then he thought about Tevis. Was the child in danger?

Reyes waited for a break in traffic and wheeled his police car around toward Los Alamos. He was going to have to risk the displeasure of the Los Alamos County sheriff.

*   *   *

Veronica Medrano sat at her desk thinking. She was almost sure the call had been from Dr. Parker.

For several minutes now she had been wondering what to do. Everyone knew that Parker was in trouble, and Castro and the security people had told them that they were supposed to report any contact with him. The talk was everywhere, and she felt very uncomfortable in Parker's office even though Theresa had assured her that she and her job were secure.

Finally Theresa walked back into the room with the coffeepot. Veronica could tell Theresa was worried too, because she never joked anymore and had hardly noticed when Veronica was late again this morning.

"I think Dr. Parker just called," she said timidly.

"What?"

"I think Dr. Parker just called Dr. Rollins. At least, I think it was his voice."

"Are you sure?"

"I think so."

Theresa didn't know what to do either. Everything had turned upside down for her, but never in a million years could she believe that David was guilty of murder and espionage.

"If you aren't sure, I think you should forget about it."

Veronica said nothing and went back to her desk. Still, it bothered her. She kept thinking about her job; she couldn't afford to lose it.

"I going to the bathroom," she said, walking out.

Theresa only stared. Veronica wasn't sure if Theresa knew what she was going to do or not. She walked quickly down the hall to Security's offices and asked for Castro.

"He's meeting with Mr. Poole right now," the secretary said.

"It's about Dr. Parker."

The secretary buzzed the inner office and said something. A few seconds later, Castro came out.

"I think Dr. Parker just called," she said.

"Come in." He motioned her inside the office. "Mrs. Medrano says that Parker just called his office."

"Parker?"

"I think it was him," she said with hesitation.

"Well, was it?"

"I'm pretty sure."

"He called for his secretary?"

"No, for Dr. Rollins."

Poole leaned forward in his chair. "When was this?"

"It was five, maybe ten minutes ago."

"Damn!" he said. "Has Rollins left the office?"

"I think so. I saw him walk out of his office right after he took the call."

Poole fell back in the chair. "Damn!" he shouted again. He jumped up from his chair. "Call the security stations and see if Rollins has left the building. Does anyone know what kind of car he drives?"

"I can ask around."

Then it hit him. "What about the phone taps?" he shouted.

Castro picked up the phone and dialed a number. Poole watched him talk and then frown and hang up. "They dropped the tap this morning. No explanation."

Poole threw up his hands. He sat back down and tried to calm himself and sort out the alternatives when an assistant stuck his head in the office.

"The east station says they think he left a few minutes ago. No one in his office knows where he went."

"Oh, great," said Poole, picking up the phone. Would Doty finally take his call? he wondered.

He had telephoned first thing this morning, as soon as he had the coroner's report with Berriman's time of death. The report put the time somewhere around eleven o'clock in the morning. That theoretically gave Rollins time to kill Berriman and rush to the laboratory and to sign in for the record. It was tight, but possible.

Somehow he had to persuade Doty to listen to him.

chapter

24

TUESDAY MORNING

A light rain was falling, more like a mist, but just enough to make it necessary to use the windshield wipers. The blades were so worn on the Volkswagen, however, that they created a thin film of rain and dirt that forced Parker to turn them on and off every few seconds.

He didn't have much time, he knew, but he wanted desperately to talk to Elisha. Just as a precaution, he drove west toward Bandelier National Monument and a pay phone that he knew was close to the road. If they could trace his call, he didn't want them knowing he was in White Rock.

He fumbled around and found a quarter and dialed his home. The phone rang four times before it was picked up.

"Yes?" said the voice. It was Elisha.

"It's me," he said.

"Oh, David, thank God! Are you all right?"

"Yes. Don't worry. I don't have much time." He watched a car pass slowly by.

"Listen. I'm coming in. Tell the FBI. I'll be there as soon as I can." He was stalling, but maybe he could buy a little more time.

"Is it safe?"

"I hope so."

"David, listen. There's something else. Tevis is missing."

"Oh Jesus."

"He left this morning for school on his bike, but the secretary just called and he never made it."

Parker felt a wave of nausea spill over him.

"He left a note."

"A note?"

"Yes, it said something like, 'I've gone back to fix everything. Don't worry about me, I'll be back.'"

"Do you know where he went?"

"I don't have any idea. He said," she began, the emotion rising in her voice, "he said, 'Don't be mad.'"

Parker tried to think what to do. "All right, listen. Don't worry. We have to trust him. Okay?"

Another car drove by. "I've got to go. I'll see you very soon." He hung up with her crying "David" on the phone.

As he drove back, he tried to imagine what Tevis had meant by "going back." Back to where? Ahead of him was the entrance to the grocery store. Right now, he would have to pray that Tevis was all right.

Rollins was glad he wore his helmet with the visor. The rain was just heavy enough to be painful without protection.

He drove comparatively slowly, partly because of the rain-slick highway and partly because the last thing he wanted was to be stopped by the highway patrol. To be safe, he took the truck route down from Los Alamos, the one that went by the giant underground accelerator.

This was one shitty day, he thought. First Angela, and now Parker. He felt he was at the end of his rope; he was ready to chuck it all and leave. Maybe he'd go to California to find Angela, maybe Mexico. He just didn't care that much anymore.

Angela was the main thing. She had really left this time, saying he could join her later. They fought about it last night until they both couldn't say anything else. It was too dangerous to stay, she said; her presence might bring the police and compromise him.

Crap! She was like his mother and all the others; they all had left him too.

Now he had to contend with Parker. The son of a bitch had found the compass and something else. Could it be the computer printout hidden in the garage? Something left by Angela? Maybe Parker was bluffing, but he couldn't afford to take the chance. Not now, when everything was almost over.

He began to slow down as he neared the intersection of the truck route and Highway 4. As he stopped and waited for the traffic to pass, he suddenly noticed a young boy in a red windbreaker riding a bicycle and heading toward Española. He wasn't sure at this distance, but he thought he recognized the kid: it was Parker's young son.

What in the hell was he doing here? he thought. Was he part of Parker's plan?

As the boy disappeared over the hill, Rollins slowly pulled onto the highway and followed him. Not more than a quarter of mile ahead he saw Tevis pull off the road on the right and walk his bike over to the fence.

Rollins stopped on the side of the road and watched. The kid slid his bike under the fence and rolled it to a clump of trees. Son of a bitch! thought Rollins, the boy was going to Tsankawi.

There was no doubt about it. Even from here, Rollins could spot the ranger building at the entrance. He could just make out a new gate. Rollins smiled; he'd bet anything the kid was going back to the cave. It must have been the little bastard who stole the wood figures!

He pulled around and drove through White Rock, aware of Smith's on his right. He hesitated at his driveway before he went to the garage; it seemed deserted. He pulled the canvas tarp out from behind the paint cans; inside was the computer printout.

Now he would see just how clever Parker was.

"What have you got?" Doty tried to make himself comfortable in the chair.

"A secretary in Parker's office took a call from a man she believed was Parker. The man, who didn't identify himself, asked for

Bob Rollins, a member of Parker's staff." Poole laid it out calmly, covering his analysis of Rollins's background and activities.

"How certain is she that it was Parker?" Doty asked, trying to find a comfortable spot in the chair. He had just come in from a session with Borne and was confronted by an excited Ed Poole.

"She's not positive, but after all, she's worked in Parker's office for some months now."

"She's not certain?"

"No." Poole felt suddenly deflated. This wasn't the response he expected. "She's been with the lab for almost two years, and in Parker's office only four months."

"How old is she?"

"I don't know, but does it matter?" He calmed himself. "If the caller was Parker, then the call to Rollins could be very significant."

"I agree," said Doty, "if the young woman is correct." He massaged his chin. "What about the call? Do we have a transcript yet?"

"The tap was dropped on Rollins's phone sometime this morning." Poole saw no change of expression on Doty's face. Doty flinched, but there was no explanation. "But the point is, Rollins could be the other man we're looking for, or maybe," he said, pausing for a moment, "maybe someone whom Parker suspects."

"Suspects?"

"Yes, if Parker is innocent, then someone could be setting him up. Rollins could be that man."

"Perhaps," said Doty, looking at his watch. "When was this?"

"Almost forty-five minutes ago."

"Well, Parker called his wife about thirty minutes ago and said he was turning himself in."

"Do you believe that?" asked Poole.

"I'll believe it when I see it."

"What about Rollins?"

"I agree he deserves checking out. But right now, we're trying to find Parker."

"What if they're planning to meet somewhere?"

"Do you know where?" asked Doty.

"Of course not, but still?"

"Where would you look?"

"Well, they can't meet at Parker's house and not in Los Alamos. What about at Rollins's house?"

"Where does he live?"

"White Rock."

"All right, I'll get the word out to bring him in. But we're stretched tight right now. It may take some time."

Poole nodded. No one from the FBI was going to White Rock anytime soon.

Doty stopped at the door. "Parker's son is missing too."

"What?"

"Yes, he left on his bike for school but never got there. We've put out a police bulletin on him as well."

"Do you think he's trying to make contact with his father?" asked Poole.

"Perhaps. We don't know. The boy might just be frightened by all that's happened. He'll show up."

Poole watched Doty disappear into the temporary offices down the hall. He called to Castro.

"Get us a car. We're going to do a little traveling on our own."

Parker sat nervously in the Volkswagen, carefully watching through the rearview mirror everyone who entered the store's parking lot. More than three-quarters of an hour had passed since his call to Rollins. Was he going to show up? Parker wondered if he hadn't made a great mistake. Perhaps it would have been better to have gone directly to the FBI with his discovery and let them sort it out.

In the distance, he thought he caught a flash of lightning. The air was so heavy that it could start to rain at any moment.

Suddenly, it wasn't worth considering the possibilities anymore. In his mirror he saw a large, dark motorcycle drive up with Rollins on it. As far as Parker could tell, the man was by himself.

Fortunately, Rollins parked at the opposite end of the building and began to remove his helmet. For a moment, he sat on his cycle and then got off and walked to the bank of newspaper machines.

As thoroughly as he could, Parker looked around him and saw no one else pull in. They could be there of course, but this was his only chance. He got out of the car and walked in one set of doors at the grocery and out another nearer to Rollins.

The trick worked. Rollins seemed startled to see Parker appear out of nowhere. At least, Parker thought, he hadn't recognized Maria's car.

"You came alone?" Parker asked.

"You see anyone else?"

"What the hell's going on, Rollins?" asked Parker, his voice trembling and filled with emotion.

"You tell me." Standing against the phone booth, Rollins looked arrogantly calm.

"You've set me up. I don't know why, but you've done it."

Rollins smirked. He had to be careful with Parker; the two of them were standing openly in front of a grocery store. He needed to get Parker away from here, somewhere out of sight. Then he remembered Tevis.

"We're not gonna talk here," said Rollins, pushing himself away from the booth.

"The hell we aren't," shouted Parker, his voice rising. He grabbed Rollins's arm.

Rollins shook it off, and stared directly at Parker with his intense blue eyes. "Not here."

"Why?" Parker could sense Rollins's powerful body tensing underneath his leather jacket.

"Because I have your son," he replied.

Parker felt like he had been hit in the stomach. The breath literally went out of him and he was speechless. Could Rollins somehow have kidnapped Tevis?

"What have you done with my son?"

"He's all right."

"You son of a bitch!" Parker hissed. *"Where is he?"*

"Down the road." Rollins got on his motorcycle, put on his helmet, and flipped the key. Gunning the engine, he shouted, "Tsankawi."

Parker was left standing by himself as Rollins raced out of the parking lot and down the highway. Out of the corner of his eye, Parker caught the black and white pattern of a highway patrol car. He stepped back into Smith's, suddenly very aware of how conspicuous he was: yesterday's suit was dirty and torn at the knee where he had fallen and his hand was bleeding through the white paper towel.

He would have to risk taking Maria's car, but he would have to wait until the highway patrol left. It would cost him valuable minutes.

Reyes was driving past the airport, at the eastern end of Los Alamos, when the second all points bulletin blurted over the radio.

This time he was surprised to hear Tevis Parker's name. Again, he turned up the volume and listened as the Los Alamos police called for assistance in locating a ten-year-old boy, white male, named Tevis Parker, believed to be in the Los Alamos vicinity on a bicycle and possibly looking to contact his father, David Parker.

Now father and son were missing. It didn't seem likely that Tevis would be looking for his father, but where else would he be? The conversation with Tevis suddenly flashed back into his head, and Reyes thought he knew the answer.

He made a quick turn into a gas station and pulled out again, running over the side of the curb and bouncing back onto the street. He had to quickly retrace his path and get down off the mesa and on the road to Tsankawi.

Poole stared out the window in silence as Castro drove. He was running through the legal implications of a confrontation with Rollins. If, he thought, they could find him.

The call from Parker to Rollins concerned him, although he wasn't exactly sure why. The secretary could have mistaken the voice, or the call could mean nothing. But Parker knew he was a wanted man; if he was planning to escape, why would he jeopardize his chances by making a call to a member of his staff? Especially Rollins, who had a reputation for being unfriendly.

No, Poole thought, Rollins was connected in some way. Either he was an accomplice with Parker, or Parker wanted to ask him something.

"How far away are we?" he asked.

"Just a few miles," said Castro. He turned off the highway on Kiowa Street and slowed down to study the street numbers. "This is it," he said, pointing to a house set back from the road.

"Pull in," ordered Poole. Unconsciously, he checked the gun he carried in his shoulder holster. It was the first time he had worn it in years.

"Doesn't look like anyone's here," said Castro. The garage sat empty, its door folded up against the roof. Castro tapped Poole's shoulder and pointed. There were fresh tire tracks from at least two different vehicles visible on the ground.

"Let's try the door." Poole motioned Castro to one side and he took the other and leaned over and pushed the doorbell. Inside, a chime sounded once, twice, in lyrical tones. He pushed it again.

"There's no one here."

Poole waved his head in the direction of the rear.

"Look at this," he said at the back porch, "blood." Scattered on the wooden porch were slivers and pieces of broken glass. There were bloodstains on the few pieces of remaining glass in the door. "Someone broke in." He touched the blood. It had coagulated, but it was still liquid. Whoever came in this way, he thought, hadn't been gone too long.

"Let's go," he said, cautiously stepping into the kitchen.

"Are you sure we should?" asked Castro. He had never seen his boss like this before.

Poole never bothered to answer. Carefully, he walked from room to room and looked around. There was no sign of a fight or struggle. Only in the master bedroom did he see the drawers pulled violently out of the chest and the desk.

"Look in here," shouted Castro. He was standing in the doorway of the middle bedroom.

"What?" asked Poole. It looked like a study.

"There," said Castro, pointing to a shelf of books.

Poole walked closer and stared. The shelf was filled with books on archaeology and Indian culture. He immediately thought of Berriman and Sandys and the serpent figure drawn in blood.

"No one's here," said Castro.

"No. If Rollins and Parker set up a meeting, it wasn't here."

"Why a meeting?"

"Just a hunch."

They walked back outside to their car. As he got in, Poole shook his head. "We're too late," he said.

chapter

25

TUESDAY MORNING

Tevis made his way up the well-worn path toward the caves. The morning's misting made the path slippery in spots, especially where the plateau's volcanic rock was exposed on the trail. The air was rich with the scent of piñon and rabbit bush, and the mountain mahogany glistened with rain.

He had come to put things right. He was going to put the *pahos* back in the same cave he had found them in. In his backpack were some other items he planned to leave: some cornmeal borrowed from Maria, a feather that Tevis hoped had come from an eagle, and pollen from plants outside his house. They had religious significance, he knew, but precisely what he wasn't sure. He hoped it would be enough to satisfy whatever spirits were involved. Perhaps then his father would be safe. Tomorrow, or maybe the next day, he would talk with Reyes. *He* could tell if everything was done right.

Tevis climbed through the great split in the rock where the early Indians had carved tiny steps and toeholds and then followed the path as it curved to the left around the rim of the ledge. It was near here, he remembered, where he first saw the fleeting figure of the Shadow Man.

At last he saw the row of dark holes in the face of the cliff ahead of him. The path to them was wet and gooey, but he made it up without difficulty. Now he had to find the right cave.

That was harder than he thought. It had only been two weeks since he had been here, but all the entrances and all the cliffs they sat in looked the same. He went to one, then another, before he found the right cave. On the floor at the entrance was the wadded remainder of the yellow ribbon the police had tied across the outside.

Tevis stepped cautiously in. It was hardly bright outside, but still the cave was fairly well lit. There was no one inside. He was reassured to see that one or two of his footprints still survived from his last visit, until he saw that there were other footprints as well, adult ones.

For a moment, he wanted to run away, back to his house where it was safe. Suddenly he heard voices whispering and the cave seemed to get darker. He had to force himself to remember how the wind could suddenly fill the small rooms with strange sounds and then stop inexplicably. His father explained it to him once. Taking a breath, he looked around for openings or fissures from which spirits from the Underworld could emerge.

Tevis searched about the room for the exact spot where he had found the prayer sticks. In his mind, he re-created the scene and decided he could do no more than approximate the location. Hopefully, that would be enough.

Out of his backpack he pulled the small zip-lock bag of pollen and the other one of cornmeal. Then he searched for the feather. In the darkened room, it was hard to see what was in his pack.

Suddenly he heard a noise outside. It wasn't a voice, but a shuffling sound like someone or something making its way toward the cave on the slippery mud. Then he heard someone breathing hard. Tevis froze where he was, afraid to leave and draw attention to himself.

As he squatted near the rear of the room, a hooded, faceless figure drifted into the entrance. With his eyes accustomed to the semidarkness of the cave, Tevis saw the tall figure bend over and peer into the room. To Tevis, the form was as featureless as it was black against the brighter background of the sky. From its head, a hundred little lights turned on and off as it moved slowly from side to side. It was the Shadow Man!

Tevis let out a shriek. The figure itself leaped back for a moment and then slowly came closer, the right hand tearing something dark from the even darker form of the body.

As quickly as he could, Tevis scrambled back against the wall, wishing desperately that he could melt into the wall of the cave and disappear into the Underworld. The figure only stood there, gradually taking on detail. Slowly Tevis could see the elements of a face, and strangely, a vaguely familiar one.

"Is that you, Tevis?" said the voice calmly.

He said nothing.

"It *is* you, isn't it?" The figure moved another foot or two into the cave itself. "Good," it said.

With the figure out of the light and into the shadows, Tevis saw that it was a man in a windbreaker with the hood speckled with drops of rain.

"Who are you?" Tevis asked, shaking, since the man knew his name. His face was somewhat familiar but the voice was not. It wasn't an Indian voice, however; it belonged to the sort of man that worked with his father in Los Alamos.

Even in the shadows, Tevis saw the man smile. "I'm a friend of your father's," the voice said, "and I've come to take you to him." The figure moved closer, and Tevis scrunched back further against the fire-blackened wall.

Tevis's heart was beating faster than he could ever remember. Somehow, he knew that his father wouldn't send someone like this to fetch him. Not here, not at Tsankawi where nobody knew he had come. But how could he escape? The man partially blocked the entryway and looked too big to beat in a race for the outside.

"Where is my father?" he asked.

"Nearby. Let's go to him."

Tevis got up and grabbed his backpack and tossed it over one shoulder. It seemed heavier than before. Then he started to walk out but noticed the man begin to tense. As calmly as he could, he paused at the entrance. "This way?" he asked, stalling.

"Yes," replied the man. Tevis saw him put a gun back into a coat pocket. No spirit needed a gun, he thought. On the floor near the wall were the items Tevis had brought to offer to the spirits. Hopefully, *they* would understand.

Out of the corner of his eye he saw the man's hand come toward him. This was it! With as much speed as he could muster, Tevis dashed out of the cave and scrambled along the ridge away from the road. He slipped and fell and slipped again. Behind him, he could see the tall man breaking out of the cave and moving rapidly toward him.

"Goddamnit!" the man shouted as he slipped and hit the rocky pathway with a thud.

Tevis ran on as quickly as he could on the wet surface. He didn't dare look back for fear of losing even a second's time. He planned to run around to the other side where maybe he could hide in the ruins or kivas. From behind him, he heard the sound of heavy footsteps getting closer, scattering rocks and pebbles as the feet hit the ground.

Suddenly there was a gunshot, one that echoed off the cliffs once or twice and then died. It hadn't come from the tall man; the shot was too far away for that.

"Rollins!" a voice shouted. It sounded like his father!

Tevis kept on running but slipped once more and fell down hard, momentarily knocking the wind out of himself. He felt his leg and knew he was bleeding.

When he looked up, he saw the tall man stopped dead in his tracks a dozen feet away, staring at something on the path down below.

"Dad!" he cried and got up.

"Are you all right?" Parker was fighting hard to catch his breath; he had fallen several times himself and his suit was now torn and muddied in several spots. It felt like his heart was in his throat.

Tevis nodded. "I'm okay." He started to walk but stopped. The man was on the path between himself and his father. Then he saw the tall man's hand move slowly to the pocket of his jacket.

"Dad!" Tevis shouted. "He's got a gun!"

Parker fired another shot that hit somewhere to the left of Rollins on the cliff behind. In that same moment, Rollins pulled out his pistol and fired a shot that hit less than two feet from Parker's head. Parker dropped to the ground and scrambled for a clump of rocks nearby.

"Run, Tevis!" he shouted, angry at himself for presenting so obvious a target. When he looked up from the rocks, seconds later, he knew that he had failed. Rollins had moved in that brief moment to grab his startled son. Clutching the child's neck with one hand, Rollins stood defiantly with the gun in the other pressed against Tevis's head. Even from here, Parker could tell the child's eyes were wide and filled with terror.

"Throw it down, Parker," Rollins said.

It was the hardest decision he ever made. A part of him inside wanted only to kill Rollins, no matter what the cost. But with his hand trembling, he threw the gun over the rocks and stood up.

"Stay there," shouted Rollins, pushing Tevis forward with his leg.

Still holding Tevis by the neck, and slightly stooped over, Rollins made his way to the pistol. Releasing Tevis, he quickly bent down and picked it up. Tevis ran to his father and clutched him around the waist. Fighting back his own fear, Parker smoothed his son's hair.

"You can't do this, Rollins. They're going to find out."

"Oh? We'll see." He stuffed Parker's gun in his coat. "We'll need this in a minute," he said, "but this is the one that counts, Parker." He held his own gun up. "It's seen action before, you know."

"You can't go back now; they'll be waiting for you. I left word."

"I can go back with the right story. I have to take the risk."

He motioned for them to start back up the hill to the caves.

Parker suddenly understood what Rollins intended to do. Both of them would be killed and Rollins would go back for help, saying he had been lured to Tsankawi by Parker and forced to defend himself. Or he could pretend he knew nothing. Everything else would be obvious.

"Move it," said Rollins.

Parker had to try to drag it out. Maybe someone had heard the shots and would come along. Maybe Rollins would stumble or fall. He had to try for it. He put Tevis in front of him, noticing in the touch that the child was trembling. If he had any chance at all, it would have to be soon.

*   *   *

The blue police car with the symbol of the San Ildefonso Pueblo on the door pulled slowly up to the entrance to Tsankawi ruins. A new metal gate was chained closed and a white metal sign announced the ruins were closed to the public. There was only a Volkswagen Beetle parked near the gate.

What he expected to find hidden on the other side of the fence was a child's ten-speed bike. He wasn't disappointed. Ten feet from where he had seen it two weeks ago, was Tevis's expensive bicycle chained to an old juniper tree. He got carefully out of his car, taking with him the shotgun that normally was locked in a metal frame on the dashboard.

Next to his car he saw fresh motorcycle tracks make a U-turn to the other side of the road and disappear behind a large outcropping of rocks. The tracks stopped behind the rocks. Reyes could tell they were very fresh.

He quickly jumped the fence at the lowest point he could find and ran along the paved path until it turned to dirt and then stopped for a moment, breathing heavily. There were fresh footprints that suddenly blended together; from what he could tell, they belonged to a child and two adults.

He tried to formulate a plan. More than likely, Tevis was headed for the south rim of the mesa, the one with the caves. A far shorter route, however, was along the upper path, one from which he could overlook most of the southern path below. That meant, however, that he might not see Tevis, or the others, if they were in the caves. He had no choice but to take the lower path, although it would take longer and he could be more easily spotted.

He checked his .38. It was fully loaded. He cocked the shotgun and took off down the trail.

The kachinas may have brought Tevis here, Reyes thought, and they had their own magic. But Reyes was human and couldn't count on magic. He felt sure he was going to need his wits and his guns. Hopefully—and he prayed God it was true—the kachinas would help.

They had nearly reached the first string of dark openings. Parker was near panic; so far, there hadn't been a chance to do anything. Rollins kept a respectful distance behind them and although he couldn't see it, Parker felt the barrel of a gun pointed straight at his back.

It was at that moment that Tevis slipped and fell, banging his right knee on a sharp rock on the path. He cried out in pain.

Parker immediately bent down and held him and then tenderly took Tevis's leg and examined it.

"Keep going," Rollins shouted.

"Just a goddamn minute!" Parker looked at the torn pants and the splotch of blood seeping through. "Are you all right?" he asked softly. Maybe he had bought a few more minutes.

Tevis nodded, tears welling in his eyes.

Parker searched his pockets and realized that he didn't even have a handkerchief on him. He gave him a hug. Not six feet away was the entrance to a cave.

Rollins apparently changed his mind. "Okay," he said, "this'll do." Keeping his eye on Parker, he reached in between his coat and his shirt and pulled out what looked to Parker like a folded computer printout.

"Recognize this?" asked Rollins.

Parker stared at him. Tevis had released his grip on his backpack. Pretending to comfort Tevis, he lifted the backpack; it was surprisingly heavy. Very carefully, he put it next to him and whispered to Tevis. "Head for that cave when I give the signal."

"Here," said Rollins, throwing the report at Parker's feet. It landed with a splat in the filmy mud.

Parker picked it up and knew instantly what it was. It was a computer printout, probably the one taken off of Berriman's printer. It contained the theoretical configurations for the Nemesis test.

Parker looked back at Rollins. "This is very valuable now," he said. "Are you sure you don't want it?"

Rollins smirked. "I can get another copy," he said.

Parker was confused. None of this made any sense; people had killed for this? "Why did you do it?" he asked.

Suddenly Rollins laughed. "You wouldn't understand." He thought of Angela and Tommy. "Maybe just for the hell of it." He pointed to the printout with the tip of his gun. "Put it inside your jacket," he ordered.

Parker stared at it for a moment. This was the last piece of the puzzle. He was sitting on his legs and shifted slightly to place himself in front of Tevis as best as he could. He looked at the report and then at the backpack.

"Here," he said, "I don't need it," and threw the printout back to Rollins.

Rollins started to bend down to pick it up when Parker made his move. In that split second he realized that his balance was skewed by squatting. He had to lunge forward to straighten himself. It was just enough warning for Rollins to catch the movement and fire his gun.

The sound of the shot reverberated off the walls and in Parker's head. At first, when the bullet struck his thigh, it only felt like he had been hit by a rock. It didn't even hurt, it only seemed to push him backward slightly. Then almost immediately he felt the pain; it was a searing fire that seemed to pierce through the fleshy part of his leg burning with an intensity that left him stunned.

"You stupid son of a bitch!" shouted Rollins. He aimed his gun and then caught himself. "Not just yet," he yelled. "Get up, goddamnit!"

Parker touched his leg and felt the warm blood oozing out through the hole in his pants. He could barely stand it, it burned so much. For a moment, all he could do was sit there, Tevis hiding behind him in shock.

"Get up! I said."

Parker nodded and tried to move. Drawing upon every ounce of energy and will he had left, he forced himself up with one hand to a semistanding position. The pain was easing, but it still burned like hell.

Then everything seemed to happen at once. From below them, a voice shouted something that Parker couldn't understand. But it must have been a name, because Rollins turned suddenly around, hesitated, and then fired once, twice. Again the sound was overpowering, flying off the walls and shattering the air with echo after echo.

From the bottom of the path, Reyes saw Rollins lift his weapon and fire. The slug whizzed by his head and hit somewhere behind him. He had already started to drop to the ground when the second shot seemed to come even closer.

Jesus! thought Reyes, the man was a damn good shot. He rolled over to put himself behind a small rock; he had lost valuable seconds. *This bastard is gonna kill me!*

Parker witnessed it all with a head still ringing from the shots and a leg burning with pain. Without even thinking, he picked up Tevis's backpack and, with all the strength he could muster, swung the pack at Rollins, hoping to God that it would hit him.

It did, barely. Rollins had just turned around enough to catch Parker's movement when the pack containing the two ancient prayer sticks and a thick archaeology text hit him between the jaw and the shoulder. For an instant, he seemed to stand there, unaffected, when suddenly he slumped down and hit the ground with his knees. He was lifting his gun to fire again when Parker stumbled over and kicked Rollins below the rib cage with his wounded leg.

The additional pain was too much for Parker, and he fell back clumsily against the rocks. It seemed like a dozen little knives were thrust into his back and shoulders.

The force of the kick was just enough to send Rollins back over the ledge of the path and tumbling down a dozen feet to land with a thud against a large rock. Still gripped tightly in his hand was Angela's gun.

For a moment, no one moved. Tevis was first to react, rushing to his father. Reyes stood up, his shotgun aimed at the twisted and stunned body twenty feet in front of him. Somewhere between Rollins and Parker a computer printout lay flattened in the mud.

"Are you all right?" shouted Reyes. Suddenly he remembered the all points bulletin. What in the hell was he supposed to do with Parker?

Parker looked at Tevis. He weakly waved his hand.

Reyes carefully walked over, kicked the gun from Rollins's hand, and picked it up by the handle. The body made no movement. He walked to Parker and Tevis and looked at Parker's leg. Then he noticed the patch of red on Tevis's pants.

"How's your leg?"

"Okay." The boy's voice was weak and frightened.

"Can you walk?" he said to Parker.

"I don't know."

Reyes shook his head. "I'll go call for help." He stopped to handcuff Rollins and then looked back at Parker.

"Don't worry," Parker said, "I'm not going anywhere. And I need him *alive*."

"The prayer sticks," shouted Tevis, "from the cave; they're in the backpack."

Reyes smiled. Now he knew why the boy had come to Tsankawi.

Tevis grabbed his father's arm. "What about the printout?"

Reyes looked at what Tevis was pointing to. Was this what it was all about? he wondered.

For a moment, Parker was tempted to say "leave it." Then he looked at Reyes. "Why don't you take it with you? I think someone's looking for it."

chapter 26

WEDNESDAY AFTERNOON

Reyes sat on a bench in the shade sipping a cup of coffee. Not far from him, Jenny was working her clay, magically turning the coils with her hands into the recognizable shape of a pot. Every now and then, she looked up from her potting wheel and smiled at him. Only once did her face darken.

"Do you think they'll catch her?"

Reyes nodded. "Yes. It's just a matter of time."

"Why did they do it?"

"I don't know, really. She seems to have done it for money; he, because he loved her." That was too simple, he knew.

"And Johnny?"

"He was caught in the middle." That wasn't exactly true either. But now it didn't seem to matter much.

"And the little boy?"

"He's fine, I think." Reyes thought of the two *pahos* in Tevis's backpack. Both of them were now in Reyes's desk drawer waiting to be returned to the proper place. Maybe a cave somewhere with its spiritway to the interior of the earth, or a family shrine near Black Mesa. "Well, he may be a little disappointed."

Jenny looked up from her work. "Why?"

"The ghosts he thought he saw turned out to be only men." He didn't say it, but he felt a little disappointed himself.

Jenny stared at him for a moment. Unconsciously, her hands continued to massage the clay, expertly seeking out the tiniest imperfections and smoothing them out. Soon the pot would be ready to decorate. "And you?" she asked.

Reyes looked across to her and smiled.

His first impression on waking was the smell. Chemical. The second was that of someone holding his hand.

He was groggy and his head felt thick and unwieldly. For a moment, all he could do was lie there and try to concentrate on the smell. It was then he realized that he was in a hospital and that it was Elisha holding his hand.

"David?" she said.

He really didn't want to talk but he was so glad to see her. He squeezed her hand.

"You're just waking up. You've been asleep for almost a day."

Then he remembered, vaguely, being brought down from the caves on a stretcher and the long ride in the ambulance to the hospital in Los Alamos.

He tried moving his lips but they were stuck together. He licked them as best as he could.

"Tevis?" he croaked.

Elisha smiled. "He's okay. A bad cut on the knee and just a bruise or two. He wanted to come, but the hospital wouldn't let him. He told me to tell you that he loves you and wants you to come home soon."

Parker nodded.

"He also says you're a hero now."

He wanted to laugh, but he was afraid his head would break at the slightest movement.

"David, Francis is here. He would like to speak to you for just a minute."

Parker shook his head slowly. "No," he whispered.

"Just for a minute? He says it's important."

Greenberg came in, grave but somehow looking relieved.

"How are you?"

Parker nodded his head, feeling the pain when he did it.

Greenberg patted him gently on the shoulder. "I'm sorry about all of this, David, I really am." His eyes were moist.

Parker believed him.

"Merritt sends his regards. Really. We all do." He studied Parker's face. "For what that's worth," he added. He bent closer. "He—we, actually—want you to come back to work as soon as you can. When you're fit, of course." Greenberg cleared his throat. "You're important to all of us."

Parker only stared. He was thinking about Rollins and the cave at Tsankawi.

"The FBI has Rollins. In fact, he's just down the hall with about fifty guards around him."

Greenberg looked at Elisha and then back at his colleague.

"Merritt wants to talk to you when you feel better."

"Merritt?" Parker's voice was barely audible.

"Yes. I know he's embarrassed by all of this, but he's an honorable man. I really believe that."

"Francis?" prodded Elisha.

"I've got to go. We'll talk soon, okay?"

Parker forced a smile and watched Greenberg give Elisha a hug.

When Greenberg was gone, Elisha gingerly took his hand again.

Parker looked at her and smiled and then painfully turned to look out the window. Somewhere out there was his son. I wonder, he thought, how much Tevis would mind moving.